A
ROYAL GENTLEMAN

THE PARTING.

A ROYAL GENTLEMAN

[ORIGINALLY ENTITLED "TOINETTE."]

A NOVEL,

BY

ALBION W. TOURGÉE.

AUTHOR OF "A FOOL'S ERRAND," ETC

THE GREGG PRESS / RIDGEWOOD, N. J.

First published in 1874 by Fords, Howard, & Hulbert
Republished in 1967 by
The Gregg Press Incorporated
171 East Ridgewood Avenue
Ridgewood, New Jersey, U.S.A.

Copyright© 1967 by
The Gregg Press, Inc.

Library of Congress Catalog Card Number: 67-29281

Printed in United States of America

AMERICANS
IN
FICTION

INTRODUCTION BY PROFESSOR CLARENCE GOHDES

Editor of *American Literature* Magazine

In the domain of literature the play may once have been the chief abstract and chronicle of the times, but during the nineteenth and twentieth centuries the novel has usurped the chief place in holding the mirror up to the homely face of society. On this account, if for no other, the Gregg Press series of reprints of American fiction merits the attention of all students of Americana and of librarians interested in building up adequate collections dealing with the social and literary history of the United States. Most of the three score and ten novels or volumes of short stories included in the series enjoyed considerable fame in their day but have been so long out of print as to be virtually unobtainable in the original editions.

Included in the list are works by writers not presently fashionable in critical circles — but nevertheless well known to literary historians — among them Joel Chandler Harris, Harriet Beecher Stowe, Thomas Bailey Aldrich, and William Gilmore Simms. A substantial element in the list consists of authors who are known especially for their graphic portrayal of a particular American setting, such as Gertrude Atherton (California), Arlo Bates (Boston), Alice Brown (New England), Edward Eggleston (Indiana), Mary Wilkins Freeman (New England), Henry B. Fuller (Chicago), Richard M. Johnston (Georgia), James Lane Allen (Kentucky), Mary N. Murfree (Tennessee), and Thomas Nelson Page (Virginia). There is even a novel by Frederic Remington, one of the most popular painters of the Western cowboy and Indian — and another, an impressive minor classic on the early mining region of Colorado, from the pen of Mary Hallock Foote. The professional student of American literature will rejoice in the opportunity afforded by the collection to extend his reading of fiction belonging to what is called the "local-color movement" — a major current in the development of the national belles-lettres.

Among the titles in the series are also a number of famous historical novels. Silas Weir Mitchell's *Hugh Wynne* is one of the best fictional treatments of the American Revolution. John Esten Cooke is the foremost Southern writer of his day who dealt with the Civil War. The two books by Thomas Dixon are among the most famous novels on the Reconstruction Era, with sensational disclosures of the original Ku Klux Klan in action. They supplied the grist for the first great movie "spectacular" — *"The Birth of a Nation"* (1915).

Paul Leicester Ford's *The Honorable Peter Stirling* is justly ranked among the top American novels which portray American politics in action — a subject illuminated by other novelists in the Gregg list — A. H. Lewis, Frances H. Burnett, and Alice Brown, for example. Economic problems are forcefully put before the reader in works by Aldrich, Mrs. Freeman, and John Hay, whose novels illustrate the ominous concern over the early battles between labor and capital. From the sweatshops of Eastern cities in which newly arrived immigrants toiled for pittances, to the Western mining camps where the laborers packed revolvers, the working class of the times enters into various other stories in the Gregg list. The capitalist class, also, comes in for attention, with an account of a struggle for the ownership of a railroad in Samuel Merwin's *The Short-Line War* and with the devastating documentation of the foibles of the newly rich and their wives in the narratives of David Graham Phillips. It was Phillips whose annoying talent for the exposure of abuses led Theodore Roosevelt to put the term "muck-raker" into currency.

While it is apparent that local-color stories, the historical novel, and the economic novel have all been borne in mind in choosing the titles for this important series of reprints, it is evident that careful consideration has also been given to treatments of various minority elements in the American population. The Negro, especially, but also the Indian, the half-breed, Creoles, Cajuns — and even the West Coast Japanese — appear as characters in various of these novels or volumes of short stories and sketches. Joel Chandler Harris's *Free Joe* will open the eyes of readers who know that author solely as the creator of humorous old Uncle Remus. And there is a revelatory volume of dialect tales, written by a Negro author, *The Conjure Woman* by Charles W. Chesnutt.

In literary conventions and the dominating attitudes toward life, the works in the Gregg series range from the adventurous romance illustrated so well by Mayne Reid or the polite urbanity of Owen Wister to the mordant irony of Kate Chopin and the grimmer realism of Joseph Kirkland's own experiences on bloody Civil War battlefields or the depressing display of New York farm life by Harold Frederic. In short, the series admirably illustrates the general qualities of the fiction produced in the United States during the era covered, just as it generously mirrors the geographical regions, the people, and the problems of the times.

PREFACE.

THIS tale was written in 1868–9, amid the scenes and shortly after some of the veritable incidents which it describes. It was originally published in 1874, under the title of "Toinette," the name of the principal female character, although not the pivotal person on whom the whole action of the drama turns.

The book was written because its incidents, in effect, had passed before my eyes with such vividness that I could not but write. At that time (1868–9) I had no idea of publishing. The simple delight of portraying what I observed was my only motive.

In the summer of 1865, before the battle-smoke had well cleared away, I settled near Greensborough, N. C., in the hope that a milder climate might aid me to prolong a life somewhat shattered by the shocks of war. My idea of Southern life was mainly derived from the literature of the era before the war. It is true that service in the army had somewhat modified it, but in the main I venture to say that it was a fair reflex of the idea and sentiment of the intelligent Northern man of my age at that period. After I went South, the contrast between these pre-notions and what I saw of the life around me, and the fresh relics of the life which had just passed away, impressed me keenly, and soon became a subject of engrossing interest.

I saw, or thought I saw, that the *conscious* evils of slavery—the cruel lash, the impossible task, and what-

ever of opportunity for malice the system gave rise to—
had been, if not magnified, at least disproportionately
dwelt upon by the anti-slavery writers of the North.
At the same time, as I conceived, the *unconscious* evils of
the system—those which warped the brain and heart of
the master as well as dwarfed the soul of the slave—had
been allowed to drop out of sight in the heat of par-
tisan advocacy.   I noticed, too, that these unconscious
evils were the very ones which had left their marks
upon character, and that every one who had been submitted to their influences was more or less scarred by
them—especially the master race; and that these influences were a part of slavery which could not be
"abolished."   It was beyond the power of Military
Proclamation, Constitutional Amendment, or legal enact-
ment—immortal as the essence on which its impress was
inscribed.   I found, too, that the non-slaveholding whites
of the South had been unfairly massed, and represented
to the Northern mind by the terms " poor white," "mean
white," and "white trash;" while in fact they ranged
from this type up through the better class of "crop-
pers"—the *metayers* of the South—to the small farmers
and even considerable land-owners, who depended on
their own labor and that of free-born " hirelings" for the
cultivation of their crops.   Impressed by these and
other differences, I wrote, setting down naught in anger,
nor contriving aught of malice against any man or system—and not, indeed, for the public eye, but for my
own pleasure merely.   The manuscript knocked about
my library—a fragment of it now and then being read for
the entertainment of some friend—until 1874, when one
whose name is itself an authority urged its publication.

The story is the delineation of a romantic sentiment,
having its root in slavery, but its flower and fruitage in

freedom, and concerns itself with Slavery only in order to mark the growth of character under that influence, and show the natural and necessary sequence by which later developments arose. It carefully traces only those unconscious influences which shape and mold mental and moral qualities, and through which *Slavery still lives and dominates*.

Since the first publication of this book the impulse to go further, and to include more broadly—both in number and in representative character—the impressions made upon my mind by the various elements of life in our Southern States, has, very naturally, but without intention, resulted in a series of these pictures. The past quarter of a century has been a remarkable era—the meeting point of divergent systems, the arena where antagonistic civilizations struggled for mastery. Knowledge and ignorance, slavery and freedom, Northman and Southron, Caucasian and African were the opposing forces and contrasted elements. Scarcely any age or nation presents so rich a field of romantic incident as the conflict of these forces, viewed at first by the glare of battle and afterward by the fitful gleam of the embers of revolution.

The relations between a subject and a dominant race are always fruitful of romance. Inequality of rank (which may be said to culminate in the relation of master and slave) is the burden of nearly all romantic fiction. In our Southern States, since the legal status of the two races has become identical, it is a task of extreme delicacy to trace the line of previous habit and note its continued strength. What the observer may clearly recognize it may be difficult to convey to the reader's mind, because the life of the present is engrafted on the root of the past—because Yesterday binds with fetters

of brass To-day.   Yet this very difficulty adds a kind of
zest to the task, and the student of history may well
pause to consider carefully these strange and strongly
contrasted elements while yet they are incongruous in
their new relations, and before the Old shall have gradually given way to the irresistible New.

"*A Fool's Errand*," written in the summer of 1879,
deals chiefly with the turbulent era of what has been
called "Reconstruction," and, naturally, depicts the
typical elements that were prominent in that seething
caldron of politics heated by the fiery passions of caste.

"*'Zouri's Christmas*," which is included in the present
volume, gives another view—a brighter and pleasanter
one, showing the kindly feelings between the freedman's
family and the former master and mistress, a case in
which continuing relations of dependence, though no
longer of bondage, preserve in the dominant race all the
generous cordiality which they feel for the negro "in his
own place."   Its importance as a social study is not
indicated by its brevity.

In "*Bricks Without Straw*" some aspects of the present
condition of the colored race (1880) and their relations
to the whites in the great matters of Labor and Education
afford still another point of view, and present still new
types of character and romantic interest.

No one of these pictures professes to be a complete or
perfect representation of the whole era, but only of portions of it, and of the types selected, each picture being
taken from a standpoint peculiar to itself.

A new edition of the present work has been
called for, and, in order that it may take its
proper and permanent place in this unpremeditated
"series," as setting forth the prime and simplest elements of the whole system of the Southern civilization

—the Master and the Slave, separated by the whole
diameter of the social sphere, and yet united in a common destiny by that universal human passion, love—I
have revised it, eliminated some extraneous matter,
restored the original plan of the work, which followed
the facts in leaving the central problem unsolved, and
have given it the title which its main character naturally
demands—"*A Royal Gentleman.*"

For the types portrayed I claim only the utmost exact-
ness in tracing the verisimilitude of nature. That they
do not conform to certain conventional pre-notions may
be freely admitted. If the Poor White, the Slave, the
Freedman, and the Royal Gentleman are not as degraded,
as astute, as apish, as brutal or as noble as we have
been wont to have them pictured for us, assuredly the
fault is not in the present delineator. If the *unconscious*
influences of a former *régime* are here accounted more
potent in producing the effects which we behold to-day
than the more apparent and tangible horrors of slavery,
it is only because long and patient study has taught the
fact. If the reader shall be surprised to find the idea
intimated that the dominant race suffered greater loss
from the relation of slavery than the servile one, without
any of that compensating development which the latter
received, the writer cannot admit himself in error, however startling the proposition. If the typical Royal Gentleman shall apparently lack some of those regal attributes with which our fancy has been wont to clothe his
class, the writer can only regret that the term has not
been more sharply defined or the attributes of the class
more clearly and justly analyzed hitherto.

In examining the many press notices, letters, etc.,
which the original issue of the story called forth, it has
been amusing to note that points of the book which at

the North are accounted defects, at the South are considered excellences, and *vice versa*. Perhaps few things have been more sharply criticised at the North than the putting of the popular dialect into the mouth of Manuel Hunter, who is represented as an able and accomplished lawyer, and a politician of national eminence. At the South, on the other hand, the truth of this representation has been universally recognized. So life-like, indeed, is this picture, that hundreds of readers without hesitation pitched upon one who was among the most eminent and accomplished lawyers of his day and State as its original; not from the circumstances of his life, for these did not accord, but from the close imitation of his language and manner. One of his contemporaries, writing to me, says: "I can see ———— in every line of Manuel Hunter. He was a grand man, and you have drawn him to the life. I believe no one has ever noticed before how our old-time country lawyers affected the vernacular, or *dialect* rather. I suppose they did it to enhance their power of presenting facts to the jury." To the Northern mind this rugged, quaint, but very English dialect is the ear-mark of the " poor white," by whom it is supposed to be employed simply from ignorance; like the traditional dialect of Brother Jonathan—having a possible parallel among the most ignorant country folk, but not to be thought of in the temples of justice or the *penetralia* of " first families." After an experience of many years at the bar and on the bench of the South, I can honestly say that many of the finest and most eloquent appeals I have ever heard addressed to court or jury have been very largely clothed in this rough and peculiar but wonderfully strong and pungent dialect.

The trouble is that the Northern man has made up a South for himself, and, without the least hesitation, criticises any departure from the original of his own imagination as untrue to life.

The same stricture has been made as to Betty Certain. She sometimes uses the vernacular dialect and sometimes does not. This would be unnatural at the North, where such a dialect would be considered evidence of ignorance, of which every one is anxious to avoid the imputation. At the South, however, it will not do to judge any man's position, wealth, or culture by his language, the clothes he wears, or the house he lives in.

A similar state of facts is true as regards Chapter XXXVII., "In His Mark." It has been severely denounced at the North as a piece of unnatural and impossible cruelty of spirit. At the South it has received, perhaps, more universal commendation than any other part of the book. I quote from the letter of one of the most accomplished lawyers, descended from one of the most cultivated and influential families of North Carolina. He says of it: "It is one of the truest and subtlest studies of character I have ever read. I would like to know the incident on which it is founded, as it is quite beyond mere invention. I can see how it would seem despicably mean from a Yankee stand-point—and it was mean, considering all its relations; but just think what a provocation—what an *abomination*—the conduct of the heroine seemed, to one raised as he had been!"

Finally, I must add that this story is in "advocacy" of nothing whatever; *it is a picture of facts.* Farther it does not go nor lead. Its pages were written because "I looked, and saw, and a voice said 'Write!'" They were published after many days, asking but the favor of

"one moment
Of the busy world's attention;"

which has been kindly accorded in the demand for numerous editions.

Issued under the title of "*A Royal Gentleman*," the story simply takes its place in the series alluded to, comprising works already published and others in course of preparation. In putting forth this edition, the author desires to acknowledge his indebtedness to the public for exceptional favors, and to express the hope that the interest thus shown may result in a just and righteous comprehension of the questions which now press upon the nation for solution, and to which he has tried to contribute some light.

ALBION W. TOURGEE.

NEW YORK, *May* 1, 1881.

CONTENTS.

LIST OF ILLUSTRATIONS.

A ROYAL GENTLEMAN.

CHAPTER I.

MANUEL HUNTER.

IT was Christmas Eve in the year of grace 1858.
Manuel Hunter sat in his private room, half office
and half library, connected with his spacious mansion
by a covered way, latticed at the sides and overgrown
with vines. The building was a substantial brick one,
its front door opening on the main street of Perham,
a pleasant county-town of Carolina, which lay in the
midst of broad plantations and noble outlying country
mansions, a rifle-shot from the banks of the Cold
Spring, a sparkling tributary of the impetuous river
which sweeps through the Piedmont valley. It was a
rambling town of the olden time, with a history that
went back into the ante-revolutionary days, when it
was one of the boroughs which were honored with a
delegate in the Colonial Assembly. Its wide streets
were lined with ancient oaks and graceful elms, and
paved with a rude flagging which was said to have
been laid by the hands of British soldiers.

The interior of the room had that strange blending
of business and leisure, of office and library, so frequently met with in the den of the Southern legal practitioner; for Manuel Hunter was a well-to-do lawyer,

and still the leader on the circuit where he practiced, though now well past threescore. An immense fireplace upon one side, piled full of hissing logs, spread a genial radiance over the room, which was also lighted by a tallow dip stuck into a candlestick whose shape and substance were effectually concealed by greasy laminæ, resulting from the expiring agonies of an unnumbered succession of tallow dips consumed therein. A collection of red and brown clay pipes of various patterns and sizes, with their long reed stems, so familiar to the smoker of that section, adorned one corner of the fireplace, and several shorter editions of the same were stuck in an open cigar-box upon the mantle, in which was a goodly supply of tobacco—a thin plug of which also peeped from the capacious pocket of the owner's coat. The table was covered with a miscellaneous array of books and papers, the usual legal paraphernalia, mixed with pipes, matches, and almost anything else for which it afforded easy lodgment—a part of which débris had been pushed aside to make room for the large server brought by a sprightly slave-girl, and which she was then in the act of taking from her head and depositing thereon.

It had covers for two, and a plentiful supply of goodly viands.

The girl removed the napkins, arranged the dishes, poured out the coffee and set the urn upon coals dragged from the fire to keep it warm, and then stood by as if awaiting orders.

The master fumbled in his pocket awhile, and finally, dragging forth a bunch of keys, selected one, and handing it to her, motioned towards a sort of side-board on which stood a water-bucket and a drinking gourd. The girl opened the cupboard, took out a decanter and glasses, and placed them upon the table.

" That 'll do, gal. I 'll call ye to take 'em away," said the master, and the girl retired and closed the door.

Manuel Hunter, by the light of the tallow candle upon the table and the flashing fire, was a man of goodly presence, sixty or more, half gray, somewhat inclined to corpulency, fidgety in his movements, and rather roughly and negligently clothed. As he sat there in his splint-bottomed easy chair, he was a fine sample of a Southern country attorney at home. He had been a figure at the bar in his day, and was a man of no mean acquirements in the law.

He had had his share of honors too. In the Legislature of his native State, and in the national Congress, he had represented his county and district. His faculty of keen observation, thorough good sense, and naturally strong logical power, with a sort of quaint humor and half-affected roughness of expression and manner, made him a power upon the stump, and a wheel-horse of his party in the section where he resided. There were current rumors that more than once, and that, too, in important crises of his party and the nation, this uncouth country lawyer had been offered positions of the first importance in the government. Certain it was, that in one of those massive cases in the office, there were piles of letters bearing the frank of more than one of our great party leaders, and of the heads of more than one administration. If, however, he had received such offers, they had never been accepted by him. Though he had served one or two terms in Congress, he had come back to his old mistress, ·the law, with renewed diligence after each absence, like a penitent truant to his task. There seemed to be something in the intricate subtlety and ever-varying analogies and differences, agreements and conflicts, of the common law, which gave it an unfailing charm to his mind. Whether it was the force of long established habit, or because the rugged energy of his nature delighted in its obstacles, it would be difficult to determine. True it was, and also true that he looked to his achievements at the bar as the solid ground of whatever remembrance he might receive among the people. His political triumphs were mere incidents of his career. They were sports, though they might be the sports of a giant.

"Well, Geoffy, son," he said, taking off the high-crowned hat which comported oddly enough with the jeans he wore, and removing from his mouth a masticated segment of the plug in his pocket, "fill the glasses. You 're young and peart. Yes, sugar. Only a drop of the whiskey, though," he added, as the liquor approached the brim. "There, there—not too much. You want to make your old daddy drunk. Stop, stop, you knave!"

He took the glass, and half its contents disappeared at a draught.

He was one of those who are so often termed the "old style" of men, who were not afraid of a glass of grog; who took their whiskey "straight," and knew it was pure, because distilled by themselves or their neighbors. Since the days of temperance societies, temperance revivals, and prohibitory legislation, the old man had been frequently cited as a strong argument against all such anti-convivial ideas and measures. Whether it was the sturdy constitution unimpaired by the excesses of previous generations, the quality of the liquor which he drank, or the fact that he *was* "one of the old fellows," which preserved him from the effects of life-long potations may well be left to the decision of those oracles who preside at the veiled mysteries of modern temperance—that shyest of all virtues, which hides itself, not in the enticing grove or the darkened cloister, but under the seductive veil of secrecy in the oath-bound Lodge—which unites with exquisite mimicry the solemnities of the sanctuary and the gayeties of the festival.

"No! no more," said he, as his son held the bottle towards him again. "Well, yes, you may—just a little. This is more 'n half water, anyhow," with a gesture toward his glass. "That's good whiskey, though— some of the real old style, made by an old Dutchman at a little spring-still up the country. I got it for a fee—half a barrel on 't—six or eight years ago. By the by, I missed a mighty plain pint of law in the case and got non-suited. My client, old Quarles, you know, son, was powerful mad, as who could blame him, and, reaching over the bar, he caught my collar, drew me down, and said, 'How's this, Mister Lawyer, they say I am non-suited?' 'Sho, sho!' says I, 'didn't you hear what the judge said?' 'No,' said he, somewhat dubiously. 'Why, sir,' says I, pompously, 'he said it was *coram non judice*, sir, *coram non judice!*' 'Did he say that?' said old Quarles, 'then, of course, it's all right.' He went off satisfied, and I kept the whiskey. I hed clean forgot it till just t'other day."

The old man chuckled at the remembrance of his joke. His son refilled the glass, and while it is being emptied let us look at him.

A face over which twenty summers might have passed, a light brown beard and moustache, clear gray eyes, a broad brow, and hair darker than the beard. Above the middle height, with a rather full figure, dressed in fashionably cut garments of rich material, but with something of his father's negligence of wear. As he sat carelessly leaning on his elbow, sipping his whiskey, and gazing dreamily at the fire, one would have said of him that life had been easy to him thus far, and, in the main, pleasant; that his future was—as chance should make it. He was a man of good possibilities, of dormant powers. For the present, cultivated, indolent, dreamy, and yet of keen perceptions and quick sensibilities; somewhat haughty of manner but frank and free among his friends, and of generous impulse; not unselfish or self-sacrificing, but ready to give of his abundance, and to scatter profusely what his thrifty father had carefully gathered. The whole county knew him for " a right royal gentleman."

"Well, sonny, let's eat," said the old man. "I told them to bring our supper here, Geoffy, son, 'cause I wanted to have a good talk with you, and somehow no place comes quite so natural for me to talk in, as the old office. I've done a heap o' wuk here, son, in my time. Forty years—'twas logs then, Geoffrey—arly an' late, summer 'n winter. Thar a'n't no nigger 'n the State 's ever tiled harder 'n ole Manuel Hunter, not one. An' it's all been for you, too, son—you an' the gals, now Jeems is gone. Poor boy! poor boy! Don't do as he did, Geoffy, don't. Don't kill yourself with drink. Yer ole father's been easy— too easy, I 'spect, with both on ye. He must hev a little himself; always did. But don't take too much, son, don't. There, take it away, Geoffy. Put it in the cupboard there, and lock it up. It makes me sad. Poor boy! I wanted him to take my place at the bar, Geoffy. You never will. More like yer ma, poor dear. Yes, I know; you'll study—to please me, and I'm glad of it—though, as you say, thar a'n't no need on 't, as thar was for me. No, I sha'n't leave you in debt, son. The old man ha'n't talked and writ all his life to do that; and he knows how hard 'tis for a youngster, too, to start with a load on his back. But I did want the Hunter name to be kep' up on the circuit. The rogues 'll all turn honest arter I'm dead, 'cause thar 'll be nobody to clar 'em. But there, there; let 's not talk any more about business till supper is over."

As the meal progressed the old man grew cheerier and their conversation lightened till, at its close, he called boisterously for the serving-maid to remove the remnants.

"Toinette, Toinette!" he shouted. "Rot the lazy jade! Call her, Geoffrey; you are younger than I. Step to the door and call her, please."

His son did as he was bidden, and the girl soon
appeared and removed the server. The young man
filled one of the long-stemmed clay pipes, and, after
lighting, handed it to his father; then drawing forth a
large meerschaum, he filled and lighted it for himself.
and for a few moments the two men resigned themselves to a quiet enjoyment of the vaporous luxury.
Their pipes were not unfit representatives of themselves: the old man's crude and strong, but capacious
and not without a certain look of luxury; the young
man's smooth, compact, and polished — a luxury in
itself. At length the old man spoke:

"It's Christmas, Geoffrey, son, to-morrow, and you
know next week whatever plans are to be laid for the
next year's business must be settled on; and now that
you 've come home — I hope to stay — I wanted jes' to
talk things over with you quietly and set our stakes
for the year's work. I sha'n't leave you in debt, son,
as I told you awhile back, if I die to-morrow. But fust
hand me that bundle of papers in the right hand corner of the desk there. So. Now let 's see what ole
Manuel's worth, and what there is to take keer of.
Where 's my specs, child? Oh, here!"—as he drew
them down from the top of his head.

"Well, what 's this?" said he, taking the first paper
from the file. "The deed of the home place. The
plantation has been in the family ever since it was
settled. Yer grandfather left it mortgaged, though—
more 'n 'twas worth. I paid it off. There's the Gard-
ner plantation, the Culver place, the old Lovett place,
and other little parcels of two or three hundred acres

apiece, mostly lyin' on the river, and jes' as good corn and terbaccer lands as ever had a hoe in them— plenty of woodland and seventy odd niggers, besides the house servants, to tend 'em.

"You 've been livin' on the Lovett place sence you came home from college. It was lucky, too, comin' jest as Craigie took sick and I could get no overseer to look after it. And you've made a fine crap, too. How do you like plantation life, son?"

"So well," answered Geoffrey, "that I was about to ask you to let me have the Lovett place and the hands on it for Christmas Gift, and allow me to settle down into a quiet country bachelor."

"Sho, sho! my boy. Some of our high-strung gals about here would have you in their train afore a twelvemonth," said the father, laughingly.

"I am not anxious for a mistress," replied the son with a shrug, "and I like the seclusion of the Lovett place. You know, father, I am not fond of carousing."

"True, true," said the old man, hastily, "and I thank God for it. But why not come home and live with us and study here in the office?"

"Why do you so often dine and sup in the office, father?"

The father smoked a moment in silence, and then said, in a saddened tone:

"The house *is* lonely, Geoffy, since yer mother died, though your sisters have a good deal of company, and your aunt is a good housekeeper. It *is* lonely."

"You know," said Geoffrey—and his voice choked,

for his mother's memory was pure and fresh to him—
"it is not far to the Lovett place. I could ride to
the office every day, if need be."

"So you could, son," was the reply. "It a'n't
just as I'd planned it, but what's the difference?
There a'n't but three on ye, no how, an' it's all
your'n at last. You shall have the Lovett place to
your share, and I'll make you a deed on't at once—
and the hands and stock. Have ye enough there
now to do the work on't?"

"One or two more could be worked to advantage,"
said Geoffrey, "and there are no house servants except Bob and old Maggie."

"You ought to hev another house servant; a
woman. What un 'll ye take?" said his father.

"I would like it if you could let me have Toinette.
She is young and lively, and old Maggie does remind
one a little too much of a burying, sometimes," answered the son.

"Oh, we couldn't spare Toinette!" said the old
lawyer, with a sharp glance at his son, as if he were
a witness under examination.

"Very well," said the young man, without looking
up. "Any one you can spare better would suit me as
well."

"So, so; I knew it," said his father. "No, you
shall hev her. She was a favorite with Ruthy, and, as
you say, is young and lively. She'll be a likely gal
sometime, too. I'll make out all the papers and give
ye a plantation ready stocked to begin with for your
Christmas."

The young man was about to express his thanks when the father stopped him with—

"No, no, Geoffy; you've got to study hard enough to pay for this. If I set you up in the world before you are twenty-one, you've got to promise to keep up the Hunter name at the bar of the circuit."

"I will try my best, father," said the young man, but his tone did not presage success.

"I have a new edition of Blackstone that I purchased for you lately," said the father, "a right fine one, too, with a new style of type, and the most keerfully edited book I ever looked into. It's a Philadelphia edition, and just out. You may begin at once. Come over every Saturday and I'll put you through a set of questions, and have you ready for the County Court in a year at most."

Awhile longer the two men sat together—father and son: the one old and rough, scarred with many a battle with the world, yet warm and tender-hearted to his boy, as a mother to her babe. He was still a child to those fond old eyes. And the son, young, unskilled, unscathed by conflict with the world, and careless what it had in store for him.

Along the covered way to the house, and into the bright lighted parlor, they went together.

And so the plantation known as Lovett Lodge, five miles from Perham by the river road, and the girl "Toinette," with sundry other "chattels-real," passed into the hands of the young master, Geoffrey Hunter, Esq., from his father, Manuel Hunter—a Christmas Gift, princely and unconditioned.

CHAPTER II.

"CHRISTMAS GIFT!"

THE next day was Christmas; Christmas at the Great House, in which Manuel Hunter lived— "The Hunter Home," as he had jocosely named the plantation years before.

As the gray dawn crept over the hill tops, a motley crew of almost every age and shade of color came thronging up from from the row of low, whitewashed huts, which constituted the servants' quarters, to the Great House. It was the modern slave's saturnalia— the heathen festival rebaptized and christened—the week whose license was a ludicrous mimicry of freedom, with an undertone of sadness, like the refrain of a plantation melody. Clad in their Sunday's best, they thronged the piazza and hall of the House, and besieged with uproarious freedom the room where "Ole Master" slept; and then, by turns, that of every other member of the household.

"Christmas Gif, Mas'r Manuel"! "Christmas Gif"! "Christmas Gif"! was shouted, again and again, in every variety of tone, from the shrill treble of child-hood to the trembling huskiness of age. Male and female vied with each other in increasing the clamor.

Meantime the old man had risen and was calling for his body-servant.

"Dick! O Dick!" he shouted, well knowing that

Dick had gone, with Manuel Hunter's pass in his pocket, to a plantation several miles distant, to spend the Christmas. "O Dick!" he exclaimed again, angrily; and then opening the door, half-clad as he was, he called for him again.

"Where has that black rascal gone? I say, Dick!"

His appearance was the signal for renewed vociferations.

"Christmas Gif! Christmas Gif, mas'r! De Lor' bress him! H'm jus as spry 's if he was n't gwine on seventy. H'm 'll live to keep many a rogue from kissin' the widder yit! Ki! no danger ennybody dancin' on nuffin while Mas'r Manwel lives! Nebber see a hangin' agin! De sheriff's dun got so he dunno how tu tie de knot! It 's gone out of fashion on de surcutes eber sense Mas'r Manwel clar de man fur killin' tree 't wonst! Lor', Lor,' 't use to be just as common puttin' hemp roun' a gemman's neck as roun' a cotting bale, 'fore Mas'r Manwel's time, I 'members! *I* do!" said an old man, with a bald crown surrounded by pads of snowy wool, who leaned upon a staff, and seemed to be regarded as a sort of chief among them.

They knew the weak point of the old man, his repute as a criminal lawyer, and with the slave's deft flattery struck it at once, and bows and cheers, waving hats, handkerchiefs and aprons, greeted the master of threescore slaves.

"Is that you, Martin? How d'ye, old man," said the master. "Why, you 're as peart as if you were n't more 'n twenty-five this mornin'. You'll help me, won't you, Marty, boy, if that fellow Dick has run away? He

ought tu hev twenty licks for it. How d'ye, boys?
How d'ye, gals? My shoes, Martin, and stockings.
Where can that black rascal hev put 'em?"

Old Martin was down upon his knees at once, and
the crowd poured into the room, each one prying into
nooks and corners after the master's lost clothing,
while he kept on, half petulantly, half humorously,
scolding Dick and saying something pleasant to every
one whose eye he caught, alternately.

At length old Martin found one of the shoes under
the bed, and carefully shaking it, out rolled a silver
dollar, which he instantly appropriated, with a whoop
of delight and a mocking "Sarvant, sah," as he bowed
and scraped to his master, who angrily exclaimed:

"Here, you old rascal, are you going to rob me?"

"Hi! yah! yah!" laughed the old negro, still
clutching the silver, "Mas'r ought ter hev a better
pus nor dat ter keep the shiners in, else niggas steal
'em, shore!"

It seemed as if the old man's money was everywhere except in its proper place, his purse. Each
stocking held a quarter; and when his vest was handed
to him he put both his hands through the arm-holes,
in the old-fashioned way of putting on that garment,
and, by some unaccountable carelessness in swinging
it over his head, scattered dimes and half-dimes about
the room in a style that produced the utmost confusion among the dusky rabble.

"Git out, you rascals!" shouted the old man,
stamping his feet in pretended rage.

"Here, Martin, give me your cane while I beat the

knaves. There! there!" he added, as all but old Martin left the room, and he stood, hat in hand, before him, "go wake up young Mas'r Geoffrey. Here, Marty, boy, is his Christmas Gift for him. You may take it to him. I've given him the Lovett place, and put you in to take care of him. You won't let him disgrace the old name, will you, Martin?"

"'Deed I won't, sah," replied the old slave, as he took the bundle of papers, and with a very consequential air marched at the head of the chattering troop toward young master's room.

Arriving at Geoffrey's door the clamor was renewed, but was soon hushed by the barking of a large Newfoundland dog, which the young master had brought home on his return from college, and who had a decided aversion to the dusky inhabitants of the plantation, though himself as highly "cullud" as any of them.

Leon had been growling his dissent to the riotous proceedings of the morning for some time. He regarded himself as the special guardian of Geoffrey, and always shared his room. Now, as the clattering feet came up the stairs and the servants clustered about the doorway, shouting their boisterous greeting, he burst out into a full-grown, threatening, imperative bark.

"Down, Leon! nobody will hurt either of us," said his master, "be quiet, I say!"

"Christmas Gif! Christmas Gif!" shouted the servants.

"Thank you, boys, thank you; but don't disturb me now. I'll give you some tricks by-and-by," said Geoffrey, lazily.

When the clamor subsided, old Martin, rapping deferentially upon the door, said:

"Please, sah, Mas'r Manwel guv me suthin', sah, as I was to giv you, sah, for your Christmas Gif."

"Well, come in," said Geoffrey. "Down, Leon!" as the old man opened the door and walked in, carefully leaving it ajar for the accommodation of his fellow-servants, who stood without, or perhaps to facilitate retreat in case of need.

"Sarvant, sah," said the old man, bending his snowy head, with a princely grace, to the young master, who sat up in bed and held out his hand for the packet, and glancing dubiously at the still growling Leon.

"Ah! I see," said the son, "the title-deeds of Lovett Lodge, with bill of sale of twelve hands and house servants, including you too, Uncle Martin. My father is very kind, indeed. I did not suppose he could spare you."

"Mas'r Manwel says he hed to sen' ole Martin to tak' keer ov de res', an' see that young Mas Geoff 'have himself," said the old man, with a chuckle.

"You and Hulda shall have the overseer's house then; and between us we will do his work, for I won't have one of that tribe on the place," replied Geoffrey.

"It's a right good plantation," said Martin, "with a heap of good lan', an' if ye jes' let ole Martin hev his way, dat force 'll make a power o' corn an' right smart uv terbaccer."

"Well, that will do, Martin. How d' ye, boys? I'll be down to the storehouse after breakfast and see

if I can find some Christmas gifts for you," said Geoffrey.

The old "uncle," with repeated bows and "Mornin',
ʌah's," backed out of the room, like an inferior man-
darin ducking to one of higher grade, carefully closed
the door and with his friends went to salute the other
members of the family, and then dispersed to the
amusements of the Christmas time—the one week out
of fifty-two in which they caught a far-off glimpse of
freedom, the one thing that kept alive their faith in
the good time coming, the oft-predicted " Jubilee."

Geoffrey Hunter laid his head back upon his pillow and wandered off into a quiet reverie, of which
himself and his possessions formed the subject matter.
He was now a man. The careless college life, with its
aimless rambling vacations, was over. He appreciated
the force of "*meum*" and "*tuum*," as applied to realty.
On the threshold of life he was independent, yes, rich—
one of the solid men of the country; one of the aris-
tocracy of the great South, securely entrenched behind
land and slaves, the two great bulwarks of respectability. These, if managed with prudence, would yield
him a constantly increasing income, and as he grew
older make his position still more secure. He would
take care of it. He was not extravagant nor, as he
assured himself, foolish. With his books, his music,
and his pipe, he pictured to himself a quiet country
life—independent, easy, honorable.

What would he do? What was his ambition? He
had none. Why should he toil, as his father had done,
until inaction was unbearable? Circumstances would

do for him all that he desired. He had only to stand
and wait. Inaction was his best card, sure to win, and
no risk. Enjoyment was his aim. He would, therefore, be temperate, frugal, careful of his tastes and
habits, lest he should impair his power of enjoying the
good things fortune offered him. He would be a man,
not a beast; a philosopher, not a fool; and, accordingly,
would seek only cultivated and refining pleasures, not
bestial ones.

And who would enjoy these pleasures with him?
The full lip, sensuous and frank, curled into an unwonted sneer, and a half flush spread over his cheek
as the thought crossed his mind. It might have been.
It could not be again. He had told his father the
night before that he had no desire to be the slave of
any woman. He meant it. When his mother died, his
faith in womanhood died too. So he said.

A boyish disappointment rankled in his memory.
When scarce a man he had thought he loved, and
had avowed his attachment to, a woman much older
than himself. Instead of treating with respect the
passionate avowal of the young heart, and saving the
self esteem of the impetuous lad, she had laughed at
his youth and driven him into the cynicism which he
had maintained so long that it had become half real.
He had determined to abjure women and prided himself on being a woman-hater. In the expressive phrase
of his vernacular he said he had "no use for them."
He half disliked his sisters and his aunt. There were
but three women among his slaves till he added that
fly-about creature last night. What did he do that

for? He did not know. He half wished they were all men. But one thing was sure, no woman should be mistress in his house. His servants should owe no divided allegiance if he lived to be four-score; that was settled. The mouth shut quietly and firmly, the brow drooped, the eyes half closed. There was an iron will about the young nabob.

Cool, cautious, selfish, ambitious only for enjoyment, and having in the very refinement of this desire a safeguard against degrading pleasures, what will be his life?

As he went down to breakfast Geoffrey Hunter met his new chattel, Toinette. She was carrying a server to the dining-room, for her mother was the cook at the Hunter Home, renowned for skill throughout the country side.

"Christmas Gif', Mass Geoff," said the handmaiden, dropping a courtesy under the server balanced on her head.

"What do you want for your Christmas, Toinette?"

"A new dress and a white apron, if you please, sir," answered the girl, pertly.

Geoffrey smiled.

"I will give you that," he said, "and the greatest Christmas you ever had, beside."

The look of childish pleasure on her face faded into wonder as she gazed up at his and followed him into the dining-room without further question.

No one else of the family had as yet answered the bell. He leaned against the mantel and watched the girl, as with an absent manner she removed the differ-

ent dishes from the tray and placed them on the table.
He remembered his father's words, "She 'll be a likely
gal some day." There could be no doubt of that, and
quite unconsciously he began to estimate the market
value of this piece of humanity a few years later, when
Time should have ripened her charms, and developed
her fine points.

He was not sordid or unfeeling. He was simply
speculating on the probable future value of his newly
acquired possession, as the jockey calculates the
"come out" of a colt, or the milkmaid counts the
eggs which exist only in expectancy. He did not
concern himself with the humanity or womanhood
of Toinette. Much less did he consider her moral
relations with himself, humanity or God. The law
made her his slave, and he was troubled with nothing
beyond. It was the chattel, not the human being, of
which he thought. "*Homo non persona,*" is the definition which the law gives to the status of the slave,
and the hater of slavery cannot wonder that the
master should contemplate only the legal relation. It
was but natural. True, Toinette was not so dark as
many of the race who are counted the descendants of
the unfortunate Ham but her mother was—well, a
shade darker than she; and the rule of the law is
inflexible *partus sequitur ventrem.* And so Toinette
was a slave, legally and properly, though scarcely of
darker integument than her new master, and perhaps
of no meaner ancestry, paternally.

He took the bill of sale from his pocket, and
read :

"Yellow girl, Toinette, daughter of Mabel, fourteen years old, regular featured, bright complexioned."

That was the description, and Geoffrey Hunter concluded that "the fly-about Toinette," as he had termed her, "would be a fine article, worth a pretty penny in a few years," as his father had said. Just then came to his ears the voice of the chattel, as she advanced through the long hall, bringing something from the kitchen beyond. She had forgotten her perplexity, and was singing, in very forgetfulness, that noble Christmas carol,

"Brightest and best of the sons of the morning."

There was nothing ignoble in the voice. Rich and full it pulsed along the notes of this grand old anthem, wild and free. "A fine voice" he thought, as unconsciously he hummed the air himself.

As she entered the doorway her singing ceased, and she advanced to the table.

"Where did you learn that song, Toinette," asked Geoffrey.

"Of Miss Ruthy, sir," answered Toinette, without interrupting her work.

"Have you guessed what is the other Christmas Gift I am to let you have?" he asked.

"La, no, sir, dun forgot all 'bout it. I reckon you 'se jis foolin me," she said, laughingly.

"No," said he, "you are going to have a new master."

The plate fell from the young girl's hand, the color fled from her cheeks, and she gasped, "Is dat so?"

"Yes, indeed it is. Father sold you yesterday," he answered.

"And mammy?" asked Toinette.

"No, he could not spare her," Geoffrey replied.

The girl's agony was painful to witness. He did not enjoy the scene, and he hated anything he did not enjoy. So he made haste to end it, by saying. "But you have not asked who bought you, yet."

The sound of his voice seemed to have awakened the girl from a sort of trance, into which she had fallen. Quick as thought she was down before him, clasping his knees, and crying out:

"Don't, don't, Mass Geoffrey, don't let 'em sell me 'way from mammy! Don't let 'em take me 'way! I'll work, Mass Geoffrey, arly an' late! I won't never be naughty! No, I won't! Pore mammy! Pore mammy! 'Twould kill her, Mas'r Geoffrey! Think of yer own mammy; her that learned me the pretty songs, and was kind to Toinette; that said she loved her most as well as if she was her own gal! I wa'n't never bad to Miss Ruthy, Mass'r Geoffrey," and she raised her face, pallid with fright, and with the tears streaming down it—the thick brown hair falling back from the fair broad brow—and looked at him beseechingly.

"Don't, Mass Geoffrey, for yer mudder's sake, and the good Lord's sake! Don't let 'em take me 'way!" His eyes moistened at this impetuous appeal, and his voice was a little uncertain too, as he said, quickly:

"I won't, Toinette, I won't. I have bought you myself. I am your new master. I am going to live at Lovett Lodge, and you can come and see Mabel as

often as you wish. Father gave you to me for a
Christmas gift. There, there! Go now." The chattel
was kissing his hands, and exclaiming through her
tears,

"Thank you, thank you! God bless you, Massa
Geoffrey."

Somehow the master seemed to have overstepped
the legal definition, and confounded the "Homo" with
the "Persona," the chattel with the child. Very plain
distinctions are sometimes difficult to maintain.

CHAPTER III.

MABEL.

WHEN Toinette returned to the kitchen one or two of the other servants were there talking of their holiday pleasures, so she said nothing to old Mabel of her change of masters. Her agitation, however, did not escape the sharp eye of the old slave woman. There is no Lavater in the world who can compare, as a skillful physiognomist, with an observing slave.

"What was the matter in yon "—with a motion of the head toward the great house—" this morning, Toinette?" said her mother when the breakfast was over, and she was preparing for the great dinner which was to be served at the Hunter Home that evening, as the Southern people always term the afternoon.

"Mas'r Geoffrey scared me, mammy—that's all," answered Toinette, carelessly.

"How?" demanded the mother sharply.

"He told me I had got a new master now, and I thought I had been sold away from you, mammy."

"No fear of that," said Mabel. "Miss Ruthy told me you should n't ever be sold away from me, an' Mas'r Manwell sed de same, an' promise Miss Ruthy on her dyin' bed dat neither on us should

OLD MABEL.

"She sat down on the floor of the kitchen, pulled the white turban from her head and moving back and forth, moaned piteously." —p. 32.

ever be parted with, less we 's sot free, as we sartin should be when he died,—so do n't hev no trouble on dat score, chile."

"No, mammy. Mas'r Geoffrey tole me afterward that I was n't sole away, but jes made a Christmas gif to him," said Toinette.

"A Christmas gift to Geoffrey Hunter!" said Mabel incredulously.

"Yes," Toinette hastened to say; "but he is going to live on the Lovett place, and I can come and see you when I choose."

"No doubt, no doubt," said her mother, with a sneer. "Ah, chile, chile, better you had never been born. O God! O God! canst thou not leave me this one!"

She sat down upon the floor of the kitchen, pulled the white turban from her head, and weaving back and forth, moaned piteously. With her eyes closed, her long, white hair waving in the chill winter wind, her tall form swaying to and fro, and muttering brokenly, it is no wonder that the superstitious servants fled in affright, declaring that Aunt Mabel was making charms to witch somebody. Toinette having tried in vain to arouse and console her mother fled with the other servants in terror.

In an hour or two the report of Aunt Mabel's condition reached Miss Lucy, Geoffrey's aunt, who straightway repaired to the kitchen; having in constant remembrance the fact that the grand dinner was dependent solely upon the exertions of the old cook. Entering the hut which served the princely Hunters

for a kitchen, she beheld Aunt Mabel squatted on the
ground before the fire, surrounded by the implements
of cookery, still weaving to and fro, and continuing the sing-song utterances which had been taken for
incantations. And indeed there was something truly
fearful in the thin, spare figure, the stern, sad face, of
old parchment hue, and the heaving masses of long
white hair, which floated unconfined about her head.
Allied to the race whose curse she bore, remotely, if at
all, Aunt Mabel was a woman who showed unmistakable marks of terrible suffering and all but invincible
fortitude. The tall figure was unbowed, and the vigor
of maturity rather than the weakness and indecision of
age characterized her movements. It was evident that
the deep furrows on her brow and the mass of white
hair which hung upon her shoulders were the result
of sorrow and affliction, not of years. The mouth
whose nether lip had not lost its fullness, even amid
the relaxation of overwhelming calamity, yet bore evidence of unusual firmness.

"What's all this fuss about, gal?" was the greeting of Miss Lucy.

Old Mabel, for the first time, ceased her crooning,
and turned sharply on the intruder. Her brow gathered a severe expression, and her face darkened with
wrath.

"Is it true, Miss Lucy?" she said almost fiercely.
"Ye know, an' ye need n't try to fool old Mabel. Is
it true? Has Manwell Hunter"—she had forgotten
the mastership in her agony and wrath—"sole my baby,
my darlin', my las' one, that he promised Miss Ruthy

on her dyin' bed should never be sole, but stay wid
de family till he died?   He certain sed dat, ef I'd take
keer o' Miss Ruthy, an' I did—Toinette an' me nussed
her like a baby. An' Toinette learned to read—Miss
Ruthy holp her, though 'twas agin the law—so that she
might hear the blessed Gospel an' the Psalms, when
her own darters wud be gone for months, Mass'r Manwell on the circuit, an' young Mass'r Geoff away to
college, ez he's allers been nigh about. An' he promised atterwards—on'y the very day afore Miss Ruthy
died, when she was a beggin' him to set us free right
away, an' he 'llowed he would ef 't wasn't for the law
—he promised then that Toinette nor me shouldn't
never be sold, he did, an' that he'd put us in his will,
so 'z we'd both be sot free as soon as ever he died,
which he 'llowed wouldn't be long no way."

"Law, gal, there's no use to take on so. Toinette ain't sold—only given to Geoffrey for a Christmas. He'll never take her away. What does he
want of her?" answered Miss Lucy.

"Aye," broke in old Mabel, springing to her feet,
"what does he want of my gal? What did my young
master want of Mabel when she was young and handsome? When her cheek was 'most as fair an' her eye
as bright an' her step as nimble as Toinette's? Does
you know, Miss Lucy? Mabel's cheek wasn't holler
then, nor her hair bleached. What made it? There
was three of 'em and dey's all gone. Toinette was de
las' one. I ought to hev killed 'em when der lives was
young an' der souls was white an' pure. God forgive
me that I didn't. But I loved 'em, Miss Lucy, an' I

hoped. An' now *you* come an' ax me what dey want of my Toinette! "

The well-kempt mistress shrank from the uplifted finger, flashing eyes, and scathing tongue of the aroused old slave-woman, with scarcely less of terror than the servants had previously manifested.

"What an awful wicked old creature!" she muttered, as she trotted back to the house, glancing over her shoulder half-fearfully as she spoke. Then she remembered she had said nothing to Mabel about the dinner, which had been the object of her visit to the kitchen, and, after hesitating a moment, she returned. Seeing that Mabel had resumed her old position, she gathered courage and spoke as a mistress should, sharply and peremptorily.

"Mabel, we will have dinner at half-past one. There will be at least ten, and you had better set about getting it ready."

"Ef 't was only not de las' one!" muttered the grim presence on the hearth, with a fierce side-look from under her close-bent brows which sent the blood back to her mistress's heart with renewed terror.

"Horrid old thing!" said Miss Lucy, fleeing again to the house. "I do believe she would poison us all. I shall be quite afraid to eat anything after this. Who ever saw such an ungrateful creature? After being so indulged and having her own way in everything, too. But law, it's just like these niggers!" and the good lady arranged her collar at the parlor glass, and sat down to wait for dinner and the diners.

Mabel watched her as she retreated to the house,

and then, as if a new thought had struck her, arose and
marched at once up the latticed walk which led from
the house to Squire Hunter's office, along it to the door,
and, opening this without ceremony, walked up to the
table where her master sat, and, looking him straight in
the eyes while a deep fire burned in her own, she exclaimed :

"Is it true? Hev ye sole my gal, my baby, my
Toinette?"

"Sho, sho, Auntie," said the old attorney, fussily,
"do n't be so put out! Sold Toinette? No more I
hain't! Jes' made a present of her to Geoffrey. You
know the boy is lonely out at the Lovett place, with
nobody but old Maggie in the house, an' all old folks
on the plantation, too; an' no wonder either."

"Did n't you promise the blessed saint Miss Ruthy
on her dyin' bed that we should n't ever be separated,
and that we should both be sot free when you died, if
not afore?" she asked.

"Law, yes, child!" he replied, "but do n't take on
so; I forgot all about that; I did certain, Auntie, or I
would n't hev let him have her though he did ask me,
so I would n't. But, law, gal, he 'll be tired of his bargain and want me to rue, in a week. He 'll be glad to
send her back to you to get rid of her by that time.
Eh, gal?" and he attempted an unsuccessful chuckle.

"Yes, he 'll get tired of her some time an' send her
—not to her old mammy, but to de auction block!
Oh, Mas'r Manwell, what 'll ye tell Miss Ruthy when
she axes ye' bout little Toinette, that she loved most
like her own child?" said the old woman, solemnly.

"Pshaw, pshaw, gal, you 're foolish. The gal 's well enough off, an' would hev to be sold or hired some time," he said.

"Not ef you hed kep' your promise to the dead," broke in the old woman.

"That 's neither here nor there, now," he said, pettishly. "I have given a bill of sale to Geoffrey, and she 's his property now. If I 've broken my word, it 's the worse for me. But I 'll think of it when he comes in again, and see if he won't exchange her for some other gal."

"He won't do it, Manwell Hunter," she replied; "I knows the Hunter blood too well. Ef he 's set his heart on havin' the gal, the ole debble hisself could n't get him to turn loose his hold on her."

"Well, well, I do n't know; she 's his property and not mine. I 've nothing to do with it. Go away, gal, go way, and do n't bother me. There," said he, handing her a slip of paper, on which he had hastily written a few words, "give that to Hendricks, and he 'll let you have a fine calico and a new bonnet besides your regular Christmas."

Mabel had taken the paper, evidently thinking it referred to the matter uppermost in her mind, but as he spoke of its contents, she dropped it as if it burned her hand, and without looking up walked to the door, where, turning suddenly, she said in a deep, low voice:

"Manwell Hunter, may de God above do to you as you have done to Mabel's Toinette; little Toinette, dat Miss Ruthy loved an' you forgot. May de old Mas'r forgit you forever!"

She closed the door and departed. Manuel Hunter shivered in his great arm-chair before the blazing fire.

There was no dinner at the great house for the crowd of Christmas friends that day. It was a thing unheard of in the model menage of Manuel Hunter; but when Miss Lucy went to the kitchen at one o'clock, to give some trifling directions about the repast which should have been served some thirty minutes later, the great gaping fireplace was cold, pots and kettles were scattered around, and the materials which had been given out for the viands were still untouched.

Amid the confusion, Mabel was nowhere to be seen. Miss Lucy's lungs were exerted to the utmost shouting, "Mabel! O, Mabel!"

Her patience received another strain, and "the ingratitude of these niggers," was duly anathematized. Messengers were sent hither and yon among the servants to hunt up and return the delinquent under threats of various penalties. But all without success. Old Mabel had disappeared from the possession and control of Manuel Hunter. Another cook was perforce extemporized from among the servants, and two hours later a miserable travesty of the dinner expected was placed upon the board at the Hunter Home.

All this annoyance and discomfort was laid to Geoffrey's charge by his disappointed aunt and sisters, in terms which did not tend to increase his desire for their society.

"It was all owing to his foolish fancy for Toinette," they said, "that there was such trouble with
old Mabel. He was so selfish. He would have that
good-for-nothing yaller gal, if everybody went without
dinners for a year. It was just like him."

Such remarks impaired his self-complacency. He
did not like to be blamed abstractly, and especially
not for what he considered to be a mere accident.
So when *père* Hunter said to the new wearer of the
toga virilis, after ominous fidgettings and stammerings,
the next evening, "Geoffy, son, would you mind ex-
changing that gal Toinette for Mary's Cely?"

The young ex-collegian merely smoked a little
impatiently and said:

"I know of no reason why I should."

"Well, there ain't no reason, only Mabel takes on
so," replied the father.

"I don't intend to make any woman my mistress
nor allow her to control my actions—least of all a
servant," said the son. "Toinette will be as well off
at the Lodge as here, and better, too, for I sha'n't
expect her to work much. I am not a fool, and though
I don't intend to turn speculator, I know her value.
I asked for the girl because she was a favorite of
ma's and a sprightly creature. Now that you have
given her to me I shall keep her because Aunt Lucy
and my sisters have raised such a furore over my
causing old Mabel's pout, and so spoiling their dinner."

"True, true, she's your property," said the old
man with a tone of disappointment, and so the subject
was dropped.

It had been Geoffrey's intention to remain at the
paternal mansion during the Christmas week, but his
annoyance was so great that he directed his body-
servant, Bob, to have everything in readiness to return
to Lovett Lodge the next morning. He then sent for
Toinette and bade her make preparations to accompany
him. Seeing that the girl's face was clouded, and
divining the cause, he said:

"Don't be put out at Aunt Mabel's huff. She feels
badly at your going away, no doubt, but when she
finds how much easier you'll live at the Lodge than
here, she'll be glad you've gone."

Toinette was young and fond of novelty. To be
the property of Geoffrey, the son, instead of Manuel,
the father, was by no means a terrible thing in her
eyes. Her alarm on learning that she was sold was
the result not of a change of ownership, but of fear
of removal from her mother and acquaintances. Her
memories of Geoffrey before his collegiate days, and
during vacations since, were not unpleasant. He had
always been a favorite among his father's servants, and
was reported by the hands on the Lovett place to be
a good, kind master, and especially opposed to the
cruel regime of so many masters and overseers. They
even reported that the tobacco crop had been housed
that year and cured in fine style without a lick being
struck, or hardly an ill word being uttered; that they
had been well fed and fairly worked. Indeed, she
knew that very many of both sexes who had control of their own hiring had applied to "Young
Mass' Geoff'" to put in wid him for de nex' year."

But she remembered her mother's grief, so she only said :

"Thank you, Mas'r Geoffrey, I hope we'll get on well,"—in a quick, simple manner. Geoffrey looked at her and thought—as he would of a thoroughbred colt —fine blood there. She would be a lady if she wasn't a nigger. Yet she was a nigger. He knew that, and his property, too. She stood fondling old Leon's ear while their master mused. The dog had become very fond of the young girl who was making such trouble to others. At length Geoffrey said,

"But I promised you a new dress and apron,—I will do better; there," handing her a paper ; "is an order on Hendricks for a full rig; dress, shoes, apron, and other toggery, as a sailor would say. Get a nice Sunday suit, and never mind the price. Bob will go round with you."

The order read :

MESSRS. HENDRICKS & SON.—Please furnish my girl Toinette, the bearer, with as fine an outfit as your stock affords, regardless of cost, allowing her to select, and send bill by Bob.

                    GEOFFREY HUNTER.

"If I choose to make the gal a doll it's nobody's business. She's mine," said he to himself, as Toinette went out. The idea seemed to strike him with peculiar force. He would dress this slave girl as a lady, and people should count it among the eccentricities which already they attributed to him. She and Leon should be his pets. People should not say he did not show good taste in his selections. The idea pleased him wonderfully. He went himself the next morning to Hendricks & Son to see that his order was not taken with a limitation.

Old Mabel did not come back to the kitchen of Manuel Hunter during the Christmas, and all search for her proved unavailing. Miss Lucy declared that the overseer should give her "twenty licks" for every day she was absent, a report which Manuel Hunter instantly negatived upon hearing it,— informing Miss Lucy, somewhat sharply, that no one should strike his niggers, except by his direction. He asked every morning if she had returned, and seemed greatly troubled when answered in the negative. His neighbors said that "he sot a heap by that ongrateful old nigger." The servants "'llowed he was afeard he'd lose de bes' cook in de State."

Which was right? Was it the loss of his dinner or the loss of his chattel that troubled him, or had conscience stripped the husk of mastership from his soul and impressed upon him the humanity of his slave?

It was strange, but he made no threats, offered no rewards, and, in short, took none of the steps a master should to secure the recapture of a runaway.

4

CHAPTER IV.

FROM SIRE TO SON.

AT the time appointed, greatly to the surprise of the paternal Hunter, Geoffrey started for his new plantation,—himself and the driver, Bob, in the buggy seat, and on the oval trunk support behind, his new "yaller gal" Toinette, and—strange anomaly—her little bundle of earthly possessions, the chattels-personal, which, from a sort of necessity, adhered to the animate-personalty, the chattel-real. For, somehow, there was no legal subtlety which could deny the slave's right to some sort of an outfit.

The fourth day of "the Christmas"—for "the Christmas" to the slave reached from Dec. 25th to Jan. 1st, inclusive, the successive days being distinguished by numbering—had not opened as pleasantly as its predecessor seemed to have promised. A cold, drizzling, steady rain had set in with a sharp wind from the north-west. It was almost the first cold storm of the season. As Bob had remarked, lucidly, to the temporary cook, in the kitchen of the Hunter mansion—"Bin so warm, it jes' open de skin so 't one git full ob cold in a minit." Long wear had also opened the finger ends of Bob's gloves—"they was once Mass' Geoffrey's best pair, but that was a time ago," he had said, jollily—and, as he drove along, each dusky finger showed chill and shrunken through the worn integument. Well clad and comfortable sat the young master beside him, wrapped and muffled, smoking in quiet complacency. And behind, one hand clinging to the back of the buggy seat, the other at once holding her bundle and acting as an improvised balancing pole, sat Toinette. Her abbreviated frock, of the coarse linsey-woolsey which constituted the winter wear of slaves and poor whites, flying in the wind and her stockingless legs swinging to and fro, with the huge uncomely shoes, made for plantation use, bouncing back and forth as the wheels sank into overflowing ruts or mounted upon roots and stumps which adorned the highway, and which Bob was in no mood to shun.

Bespattered with mud, bedraggled with rain, chilled with the cold breath of the coming winter, she thought of her mother's words, "Child, it were better you had never been born." She was going away from her mother, away from home—she called it "home" and "hers." She almost laughed as she thought of it, not bitterly—she had not yet reached the dregs—but it seemed so absurd. What difference did it make to her where she was—where she went? Nothing was hers, not even herself. She doubted if her soul was. What matter where she lived? It was only so many days, and then—would she have anything, own anything, possess anything, be anything, after that great "Then"? She doubted.

How the wind blew! She almost wished the chill would reach her heart and stop its beating, before her life grew so fearfully sad as she knew her mother's must have been. The master was dreaming of the inheritance toward which he rode, and Bob was too cold to let the proud-stepping bay sleep in the traces. He looked around sometimes too, and saw the little half-clad creature behind, clinging to the seat-rail, and bouncing to and fro as if blown by the wind. He heard the low moans which came from the chilled lips, and slyly gave the bay a touch of the whip. The road was short from the Hunter Home to Lovett Lodge that day to one of the men, long enough to the bare-fingered chattel who held the whip and reins, and seemed almost endless to the drenched and drabbled creature, who was borne, chilled to the marrow, tearful and hopeless, away from slavery's childhood and a chattel mother, to a womanhood of bondage, with the protection only of Him who shields the lamb from winter storms.

Thus they went to Lovett Lodge.

"Bless me!" exclaimed Geoffrey, jumping from the buggy as they reached their destination, half-benumbed in spite of wrappings, as he saw old Leon, with his fore-paws upon the axle, licking the tear-stained face of his new friend, who clung in shivering unconsciousness to her perch, "Bless me, if the child isn't near about frozen! Maggie! O Maggie!"

The master's voice brought from the house old Maggie,—the very picture of rotund, healthy, black benignity. A form and face that bade defiance to age and trouble, and a step that showed capacity for a "heap o' work yit.'' Her best calico was doing its Christmas duty, the sleeves rolled above the elbows, to avoid mishap, while the snowiest of turbans crowned her head, whose matted locks were just beginning to show silver threads.

"Why, whoever in the world hev yo' got thar, Mass' Geoffrey?" she exclaimed, after dropping a curtsey and uttering the customary "Christmas Gif'." "Law sakes, ef t'aint Mabel's Toinette! Shakes like it had an agur fit," and the kind-hearted old slave woman folded her sooty arms about the shivering, splattered figure on the "buck-board," regardless of consequences to the best calico, and carried her affectionately into the house. Old Leon followed, contentedly, bringing the bundle which had fallen from Toinette's grasp.

There was a huge fire in the great sitting-room of the mansion, for, besides the master's absence, the fact that she was housekeeper at the Lodge, and his almost constant occupation of the Library, had given Maggie a show of reason for making herself a pretty constant denizen of this room. A measure which was attended with so many conveniences, and so prudently executed, that Geoffrey had not only come to acquiesce in, but really to approve, it.

He had all confidence in old Maggie, people said, and allowed her great privileges. Why should he not? Those strong arms had been his cradle, and from that bosom he had drawn the strength of his young life. She was his old nurse, and she loved him as her son, aye, even as she loved that son whose lips had been taken from her breast, and who had been sold to the trader, that she might give more at-

tention and care to the young heir of the Hunter
family.

"There was no trusting them," the sage Manuel
had said, when remonstrated with by his feeble wife.
They would neglect the children they were nursing,
as long as their own brats were in reach. It was a
likely young nigger, and would n't bring anything now,
scarcely; but it was better to sacrifice something, to
make sure the boy—his boy, the hope of the Hunter
name—should receive proper attention.

So the black baby was taken from the clinging arms
and yearning breast, and the puny white one placed
there instead. How the arms loathed it! How the
swelling breasts shrank from it, and refused it sustenance until its wailing cry minded the mother of her own
lost treasure. Then the arms clasped it close, the breast
yielded its wealth, and the slave mother supplied with
tearful assiduity the wants of her infant lord and master. She had a foolish notion, that as she cared for
her nursling so would the Good Master in Heaven care
for her own motherless boy. Of course it was foolish.
God cared nothing for the little nigger brat. But it
consoled her, and she had always kept up the delusion.
It made her feel better, and kept her from giving up
entirely. Thus the white baby had come almost unconsciously to take the place of the black one she had
lost, or, rather, since the latter was never forgotten, the
Caucasian master-child had come to be a twin existence, in the memory of the chattel-mother, with the lost
African slave-brat. So that when the actual baby in
her arms was christened, with abundant ceremony,

"Geoffrey," with loving tears she had baptized the dusky mannikin she nourished still in memory, "Jeff."

Before the huge fireplace sat a large splint-bottomed arm-chair, from which Maggie had risen when called by Geoffrey, and here she now deposited her burden, and had removed the dripping bonnet when Geoffrey appeared, bringing in the Christmas gifts which, carefully bundled up, had been stowed under the seat, during the ride.

"Pore thing, pore thing," repeated old Maggie, "whatever did you bring her fur, in dis awful weather Mas'r Geoffrey?"

"Why, to see you, Maggie, and be a little company for you," replied the young master.

"Wal, wal!" laughed Aunt Maggie, for she was not proof against flattery, especially from Geoffrey, and when it assumed the form of considerate kindness, "but ole Maggie's not so bad off fur company while young Mas'r Geoff's about that you need to go and freeze dis pore gal to death jes to bring her out to visit me, though I da'say she wanted to come an' see old Maggie. Dey all takes to me, black an' white—even de ole dog hisself. Why, whatever has he got now?" she exclaimed, as Leon came waddling up to her with a somewhat cumbrous bundle in his mouth. "Law sakes! ef 't tain't the pore chile's duds! What does it all mean, Mass'r Geoffrey?"

"Simply that my father made me a very bountiful Christmas gift, including the Lovett place, my old nurse, and about a dozen other servants," said Geoffrey, with a poorly-assumed air of confident indifference.

"Wal, wal, I'se jes de same as bin yourn' dis one an' twenty years," replied Maggie, "but dat don't 'splain Toinette's bein' here."

"Toinette was a part of the present," said Geoffrey.

"Wal, wal, I nebber! Toinette a part of de gif'!" said the old nurse in amazement.

"Why, what is there so surprising about that?' asked Geoffrey.

"Oh, nuffin, nuffin, only I heard Mass'r Manwel promise Miss Ruth that he never would sell or give 'way Toinette ner Mabel, an' when he died dat dey sartin should be sot free," answered Maggie.

"Did my father promise my mother that?" asked Geoffrey.

"He did, chile, sartin shore; shore 's ole nuss tells ye, an' ye know she wouldn't tell a lie fur de hull worl'," Maggie replied.

"No, Aunt Maggie, you never told me a lie, and I don't think you 'll begin now. This explains something though," said Geoffrey, and he began to pace the room with a disturbed countenance.

"What is it, honey?" said old Maggie, as she paused in her task of restoring consciousness by rubbing and warming Toinette's chilled limbs.

And then the young master sat down near the old servant and told her all that had occurred during the two previous days at the Hunter mansion. When he had finished the old nurse looked grave for a time, and then, turning sharply upon him, asked:

"What made ye ask Toinette of yer father? Ye

know he can't refuse ye, an' what do you want o' de
gal, anyhow?"

"I hardly know," he answered; "I had a fancy for
her. She is so full of life, quick and intelligent. I
believe if my motives had been analyzed at the time
they would have been found to be, to give you a little
help and a good deal of company."

"An' nuffin' else?" she asked, eyeing him closely.

He hesitated a moment, flushed angrily, and then
replied, "Nothing else. You don't think I mean to
turn speculator?" and added, "Now that you have
told me my father's promise to my mother, I am determined that it shall be fulfilled. I will keep the girl
and take good care of her as my mother did, and when
my father dies she shall be emancipated. She will
be quite as well off here as at home. I do not care to
have everybody know my intention, but I will attend
to it at once."

And so Toinette's future was mapped out before
she had recovered her consciousness. This Christmas
was likely to be an eventful one to her, at least.

Meantime but little progress was made in the process
of restoration. The chill was so severe as to threaten
serious results, and Geoffrey more than once suggested
sending for a physician. Aunt Maggie, however, declared it unnecessary, and merely redoubled her own
efforts, saying that she "knowed better nor any doctor." After a time the opening of Toinette's eyes, and
some wondering questions as to her whereabouts, veri-
fied the truth of the assertion. "It was only wrappin'
and rubbin', an' a good fire an' a little toddy she

needed to bring her all right," Aunt Maggie said, as she forced another dose of the latter down the girl's unwilling throat.

She soon brightened, partook heartily of Aunt Maggie's bountiful dinner, and was ready to begin prospecting in the new dominion of her new master. Having learned the interest manifested in her by Leon, she at once established a sworn friendship with the noble old Newfoundland, and from that day on they were almost inseparable companions.

The young master watched her thoughtfully, as she alternately petted the dog and inspected narrowly her surroundings. The old nurse had arrayed her in the best of her slave garments, instead of the old and soiled one in which she had made the journey. Thus clad, and the wealth of black hair brushed back from her forehead and hanging in loose curls upon her shoulders, with dark, liquid eyes, full of childish wonder, and the red flushing the clear, soft olive of her cheek, it was no wonder that Mr. Geoffrey Hunter more than once thought of his father's remark—"A right likely gal." But somehow he was not much inclined to estimate her value now. He had an idea in his head which pleased him better, and was going to carry it out.

Why should he not? he asked himself. He could afford to. His mother liked this girl—half child yet— who had attended her in sickness with such unusual devotion—*loved* her almost as if she had been her own daughter; and it was her desire that Toinette should be emancipated. It should be done. Of course, his mother would not have desired that she should receive her freedom until she was prepared to preserve and enjoy it. She should have freedom, and he, Geoffrey Hunter, would prepare her for it. He would do this in honor of his mother's memory. He knew that she would approve the act could she but know of it. The child was all but white, anyhow. It was a shame to hold her a slave. He would educate her and fit her for freedom, and when his father died—perhaps before—she should be free.

It was a generous resolve which warmed the heart and moistened the eye of the young man. It brought the reward which the very contemplation of a good act always brings—the pay in advance which the Lord gives to them that do right—a lightened spirit.

"Well, Toinette," said he presently, "did you get a Christmas gift to suit you?"

She lifted her eyes to his face and answered blunt and straight:

"No, sah, did n't get any."

"Not get any, Toinette!" he said. "Why not?"

"Mass'r Hendricks would n't let me have what I wanted, so I come off widout anything," she replied.

"That's strange. I told Hendricks to let you have whatever you liked, if it was the best in the store," Geoffrey replied.

"That's what he tole me, sah," said Toinette.

"And yet he would not let you have what you wanted?" Geoffrey asked.

"No, sah."

"I do n't quite understand that. Tell me how it was," her master said kindly.

"Well, you see, sah," said she, coming nearer, and speaking earnestly, "I went to de store wid Bob, an' giv' Mass'r Hendricks de order, an' tole him I wanted a Christmas dress an' apron. He said, 'I understand, I understand,' an' then begun to take down the prettiest goods in de store, real splendid—like Miss Lucy an' Miss Mary wears—all soft, an' warm, an' nice. An' I kep' lookin' at one piece an' another, an' wishin', an' wishin' I was some great lady to wear such gran' close till I mos' got to thinkin' I was. I stood there, an' kep' sayin', what a pretty dress this would make, an' what a fine mantilly that; an' Mass'r Hendricks he kep' sayin', 'Which do you like bes', dis one or dat one?' an' of course I'd tell him; an' I do n't know but I'd stood there till now if it had n't been for Bob." She hesitated, and Geoffrey asked:

"Well, what did Bob do?"

"Nuffin', only "—and she hesitated.

"Only what?" asked Geoffrey, evidently enjoying the girl's story of her exploit.

"Well, he jis said to one of de men in de store, 'Lor' do n't she make Mass'r Geoffrey's money fly, for a young un.' But I had no idea of buyin' them nice things for myself, Mass'r Geoffrey, not a bit. So I tole Mass'r Hendricks I jis wanted some good calico, an' was only lookin' at these nice things;—tho' t he was only showin' 'em to me for de fun. He only said, 'Yes, yes, I know,' an' would n't show me any calico at all. He said 'twas Mass'r Geoff's orders, an' Mass'r

Geoff knowed what he was about, ef he was n't as old
as a bald eagle.' An' the long an' short of it was, he
would n't let me have calico, an' I would n't take anything else."

"And so you got no Christmas gift?" said Geoffrey.

"No, sah," Toinette replied.

"What is this then?" he asked, taking the one he
had brought in from the sideboard. "Bob said it was
your things, and here is Hendrick's bill of articles—
'Bought by Toinette'; this must be yours."

He unrolled the package and displayed the goods—
soft, rich merinos, with dainty trimmings, and fresh,
pure muslins, seeming like the work of fairy hands beside the coarse dress she now wore. A pretty hood
and elegant shoes completed the outfit. One by one
they rolled from Geoffrey's knees to the floor at the
feet of the wondering child. "It was not strange she
wished herself a lady," he thought, when he compared
the slave costume with the elegant goods upon the
floor. They did credit to her taste, too. No harsh,
glaring colors, but, as she said, "soft, and warm, and
nice."

"So these are not your things?" he said; "you did
not buy them?"

"Oh, no, sah! Mass'r Hendricks knows I did n't.
I tole him I only wanted calico," she answered, with a
frightened look.

"Then I must send them back, I suppose?" said he.

"I reckon so, sah. He mus' a known I did n't want
such goods ez these," she answered, meditatively.

'Of course; but suppose I give them to you, would you not like to wear them?" said Geoffrey.

"Oh, Mass'r Geoffrey!" said the girl, in confusion, "oh, Mass'r Geoff, I'se only a ——." The blood rushed over neck and face in a sweeping flood of shame. Her limbs tottered, and her breath came quick and chokingly. Of course he knew she was "only a ——." As if she should think of being anything else. Oh, why, why! Her soul was beating against the prison bars already. She knew that such garments were not befitting "a ——." Somehow the confusion got into Geoffrey Hunter's face too. It was hot and flushed. He was glad she did not finish the sentence. It was doubtful which was the most nonplussed, the newly-acquired slave or the newly-fledged master.

"Pshaw, pshaw!" said he, petulantly, "they are yours, child. Take them, take them!" And he arose and left the room.

"'Only a ——.' Gad, I was afraid she'd finish it and say 'nigger.' I should have told her 't was a lie if she had. Damned if I believe there's 'nig' enough in her veins to keep a musquito alive two seconds!"

CHAPTER V.

MORTUA MANUS.

GEOFFREY HUNTER was not a man to sleep upon his intentions, good or bad. There was no hesitating, waiting, or trifling in his composition. Direct and earnest, he went like an arrow straight to the mark. Accordingly the next day saw him alight at the street door of his father's office.

"Howdye, son, howdye? Anything wrong at Lovett's?" asked the old man, anxiously.

"All tolerable there, I thank you; I just came over on business," said the son.

"Oh, something you need at Hendricks', I suppose," said the father.

"No," replied Geoffrey, "my business is with you. I want a deed of manumission."

' Hey, Geoffrey," said the old man in surprise, "you are not turning Abolitionist, are you? You crazy boy, you frighten me!"

"No, I am not turning Abolitionist, and you need not be frightened on that score, for I am not likely to; but, nevertheless, I want a deed of manumission drawn, and if you will not do it for me I will go over to Perkins and employ him," said Geoffrey, laughing.

And then Geoffrey Hunter explained that having learned it to be the desire of his lately deceased mother that Toinette should be manumitted, at least on the death of her former master—he, her present master, conceived it his duty, in consideration of his dead parent's wish, to make provisions for her emancipation according to his father's promise, if not before.   He was strengthened in this resolution, too, by an unwillingness which he felt to hold as a slave, or sell, one who evidently had a strong preponderance of Saxon blood.

"Yes, Geoffrey," said the old man, earnestly, "your mother did wish the gal and her mammy sot free, and spoke to me about it times without number, in her later days.   I did 'low to have it done then, but her sister Lucy kept insisting that Ruthy was crazy, and her conceits did n't signify; that if I 'd only jest promise, so 's to satisfy her, it would all be right.   I know I promised her once that they should be free at my decease.   And I did make that provision in my will, as you will find when you come to be my executor, as I spect you will afore long, Sonny.   However, it does not matter now, for that part of the will can never be executed.

"You see, the General Assembly last winter took it into their heads to regulate the matter of emancipation, on the idea that the institution of slavery needed another restriction to keep it in life.   Besides that, this abolition business at the North is playing the wild with our people's notions.   They think because those fanatics are trying to free all the niggers, it is our business to turn in and prevent any of them from getting their liberty.   We hav' n't got quite so bad as that, Geoffy—not here. In some of the States they have gone to even that length. There is enough regard left with us yet for the very name of freedom, *that* freedom so dear to the common law that it never would take kindly to the system of slavery—there is just enough of that left, so that a kind intention toward a faithful or favorite slave can yet be carried out, if a man is only rich enough to make a deed of gift without his creditors interfering. Even then, however, he must get leave of the Superior Court and give bond, with good security, in the penal sum of a thousand dollars, conditioned that the manumitted slave shall leave the State in ninety days thereafter, and never return thereto. This has been the law in effect since '35, when the Constitution was amended and the 'free niggers' deprived of the elective franchise. One always had the right, though, to manumit his slaves by will, the executor complying with the statutory conditions, till last winter, when the Legislature repealed that part of the law and made all testamentary emancipation void. I'm sorry for it, too. It looks like an admission of guilt—as if slavery was afraid of the twinges of conscience on the death-bed an' couldn't hold its own when the soul began to shrivel into nothingness in the view and presence of the Infinite.

"I don't know, Geoffy, where all this matter of legislating about slavery, *pro* and *con*, in the States and the general Government too, is going to end. I can't help being afeard that trouble will come on 't sometime. At first, things went agin the South in this matter, and it seemed as if slavery was going

to lose its foothold in the nation. I 'm sorry sometimes that it did n't. We 'd been better off, Geoffy—
better off. You remember Jefferson was dead down
agin it, as were a good many of our best Southern men
at first. You know, of course, what Jefferson said,
for the Abolitionists hev made a great handle on 't for
years, but perhaps you never heard that Kosciusko—
the Polish hero who fought for the Colonies in the
Revolution, and who certainly had no prejudice in the
matter—you may not have heard that he left his entire estate to be used in freeing and educating niggers. He spent most of his time with Jefferson at
Monticello, was a great friend of his, and made him
his executor. Jefferson declined the trust, on account
of his age, he said. I was over in Albemarle a few
years ago, an' went to the clerk's office to see the
original will. It 's there, and it seemed strange enough
to read the brief, quaint instrument and reflect that
the institution which this patriot so feared and de-
tested in its infancy has since grown up and over-
shadowed the whole land. It 's odd, too, that the very
party which Jefferson founded has been the jealous
guardian of slavery and its propagation. The centrif-
ugal force—the dispersion of power—which was his
favorite idea, has been the nurse of the institution
which he dreaded and condemned. Had the principle
of Hamilton—the centripetal tendency of power—prevailed, there is little doubt that slavery would have disappeared long ago before the numerical preponderance
of the North.

"Marshall, too, the great expounder of our constitution, was never kindly disposed to slavery. Though he had to pronounce it legal, from a conviction that the young Republic could not endure the shock of an adverse decision, there was an undertone went through the entire case that was more convincing than the text. You will find it in 10th *Wheaton*, and it 's worth reading.

"The fact is, Geoffrey, those old fellows were the right kind of Abolitionists. They owned niggers, and wer' n't meddling with what they had no interest in, or, like the old Sarmatian, were too high-minded to have any but a noble motive. If there had been more of them they would have found some way to get rid of the trouble long ago. I 'm more 'n half of the notion it would hev been better if they had.

"After this, everything turned in our favor, and slavery has certainly been 'cock of the walk' since '32 or thereabouts. I 'm afraid it 's not for always, though. The institution aint what it once was. Years ago, when our fathers fust held slaves, they were poor an' hard-working themselves, the majority of them. And even the richest had to hev a keer over things we do n't give 'em now-a-days. The system was patriarchal then, sure enough. These poor heathen niggers had all the privileges of a Christian family. Sometimes they learned to read and write. They were kept and cared for, and taught to work and obey the law. Those were great things, Sonny, to teach a heathen to work and behave himself—an' I 've always thought that slavery in the United States was as divinely ordained as the church itself. I 've no doubt time will prove it so. I do n't know why it was, for there 's a heap of bad things come with it, or with its abuse, certain, but my word for it, Son, it wa' n't no accident ; God meant it—an' meant it for some good, too. And when it 's done its work, he 'll find a way to end it. I 'm afeard it 's coming to be such a high-pressure system of speculation,* that it will bring up at the bad yet. The pesky Abolitionists fussing and jowering about what they know nothing of an' haint no more interest in than a dog in a cider-mill, to my notion, are just making a bad matter worse all the time. They give an excuse to bad men to make our slave-laws harsher and our practice rougher every year—an' at the same time they provoke good men, by their lies an' slanders, to sit still and see this done without objections.

"There seems to be trouble brewing now, and I think we are just at the fust on 't. But there, there, do n't let 's talk about it any more. It 's an unpleasant thing to think of at the best. It 's like everything else in politics, brings a heap more trouble than comfort or profit. Do n't ever touch 'em, Geoffy, boy. Whatever other mean thing you may do, keep out of politics. It spoils any man, and kills a lawyer quicker than arsenic.

"But how about this matter we had in hand ?

"I knew the will was of no account arter the act of last winter; so when you took a fancy to the gal, just out 'o weakness or laziness—to avoid the trouble of arguing you out on 't—I let you have her. So

---

* The word "speculate" and its derivations were applied at the South exclusively to the traffic in slaves.

now I own the mother, an' you own the gal, both of whom I promised Ruthy should be emancipated at my death. Now, as the law forbids my emancipating Mabel by will, and you want to give Toinette her liberty, jes' get yer pen, and sit down here, an' we 'll take the fust step toward fulfilling yer mother's request, pore dear. She 'll nigh forget the joys of Heaven when she sees her old Manuel an' our Geoffy remembering her last wish, an doin' on 't. Now, let me see: the first thing is a petition under ch. 107 of the Code, sec. 45· It 's not done often, so that a lawyer is not usually required to draw more than one in a lifetime, and not one in a hundred of the profession could tell whether it was right or wrong without consulting the statute.

"Now write the usual heading—

'STATE OF NORTH CAROLINA, ⎫ *In the Superior Court.*
COUNTY OF COLD SPRING. ⎬
                         ⎭ *Spring Term,* 1859.
' *To the Honorable, the Judge of said Court:*'

("Put in your colon, Son. Never forgit yer colons an' brackets in heading a paper. It has been decided that punctuation is no part of a statute; but I tell you, Son, it is a part of a legal instrument. You mind what has been said about pleading, that 'he who knows how to use the words "said" and "aforesaid" is a good pleader'—not because these words are more important than any others, but because a knowledge of their use implies knowledge of a thousand other important things. So, he that knows how to divide and distinguish properly between the different parts of a written instrument —what may be well termed legal punctuation—is a

good draughtsman, and no one else can be. Now
go on.)

"'Your Petitioner, Manuel Hunter, respectfully rep-
resents unto your Honor, that he is an inhabitant of
the State and county aforesaid;' — (You see, Son, the
statute requires the petition to set forth that fact, before the court can have jurisdiction. The ordinary
form uses "citizen" or "resident," but the term employed in the statute is "inhabitant." It is a word
somewhat rare in our State legislation, being generally
confined to international law. I have spent some time
in trying to make out what reason there might be for
its use here, but have never been able to discover. It
is used, however, and a draughtsman should always
follow the statute. Remember that, Son)—'that he is
the sole and separate owner of a certain female slave
named Mabel, of the age of fifty; or thereabouts'—
(I never know'd her age exactly; but with that white
hair she'll bear fifty as well as any other figure, and
there's generally less objection to freein' a slave of that
age, than one younger, 'specially if it's a woman,)—
'that the said petitioner is desirous of emancipating
the female slave aforesaid, in the manner prescribed by
law, and is ready, willing, and able to comply with the
conditions legally attaching to such emancipation.

"'Your Petitioner further shows that he has given
due notice of his intention, by Public Advertisement,
in the manner and torm required by law.

"'Your Petitioner, therefore, prays this Honorable
Court, to grant to him leave to manumit and set free
the aforesaid female slave, "Mabel," upon your Peti-

tioner entering into bond with sufficient security, conditioned for the good behaviour of said slave, while
she shall remain in the State after her emancipation,
and that she shall depart therefrom within ninety days
from the granting of this Petition, according to the
statute in such cases made and provided.

'And your Petitioner will ever pray,' &c.

"There, now, let me sign it," and the old man took
the pen, and wrote in characters whose strength was
somewhat marred by the uncertainties of age, "Manuel
Hunter."

"Now for the advertisement, for this is only half,"
said he, as he removed his "specs" and leaned back
in his easy chair.

Geoffrey resumed his pen, and wrote to his father's
dictation as follows:

"To whom it may concern:

"You are hereby notified that the undersigned, being
the sole and separate owner of a certain female slave,
named "Mabel," will petition the Honorable Superior
Court to be held in and for the County of ˙Cold
Spring, at its next term, to be held on the sixth Monday after the first Monday in March next, for leave to
emancipate the same."

    Signed,   MANUEL HUNTER.

"Now you want to draw up exactly the same papers, in Toinette's case, only changing the names and
age," the old man said. "The advertisement you must
publish for six weeks in the *Gazette*—there's just time
to do it before the term."

And so the papers were duly prepared, to set in motion the machinery of the law, which was to transform the chattels-*real*—Mabel and Toinette—into *self-directing* human beings; and the same were duly filed in the office of the Clerk of the Superior Court of the County of Cold Spring, at the Courthouse in Perham, in the good State of North Carolina.

The road to Lovett Lodge seemed shorter than ever before to Geoffrey Hunter that night. The silly fool flattered himself that he was doing an act of most unusual charity towards a fellow-creature, who had appealed strongly and peculiarly to his sympathies. He did not think the act would be a curse to the girl. He did not expect her to regard it in that light, and, strangely enough, he did not once dream that she would refuse the charity he designed to offer her. But he did not mean she should know it at present. It would do her no good. She would just grow lazy and dissatisfied with her present condition if she were told. It would be time enough to inform her when the act of emancipation was completed.

He did not consider that he was a dangerous Jacobin, thus to break up and disturb the normal condition of things in the patriarchal South; that his act was a step toward the recognition of "the nigger" as a human being, an independent moral entity, instead of an article of merchandise; that he was striking a blow at the relations of master and slave on which the harmony and prosperity of society depended; that he was, in short, in great danger of becoming that terrible thing, an Abolitionist. He did not think, in reflecting

upon what he had done for Toinette, of the incapacity
of her race for self-support and self-protection. He
did not conjecture the possibility of her becoming a
vagabond, houseless and homeless, without means, character, or friends, because she had no master. And yet
this is the picture any one of his gentlemanly neighbors
would have drawn for him.

As he rode home that day, Geoffrey Hunter pictured to himself a little cottage in one of the Western
free States, nice and cosy, with fruit and flowers, where
Mabel and her daughter Toinette, the faithful servitors
of his dead mother, should live in peace and content-
ment. More and more, as he dwelt upon the idea, was
he inclined to forget the monstrous anomaly which the
common law borrowed from the Roman, "*Homo sed
non persona,*" and applied with redoubled stringency
to the American slave. Was it because he recognized
instinctively its falsity? Or was it because Geoffrey
Hunter was eccentric—all the Hunters were—and this
was an eccentricity?

CHAPTER VI.

NOT IN THE BOND.

THAT night Geoffrey called old Maggie to the library, and told her his plans about Toinette, as far as he knew them. Overwhelming astonishment closed the old nurse's mouth, or she would have interrupted him frequently during the narration. As it was, only short ejaculations of surprise and gratification escaped her; but, when he had finished with the question:

"And now, Auntie, do you understand my idea?"

"Oh law, yes, Mass'r Geoffrey," said the old woman. "De good Lor' be praised! Understan' you? I reckon I does. You jes' wants tu larn Toinette to be a lady an' not let her know all de time but what she's a slave. It's a mighty hard ting tu do, Mass'r Geoffrey, but we jes try, de bes' we knows. Dat's all. Lor', Lor', how proud I is! De boy I nuss gwine tu do dis ting! Ole Maggie feel mos' as good ez ef she was a gal agin an' gwine to be sot free herself. She don't want to be free now "—seeing an inquiring look on Geoffrey's face. "She's tu ole, an' 'sides dat she could n't leave you, Honey. No more she could n't, now she's got you back again." "But," said she, returning to the subject she had left, "whar's ye gwine to put Toinette? She'll hev tu lodge somewhar besides with ole Maggie, if she 's gwine to be free ? "

"Yes," said Geoffrey, "I wish her to be lodged and treated in accordance with my plans for her future, and so as to promote them as much as possible."

"Dat's what I thought," said Maggie, "an so I 'll jes fix up a room over the dining-room for her. Ther 's one right comfortable an' tidy thar. An' that minds me, Mass'r Geoffrey, dat I foun' annudder room in dis house to-day, jes by accident, dat I reckon you nebber saw."

"Another room!" said Geoffrey, "you don't mean to say that there 's any secret closet about the Lodge, do you, Maggie ? "

"No, not 'zactly a closet, but a room dat I nebber dreamed of afore," said the old nurse.

"A secret room, where is it ? I thought nothing could be hidden here. I must see this curiosity at once," said Geoffrey.

"Oh, not to-night, Honey ! Wait till mornin'," said the old nurse, hastily. "I 'll show it tu ye in the mornin', honey. Ole nuss' rheumatis proper bad to-night."

"O, Pshaw on your fears, Auntie," said Geoffrey, taking up the tallow dip from the library-table, "the room is not haunted as well as secret, is it ? "

"De good Lor' only knows dat, shore, but ole Maggie does n't want to go dar to-night, nohow, Mass'r Geoffrey," said the nurse.

"Well, well, only show me the door, and you need not go in. I 'll go in alone. Come, where is it ? " said Geoffrey.

"De door opens right out of dis room," she answered, without getting up.

"Out of this room! Impossible," said Geoffrey.

For a full understanding of the references which will
be made to Lovett Lodge and its architectural features, a description of that structure will be necessary.
It was of a style very frequent in the region where our
tale is located. The main building was of brick, two
stories high, built upon base-wall of considerable elevation, so that the porch, which ran along the front on
a level with the ground-floor, was raised upon brick
pillars three or four feet high.

There were three large rooms below, two in front,
—the "living room," as it is called, or sitting-room,
and parlor, with a wide hall between, which opened on
a porch running along one side of the great dining-
room in the rear. A servant's lodging-room and a
great pantry or store-room opened off the dining-room.
The rooms were all large and high, evidently built for
coolness, rather than warmth. Each gable was bisected
by a huge chimney built upon the outside of the house
and opening its capacious jaws upon a line with the
walls of the room, so that the fireplaces were not *in* the
several rooms, but adjoining them.

The library was of wood, a story and a half high,
and abutted on the east side of the sitting-room. Its
floor was of the same level, and it was supported on
brick pillars like the porch. It had been used as a
library before the Hunters came into possession of the
Lodge. It had evidently been built at a later day than
the main building, and seemed to have been constructed

for the very purpose for which it was used. It opened on the portico which ran along in front, and also had a door communicating with the sitting-room. It had but one window, a large one, reaching to the floor, on the east end. Upon either side of the front door-way was the counterpart of this window in appearance from without, but the wall was solid, and the green blinds outside were only an illusion. There were two of these false windows also upon the back side of the building, and one upon the east end, designed, it was supposed, to break the monotony of the blank wall. As one stood in the front door-way the fire-place was in the right-hand corner, opposite, and its flue ran up into the great chimney of the sitting-room, though the two were separate below. To the left of this was an immense oaken wardrobe, which looked as much a part of the framework of the house as the chimney itself, reaching from floor to ceiling, and from the side of the chimney to the wall opposite. Upon the side towards the chimney it was divided into shelves and cupboards for papers, and in the corner next the wall it was wardrobe proper—a very convenient piece of furniture to occupy a place in a country gentleman's private office and library. The rest of the walls were covered with open book-shelves.

"You 've been dreaming, Maggie. There 's no door opening from this room except into the sitting-room and porch," said Geoffrey.

"Yes, dar is," said the old woman positively. "Ole Maggie wa' n't a-dreamin' when she found it. But wait till mornin', Honey—do now, dat 's a dear—jes to

please de pore ole nuss, dat 's got de rheumatism
so."

" Oh, bother the rheumatism, Auntie. It won't be
any better by daylight than now. I am going to see
this curiosity before I sleep, so where 's the door ? "
said Geoffrey.

" In de wardrobe, Mass'r Geoffrey, ef ye mus' know ;
but do n't go in dar to-night—do n't, please. De ole
Boy hisself may be in dar, fur all ole nuss knows t'
contrary. Oh Lor' ! oh Lor' ! " she exclaimed, as he
opened the door of the wardrobe, springing from her
chair and running toward him in a style that promised
well for her speedy recovery. " Did n't ye hear dat,
Honey ? Do n't, do n't, Mass'r Geoffrey ! It 's de
den o' sarpints, shore."

" Hear what ? " he asked, listening and looking at
her frightened visage. " I heard nothing but your confounded clatter. There 's no door here," he continued,
holding the candle above his head and inspecting the
interior of the wardrobe.

" Dar, dar," said the old nurse, in desperation, " ef
ye mus' go to de debble, go. Lift dat knob dar, 'n
see ef ye do n't bleve ole Maggie den."

She pointed to a wooden knob precisely like the
others, and apparently designed for the same use.
Raising this a short distance, the back of the wardrobe opened and disclosed a small but comfortable
room, with a wood fire burning on the hearth and a
chair standing before it. The rush of air from the
sudden opening of the door put out the light, and
Geoffrey, after standing a moment to recover from his

astonishment, went back to the grate to relight it, old Maggie clinging to his coat and calling upon the Lord with exemplary energy. Having relighted the candle, he returned and examined the newly-discovered room. It had once been considerably used, as was evident from its aspect; and the furniture, though now scanty, had been of the best quality of the olden style. It contained a bed and a small dressing-case with a mirror, a table, and two chairs. The fire had evidently been burning for several hours, though Aunt Maggie declared she had seen none when she was in the room. There did not appear to Geoffrey, after careful examination, to be any other door than the one by which they had entered.

How Aunt Maggie came to find this room she could scarcely tell. "Jes by accident," she said, "cos Mass'r Geoffrey's coat hung to de knob when I went to take it down." She had lighted a candle and came cautiously into the room; looking hastily about. She said there was wood in the fireplace but no fire at that time. Geoffrey arrived at the conclusion that she must have accidentally lighted it and had forgotten that she had done so, thus producing this startling appearance of occupancy which met them on their entrance. He also concluded that the room had been unused for several years—perhaps its very existence unknown to those who had lately occupied the mansion. Thinking it might be well that the existence of this room should be kept as quiet as possible, he cautioned Maggie to say nothing about it, and, on going out, locked the wardrobe door and put the key in his pocket.

What the room had been used for he did not know,
but it occurred to him at once that here was a place
where he could conduct the education of Toinette and
no one be the wiser but herself. He was determined·she
should be educated, and although it was all well enough
that his mother, then a helpless invalid, should teach
a little "yaller" gal to read, that she might spell out
the Psalms and Gospels to her sick mistress, he knew
very well that it would not do to have it known in
the country that Geoffrey Hunter had turned tutor to
one of his own "she-niggers." He might work her night
and day, flog and starve and make her the mother of
his children, tear them from her breast and sell them
to toil and shame again, and all would be well—the
foundations of society would still be secure; but teach
her to read and write, educate one of them! Oh, he
knew! He was Southern-born and was only trying an
experiment for the simple fun of the thing. He believed in slavery himself—not so firmly as some, perhaps, not so clearly as he did in his own existence,
nor carried to its worst lengths, but enough for all
practical purposes. He hated the "speculator" and the
overseer. They were excrescences of the system and
arose from its abuses. He held that when slavery became gregarious, when it passed beyond the stage in
which the master and slave were in some sense—often
a kind and intimate one—members of the same family,
then it became unchristian and barbarous. The great
barracoons of the richer planters, termed "quarters,"
with the entire system of overseers and drivers, he
looked upon with distrust. It was stripping the slave

of all humanity and extending the idea of chattelism
to a point too close to that of irrational beasts for
him to approve. He remembered to have heard that
his father had advocated the same ideas very strongly when he was young, though he had considerably relaxed in practice of late years. Was it because
Manuel Hunter was richer now? He, Geoffrey, was
not going to do anything for the negro race; he would
have scorned the imputation : but he meant simply to
carry out his own idea, his whim; and, of course, to
fulfill his mother's request.

This Christmas time had more than its usual share
of strange and ghostly experiences. A weird presence, that of a woman, clad in gray, with noiseless
footsteps, and who made no shadow in the winter
moonlight, had terrified the servants at " The Home,"
and some rabbit-hunters had beheld a similar presence
sitting on the ruins of an old house near Lovett
Lodge. It seemed as if the nights of "that season
wherein our Saviour's birth is celebrated" had not
only ceased to be "wholesome," but had become the
very carnival time of ghostliness.

Toinette was soon a fixture at Lovett Lodge.
Maggie installed her in one of the upper back rooms,
and a white woman who lived in an old log-house on
Geoffrey's land, obtaining her sustenance by taking in
sewing and various other uncertain devices, was sent
for to come and make up the Christmas gift for the
new pet. Aunt Maggie had the management of the
affair, and seeing that the woman's curiosity was excited, she did not hesitate to tell her that it would be

6

well for her to use due discretion in speaking of the
matter, or she "would git out o' dat' ar house mighty
quick an' git prosecutioned besides."

"Oh, no danger of me," the woman said, with a
leer, and rubbing her dipping-stick about in the box
of snuff she held. "No danger of her; she had lived
on that place nigh twenty years, jes becos' she could
hold her tongue. People might do what they pleased.
She did n't keer so long 's they did n't 'lest her. An'
she *had* seen strange things thére in her time, but
't was none o' her business. No, she was n't gwine to
tell on 't, though them as did 'em was dead an' gone,
or dead at least—p'raps not gone 'zactly. She'd heard
—but then it wa'n't none of her business. They'd find
out soon enough. 'T was n't the fust time she 'd come
there to make ladies' dresses, for them as wa'n't all
white, an' might n't be the last. She'd always been
well paid for 't, an' that was enough. She was hired
to sow clothes an' not to sow tares—as the Hard-shell
minister used to talk about. He, he!" The well-
laden snuff-brush, with its burden of "Carolina Belle,"
found its way into her mouth, the blackened fangs
closed on it, and cut short the chuckle.

So Toinette was domesticated at the Lodge, apparently as a sort of sinecured assistant of old Maggie, with next to nothing to do, and every possible
liberty; as the protegée and pupil of Geoffrey Hunter,
according to his own dictum, when speaking to himself
in the library; as his present pet and future mistress,
so said the little world which knew something of the
internal economy of Lovett Lodge. Which was right?

The young visionary, or the cool, calculating world, which judges others harshly because itself so vile?

Affairs progressed satisfactorily for several weeks. Toinette—half child, half woman—accustomed to privilege, as the petted servant of Mistress Ruth in the Hunter·*ménage*, was not long in falling into the niche which Geoffrey had designed for her. In her new and becoming clothing she had more the appearance of a bashful child than a privileged servant. Old Maggie wondered how the girl could unconsciously adapt herself to the required position so easily. But the effort on the part of the young master was most apparent. He could not, consistently with his own views, treat her as an equal, nor did it suit his purpose to regard her altogether as a menial. Her easy acceptance of the role of petted slave-child and her artless trust in him and affection for his brave Newfoundlander were probably all that saved him from a renunciation of his scheme, as soon as he came to realize the difficult role it imposed on himself. He soon found that she could be allowed to regard his purposed preparation as a sort of play on her part, and as there was but little company at the Lodge, there was no fear of her being seen while engaged in the dangerous act of spelling out the Cadmean mysteries. So, while Geoffrey sat in the library engaged in mastering the rusty lore of the common law, Toinette was intent upon the tasks which Mass'r Geoffrey imposed, "to keep her out of mischief," he said. After supper in the great room, while Maggie cleared away the things, he would question her upon her day's studies. It was not very dignified, a young country squire teaching one of his "yaller gals;" but somehow he soon grew fond of his evening task, and was irritable if anything prevented him from discharging it.

Old Maggie would finish her work and sit down in the corner of the fireplace, with her high turban and sooty face, beaming with benignity, and between the whiffs on her short pipe, exclaim, "Law sakes! how dat ar chile du larn!" And Geoffrey himself was forced to acknowledge a wonderful capacity for acquisition in "that fly-about Toinette."

CHAPTER VII.

MYSTERY.

GEOFFREY HUNTER'S favorite recreation was music, and of this he was passionately fond. Besides possessing a fine tenor voice, which had been trained and cultivated under the best masters, he was a skillful performer upon several instruments. Almost the first piece of furniture he had brought to Lovett Lodge, when he came to superintend the plantation, was a piano, which occupied a corner of the great sitting-room. It had been a favorite amusement during the summer and fall, to open the doors and windows and play for the entertainment of the servants and any friends they might have visiting them. Not unfrequently the porch and wide gravel-path in front were the scene of a jolly break-down, executed by the delighted darkies.

After the first harsh weather of Christmas had continued a day or two, it moderated, and that glory of a Carolina winter came on, a period of vernal mildness and loveliness, when we look for chill and gloom—the days bright and balmy as April, and the nights frosty but clear and radiant as September.

Bob was therefore commissioned by the other servants to ask Mass'r Geoffrey to give them permission to dance on the porch and in the yard during the

Christmas, and to get him to play some of "dem nice jig tunes on de pianner." The leave was readily accorded, and during the rest of the holidays the nightly carousal of the blacks was sure to begin with a breakdown on the porch.

At these times Geoffrey could not but notice the rapt attention his *protegée* gave to his performance at the piano. When he could overcome her shyness sufficiently to induce her to accompany him in some of the familiar tunes his mother had taught her, he was surprised at the vocal power she displayed and at the wonderful facility with which she acquired both words and music. He was a good musician, and, like most performers fully appreciated the silent tribute of the slave girl's admiration, whom he soon began to recognize as one equally gifted with himself in musical capacity. Whatever precept or example offered her, she seized with an amazing avidity. Ear and voice seemed equally faultless, and Geoffrey Hunter felt the pride an artist always has in a gifted pupil, as he taught her, one after another, his favorite songs. The girl, if properly trained, he admitted, would need nobody's care when freed. That glorious voice and rich physique would, when fully developed, prove a fortune on the stage. In addition to a correct ear and fine voice she seemed also to have that faultless intuition which ever gives to genius the power of rendering feeling correctly. His surprise soon began to ripen into a sort of respect, and he was daily in danger of forgetting that the gifted being, whose powers were unfolding under his kindly touch, was a creature of an inferior race, and, withal, his property. Every now and then he caught himself picturing for her a great and enviable future, the reward of her own powers developed and utilized. He came to look forward to their cheerful evening concerts, when the supper had been cleared away, in the great room, with no little anticipation.

Meanwhile Toinette seemed to have lost all other thought except that of rapt admiration, almost worship, for Geoffrey Hunter. She never forgot that he was of a superior race. She remembered it, and hated and loathed the drop of darker blood which like the "juice of cursed Hebanon," coursed through the natural gates and alleys of her body, transforming and degrading all the nobler blood. She paid daily and hourly tribute unto Cæsar, the myriad-minded monarch, whose perfections charmed her inexperienced thought, and, to her eyes, crowned his brow with the beauty of an unattainable perfection. With great wondering eyes she watched him as he played; with enraptured ears she listened while he read; and when he spoke

" It seemed that an angel had brightened the sod,
And brought to her bosom a message from God."

In everything he was to her a great glorious being— a revelation of immaculate, white humanity—her Master. She felt a sense of ownership in him. He was *her* Mass' Geoffrey! What a privilege to have such a master! How gladly she obeyed him, and when anything pleased him how carefully she noted it! Was it not enough to be the petted servant of such a divinity! *Her* mind was not disturbed by any "common humanity" theories. She was content to be a

slave if she could only serve Mass'r Geoff. She never
dreamed of being the "equal" of her demi-god. She
would like to be, of course; but then she was not
She was only a "nigger," with a little white mixed in.
God only knew what for, and yet she was glad it was
there, for she had an idea that she would not have
been permitted to behold the unveiled glories of human
perfection, in the person of Geoffrey Hunter, if it had
not been for this admixture of Saxon blood. Thus,
the master was losing the arrogance of the owner in the
interest of the instructor, and the slave was merging
the servility of the chattel in the absorption of the
devotee.

A month had passed, and it seemed to Toinette
but a day since she had come into that paradise for
"pet niggers," Lovett Lodge. One night after they
had been practising a favorite song which Geoffrey
was teaching her, he praised her effort, and told her
if she were attentive and tried very hard she would
sometime be as good a musician as himself. She stared
incredulously. Nevertheless, she was gratified, and
when he dashed off in a merry waltz, which woke old
Maggie, who had been nodding in the corner, with a
start, she seized the paws of old Leon and danced
about with him for a partner, until both the lookers-on
were convulsed with laughter at their antics. Happen-
ing to go near one of the large uncurtained windows
opening on the porch, and chancing to glance up at it,
she stood an instant as if frozen in her tracks, and then,
with shriek after shriek, fled behind the player, exclaiming: "Don't let 'em! don't let 'em, Mass'r Geoff!"

THE TWO PETS.

"*And when he dashed off in a merry waltz, she seized the paws of old Leon and danced about with him for a partner.*"—p. 8c

Almost simultaneously old Maggie made her first effort -in tragedy, and, considering her previous training, the *début* was certainly successful. Rising from her chair with that sickly pallor and rigidity of feature which intense excitement produces in the African, leaning forward and gazing with a terrified stare at the window, she pointed toward it with her hand and exclaimed in a half-whispered shriek : " Dar, dar, Mass'r Geoffrey! Look dar! Oh, de good Lord! Lord save us! O Lo'ddy! O Lo'ddy!"

Geoffrey stopped playing, with a start, and glanced at the window to which Maggie pointed, not because she was pointing there, (for he did not look to see the direction of her hand,) but from that instinctive impulse by which the eye is ofttimes guided to see the horrible or supernatural. He caught a glimpse, only, of a figure moving swiftly and noiselessly along the porch.

Geoffrey Hunter was no coward, but the superstitions of his native South were woven in with the warp of his existence. The tales which rest upon the lips of every ·slave-nurse had constituted a large part of the fairy-land of his young thoughts. He had outgrown his fear of "ghosts and spirits," as a deliberate thing, and would have laughed at such an accusation, if it had not enraged him ; but sprung upon him suddenly, the bias of childhood showed its power. His hands were glued to the depressed keys, his heart gave a great start, cold chills ran over him, and with bristling hair he sat gazing at the window. Behind him on the floor, sobbing and quaking, with hands pressed over her eyes, was Toinette; before the fire, sunk now upon her knees, was Maggie, uttering incoherent prayers. Outside, the moon shone, clear and cold, upon the porch, and the squeaking noise made by the arm of the climbing rose, which reached over and rubbed against the window, was the only sound. Even dauntless old Leon was crouching with a cowed look at his master's side.

It was but a moment. Manhood, firm, strong and re-assuring, came rushing to the rescue and drove credulous, superstitious Boyhood back into the dim past. He sprang to his feet and rushed upon the porch. He ran to the end and looked up and down the enclosure. The light of the full moon lay still and clear over all, and there was no opportunity for concealment. The figure he had seen was certainly going in that direction, and could not have left the porch without having jumped the railing and fallen some six or eight feet. He was puzzled. To add to his quandary, there, only a few yards from the foot of the steps, lay a large mastiff, a present from his father, who had especially recommended him as a remarkable guard-dog, looking quietly up into his master's face as if inquiring the reason of this unusual visit to his post of duty. No one could have passed down the steps without being seen by this dog, and it was a thing unheard of, for any one to come inside the enclosure without his giving the alarm.

He thought a moment, then went back to the great room, and without speaking to the frightened women, seated himself again at the piano, and rattled off a half dozen cheery airs as if nothing had occurred to disturb his equanimity. It was like sunshine succeeding the vague uncertainties of night, to the terrified women. He turned suddenly upon the younger and said quietly:

"What was the matter with you, Toinette?"

She buried her face in her apron and said in a horrified voice:

"Oh Mass'r Geoff, don't ax me! don't ax me!"

Then Geoffrey spoke sternly, as a master should to a disobedient servant—

"Toinette, stop this foolery. Come here and look at me."

She obeyed at once. Had not her master spoken, and was it not her duty to obey? She would do his bidding though body and soul perished. She stood before him and looked straight into his eyes. This ready obedience and sudden renunciation of her fear surprised him. He had not expected and could not understand it. Geoffrey Hunter had somewhat to learn which the "favorite yaller gal" had already acquired. The teacher must learn of the pupil sometimes.

"What frightened you, Toinette?" said he, kindly.

"S'pose 'twas a spook or de Debble, sir," she replied promptly.

The quaintness of the answer brought a smile to Geoffrey's face, as he asked:

"Well, and what was the appearance of the ghostly visitant?"

"Ye know, Mass'r Geoffrey," she answered, "I was playin' with Leon, and he came atween me and the wall, close by the window thar, an' I happened to look up, and thar stood something like a woman, only so tall and white, an' with eyes that burned like coals of fire, lookin' straight at me, as ef it wanted to jes git hold o' me an' kill me dead. And then I was so scart, Mass'r Geoffrey, I run an' hollered, but I could n't help it—I could n't, Mass'r Geoff—I could n't."

All this old Maggie, with many a pious ejaculation and fragmentary prayer, confirmed, adding that "it was jes all white from top to bottom, all up an' down de winder, an' hed a face like a dead pusson, only de eyes, dey glistened like fox-fire in de night, an' jes kep' watchin' Toinette all de time till Mass'r Geoffrey stop playin' an' look up, an' den it jes wanish away like a shadder in de water. Pore chile! pore chile! She 'll not live many days. Her time 's nigh come. It 's a shore sign, so de ole uns allers tells me, when de folks comes from de dead in der grave-clothes an' fastens der cold, dead eyes on any particular pusson deys shore gwine to die. Pore chile! pore chile!"

"What did your ghost have on its head?" queried Geoffrey. "You used to tell me, Maggie, that the spooks always had their grave-clothes over their heads, and found their way about without the aid of vision."

"An' so did dis one, too, Mass'r Geoff, only de eyes burn so bright dey show right fru," protested the old woman.

"And the face," said the skeptical Geoffrey, "how about that? You saw that too?"

"Oh, well, Honey, it 's only a ghost-shroud, anyhow, an' jes show fru like glass," said Maggie.

"What do you say about it, Toinette?" asked Geoffrey of the young girl, who had stood a thoughtful listener to the conversation with Maggie. "Did you see the face?"

"Oh, yes, sah," she replied, "I saw it quite plain. It seemed cold an' pale an' hard like. The forehead was wrinkled an' scowlin', and the mouth shet close. Oh, sah, it looked mighty angry at me, an' somehow it seemed as ef I had seen the face afore, a long time ago."

"In course ye has, chile," said old Maggie. "One allers knows de sperret dat comes to warn us ov de end. It's allus de 'miliar sperret dat de Scriptur tells on. Pore chile! ye 'd better be a prayin' den standin' dar answerin' young Mass'r Geoffrey's fool questions, when ez like ez not de death-damp's comin' on yer forrid now."

"Did you see the hair, Toinette?" continued Geoffrey.

"I can't jes remember, sah; kind o' 'pears like I did, an' then again I do n't know. There was n't no cap or bonnet on her head, an' ef there was any hair 't was white as snow," answered Toinette.

"Shore 'nuff, shore 'nuff," said old Maggie, with a start. "Wal, wal, it mout hev ben!"

"And so," said Geoffrey, "you two silly women have made all this hubbub because some old woman happened to come and look in at the window."

"Who ever knowed anybody to come inside dis yard an' ole Tige not bark at 'em?" said the nurse, contemptuously.

"Oh, Tige was asleep and did not see her," said Geoffrey.

"Tige nebber sleep arter sundown," said the old woman, stoutly.

"It's strange how she came and went without being seen," he began—

"Or heard uther, Mass'r Geoff. Who ever knowed any mortal man or woman to go 'long dat dar porch an' nebber make noise 'nuff to be heard in dis yer room when ebbryting was still 'nuff to hear an acorn drop off de furdest tree in de yard?" interrupted the stubborn old servant.

Geoffrey could not answer the question, and yet his reason assured him of two facts: First, the figure at the window was no illusion. His own view of it had been indistinct, but Toinette and old Maggie agreed in all the essential particulars, and their testimony was consistent. Second, he was convinced that it was no apparition. The grounds for this belief he could not have stated satisfactorily. He could not account for its sudden and noiseless disappearance, nor for the unusual silence of the dogs, and yet he could not bring himself to recognize their strange auditor as of a ghostly nature. Somehow the incident connected itself in his mind with the secret room back of the library. He had not been there since the night he had first examined it. For some unaccountable reason he had shrunk from entering it again. He put his hand in his pocket and felt the key of the wardrobe. He would go and examine it now. He rose, and, taking the candle from the table, went into the library. Old Maggie seemed to divine his purpose, and cried out:

"Oh, Mass'r Geoff, don't, don't! Not to-night,

wait till mornin'. Do, please, Mass'r Geoff. Dat boy's contrariness will be his death, dat's shore. Den what will Mass'r Manwell do to ole nuss, 'cause she did n't take keer of one dat's jes' as headstrong ez de ole debble. 'Pears like dat boy nebber would hear to nobody's 'vice at all. Jes' will hev his own way 'n' it 'll be de ru'nation ob him, shore. Good Lor'! I 'm glad dat great dog's gone wid him. 'Pears like de critter knows most ez much ez a human, eny how. He hez got a heap o' sense.''

Geoffrey went into the library and shut the door. He was alone here, at the Lodge. Granting that his hypothesis was correct, and that the mysterious figure at the window and the secret of the room which opened from the library through the wardrobe yonder had some, to him, occult relation to each other, what was it? He sat down by the dying fire upon the library hearth and asked himself this question. Was it good or ill the apparition boded? Did that mysterious watcher have some sinister design against himself that it thus pried into the secrets of his hearth and made itself or herself—if, perchance, it was a woman, which he did not for a moment believe—an occupant of his house? For, somehow, he had never yet been able to convince himself that the fire he saw burning in the secret room had really been kindled by old Maggie's carelessness, or by the hand of any legitimate inhabitant of his domicil. Often, since he had examined the room, he had been haunted with the impression, as he sat reading in his great library chair, that some one just beyond the wall was keeping up a constant and by no means friendly espionage upon his acts. This night was not the first time that he had experienced a feeling that hostile eyes were gazing at him through the window of the sitting-room, as he sat at the piano or heard Toinette's lessons. Several times he had thought he caught a vanishing glimpse of a figure, and once in particular of what seemed flowing white hair or beard. It all came to him now, and he reasoned upon the data carefully and coolly. The white, snowy beard or hair were adopted for the occasion. They were a part of, or, at least, in fine keeping with the traditional get-up of a ghostly character. It was all clear to his mind, except how it was managed and what was the motive. He was there alone—the only white man on the plantation, and, for the matter of that, within a circuit of a mile or more. He was reported rich. Was robbery the crime intended? Hardly, or it would have been perpetrated long ago; for he was convinced that this system of espial was a month old or thereabouts. What then? He had not an enemy in the world. No man could claim that he had ever acted dishonorably towards him, or woman lay any evil at his door. What could be the motive? It troubled him.

All at once he thought of a solution. Lovett Lodge was a desirable piece of property, and some sharper, knowing the secret of the hidden room—perhaps a descendant of the builder—had devised this trick to give the premises an unenviable reputation, a reputation which he knew would greatly depreciate its value among the superstitious people of the country, especially as

it would render it almost impossible to keep the ignorant and cowardly slaves upon a plantation which was
believed to be haunted. Perhaps, too, it was calculated
that this annoyance would prove too much for his patience, and incline him to dispose of it at a moderate
price. The theory pleased him. He ran it over in
his mind two or three times, pacing back and forth in
the library. He would show this ingenious trader his
mistake. He would let him know that Geoffrey Hunter was not to be fooled by any such shallow trickery.
And if it were not more cautiously played, he would
make it a sad game to the actor. He took a revolver
from a drawer in his desk, examined the caps, cocked
it, and, taking the candle, advanced to the door of
the wardrobe. Old Leon was lying before it and
seemed to be eyeing it dubiously. Geoffrey turned
the key in the lock and opened the wardrobe door.
The door into the hidden room was closed precisely
as he had left it. Mindful of his previous experience,
he took the revolver in his right hand and held the
candle at arm's length outside the wardrobe while he
moved the knob. The door opened suddenly as before and Leon at once sprung into the room. Geoffrey
followed, holding the candle above his head. It was
cold and empty and there were no signs of its having
been lately occupied. The ashes in the fire-place
looked as if they had been undisturbed since his previous visit. The bed-clothing and furniture told no
tales of use, but seemed to be in precisely the same
condition as when he last saw them. And yet he could
not rid himself of the idea that the room had lately
7

been inhabited. Leon seemed to be of the same opinion. He snuffed about the room eagerly, and finally
concentrated his attention upon a spot near the fire-
place. After searching about the room he would return
each time and re-examine this spot, until apparently
confessing himself balked, he lay down and looked up
at his master's face inquiringly.

"Well," thought Geoffrey, "I'm in here now, and
I'm bound to know if there's any other outlet to this
infernal den."

So he set to work and examined minutely every
portion of the room. He moved the bed and searched
the floor for a trap-door. He could find none. The
wall was a plain plastered one, and he sought along
it vainly for any evidence there might be of a joint.
And so he went around again and again, but could
find no opening save that by which he had entered
and the immovable windows with the fixed, unyielding
shutters on the back side. He went out, closed the
door, brought sealing-wax and placed his seal upon
it, and closed the door of the wardrobe, which he
locked and sealed also.

"There," said he, "if that den is occupied, no one
shall come in here without my knowledge."

And so he returned to the great room thwarted,
but not convinced nor even discouraged. His hypothesis of the mystery was fixed and clear, and he should
not endanger his chances of eliminating the truth and
detecting the knave by imparting it to anyone.

CHAPTER VIII.

FAITHFUL UNTO DEATH.

THE next day Maggie put paper shades upon the windows of the sitting-room. Geoffrey set himself to work out the mystery upon his hypothesis, and adopted several clever devices to entrap the intruder, without success. Nothing more was seen or heard to throw light upon the matter, until the night of the succeeding Sabbath; then indeed the question in regard to the character of the mysterious visitant received a terrible solution.

It was past midnight. The moon was shining clearly upon the straggling mass of buildings which formed Lovett Lodge. Its soft light came into the room occupied by Geoffrey Hunter, which was across the hall from the living-room, and had once been the reception-room or parlor of the Lodge.

Geoffrey Hunter was sitting on the side of his bed, a look of mingled perplexity and terror upon his face. Old Leon was going back and forth from his master's bed to the door, whining piteously. Geoffrey had awakened from his sleep overwhelmed with terror. It did not seem a dream. He could not remember any definite thought which had caused his fright. He could only hear the low whining of Leon. He called him, softly. The dog came and licked his hand, trembling with excitement.

"What is it, fellow?" said Geoffrey, whispering and putting his hand on the dog's neck. He held his breath and listened. The dog grew restive. "Hist, hist. Be still," he said under his breath. He heard the old clock in the room across the hall tick the seconds slowly. The silence was terrible. It seemed as if nature never slept so deeply before. The night was one dead sea of silence. Even the moonlight was oppressive—a dull, ghastly glare. He was wide awake, but still the horrible, nameless fear brooded over him like a nightmare—a terrible foreboding waiting to be fulfilled. He rose and began to dress, hurriedly, but noiselessly, stopping every now and then to listen. Every instant suspense and apprehension grew more fearful. An overturned shoe made him start, gaze wildly around, and grasp the revolver lying on the table. He smiled—a faint and sickly smile—at his own terrors, but still clutched the revolver, and looked cautiously around. The dog was growing more restless. Strange that he should act so! He never did before. Should he let him out?

He started towards the door to do so, moving stealthily in his stockinged feet, as if afraid of his own foot-fall. Suddenly shriek after shriek of mortal terror rang through the house. A woman's voice, strained to its utmost pitch and freighted with an agony of fear. It made the silence populous with shapes of terror. The ear which was oppressed with stillness a moment since was overburdened with echoing horror now.

There was no more uncertainty; all was sharp, clear, definite. Evil, crime, a life in mortal peril, was the unmistakable language of those cries. Geoffrey's fear was ·gone. Leon bounded at the door and began tearing it with his teeth. Geoffrey hastened to undo it, and the faithful brute sprang like an arrow down the long hall, and Geoffrey heard him ascending the stairs towards Toinette's room almost before he had stepped outside the door. All at once the shrieking ceased. The terrible silence, pregnant of evil, came again for an instant. Geoffrey's heart almost ceased beating as he ran at his utmost speed along the hall. Every sense seemed trebled in intensity and power. He tried to shout to the dog, but no sound came from his lips. Now there was a short, sharp, anxious yelp, a loud, angry roar, and then the terrible silence came again as Geoffrey reached the foot of the stairs. He mounted swiftly, clutching the revolver, anticipating an encounter. It was strange he did not hear Leon, he thought. He reached the top. It seemed an age since he was at the bottom. All silent still. He half paused. "Take 'em, Leon, take 'em, boy," he shouted with an effort, as he rushed into the long, dark hall leading from the landing towards Toinette's room, braced for a desperate struggle. There is a rustle behind him. His strained ear catches it. He turns and sees a tall figure gliding swiftly down the stairway. He wheels, and pursues, clears the stairs almost at a bound, rushes along the side-hall into the great one leading to the front doorway, and there, just passing through the open door—How came it open?

Maggie kept the keys—with a swift, gliding motion, sees the tall figure he had seen before—the ghost of Lovett Lodge.

He raised his revolver and fired quickly. . Without looking around or changing its pace in the least, the figure kept on, and before he could fire again had passed the door and turned toward the eastern end of the porch. He redoubled his efforts, and caught a glimpse of it, as he reached the door, descending the flight of steps which led down from the porch. Another shot, with like effect, and Geoffrey Hunter was stand- ing where the figure had been ten seconds before looking to the right and left in the moonlit enclosure, seeing nothing but the dog Tige, who was crouching, silent and cowed, at the foot of the steps. He felt the horror of his waking moments creeping back upon him. Could it be that this mysterious entity was in- deed ghostly in its character? He went down the steps slowly and thoughtfully. He peered beneath the porch. The clear moonlight, streaming in at the west- ern end, showed the brick wall and narrow brick col- umns on which the porch rested with great distinctness. A child of five years old could not have hidden from his sight there. He passed around the eastern end of the dwelling to the rear, peering into every shaded nook, saying over and over again to himself, " It cannot be far off." And yet he saw nothing, and his strained ear caught no sound except the uproar in the servants' quarters among the aroused and wonder- ing inmates, and the outcries of old Maggie, who was calling upon every individual in her vocabulary of

names, whether of earthly or unearthly nature, for aid.
He paid no attention to them. He heard the noise
as an operative hears the clatter of machinery by
which he is daily surrounded—without heeding' its
existence. The lightest footfall in the front enclosure would have drowned them all to his ears. There
was none. He went back to the steps, peered under
the porch again, ascended, walked along the porch,
let down the hammer of his revolver, and went to his
own room. Striking a light at once, he passed along
the hall to the door of the housekeeper's room. Opening it, he entered, and beheld old Maggie on her knees
in the corner, exclaiming frantically.

"Oh Lor', Lor', help us! an' ef de Lor' won't help
us, Jesus Christ help. Do help, do Lor'!"

Seizing her by the shoulder, he shook her roughly,
saying:

"Stop this nonsense, Maggie."

"Oh, Mass'r Geoffrey, *whatever* is de matter? Oh
you need n't shake de ole nuss's bones out of her black
skin!"—as Geoffrey continued shaking. "What *has*
happen'd?" Another shake. "Has-de-gho's-come-agin?"

"Shut up, or it will." And shake followed shake
too fast for utterance upon her part.

"And now," said Geoffrey, when she was finally
silenced, "do as I tell you. Go and tell Bob and Martin to come here at once, and the others to go to bed.
D 'ye hear?"

He was gone before she could find breath to question. Not daring to remain alone, she hurried off to
the quarters to perform her master's bidding.

Geoffrey passed quickly down the hall into the side one, where he half-paused to listen. There was no sound above. He passed up the stairs quickly, but quietly. It seemed strange that he felt no such apprehension as when he last ascended them. His revolver was in his pocket but he did not think of it. He anticipated no struggle, and yet was oppressed with fear. He paused at the head of the stairs, intending to wait there till Bob and Martin came. He dreaded to see the unknown horror, which waited him in the obscurity of the hall. The boys would come in a moment. It was here he had shouted to old Leon. What had become of the dog? He held the candle above his head and stood peering into the darkness. He would call him. He did so and listened. Was that a sigh he heard? It came again, piteous, pleading, feeble. Was it human? He could wait no longer, but walked rapidly down the hall. His foot slipped and he almost fell. He lowered the candle and looked. It was blood—a great pool of it. And then it went in an irregular, zigzag line down the hall towards Toinette's room. He followed it. Sometimes draggled, and splashed, as if something had been dragged through it, and then narrow and deep as if it had gurgled from a wound. Geoffrey watched it and wondered. Still he went on, tremblingly. He had never looked on murder, but now he felt that he must meet it soon. There was a track of Leon's foot. Where *could* the dog be? He heard, as if in a dream, the voice of Bob in conversation with old Maggie, at the foot of the stairs. He was at the door of Toinette's room now. It was ajar, and splashed at the bottom with blood. He paused a moment, then opened it and entered. Almost at his feet lay the form of Toinette, her face, pale and rigid, turned towards him, her night-dress dabbled with blood; and close beside the white-robed figure of the unconscious girl, was the form of the noble old dog. The faithful animal looked in his master's face, with a beseeching gaze, flapped his tail in recognition, and then licked the pallid face before him tenderly.

Geoffrey stooped and put his hand on the pale brow. There was no pulse in the temple. He sought for the heart-beat, and, when it was withdrawn, his hand was stained with blood. It moved him strangely. He could not decide whether she was dead or not. He stripped the dress from her shoulder, and there, just below the collar-bone, was a small blue puncture, from the narrow blackened lips of which a small dark stream trickled down over the fair white bosom. He watched it a moment and thought it flowed irregularly, as if she still breathed. He stooped to raise her from the floor, when his attention was attracted to old Leon. Now that he was in front of him, he noticed that the white breast of his noble pet was dark with blood, and that a great puddle of it had collected where he lay. He seemed to be gnawing at his breast.

"Poor fellow," said Geoffrey, "are you hurt too?"

He put his hand on the dog's breast and felt the hilt of a dagger buried deep in his chest. Then it all flashed upon him: how the girl had been stabbed in

E

her room the flight of the criminal, intercepted by the
dog; the short struggle in the hall, when the murderer's knife, buried in the breast of the brave assailant, had slipped from its owner's grasp. This
explained the trail of blood in the hall, and the after
silence of the dog. He had met the murderer and
received the fatal blow. Then, with his life-blood
flowing from the wound, in the very anguish-throes of
death, he had dragged himself to the side of the play-
mate for whom he had fallen. It came to the mind
of Geoffrey, too, that he owed his own life to the
faithful brute. The dagger was evidently the weapon
relied on, perhaps the only one used by the criminal,
and this being lost, he was not attacked, though he
must have passed within striking distance of the assassin.

"Poor fellow," said Geoffrey. The dog looked at
him wistfully, tried feebly to grasp the dagger-hilt with
his teeth, then laid his head upon the neck of the unconscious girl and died. One of Geoffrey Hunter's
truest friends would watch over him no more.

He drew out the dagger and wiped it on Leon's
shaggy coat. It was a delicate affair, blue-bladed and
silver-hilted, like a lady's *bijou*, but a strong arm had
held it, and a cool head had directed the fatal stroke.
It was no chance blow. The point of attack was
selected, and the blade sent home with a will. He
put the dagger in his pocket, patted the noble head,
and, lifting it tenderly, laid it on the floor. Then,
gathering Toinette in his arms, he started along the
hall to the stairway. Carefully as if she were a woman

FAITHFUL UNTO DEATH.

*" Patted the old dog's noble head, and lifting it tenderly laid it on the floor.
Then, gathering Toinette in his arms, he started along the hall."*—p. 98.

and a sister, Geoffrey Hunter carried the lax form of
the stricken girl. Did he forget that she was a slave,
and only remember in that fearful hour the humanity
and womanhood of the "yaller gal Toinette"? It could
hardly be, yet when he came to examine the wound,
after he had laid her on the sofa in the great room, he
did not ruthlessly expose her bosom, but folded back
the gown with care, and put on the bandages deftly
and tenderly, as if she were a woman rather than a
chattel.

As soon as this was done, he directed Bob to send
a boy for a physician, and himself, with three or four
of the most trusty hands, to keep watch about the
building, and see that no one left the premises until
morning. The blood from Toinette's wound was
stanched for the time, and, through the influence of
stimulants, she at length recovered from her swoon
and looked inquiringly at Geoffrey, who sat by her
with his finger on her pulse. She seemed bewildered
at her novel situation, and would have spoken, but the
effort was so painful that she swooned again, and the
wound began to bleed afresh.

When she had revived somewhat Geoffrey said:
"You must not try to speak, Toinette. You have
been badly hurt, and must keep very quiet indeed!"

He spoke tenderly and soothingly, and Toinette's
great dark eyes turned upon him wonderingly and
searchingly. Something in the expression of his face
seemed to satisfy her, and she closed them again with
a smile of contented weakness.

CHAPTER IX.

A "POOR POLL."

MEANTIME, Aunt Maggie had been petitioning for Geoffrey's leave to send for Betty Certain, a neighbor woman, who had achieved a local reputation for steadiness of head and skill of hand in important crises of sickness and misfortune in the vicinity of the Lodge.

She was said to be a woman of somewhat eccentric disposition, neither young nor old, living alone upon a little farm adjoining the Lovett Lodge plantation, and known as the Old Certain Tract. It jutted into the Lovett plantation, and the owners of the Lodge had at various times offered unreasonable prices for the bit of barren ridge, but their offers had invariably been met with an almost angry refusal.

The woman, though a landowner in her own right, did not belong to what was known in the community as the better class of people. Her parents and forebears had been " common livers," who had never owned slaves, but relied solely upon their own labor for subsistence. As a consequence the little tract of land had grown poorer and poorer year by year, and its occupants had kept pace with it in deterioration. So Betty Certain—Mistress Certain, as she was frequently called, no one seemed to know why—was a "poor

white," but, withal, one without imputation of the vices
not unfrequently attaching to the females of her class,
and held in considerable repute for sturdy uprightness
as well as for unpretending kindness of heart.

Geoffrey Hunter was unwilling to allow any one to
know more of the interior happenings of his household
at this juncture than was absolutely necessary, "especially," he said, "any poor white woman of whom he
knew nothing."

Old Maggie's entreaties finally prevailed, however,
upon the condition that Mistress Certain should first
report to him in person; and if, after examination, she
seemed to him worthy of such honor, she was to remain, otherwise not.

Geoffrey was sitting by the table in the library when
she arrived. It was broad daylight without, but the
solid shutters were closed and a candle was burning
within. He was examining the dagger which he had
drawn from Leon's breast, when a servant came to say
she was waiting. He dropped it into a drawer of the
table and bade her enter.

She was by no means prepossessing in appearance.
A tall, large woman, of perhaps forty years, of lean,
muscular build, with a certain masculinity of appearance which, as well as her apparent height, was doubt-
less enhanced by the coarse, scant, homespun dress,
which did not reach low enough to conceal the heavy
brogans and a part of the gray stockings which formed
her foot-gear. An old sun-bonnet, of the same dull,
uncertain color as her dress, adorned her head, and
under it the masses of her dark hair were gathered in

heavy, shining plaits, contrasting strangely with her somewhat coarse features and negligent attire. There was nothing especially repulsive about the woman, and her face had a sturdy resoluteness of aspect rather pleasing than otherwise, when narrowly scanned.

Bidding her "How d' ye, ma'm," Geoffrey motioned to a chair near the hearth.

The woman seated herself, stretched her feet toward the fire, and gazed nonchalantly at the blaze. She was evidently no whit abashed in the presence of the wealthy young planter who deemed himself so infinitely superior to any of her class. There was no curiosity or nervousness in her demeanor — just straightforward independence. Neither voice or manner asked a question. Geoffrey noted the fact and it suited him.

"This is Mrs. Certain, I suppose?" said he.

"I 'm sometimes called that. Betty Certain 's my name," she answered, without looking round.

"I have sent for you, Mrs. Certain," said Geoffrey, "because I am in need of some one to—that is—Maggie desired me to send for you to come and remain at the Lodge for a few days."

"So I heerd," said the woman, quietly.

"At this time," continued the master of Lovett "I could only with great reluctance consent that any stranger should enter my house"—

"I 've been here afore," she interrupted.

"Yes, but we do not happen to be acquainted," said he.

"Not 'specially."

"And at this time it is very necessary that all my—

all who are in my house," he said, correcting himself, "should be entirely trustworthy."

"Betty Certain never stole nothin'," said the woman, shortly.

"Oh, no! I"—beg your pardon he would have said, but she was a "mean white"—"I did not mean that; but can—can I trust your prudence, your discretion, Mrs. Certain?"

"I do n't ask to know your secrets, Geoffrey Hunter," said the woman, sharply. "I 've known many a one connected with this house, and got too poor pay for it to keer to hear more," and she looked round the room with a quiet familiarity that puzzled Geoffrey Hunter. This ignorant, poor, "mean white" woman would not be patronized, and was fast changing places with him and assuming the air of careless condescension with which he had set out.

He thought, however, that her allusion to payment had given him a key to her character. He would try again. So he said :

"I think I can trust you, Mrs. Certain, and I am willing to pay you well Here is the first installment," and he took a half-eagle from his drawer and held it towards her.

The woman glanced at the money, then rose, gazed searchingly at Geoffrey a moment, and said:

"Geoffrey Hunter, I'm a pore woman, an' I s'pose folks tells sad tales on me—tho' I do n't keer fer that— but there's some things I won't do, not fer no man's money; an' 'fore I takes yours, ye mus' give me ver word that there ain't no crime in what ye want done—no blood, nor anythin' that 'll make one think atterwards that the devil's got a mortgage on ther soul. I hed enuff o' that years ago, an' tho' I ain't no better nor I should be, at the best,' more 'n other folks, I promised the Lord that if He would show my hands clar o' that ar trouble, as they were, I 'd never git into any more sech, an' I won't. An' so, sir, if ye 've got anythin' to do that or'tn't tu be done, ye'd better du it yerself, or git somebody else. I wo'n't du it.

"But if you'll promise me there ain't no blood ner wrong in the matter that ye want my help in, why, I'll stay an' du it. Ef not, I 'll jes' go home. I know 't ain't no common thing that's made young Geoffrey Hunter sen' fer Betty Certain afore day in the winter time. I ain't ter be fooled. Fa'r 's fa'r. Come out squar' an' strait, an' ye can 'pend on my totin' right, but ef ye try ter chaff me, an' git me inter trouble, ye'll be sorry, shore."

Geoffrey was astounded. There was no chance of patronizing this woman, if she was a "mean white." She would have been strong-minded enough had her station in life been different. She had taken the reins from his hands, and put him in the shafts. She was evidently the master of the situation, and he must sue for terms, or let her go home, as she proposed. He was now as anxious that she should stay as he had been that she should not come.

"Well, Mr. Hunter," said the woman, "yes or no. Will yer give me yer word?"

"There is no crime or wrong in this affair," said Geoffrey slowly and emphatically, looking steadily in hei eyes, "of my seeking, aiding, or desiring. Will that do?"

"There *is* crime in it then," said the woman cautiously, "perhaps blood?"

"Crime and blood," he assented.

"More blood, more blood! An' in this house perhaps?"

"In this house!" he answered.

"I was afeard," she said, shaking her head. "It hed a bad start at fust. I don't want ter be curus, but perhaps ye-wouldn't object tu tellin' me whose blood it was?"

"Toinette's, my girl Toinette's," he said.

"An' you didn't do it, nor don't know who did?" she asked.

"I would almost as soon have thought of shedding my own," he answered, solemnly.

"Dead?"

"Not yet."

The woman took off her sun-bonnet and laid it on the chair, smoothed her front hair, and felt the shining knob in which it was gathered at the back, caught up the recreant locks about her ears, and replaced an obtruding pin with a motion that made Geoffrey think of a dagger-thrust. Then she spoke, in the quiet, practical tone of one who is ready for work.

"Well, Mr. Hunter, ef I can be of any service I'm ready to begin."

Geoffrey picked up the coin from the table and offered it to her again.

"Wait till it's arned, Mister Geoffrey. Time 'nuff
8

then," said the woman, waving it aside. "Besides, the son of Manuel Hunter has a right to ask some favor of Betty Certain without pay."

Geoffrey asked her to be seated again, and briefly related the events of the past night. He said nothing of the previous occurrences, the apparition at the window or the secret room, as he had no evidence to connect them with the crime, though they were constantly in his thought.

When he had finished, Betty Certain drew a long breath, and said:

"Strange things hez happened in this house afore, which nobody could explain, though I've always thought I could guess at most on 't; but this yer thing beats me. Hevn't ye any idea, Mister Geoffrey, whose work it is?"

"None," he answered, "except that it must have been the work of an enemy—a bitter enemy."

"An' what enemy hev ye?" she asked.

"I did not know that I had any," he replied.

"Could any one hev been jealous of the gal?" eyeing him keenly.

"Impossible," he replied.

"Hev' ye looked fer any traces whar the gal was stabbed?" she asked.

He replied in the negative, and suggested that they should do so at once. They accordingly passed out upon the porch, and as they went along he pointed to the spot where he had last seen the figure. As they went through the front door-way, they noted where his shot had grazed the post, passing clear to the right

of the figure, which had not then reached the door.
In the hall Mrs. Certain called attention to the bloody
imprint of a foot. They followed it on, up the stairs,
and to the room occupied by Toinette. It was a
small, narrow, delicate track, such as might have been
made by the slippered foot of a woman.

"Not bigger'n fives, at the outside," said Mrs. Certain, putting her broad pedestal beside it.

Further on, they found a small piece of gray cloth,
which Mrs. Certain pronounced to have been torn from
the sleeve of a woman's dress—"and somehow," said
she, "it seems as ef I hed seen sunthin' like it afore,
but I can't jes now remember whar."

The dog had evidently torn it from the assassin in
the struggle and carried it on in his mouth as he
dragged himself, bleeding and dying, towards the friend
for whom he had given his life, an unavailing sacrifice.

Entering the room where the crime had been committed, they found that Toinette had been dragged
from her bed, across the room, almost to the door,
where she had finally been struck down. Here was
the form of the noble old Newfoundland stretched stiff
and stark upon his side, where his own life-blood had
mingled with that of the young slave-girl whom he had
sought to defend. His white breast was clotted with
blood, and his paws, thrust forth appealingly towards
his young master in that last moment of his life, had
been frozen there by the icy touch of death.

Geoffrey loved the old dog, who had once saved
him from a watery grave, and afterwards been the inseparable companion of his college days. He bent

over him, patted his curly neck, and said with tearful eyes, " Poor fellow! poor fellow!" On the plantation Leon had been a sort of Grand Turk, whose
ways were never questioned,—going wherever his master went, lying by his chair while he studied, and
keeping watch at his bedside while he slept. Is it any
wonder that Geoffrey Hunter dropped tears upon the
shaggy coat of his old friend—the truest and most devoted he had ever known?

There was nothing more to be learned here. In
fact, the mechanism, so to speak, of the attempted
murder was very simple and easily apprehended, except one thing—the opening of the front door. The
doorway from the back porch into the hall at the foot
of the stairway, as is usual in Southern houses of this
character, was seldom locked at night, and anyone desiring merely to reach the room occupied by Toinette
might have entered there and passed up the stairs entirely unmolested. Instead of doing so, it was evident
in this instance, as Geoffrey thought, that Aunt Maggie's room had first been entered, the key taken from
the nail at the foot of her bed, the door unlocked, and
the key returned to its place.

Geoffrey remarked this as he passed through the
hall with the woman, on their return. She was still
twisting the blood-stained piece of gray cloth about
her finger in an absent way.

"So yer think whoever 't was must hev come in at
the side door, gone to Maggie's room for the key, then
'long this hall to the front door, an' back an' up the
stairs, afore she hurt the gal," said Mrs. Certain.

"Certainly," replied Geoffrey; "how else could it have been done?"

"Why not hev come in at the back door an' gone up the stairs without coming in here at all?" she asked.

Geoffrey started, and his surprise did not escape the keen, gray eye of Mrs. Certain, who seemed almost instinctively to be dragging his unacknowledged thought to light. Unconsciously Geoffrey had, in his own mind, connected this act of violence with the apparition which had alarmed Toinette, and which had been seen only in the front of the house, to such an extent that he had failed to inquire *why* he had elaborated the hypothesis which he had adopted. This latent premise being absent from the mind of the woman, she had naturally inquired, why should the would-be murderer turn away from the intended victim, enter the old servant's room, pass along the corridor, unlock the front door, return the key, and then proceed to the chamber of Toinette, to commit the deed? And this thought found expression as the woman, watching him narrowly, continued:

"An' what would anyone carry the key back into Maggie's room fer?"

No reason was apparent. The young aristocrat saw at once that this poor woman, whom he had contemned and distrusted, had taken the lead in the investigation, and that he must follow. It irritated him, and he answered shortly:

"How should I know why? It must have been done, however."

The woman did not seem to hear him. They had

stopped in the hall while speaking, and she stood leaning back against the balusters, looking absently at the
wall before her.

"Whar did you say you slept?" she asked, at
length.

Geoffrey indicated the room by a gesture.

"In thar?" exclaimed the woman; "an' was the
dog with you?"

"Yes," he answered.

"An' war' he quiet afore the gal screamed?" she
asked.

"His restlessness and growling wakened me."

"Geoffrey Hunter," said the woman, with startling
earnestness, "ye'd best git out o' this yer house directly.
Them as entered here las' night came in by that ar
door,"—pointing to the front way—"an' it's my notion
that they meant harm tu you, mor'n tu the pore gal in
yon. It's not the fus' time the devil's played quare
pranks in this yer house, to my knowin'; an' bolts an'
bars ain't no account 'gin sech as went 'long here las'
night. Ef't hadn't been fer that ar dog, it's my notion
ye'd not been here to tell about it now. .An' now, ef
ye'll take my advice, ye'll not sleep in that thar room
ary other night, an' fur that matter, you'd be safer
sleepin' away entirely. No good'll come o' yer bidin
here." She was twisting and untwisting the bit of cloth
around her fingers absently, as she spoke.

Geoffrey was silent a moment.

"Come," said he, and they entered the room where
Toinette lay.

As they approached the sofa the woman's face again

assumed a look of indefinite, struggling surprise. It seemed as if memory were engaged in an unsuccessful effort at recognition.

With a half-despairing shake of the head she approached closer, and said:

"So this is the gal ez was hurt, is it?"

She did not seem to expect an answer, but wrapping the bit of cloth about the forefinger of her left hand, she began to undo the dressing and examine the wound. A thin red line, slightly broader in the center, with the pallid lips and purplish ring surrounding it, which marks the wound made by a dagger, showed itself upon the left breast, just above the girlish bosom.

"'Twas a close call," said the woman, after regarding it a moment, "an' I'll be boun' 'twasn't no or'nary knife cut that ar hole."

As she replaced the bandages, nodding her head in approbation of what had been done, Toinette opened her eyes, and gazed wonderingly at her. The effect upon the woman was marvelous. Surprise, incredulity, fear, seemed at once to possess her countenance. Her face flushed and paled by turns. With a quick movement, the left hand, containing the piece of cloth she had picked up in the hall above, was withdrawn from Toinette's shoulder, and thrust under her apron. At the same time she glanced furtively at Geoffrey. When she drew forth her hand again the bit of gray cloth had disappeared.

"Hush, chile," said the woman, as Toinette would have spoken. "You'd better save what breath ye have. Ther's no knowin' how long any'll be lef' ye."

"I'm to take keer o' her, ye said?" Geoffrey nodded assent. "Then I may ez well begin," she said, as she addressed herself with something of unnecessary stir to the duties of nurse.

Geoffrey retired from the room, and Toinette soon sank into a quiet slumber.

Then Mrs. Certain sat down and drew from its hiding-place the piece of cloth. She smoothed it out upon her knee, and gazed upon it long and earnestly.

"It's the very same," said she. "It's been many a year since I see'd it, but I would a-knowed it anywhar. I'd good reason to remember it, though I never thought to see it under these circumstances, never!" Then she sat a long time apparently absorbed in thought.

While she sat thus the doctor came to look at his patient. He was simply an old and garrulous practitioner of the country neighborhood. Geoffrey had told him as much as he thought necessary for him to know, no more. The girl had been stabbed. That was all that could concern the medical attendant.

"Some of the niggers been quarreling with her, eh? An' cut the gal, ye say? Bad, bad! They allers will cut, ef they can get a knife when the fit's on."

He felt Toinette's pulse, and, removing the covering, adjusted his spectacles and looked at the wound. He started—

"Eh! What's this?" looking minutely at the small, dark puncture. "Who d'ye say did this?"

Geoffrey told him that the perpetrator was unknown.

"Don't know who did it, Mr. Geoffrey!" said the old physician, looking keenly around. "Well, then, look here. Let me tell you this is no common wound —no cut made with a plantation-nigger's knife. It was a genteel weapon did that, and a steady hand that held it, too. I 'd wager money it 's not the first time that blade has tasted blood, nor the first time that hand has guided it."

Geoffrey then told him of the occurrence of the night more minutely, and brought him the dagger drawn from Leon's breast.

"Yes, yes," said the doctor, "this is it," comparing it with the wound. "But where 's the dog?"

Geoffrey informed him that the servants were then taking him out for burial. They went together and examined the body, and then returned.

"Yes," said the Doctor, "it was a steady and practiced hand. Not one in a hundred of the coolest of men—I say men, for somehow I allus thought it was a woman's hand that used that dirk—could have made that stroke. As I 've said, it 's not the first time I 've seen that style of cut, an' in this very house too. Ah, Mrs. Certain, I see you remember it. What! Never heard of it, Mr. Geoffrey? Yes, you were away at school at that time, or too young to know about it if you were at home, I reckon. Well, let 's have breakfast, and over our pipes afterwards I 'll tell you about it. I never let anything interfere with eating and digestion. Yes, the gal 's well enough. Rest and quiet—Betty Certain knows how to nuss her. I 'll leave her a little soothing powders, an' drop in towards night again. I allow she 'll get well if she aint hurt any more. It was a narrow miss, but she 's young an' strong."

CHAPTER X.

APOLLO'S ORACLE.

BREAKFAST was over, and the doctor and Geoffrey were seated in the library, each with a long-stemmed pipe, and a box of light russet-yellow tobacco between them.

During the meal, the doctor had, according to his previously declared maxim, studiously refrained from all reference to the present exciting events at the Lodge, or previously enacted ones of which he had intimated some knowledge.

"So you never heard the history of this house, Mr. Geoffrey?" said he at length, as the clay pipe glowed and puffed, and clouds of soft, bluish-white smoke rolled from his mouth.

Geoffrey answered that he had not, and the old man went on:

"Well, it's queer. I've been practicing on the river here for nigh about thirty years. Let me see— I came here in '30 or '31, and this house was built a few years later. Lovett—Arthur Lovett built it. He came from somewhere down in the low country, and was kin to the Loyds, and through them to the Petrees and some other families in the country round.

"He was a man of somewhat unsocial disposition

but finely educated and very well read. These books about us bear testimony to his taste, for most of them were his familiar friends. I see you have put your law-sheep into that corner rack which he had filled with a class of publications not very common nor popular in our part of the country, which were probably removed before your father bought. It was a collection of works on the institution of slavery. I reckon it contained every book that had been published on the subject in any language up to that time.

"Mr. Lovett was supposed to have peculiar notions on this question, but so far as I know he never expressed any opinion at all here, but just went on about his own matters, kept his niggers at work, and raised just as big crops as any of his neighbors. So they generally let him alone. Once, however, the circuit-rider stopped here over night and got a glimpse of some of these books, which I had seen many a time—and had even read several of them which bore somewhat on professional matters—without a thought of speaking of them, thinking it none of my business to attend to anything pertaining to my patients except their diseases. No sooner, however, did the preacher see them than he began to tell about the country that Mr. Lovett was not sound on the slavery question—was a seditious, dangerous, and objectionable person.

"By itself, this report would, perhaps, have passed for very little, but taken in connection with certain facts in the *ménage* of the Lodge, it gave him no little notoriety for a time. One or two committees waited upon him to regulate his doctrines and practice, but it was generally believed that they found the quiet recluse less of a coward than they had presumed, and were, in fact, badly outdone at their own game.

"He was a bachelor, of perhaps thirty-five or forty years old when he first moved here, and had for a housekeeper a young quadroon woman of remarkable beauty as to whose status there was, for a time, considerable discussion.

"It was said, and the revelations of a celebrated action at law which you have probably read afterwards proved the correctness of the rumor, that this man, Arthur Lovett, had, at an early age, become enamored of the girl, then his father's slave. Several children were result of their intimacy, and so great was his infatuation that he finally persuaded his father to execute a deed of manumission for her and her children, and he, thereupon, conveyed to them the major part of his own estate, and continued his former intimacy. A doubt having been intimated by an eminent attorney as to the legality of the deed of manumission, Arthur persuaded his father to take Belle and her children to New York and have them freed according to the laws of that State. This was accordingly done, but the woman, after a time, returned to this State, and entered upon her old relations with him.

"He seems to have been perfectly infatuated with this yaller gal, and at one time to have imbibed all the pestiferous doctrines of the Abolitionists. People were very lenient upon this subject then. It was regarded as a possible contingency that the slaves might, sometime, be freed. Very many masters taught their people

to read and write. The free negroes were then voters,
and were allowed a larger liberty than is now permitted
them. That was changed in '35, you know. Before that,
I have heard that some of them were ministers, regularly
ordained, and teachers of no mean efficiency. I have
understood that one or two of our Governors, and perhaps Judges of the Supreme Court too, were, for a
time, under the tuition of a certain free negro, and perhaps were fitted for college by him. There is a tale
which I have heard among the country people, that once,
when he came unexpectedly to a place where some of
his old pupils were at dinner, they compelled him almost
by force to sit down and eat with them, declaring
themselves honored by his society. I reckon it was
true too, for, by all I hear, he must have been a most
extraordinary man. I suppose the old fellows would
deny it now, though I have heard another ex-Governor
own that he had mustered in the same company with
free-niggers many a time in the old days; and I've
seen hundreds of our best men do the same thing. So,
people did not make so much note of Arthur Lovett
allowing this girl to read and write and have all the
accomplishments of a lady as we would now.

"But the relationship which existed between them,
after a time, began to occasion remark in the community, for it was too plainly one which no law-abid-
ing, Christian people could endure. They were indicted, and, as is usual in such cases, prosecution became
persecution. People were not content to prosecute
them for adultery, but also set upon them, under the
law just enacted, for inciting slaves to sedition, and

for circulating seditious publications. It created a great
excitement in the region where they lived and I have
heard that the old man Lovett had to pay a pretty
sum to stop the prosecutions, which he could only do
upon condition that the parties should leave the county
for good.

"Thereupon, Arthur came here and bought this
place, taking a deed to himself 'as trustee for Belle
Lovett, a free person of color, and the children born of
her body,' as your law books phrase it. He built this
house, as I said, superintending it all himself and putting into it all his whimsical notions.

"On coming here, Arthur Lovett seemed to have
determined to avoid any of those damaging suspicions
as to his relations with the girl Belle which had given
him trouble in the low country. It is true that he
lived in the same house here with her, and was very
attentive in his care of her children, who were really
bright, beautiful creatures. Beyond this, however, not
the most rigid scrutiny could detect any sign of familiarity. The girl occupied some well-furnished apart-
ments in that part of the house where the cutting was
done last night, and had absolute control of all that
pertained to the culinary department of the household,
being reputed to be something extraordinary in that
line.

"Thus matters went on for some time without
change. At length the old man, Peter Lovett, died.
It was said that his death was caused by anxiety arising
from pecuniary losses, but this was perhaps an after-
thought engendered by the deplorable condition in

which his estate was found to be after his death. It proved to be utterly insolvent. His creditors seized upon everything except the meager year's provisions for the widow and her dower in her husband's real estate, which the law allowed her to hold during her life. Except for this, the mother and two unmarried sisters were reduced to penury, and now it was seen how thoughtless Arthur had been in yielding to his infatuation for Belle. His mother soon died, and his sisters came to live at the Lodge. They constantly upbraided him with unkindness, and an utter disregard for their comfort and interest. In fact, there was the worst kind of a chronic family quarrel, in which the quiet, studious young epicurean had decidedly the worst of the encounter.

"The gal who had caused all this trouble seems to have behaved better than any of the rest. I have been told that she offered to waive all her rights under the deed of trust in case she was taken North with her children and given a reasonable settlement there. The girl evidently thought she was making a liberal offer, as she certainly was if she had actually been a free woman, as everybody at that time supposed her to be. It seemed, however, to enrage the whole family against her, who at once set upon her with redoubled violence. You know how they would act in such a case. The gal's old mistress, Nannie, was dead, and she had to fight the other two sisters single-handed, or rather single-tongued, for Arthur would not allow them to strike the gal.

"As for Arthur, he was near about distracted. It is

reasonable to suppose that the heat of his passion had
somewhat cooled, and that he began to see the folly
of his course. At any rate, he kept himself locked in
the library here, and smoked and cussed in grim solitude.

"About this time the administrator of the elder Lovett's estate conceived the idea that the girl Belle and
her children might be held for the benefit of the estate. He, therefore, brought suit against Arthur, in
whose possession he alleged they were, for their recovery and also to compel him to account for their use
and profit for several years.

"After a great deal of litigation, the gal and her
children were adjudged to be still the property of the
estate, and were taken to the low country by the administrator and sold at public outcry, to make assets for
the payment of creditors.

"Meantime, Arthur seemed to have become thoroughly ashamed of his early life, and to have done all
in his power to shake off its memory and influences.
The deed to this plantation, which had been made as I
told you, had never been registered, and after the gal
had been taken as a slave, he made search for it, with
the intention of destroying it, I think, but without avail.
Your father's advice was asked, and he counseled the
making of a new deed directly to Arthur Lovett, with,
out any trusteeship expressed. The simple-minded man
of whom the plantation had been purchased was informed that his former deed was lost and a new one
required, and for a slight gratuity executed another as
directed, making no inquiries. Indeed, he would have
been no wiser if he had.

"Then affairs settled down, and people were beginning to forget the occurrences which I have narrated, when, all at once, we were startled with the announcement that Arthur Lovett was about to marry Betty Certain—the Mistress Certain in the other room. Such a marriage was hardly less remarkable than his *liason* with the pretty quadroon.

"Betty Certain was a girl of perhaps twenty-one or two, buxom and rugged, but of a very *un*-certain position in society. Her father was not exactly a poor white, for he owned a little piece of land and was a comfortable liver, but they were not, by any means, of the class in society to which the Lovetts belonged.

"She had, somehow, obtained the *entrée* of the Lodge when Arthur first came, and was a sort of privileged character here ever afterwards. She was a strange, blunt sort of creature, of a good enough character, with a kind of man-like fearlessness of consequences which made her more dreaded than loved in her own circle in life, and rendered it even more strange that Arthur should have chosen her. Yet she was a sort of favorite. One could hardly meet the fresh, sturdy girl without being impressed with her good nature and her good sense. She came of a tolerably fair stock, too. Her grandfather, Ezra Certain, was the agent of 'the Earl' in the old days, when that dignitary owned a grant which might have been an empire, if he could have held it. He had a bee in his bonnet though, and his oddities came out in his children pretty strong. There is a story in the country that the family name is not Certain, but I don't know how true it is.

" People generally thought the bride would be good
enough for the groom; but I always distrusted her, and
not unfrequently speculated as to how she had brought
the matter about, for it was evidently her own work.
There was a rumor that certain disclosures in reference
to their previous relations, made by a set of rough characters who organized themselves into a committee of
vigilance for the purpose of whipping the gal—Belle—
and righting affairs generally at Lovett Lodge, led
eventually to this engagement.   It was said that they
found something connected with the domestic economy of the Lodge which compromised Miss Betty.
There certainly was a meeting between Bill Price, the
leader, and Lovett, which came near closing Price's
account without waiting for it to be balanced.   I never
believed a word of this report, though, so far as it implied any impropriety on her part.   She had too much
prudence for that sort of thing.

" By the sisters of Arthur Lovett—proud and refined
ladies—Betty Certain, after her engagement with Arthur
was known, was treated with the utmost contempt, and
only seemed to be endured because they were powerless to have things otherwise.   Her conduct towards
them, and their ordinary intercourse, was such as might
be expected from what I have described—constant
abuse and recriminations upon both sides.

"Towards Arthur Lovett himself the conduct of
this woman was, to my mind, most remarkable.   It was
the farthest removed from what would have been expected of a low-bred woman, who finds a man of
position in her toils and determines to profit by the

discovery. She seemed to regard him with absolute veneration, as a being of superior mold, and yet with a constant and tender pity. Never have I seen a woman's eyes beam with that peculiar light which speaks the tender care of a watchful nurse over a beloved object more clearly than when she watched his varying moods. It was utterly devoid of the exultation you would have looked for under the circumstances, and did not seem so much passion as watchful adoration. It was the mute watching for the will of the master which you may have noticed in a favorite dog. Every motion or gesture of his form or countenance seemed to have a meaning which she was anxious to apprehend and obey, not so much, it seemed to me, from love as from pity. She shielded him from the family broils, which often raged, and was untiring in her efforts to secure an atmosphere of quiet for the eccentric recluse.

"I watched her closely, for I was convinced that she was a most consummate actress, as the proposed marriage clearly proved. One would not expect it, but that coarse, hard-featured woman, nursing that yaller gal in yonder, has powers of intrigue, self-control, and artful assumption of the garb and guise of feeling, which I have never seen equaled.

"The effect upon her of the approaching marriage was most remarkable. She seemed to be half-frightened at the success of her own schemes. Her watchfulness and anxiety towards Arthur redoubled, and even her manner towards his sisters softened. She listened quietly and kindly to their remonstrances, and told them that it was not by her desire or wish, but in obedience to Arthur's solicitations, that she had consented to become his wife. Of course they did not believe a word of it, and when they retorted with taunts and insinuations she repeated her old threats, and told them that she was not yet powerless to repay scorn with injury—though she might be when she became the wife of Arthur Lovett.

"Yet she seemed to shrink from the day that would witness her triumph, rather than to desire its advent. It was put off from time to time with apparent dread, and when it was finally fixed, she begged that the wedding might be of the most private character, and that they might start at once upon their bridal trip.

"I spoke to Lovett with regard to his approaching nuptials, one day, but he changed the subject, betraying, as I thought, a disinclination to speak of it.

"The *trousseau* for the bride was completed at last, and a portion of it spread out upon a table at the end of this room. The wedding was to have taken place the next morning. Arthur Lovett was that night in unusual spirits. He left the sitting-room immediately after tea, and sat with Miss Betty in the library here for an hour or so, attended her back to the sitting-room door, and then, as was his custom, shut himself in here for the night with his books and his pipe.

"I was quite intimate at the Lodge at that time, having some thought of marriage with Miss Bertha, the younger sister of Arthur, so you see I was not exactly a disinterested spectator of the events I am relating. However, nothing ever came of it, and, considering what followed, I am sincerely glad there did not."

CHAPTER XI.

NICOTINIANA.

"I FEAR," said the Doctor, refilling his pipe, which had long been empty, "that I have been indulging in speculations rather than narrating the events which I set out to tell. The fact is," he continued, crowding the tobacco into the bowl, "that is the invariable effect of a narcotic upon a person of sedentary habits. Tobacco does not have the effect which has been attributed to it, of depriving the mind of logical power and accuracy, though its excessive use is in many other respects hurtful enough. On the other hand, I am inclined to the opinion that the purely logical power is strengthened, or, at least, improved, by the abstraction which results from the use of the weed. Its soothing and quieting influences tend at once to the most perfect abstraction and concentration of thought. The mind, which is largely affected by the use of this narcotic, or, indeed, any other, is disinclined to leave one subject to pursue another. It seems to produce the most perfectly conservative state of mind conceivable. The victim, or subject rather, of confirmed narcotism, started upon a train of thought, follows it with the utmost persistence and pleasure to the farthest possible limit, and leaves it with the greatest reluctance.

"For instance, the religious speculations of the
Brahmins and other Eastern philosophical sects, and
the more recent but quite as marked tendency of the
German mind, I regard as an unmistakable evidence
of the effect of narcotics upon the men of sedentary
habits. The same is observable in our own country.
The brilliant speculative intellects are to be found—
at least until of late years—almost exclusively at the
South. It is true that nearly all works claiming that
character have been of New England origin, but they
have been mostly controversial and semi-religious works.
They are not properly speculative; they are simply
cold mathematical deductions, from premises either
admitted or assumed. You might as well term Euclid
speculative as Edwards and the theologic disputants
of that day. Speculation is always suggestive, inquiring—awakening the mind to thought and research,
but not satisfying its wants. Demonstration, on the
other hand, leaves nothing to be done by the reader.
Beginning to read a book of that character is like
getting on a railway train—you must go where the
train goes. The demonstrator carries you with him
like a prisoner. The speculator sends you abroad alone,
into tangled thickets of luxuriant thought, full of unseen treasures and unexplored ways, and quietly waits
for you to come back to pursue your general course
with him. The one is the man who travels because
he must get to his journey's end, the other, the leisured
and accomplished tourist, who travels simply for the
enjoyment to be derived from wayside scenes and
chance encounters.

"The former class are more apt to figure in literature and to leave a lasting record of their acts and
successes than the latter. It is for this reason that
our history presents the anomaly that it does. The
South has ruled the Government from its inception,
but the record of Northern statesmen and orators is
far more permanently brilliant and imposing than ours.

"The opponents of John Randolph—a dozen of
them—are immortalized by speeches made in reply to
his, yet how meager is our record of those dazzling efforts which it gave immortality to oppose!

"The same was true of Mr. Clay. He towered
above the giant from Massachusetts, as Webster did
above his pigmy fellows—in strength, influence, and
effective eloquence—but a hundred years from now
Webster will be read with delight, Clay with surprise
and wonder that he was ever deemed an orator. The
same is true of our Badger, and Mangum, and a hundred other names dear to every Southern heart. Their
strength was in the thoughts they suggested, not in
the conclusions they demonstrated. They were giant
minds, fitted by every circumstance of growth, training and habit for the highest effort of speculation—
the accurate delineation of the various relations which
our anomalous governmental machinery imposed upon
the Federal Union, the State, and the individual.

"Calhoun was the most powerful generalizer who
has ever appeared in the field of American political
thought. I have never been able to concur with his
views, not because I did not consider his reasoning
good, but because I did not want to admit his con-

clusions, whether right or wrong. Our Southern statesmen have always been speculators, suggesters. They
have from the first supplied our political capital. They
have been the animating influences of our national
counsels. The Northern leaders have been leeches,
robbers, stealing the thoughts of our great careless
Goliaths, as they chatted over a glowing pipe or uttered the results of years of subtle meditations in the
freedom of convivial intercourse. These diamonds of
priceless value they have carefully garnered and set
in crowns upon their brows, for the future to regard
with wonder. The issues have been ours,—the work
of our thinkers. The successes have been ours too,
the triumphs of our great intellects. The speeches,
the reports, and the personal fame, in the main, will
be theirs. We have had the past, they will have the
future. The speeches of our Northern statesmen are
their enduring monuments. The measures accomplished by our Southern giants, the rule obtained and
held by a numerical minority for two generations
against the hottest opposition, the form proud memorial
of their strength, seen but by few and appreciated
by still fewer.

"In the main, I attribute this to the leisure of the
Southern planter and the free use of tobacco. It is
true that at this time there are a few in chill New
England who are taking the highest rank as published speculators—for the best speculative minds, as
I have said or intimated, rarely leave their lucubra-
tions to posterity at first hand. These Boston fellows,
however, seem to have happily united the faculties of

the two classes. What a king of suggesters is this fellow, Emerson, and the author of *The House with Seven Gables!* I understand that Emerson does not smoke, which accounts for his writing so much. If he smoked, he would be content to talk.

"Doctor," said Geoffrey, "do n't you think you are illustrating your own doctrine pretty fully?"

"Well, perhaps I am," said he, with a laugh, "and demonstrating its correctness too. Let me see. Where did I leave off? Oh, yes. Arthur Lovett had come into the library here, the night before the marriage was to take place. There was no disturbance here that night, but as he did not make his appearance at the usual time next morning the door was forced open, and in a great arm-chair, which was his favorite seat, they found him, stone dead.

"I was called at once, and not only examined as to the cause of his death but made an investigation as to the means by which he had been killed—for killed he undoubtedly was—by the hand of another. He had been reading and smoking after Miss Betty left him, and had probably fallen asleep, for his pipe was lying on the floor beside him, and the volume was pressed between his leg and the chair arm.

"He was stabbed just in front of the left shoulder, the blade passing downward through the heart. I am of the impression that his head was held forcibly in a reclining position for a moment. His struggles were but brief, however, as he must have died instantaneously. There was no blood, except a little on his clothing about the wound, and upon a handkerchief—

part of the bridal trouseau—which had evidently been
used to wipe the dagger.

"It seemed probable, in fact almost certain, from
the direction of the blow, that the murderer had stood
behind the chair when it was struck. It was a clean,
sharp, steady blow, and, judging from the wound, made
by the same weapon that cut that dainty hole in your
yaller gal out there last night—or at least its counterpart. Two wounds could not more closely resemble
each other, except that this was evidently more hurried, and directed too far back to be fatal.

"It may be a whimsical fancy, and certainly I can
offer no reason for the hypothesis; but I cannot help
believing that this ere little toy made both those wounds,
and that the same hand held it on both occasions. It
is of elegant workmanship, and seems to be of solid
silver mounting; but it makes an ugly hole, with the
least possible strength.

"Did you ever think the Italians were philosophic
in choosing that form of weapon for assassination? It
has several peculiar merits. First, it reduces the resistance to a minimum; then it is more easily withdrawn than the flat blade; and being withdrawn, the
wound is not so liable to close and stop hemorrhage.

"But I do not mean to speculate on murder. I
have told you my story, and you can draw your own
inferences and take such precautions as you may
deem expedient and necessary. Perhaps you know
more of this than I do, and have the thread which
will guide you out of the labyrinth; but I confess it
makes me nervous. I do not like such unexplained

phenomena. There seems to be a fatality about the place of a peculiar character."

_ "Yes," he continued, in answer to an inquiry from Geoffrey, " there was a great deal of excitement and speculation over the death of Authur Lovett, and any number of theories were advanced to account for it. Your father, among others, examined the premises and the body very carefully. He was then County Attorney, and of course had an interest in the investigation of crime. He asked a great many questions of all the witnesses before the Coroner's jury; but I thought he signally failed in his attempt to elucidate the mystery."

"Was there anything peculiar about the room?" asked Geoffrey.

' No, nothing that I particularly recollect," said the Doctor. "Yes, there was; the door was locked, and the key upon the ring, with other keys, in his pocket, as he always carried it. Nothing was taken from his person that was known to have been on it, and nothing was disturbed in the room."

"What could have been the motive for killing him?" asked Geoffrey.

"Well, sir," answered the doctor, "it is hard to say. No one had any grudge against him, or anything to gain by his death, except his own family. Suspicion ran hard against Betty Certain for a time, but on investigation it was shown that she had certainly far more to gain by his life than by his death. His will was written, but unsigned, leaving everything to his intended wife, Betty Certain. It was shown that he

designed signing it before he started on his bridal
tour. Dying intestate, all went to his sisters. Besides,
it was found that his life was heavily insured—
very heavily, for those days—and they received all this
too. These things made a great deal of talk about
the sisters, and I think the general idea was that they,
by some means, compassed his death. I have never
been quite able to disbelieve their protestations of innocence, nor yet to account for the murder on any other
hypothesis."

"What did Betty Certain do and say?" asked Geoffrey.

"Betty Certain said very little. What she did was
to gather her own little wardrobe and personal effects,
carefully leaving out every gift she had received from
Lovett except her engagement ring, which you may
have noticed she still wears, and go home to her
mother's. After the property was sold, and the money
received from the Insurance Company, the sisters, by
your father's advice, I think, offered her a considerable
sum, perhaps one third. She did not take it, and when
they came to urge it upon her, told them plainly, that
she did not '*want any money of that color.*' Miss Betty
evidently believed that the manner of his death was not
unknown to them.

"The place was bought by your father at a bargain,
on account of the bad name given it after the murder,
and has been, generally, unoccupied, until you came
here."

"Its bad name!" said Geoffrey. "Does a place get a
bad name simply from a man having been killed upon it?"

"That alone," answered the doctor, "might not give it one; but there soon came to be tales abroad of spectral figures, seen moving among your oaks, to which the ordinary laws of nature did not apply. It was said that a weird shape flitted back and forth, in the moonlight, before which the dogs were silent, or howled in fear. In other words, your pleasant residence is generally supposed to be haunted. I hope you have experienced nothing of this?" noticing the start which his auditor gave, at the sudden memory of what he had seen the night before.

Geoffrey answered that he had no faith in ghostly visitants, and was not likely to be troubled by them.

The doctor smilingly assented, knocked the ashes from his pipe, and prepared to leave.

"By the way," said he, "I saw your father yesterday. He has had another touch of paralysis, and I am afraid he is failing. If there are any arrangements to be made—as to his business, you know—they should be attended to at once. There is no knowing what may happen. Good day."

And the old Doctor rode away, leaving Geoffrey Hunter with his strange problem yet unsolved.

CHAPTER XII.

A DEAD CLIENT.

ACTING upon the doctor's advice, the next day
Geoffrey went to the Hunter Home and found
his father as had been described to him. The sight
of his son somewhat revived him, and he said with a
touch of his old vivacity:

"How d'ye, Geoffrey, son. I'm powerful glad to
see you. I was jes' goin' to send a boy over arter ye.
Yes, as ye see, I'm but poorly, but I hope all's well
at the Lodge?"

Geoffrey informed him briefly of what had trans-
pired there, of the stabbing of Toinette and killing of
Leon.

"Sho, sho; ye do n't say so. Toinette, little Toinette, stabbed! Who should want to kill her! An'
her mammy, old Mabel, come back this morning, too—
how bad she'll feel! An' the dog killed! Pity, pity.
He was a fine fellow, though he had n't any nose an'
wa'n't worth nothin', only fer company-like, to you.
But he certain did think a power o' ye, no mistake.
An' Toinette, little Toinette, that yer ma loved so
well. My mind·misgave me when you asked me for
her. It was wrong, my son, I ought not to hev let
you have her. An' that 'minds me that neither of us
'tended to the petitions for the emancipation of these

gals at the last term of our Court. I thought o' it one night during the term, an' did 'low to do it the very next day, but I quite forgot it then. Of course, you thought I would see to it. You ain't ter blame. But you mus' do it next time. The Court will be here agin in November, an' you must look after it then; mind now, Sonny, I may not be here then, an' if I am, you must charge yerself with it, for the sake o' that pore gal, Toinette.

"Stabbed, too! It's queer; Arthur Lovett was stabbed in that same house—let me see—ten or twelve —yes, better than twelve—years ago. It was a wonderfully mysterious affair. I did my best to find out the truth on 't, but never could satisfy my own mind, much less another, about it.

"You see, I was his counsel and friend as well as County Attorney, and I made a thorough search arter the murderer, but nothin' ever came on 't. He was stabbed at night, sleepin' in his chair in the library. Most folks laid it on his sisters, an' at first I did, too —especially when I found he had not signed his will, which he had drawn up in his own hand and would probably have executed the next day. Indeed, he had spoken to me about it several days before, and said that he should make a will before he left on his bridal trip. He was to have been married the next day, and by his will he intended to have left everything nearly to his wife, or the woman he would have married next morning. He dying intestate, his sisters got it, including an insurance policy of twenty-five thousand dollars on his life. This made me more suspicious of his sis-

ters than anyone else; but I was satisfied that I was
wrong on seeing their absolute surprise when I informed
them of these facts. They never were knowin' to his
death, that I am sure of, but who was, or for what
purpose, with what motive, it passes me to say.

"I have got all the papers now. I was looking
them over only a little time back and wondering that
no clue had ever been found to his murder in all the
time that has elapsed since. It's rare that crime man-
ages to hide so long; I don't think I have known
another case like it in nigh on to half-a-century of
practice. We will get the papers before you leave, and
you can take them home and look them over if you
choose. You will find some in the bundle not relating
to this particularly, but connected with Lovett's business. You may find them all interesting. He was
party to one of the most important suits ever decided
by our Courts. You had better study this case thoroughly, for it may sometime involve the title of your
estate. I was never right satisfied that the decision
on which our title rests is good law. I didn't think
so when I bought, but just considered the chances
fair in my favor, an' it was goin' for nothing a'most.
The place was first deeded from old man Tommy Gray
to Arthur Lovett, as trustee for a yaller gal, Belle, and
her children, who lived with him. She had been manumitted according to the laws of New York, and was
also directed to be freed, by the will of the old man,
Peter Lovett, Arthur's father. This provision was
defeated by the codicil of the same will, which be-
queathed to her certain real property in the State, for

her use and occupancy. The Courts refused to recognize the act of manumission in New York, on the ground that Belle and her child had been removed to that State only for the temporary purpose of emancipation, and had very soon thereafter returned to this State. This was thought to be in fraud of our statute upon the subject, as it unquestionably was, so far as the motives and intent of the master were concerned. At the old man's death they were adjudged to be still slaves, and were taken into possession by the executors as part of the assets of the old man Peter's estate. You will find the case, so far as it was reported, in the eighth of Iredell.

"Now, you see at once, that if she or her heirs, at any time, should succeed in getting his decision reversed—as I am of the opinion that it would be, if it should ever be in their power to bring it up for consideration, from a different standpoint, or even in another tribunal—it might be a troublesome matter for us.

"I have often wondered what the United States Courts would do if this question should ever be fairly presented to them. The act of emancipation in New York, if regular and in accordance with their statutes, and I have examined into this case and think it was, clothed the gal, Belle, *eo instante*, with all the rights of the richest white woman in the country before the law. Can the intention of her former owner, however fraudulent, deprive her of these rights? It may be said that she was cognizant of his act, but she was then a chattel, and could not be a party to a fraud, whether

10

affecting her manumission or not. Surely her master's fraudulent or unlawful intent could not operate to defeat her of the rights which the statute of that State guaranteed her.

"It is one of those mixed questions which can never be decided with strict obedience to logic, and yet be entirely just. Or, rather, it is a question which one series of logical deductions will decide in the affirmative, and another, equally logical, in the negative. If we regard Belle as having been first, last, and all the time a chattel merely, then the decision is correct. But if we consider her as a human being, with the rights, powers and privileges of such, merely removed by the operation of law, and consider the act of emancipation as one personal to herself, then it is wrong. The effects, too, are equally inharmonious. If the decision is correct, the gal, Belle, loses the rights which the law declares—the statute law of New York, I mean,—she is entitled to maintain. If it is erroneous, then the creditors of her master lose their right to subject his property to the payment of their just debts. The real irreconcilability of these two lines of thought was first pointed out to me by Arthur Lovett, and I must say the puzzle has gone far to convince me in fact that the state of slavery was designed to be a temporary one merely, and, on account of its inconsistencies could never obtain a permanent place in the laws and institutions of a free country.

"Suppose, now, that Belle Lovett, or her children, should ever be in a condition to present this matter in a tangible form to a United States Court, what would

be the result? Candidly, Geoffrey, I don't see how we
could fail to go to the wall. I am satisfied our title
would be worthless—provided the original deed to Arthur Lovett, as trustee, should be found, or could be
proven. You see it was never registered, and, in fact,
has not been seen since the gal, Belle, was taken by the
Executor. I always thought that it was in Arthur Lovett's possession after Belle, pore gal, was taken off and
sold—though he denied knowing anything about it,
saying he had not seen it for years, and assented, or
rather submitted, to the making of another deed by
the old man Gray, to himself individually. As the parties were the same as in the former deed, this, even
when recorded, can only be of value to pass the property, in so far as it is a renewal of the original one.

"I looked over Lovett's papers carefully, after his
death, but could find nothing of the missing deed.
The gal, Belle, must have carried it off with her, or she
may have placed it in the hands of some person to
hold for her, with the idea of sometime obtaining her
rights thereby. I have been looking for a suit about
the matter from year to year.

"But the strangest thing about it is that I cannot
find the gal herself. I tried to trace her out, after
Lovett died and I had bought the place, to see if I
could not compromise the matter with her, by freeing
her and her children. I never felt quite right about
it, for I got the property for a tithe of its value because people were so sartin' that the gal's claim would
sometime be urged.

"It's a queer thing, Geoffrey, but the older you

grow the more you'll notice it, that the downright honest notions of the people ain't far from the law and equity of things. It makes little difference what prejudice or passion may say. The *vox populi* is not the voice of God when it comes in anger, rage or disappointment, with hot blood and violence. It is not *vox Dei*, but more probably the opposite, when it comes with a roar and a shout, fervid and wild. Don't trust it then, Geoffrey, never. But when it comes calm and deliberate, in the quiet chat of neighbors, or rises in a man's mind as he smokes his pipe alone, or gives his notions to his ole woman by the firelight after supper, then I've ginerally found it was better law than we ordinarily get in the Reports. When it comes in that way, Geoffrey, the people's voice is so nigh what God means, that one is taking onreasonable risks when he goes agin it. Remember that, Sonny, remember that. I took sich risk when I bought the Lovett place. I don't know why. Perhaps I had a lingerin' notion that I would, in effect, carry out Arthur Lovett's will—set the gal an' her children free, an' make myself whole out of the plantation—I don't know. He seemed to care more about that than anything else, as you'll see by reading his will.

"Ruthy always told me that if I did not make it right with the gal, an' her children, the plantation would just be a curse to us and our heirs. She never looked in a law-book, nor anything resembling one, except the Scriptures, but, queerly enough, she always used a legal phrase in describing my relations to the property. She said I was just a trustee for the rightful owner, who had been dispossessed by fraud; which you know, Son, is just what the courts would say, if her 'freedom papers' should prove good, and the deed to her use should be established.

"As I said, I tried to trace the gal and her children. They were all sold by the Executor at public auction. The two older children to a trader who dealt in fancy niggers for the Richmond market. He calculated to keep them four or five years, as they was n't quite 'prime' at that age, and then sell them high. I found out about them after Arthur died, and sent a trader from t'other side the river to buy them for me. I got the boy but missed the gal, and never could get trace of her agin.

"I took the boy, Fred, North and set him free, and left money enough in trust for him to send him to school a right smart time. He 's a bright lad, and I guarantee that if he has a fair show he 'll be no discredit to the man that set him free. I 'd like to see him once more, for somehow he 's some sort of evidence of one good deed I 've done. I 'm always glad to think I did it, too. I never told him his history, but when I am dead I want you to write to him and get a fair and square quit-claim. He is of age now and would probably give one, for I tell you, my son, he nigh about worships Manuel Hunter, and I would give more to deserve his gratitude than anythin' else in this world. I can 't bear that he should know how I hev been cheating him as it were till I 'm past knowin' what he says of my conduct."

"I am sure, father," said Geoffrey, "he has reason

to be grateful. If you are the trustee, have you not used the interest in the estate which you acquired for his good? The law made him a slave, and he would probably have remained so if it had not been for your trusteeship, as you term it."

"Perhaps you 're right, my son. I wish Ruthy could have heard her son—her favorite, too, you always were —defending my conduct in that way. I 've a notion though that she was something of that mind herself; for when I came home an' told her that I had put the boy at school, she half-started out of her chair, when she had n't stood alone for years, and said, 'God bless you, Manuel!' and then she clasped her hands, and her lips moved, and the tears ran down her poor, pale cheeks. An' that night, when she was wheeled out to supper, she looked as bright and beaming as a glorified angel. An' when she asked me not to go back to the office, but to sit an' smoke in her room and hev a cosy chat with her, I could n't refuse, though some clients war a-waitin' for me. An' so I sat by her easy-chair well into the night.

"She said she 'd never been so proud of me since I refused a fee from the prosecution an' volunteered to defend a pore gal for killin' her master in defense of her virtue. That was when I first came to the bar an' fees was scarce an' small, but I could n't prosecute that innocent gal for defending her honor against her master's lust. Ruthy never ceased praisin' me for that.

"I knew that night she wouldn't be with me long, for she was too nigh a saint to stay on earth. Oh, Geoffy, boy, ye do n't know what a woman yer mother was! It's little Manuel Hunter would ha' been on earth without her; an' if he's any hope of heaven, it's all through her. I know she's up there with the angels now, and I hope to see her soon."

The two men wept in silence over the memory of the sainted woman to whose influence so much of the good in both was due.

The old man at length broke the silence, saying: " I 'm glad we came to talk of these things, Geoffrey. Now you 'll understand my will better. I made it some years ago, as you know, but I added an important codicil only a few weeks back. It 's about that woman Belle. I can 't get rid of an impression that she 's alive somewhere, and I want her hunted up and freed; an' when that is done—not before, boy—make the best bargain with her that you can. Mind, you 're to look sharp for her. You are young and can travel. I know only this—she was sold to Buck Loyd, an' he took her to Alabama—at least I s'pose he took her there— but what came of her atterwards I never could make out. He lived a wild, roving life, an' no one could ever track him so as to find the gal. I sent down to the administrator's sale of his estate, but could get no trace of her. In fact, he had lost more 'n half the bills of sale for the niggers which he had. I bought Mabel then, because yer mother wanted a good cook and she was recommended as something extr., as she is. I saw the girl Belle several times, when she was with Lovett at the Lodge, and should know her any time if I should see her—especially by her long black hair, the finest I ever saw. Loyd probably traded her off, perhaps gambled her off, in some drunken spree, and I am afraid the chances for finding her are not good; but you 'll try, boy, won't you? That 's the only thing on my mind, Geoffy. You are my executor. You an' the gals will divide the property equally after taking out a share for your aunt, pore woman. Mabel, you know, is to be freed; remember, I promised your mother and the petition is already filed, and I promised her, too, that Toinette should be free at the same time. You 'll make yer old father glad and do it, so that I can tell Ruthy that we 've done as she wished, won't you, Geoffy? Now, do n't forget, Son, do n't forgit."

"Yes, father," answered the son, "I will attend to it at the next term, and we will have them both freed, and sent away. You will remember it if I should forget."

"Thank ye, Son, thank ye; but Manuel Hunter 'll have to answer at another bar, afore the Judge calls over the docket in the Court House yonder, again. Somehow it do n't seem as if I should see you again soon. But go home now. You 're needed there, an' keep close watch. Somehow, I think ye 'll clear up that mystery yet. Keep watch—keep watch. There's nothing like a steady eye in this world. Good bye," and the old man leaned back wearily in his chair, while his son took the books and papers that his father had referred to and returned to the Lodge.

The next day, the mind of Manuel Hunter—the clearest-headed lawyer in his circuit for many a year —had lapsed into childish imbecility, and his busy past had become to him—a dream.

That night Geoffrey Hunter sat alone in the library at Lovett Lodge, and examined the papers referring to the life and death of his predecessor in its possession, Arthur Lovett. The first was the unsigned draft of a will. In a small, distinct and peculiarly unmistakable hand, it read:

"*The last will and testament of Arthur Lovett of Lovett Lodge.*

" Being of sound mind, and of bodily health unimpaired, I, Arthur Lovett, of Lovett Lodge, in the County of Cold Spring, State of North Carolina, do indite the following as my last will and testament:

"*Item.*—I give and bequeath to each of my sisters five thousand dollars.

"*Item.*—I give and bequeath the residue of my estate, after paying all my debts and the above legacies, to my wife, Betty, to be used for the purposes, and upon the conditions, hereinafter named—to wit:

"First.—That she shall employ such portion of the said estate as may be necessary, in securing the freedom of Belle Lovett, and her children Fred, Alice, and Antoinette.

" The said Belle Lovett was my beloved and devoted servant, and the said children are my own. I had supposed her to be free, and intended to repay her devotion by such feeble reparation as our constitution of society would allow me to make. As the law has mocked my efforts in this, it is only just that I should devote my estate to securing to her and her children the liberty of which her love and my selfishness have deprived them.

G

"SECOND.—That when the liberation of the said Belle Lovett and her children shall have been accomplished, my estate shall be equally divided, one-half to go to my wife Betty, and one-half to the woman Belle and her children.

"*Item.*—I constitute and appoint Betty, my wife aforesaid, executrix of this my last will and testament, and exhort her to do, without fail, these acts of tardy justice, which my own weakness of purpose has prevented me from doing in my lifetime.

"*Item.*—In case my said wife Betty shall fail or refuse to qualify as executrix of this my will, for the purposes herein expressed, then I hereby constitute and appoint the Hon. Manuel Hunter executor and residuary legatee, in the place of my said wife, and upon like conditions, except that before entering upon the execution of this devise, I require that he shall give bond, with good security, to be approved by the Judge of the Court of Equity of the county aforesaid, in the sum of fifty thousand dollars, for the faithful performance of the conditions thereto attached.

"And in case the said Manuel Hunter shall refuse to accept such executorship, then it is my will, that a trustee be appointed by the Court aforesaid, to use, employ, and expend my estate so far as may be necessary, for the purposes and in the manner above-named; and all my estate remaining, after the said persons have been set at liberty, except a portion equal to the dower and allowance guaranteed by law to the widow, I give and bequeath in equal portions to Belle Lovett and her children—Fred, Alice and Antoinette.

"*Item.*—In case I should decease before my now intended marriage shall have been consummated, it is my will and desire that my intended wife, Betty Certain, in that event shall take and hold, under this my will, as is herein and heretofore provided for my wife Betty, the said Betty Certain being the person intended to be thus designated, both as legatee and executrix; and I desire that, in that event, she shall do and perform, all and singular, the acts and duties devolved on my said wife, and receive all the benefits conferred upon her in this my last will and testament.

"And it is my desire that the said court shall in all things order and direct the said executrix, executor, or trustee, in the faithful performance of the trust, imposed according to equity and good conscience, and according to the plain purport and intent of this instrument, and without legal subtlety.

"In testimony whereof I have hereunto set my hand this —— day of ——, 1845."

The signature that would have made this instrument valid alone was lacking. Geoffrey Hunter thought Arthur Lovett must indeed have been infatuated to become such an idiot over a "yaller gal" who had been his paramour.

"He must have been perfectly insane," was his mental comment, "thus to have put himself at variance with the laws and customs of the entire society in which he lived. It is strange! There must be something radically wrong in a condition of things which made this woman a slave and this man her master. The institution itself is well enough, but there should be

some limitation placed upon it. This woman seems
to have been a superior person. Why has not the old
Roman principle been adopted, that the noble who
married his manumitted slave raised her to his level,
without reproach. Slavery in the abstract is right, and
the proper sphere of the African race. Let the Abolitionists say what they choose, of that I am satisfied.
But in the concrete—in individual instances—Toinette
now—with harsh, brutal treatment—My God! think of
Toinette in that condition!" He groaned at the idea.
"No wonder my mother wished her emancipated. It
shall be done without fail."

And so the conscience of the weak, hesitating, dead
Arthur Lovett awoke the dormant sense of right and
justice in the soul of the prompt and strong Geoffrey
Hunter, and made him, in spirit, the executor of the
unsigned testament. Perhaps there was an analogy in
their lives, like the refrain of a remembered song,
which he had not yet recognized.

"And so," pondered Geoffrey, "Betty Certain, the
hard-faced woman in yonder, was to have been the
wife of this visionary. What did he want of her? Why
would he have married her? I cannot understand.
But of one thing I am satisfied: that proposed marriage and this draft of a will, either singly or united,
were the cause of his death. As father says, 'I feel
as if I should sometime clear this mystery up.'"

The young man was evidently becoming interested
in the events which had so mysteriously encircled him.
He filled his pipe, and applied himself again to the
perusal of the documents before him. The next in-

strument which he read was a letter from Manuel
Hunter to his client, dated some months previous to
Lovett's death:

"*My Dear Sir :*

"I have just returned from the Supreme Court,
where the cause of Albert Chasteen, Executor of Peter
Lovett, *vs.* Arthur Lovett and the heirs-at-law of Peter
Lovett has been argued and decided.

"Contrary to my expectations and positive convictions, we have been thrown. Even now I am satisfied
that we are right and that the Court is wrong. But
it is useless to argue that.

"The decision proceeds upon these grounds:

"1st. That the emancipation in the State of New
York was invalid as being against public policy, and in
fraud of the jurisdiction of the Courts of this State.
Although the act of emancipation was in the State of
New York, yet as the girl Belle was taken there for
the express purpose of being freed and soon thereafter
returned to this State, it is held that this act was to
avoid the statute of this State, and the emancipation is
therefore fraudulent and invalid.

"2d. That the clause in the will of Peter Lovett
providing for the emancipation of the girl at his
decease is void by reason of the codicil which be-
queaths certain real estate to a trustee for her use and
occupancy, which they held to be inconsistent with the
law requiring the removal of a freed person from the
State, and consequently void.

"This decision, of course, applies to all of her chil-

dren. They are slaves with her. The decision pre-
sumes everything against liberty, rather than in its favor.
It is correct enough so far as it affects the master, but
it utterly ignores the rights which emancipation conferred on the girl. It defeats the girl of her liberty
because her master intended a fraud.

"I tried to get Chasteen to consent to a sale to me,
but he said he had had so much trouble with the gal
that she and the children should only be sold on the
block, adding that he hoped they would go into the
hands of traders so that you might never see them again.

"I am satisfied he will do all he can to prevent
your recovering possession.

"I would advise that you assume indifference, let
the sale pass a short time, and then deal with the
purchasers. Besides, I wish to examine whether some
steps cannot be taken to have this decision reviewed,
which I think might be done should any of them be
sold out of the State.

"I was never more inclined to concur in your notion about the evil and misfortune of slavery than now.
It is either wrong or wrongly managed.

"Your friend,   MANUEL HUNTER."

The rough old lawyer and his somewhat pampered
son, strangely enough, seem to have felt the same truth
in considering Arthur Lovett and his quadroon. In
the practical concrete both were slaveholders. In the
abstract, they were not so far removed from the Abolitionists of that day, as either themselves or those
fanatics would have maintained.

He read several other papers, but none seemed to show any light upon the questions he sought to solve.

At length he came to the last in the package. It was carefully sealed, and a superscription covered the entire face. It was in the handwriting of Arthur Lovett, and ran as follows:

"To Belle Lovett, whom God designed for my wife, who is the mother of my children, but whom society made my slave, and my own weakness made the victim of the most terrible wrong—or to any of her children should she die before being legally emancipated.

"Let no other hand break these seals. A. L."

On the back was written, in the sturdy, irregular hand of Manuel Hunter:

"I have been strongly tempted to disregard the injunction of Arthur Lovett, to see if some clue to his murder might not be obtained from this paper but the last request of a friend is too sacred to be broken.

"M. H."

Geoffrey Hunter took his pen from the table and wrote these words underneath:

"The example of a father restrains the hand of his son. G. H."

He replaced the papers in the package and put them in his private drawer.

CHAPTER XIII.

WARNED.

BY the affliction of Manuel Hunter, the care of his entire estate devolved upon Geoffrey, he having been appointed trustee upon his father being adjudged of unsound mind.

Examination of his father's estate fully disclosed the fact that he had not boasted without cause, of his material success in life. Patient industry and unflagging zeal, united with foresight and prudence in his investments, had borne their usual fruits to the old lawyer. It was, however, soon discovered by Geoffrey, that his father's kindly feeling and accommodating spirit had led him to endorse for several parties to a very large amount, enough, in fact, to nearly swallow up his accumulations, should his estate be obliged to pay them all. There was little apprehension of this, however, as most of the principals were in good circumstances and abundantly able to discharge all liabilities.

To prepare the estate for a speedy settlement in case of his father's decease, now a matter to be daily expected, would require, however, no little time and attention. To this task Geoffrey addressed himself with the energy and concentration of purpose which marked his nature when fully aroused. For several months he did, and thought of, little else. His time was mostly passed at the Home, and the father's office

became almost as regular a place of resort, day by
day, to the son, as it had been to the father in his
busiest years.

Meanwhile the household at Lovett Lodge was still
kept up, though with only the occasional presence of
the master. Once in a week or two he would drive
over to pass the Sunday, and remain a few days to
see that matters were progressing favorably.

Immediately upon her recovery, Toinette had devoted herself to the piano, which had been opened for
her amusement during convalescence, and to such desultory reading as the library afforded, and which struck
her fancy at the moment.

The question had often crossed Geoffrey's mind,
even amid the engrossing duties of his present life, as
to what was the best preparation which he could bestow
upon this favorite, to prepare her for that freedom which
at no distant day awaited her. Her condition, even in
the North, would be anomalous, and, in his view, even
pitiable. He earnestly desired, he often said to himself, to do what was wisest. She would, when emancipated and at the North, be an outcast, nothing more —
nothing less. The race to which she was nearest akin
—he often questioned whether she was akin to any
other—would look upon her with scorn. It seemed
as if degradation awaited her in any view which could
be taken of the future. She was too light to be black,
and, of course, she could never be white. Poor girl!
it was not her fault but her misfortune.

And thus, while he speculated, she read his books,
and learned his music, and grew into a rarely beautiful
11

woman, with a quick and teeming fancy, and a demeanor neither of the servant nor of the equal, the outgrowth of her undefined position in the household, solving the question, in fact, before he could perfect his theory.

Soon after her recovery, Geoffrey had taken Betty Certain into his confidence so far as to inform her of the intended emancipation of Toinette, and she spared no pains to impart to the young slave girl, to whom she seemed much attached, such useful information as she had acquired, which, though by no means startling, was by far greater than would have been supposed from observation of her countenance and person, or from knowledge of her surroundings in life. Somehow and at some period, she had managed to pick up what might be termed "a tolerable English education," whether from one of the log school-houses not very abundant in that region, or through the charity of some teacher at the "Silk-Stocking Academy," on "Gentleman Ridge," it is unnecessary to enquire. In addition to this, she had great powers of observation, and was given to reading in an abstracted, unaccountable way —as it seemed to Toinette—the books upon the library shelves. They did not seem to be new to her, but rather, old friends, and her quaint comments showed her intimacy with the thoughts they contained.

And so for months they dwelt almost alone, the middle-aged, hard-featured, poor white woman, and the young slave girl just budding into womanhood, under the roof of the young Antinous, whose time was then given to conquering the difficulties which his new duties devolved upon him.

Time wrought a wonderful change in old Mabel. She seemed to have lost all affection for the child she had once so fondly loved. Mother and child did not meet until the Christmas came again and Toinette went to pass the season of festivity at her old home.

What was her surprise when, meeting her mother at the kitchen door, in response to her joyful greeting old Mabel repulsed her with the utmost coolness, and, despite all her efforts, refused to bestow any loving attention upon her.

" Go back to yer Mass'r Geoffrey," she said, grimly. " Yer haint been my gal since the ole lyin' rascal, that sits mumblin' yonder to hisself, an' waitin' fer de debble to answer, giv' ye to his son. I do n't want to see ye. I wish ye was dead."

" But, mother," said the affrighted girl, " do n't you know we are both to be free when Mass'r Manuel dies ? It 's in his will. Mass'r Geoffrey told me so hisself. An' then he 's going to take us North somewhere and give us a nice home."

" Free ! " said old Mabel with a sneer. " Free ! Ye like the word an' the idee, do n't ye ? I used to like it once, but I hates it now worse 'n de debble does the sound o' prayer. Free ! I 've heard it so many times that I 'd hardly believe it if the Lord God hisself, if ther' is one, should tell me so with his own mouth. I could tell ye—but whar 's the use. Yer jes' Mass'r Geoffrey Hunter's nigger, body an' soul, an' he aint gwine to give up either one till it 's ready for de debble's pickin' ! I tells ye so, an' I knows. Did n't dat ar ole liar Manuel Hunter tell Miss Ruth, as is a blessed angel in Heaven to-day, if there is sech a place, on his bended knee, an' she a-dyin', with the light of Heaven shinin' on her face—did n't I hear him tell her dat ole Mabel an' her little gal Toinette should be free' an given a home in a free land, atter she 'd done wid 'em? An' did n't I feel like goin' down on my knees an' kissin' de dust off his feet, cos I believed him? More fool I, for 't wa' n't the fust time lips like his hed lied to me—lips dat orter hev turned cold in death 'fore dey let one false word come fru dem to my ear. But dey lied, an' he lied. He jes' kep' us right on, an' when young Mass'r axed for ye, he jes' give ye away as light as a penny to a beggar.

"An' when I went to him an' tole him of his promise, an' axed him not to let ye go, he would not heed me, cos he 'd promised ye to Mass'r Geoffrey, as ef he had n't promised de dear dead saint, dat kep' de debble off his pore soul so many years by her love an' prayers. I cussed him den, an' de Lor' heard it, ef he do n't take much 'count ov us pore niggers often.

"An' now, see de pore critter! An' he aint half over it yit. His body 's here, but I tell ye, gal, he 's in hell-torment, as he ought to be. De debble made a good trade de day Manuel Hunter guv ye to his son. He 's gittin' his pay now. I loves to see him maunderin' an' putterin' about, with less sense dan de meanest nigger on de place, an' I say to myself, Dat's de man Hunter, dat give away yer chile, to go thru all dat you 've faced in yer life, agin. But he can 't pay it all. Geoff Hunter's turn 'll come some day.

"Ye pore gal, yer aint tu blame. I don't want tu

hurt ye," she said, as Toinette sobbed and wept. "De debble's got ye an' ye can't help it. It's a pity dat knife did not make an end of ye. Ye aint to blame, I knows. Ye aint yer own, but Geoff Hunter's. I do n't hate ye, gal, but jes' can't abide to see ye. Go back to yer master, an' if sin ever scotches yer white soul his'n 'll hev tu pay for 't as sure as there's anything like justice in Heaven."

That night Toinette went back to Lovett Lodge, confused, bewildered; wonderingly asking herself the question after whose solution so many have vainly groped. The infinite problem of life made her heart heavy and her head dull. What wonder if the poor child, standing in the darkness—walled in by stern necessity—lost sight of the dim spot of far away blue sky above. What if she deemed the prison walls insurmountable by hope or faith and caught at the mockeries it held to cheer her hopeless misery.

She was no more a child. She lost her girlhood the hour she bade her mother "good bye." A bright rosy glamour hung over the earth when the petted slave-child, Toinette, started to meet her mother that day;—a hot, yellow glare oppressed the eyelids of the pampered slave-woman as she returned.

The change had come, the die was cast. She could never be what she had been. She felt that dimly. What would she be? She did not know—hardly cared. Her mother had told her to go back to her Mass'r Geoffrey. She would go. He was kind to her. She thought he was the only one who cared for her now.

So she fled from the Mother to the Master.

CHAPTER XIV.

"OH, LIMED SOUL!"

GEOFFREY HUNTER had resumed his residence at the Lodge before another summer came. The burden of his father's business had either become less, or he bore it more easily, as he became accustomed to it.

The relations of the inmates of the Lodge to each other seemed, however, to have changed, when he came to be again an accustomed presence within its walls. For a time there was an attempt upon the part of all to take up the thread of life at the point where the paralysis of the elder Hunter had separated the strands, but it was a futile one. The sensuous young Epicurean was then trying to prepare, in an impossible manner, for an unheard of life, the budding mind of a slave-child. The same being, grown to womanhood, conscious of her charms, and with the memory of former intimacy and favor, constituted a whole which Geoffrey Hunter in his Utopian dreams had never fully counted on. The reader will remember that he had at first viewed her as a chattel, mentally calculating her probable market value at maturity, and afterwards as a curious toy on which he might try such visionary experiments of the humanitarian type as his fertile brain might suggest. Now, he was forced to look upon her in another light—that of

a woman. Already the country gossip had seized upon
the significant facts of his household *ménage* to couple
his name with Toinette's in good-humored banter.

The rumor was not of that character which could be,
or, in that state of society, even needed to be, put down.
There was no disgrace, scarcely an impropriety, coupled
with the relation it implied. It awakened him, however, to some facts which most probably had before
that unconsciously exerted an influence on his esthetic
nature, among which was the wonderful beauty of his
young bond-woman.

The familiarity of the child had given way to the
consciousness of womanhood, and as she passed before
his sight here and there about the house in tasks quite
self-imposed he could not shut from his mind an uneasy, indefinite feeling that everything was not precisely
as he could desire. He became moody and fitful in
his temper. He could not but see that gradually and
almost unconsciously Toinette had assumed control of
the household; that she had been placed by him in a
false position, but one which she filled with completeness and grace. He was sorry she was there, yet would
not have her elsewhere. He did not analyze his own
feelings, but only knew that he was sorry she was a
slave, yet could not bear to send her away from him.

It was no wonder that the young sybarite felt the
charm of her presence. To a form of that lithe grace
and peculiar roundness which only a life of unrestrained
freedom under a Southern sun in youth can bestow,
Toinette added a face of singular loveliness. Eyes of
dark liquid brown, heavy brows, and a wealth of flow-

ing locks, so dark as just to avoid the name of jetty,
which seemed almost to burden with their weight the
shapely head and slender neck. Her cheek had that
changeful softness which marks the perfection of the
brunette, and her manner was that rare blending of
boldness and timidity which provokes question and approach, yet baffles inquiry and courts retirement. One
of those female characters which no man can help trying to read, yet which so few are able to solve; one of
those combinations of attributes which give to some
rare instances of womanhood the power to "raise mortals to the skies," or "drag angels down."

Geoffrey Hunter looked upon this vision of loveliness and forgot that she was his chattel-real. Her
presence brought light, and her voice was music to
him. He listened for her footstep and was moody
and ill-tempered if she were absent. He did not stop
to inquire why, but her presence soothed him. He
loved to see her, to hear her sing, to have her do any
of the thousand trivial services which brought her
near him. It flattered his self-esteem, and gave him a
pleasure which he took care not to mar by too close
an analysis, when, at length, he discovered that he was
the sun of this beautiful slave-girl's life; that her
heart beat for no joy but the rapture of his approval,
and that earth held no pleasure for her fluttering
bosom to be compared with the bliss of pouring the
precious ointment of her love upon his head, though
all unheeded and unblest in return.

Of course Geoffrey Hunter knew his position in
society too well to commit the enormity of falling in

love with a slave—even if she had been pampered and petted and was destined to be free at no very distant day. But he did not repel the love which perfumed the passing moments, and so the jest of gossiping tongues was entered in the books of heavenly record as a fact; and Geoffrey Hunter was debited with the safety of that fair soul, which had lavished the treasures of its love upon him, and of other souls which might yet bear the impress of both minds. Now were they doubly master and slave—once by the bill-of-sale, among his valuable papers and effects, and once by acquisition in the market-overt, where Love is auctioneer.

It was a light thing to the young slave-owner, and Toinette did not dream of evil in her devotion. She was too happy in the privilege of loving even once to dream of sin.

CHAPTER XV.

"THINGS HID FROM THE WISE."

BETTY CERTAIN seemed to be almost stupefied with amazement at the discovery of the fact revealed in the preceding chapter. For a time she seemed quite undecided as to the course she should adopt in view of it, and for some days she wandered about the Lodge with a grotesque uncertainty of movement, taking odd and uncouth positions, sitting crosswise upon her chair, and spitting, here and there, regardless of consequences.

She was not an attractive woman at any time, and now the vague look of doubt that hung about her every limb and feature magnified her eccentricities, until they bordered on the ludicrous. After long reflection she decided upon her course. How she had come to stay at the Lodge for the past two years, since Toinette had recovered from her wounds, no one, not even herself, could tell. Geoffrey had asked her to continue there, a month or two after, when she proposed returning to her home, and from some motive quite unknown to others, at least, she had signified her assent, and the matter had never been mentioned afterward. Whatever it was, this poor white woman had evidently allowed it to enter largely into her own plans for the future, which seemed to have been utterly overturned by the newly

discovered intimacy between master and servant. Her
conclusion once reached, however, there was no more
uncertainty. She stood erect and faced the issue un-
flinchingly and promptly. Her log-house on the old
Certain tract was at once repaired under her own super-
intendence; the old shaded spring dug out, and the
entire premises made snug, cleanly and habitable. This
done, she once more sought an interview with Geoffrey
Hunter in the library. Since he had known her, Betty
Certain had manifested some characteristics, which, in
connection with what he had learned of her past life,
had impressed him with a profound respect for her
shrewdness, capacity, and trustworthiness. It was,
therefore, not without regret that he heard of her
determination to quit his roof, and he questioned
her closely as to her motive.

"I will own to you, Mr. Hunter, that I had not
thought of leaving until within a few days, and it upset
me mightily for a while to think of doing it then," she
said in reply.

"But why," he urged, "think of it at all? You
have become almost as inseparable from Lovett Lodge
as the ivy on the chimney or the ghost which is said
to cling to its bounds."

"Yes, Mr. Geoffrey," she replied, "I came here at
your bidding, not intending to stay at all, but jes'
to let you know that a pore white woman could n't
always be bought. But when I seed that poor, tender
critter just at the point of death, an' seed that your
consarn for her was more like a father than that ov
a master, I concluded to stay, for a while, at least.

Then atterwards I staid on, for a reason which I
need n't speak of now. Till by-and-by I begun to
love the gal Toinie as I should my own darter, if I 'd
had one, I suppose. An' then you told me how she
an' old Mabel, her mother, was to be sot free ez soon
ez ever Manwell Hunter died, an' I 'lowed that I 'd
jest stay here with her till that time, and then pick
up an' go North with you all, when you tuk' em away,
an' see if I liked it any better than this country. I
wanted to be nigh Toinette, anyhow."

"And why not do it yet?" asked Geoffrey.

"Things hez changed since then, Geoffrey Hunter,"
said the woman quickly; "Toinette will never be sot
free, now."

"Toinette not liberated? Why?"

"Do n't ask me. You knows better than I can tell
you," said she, coolly.

Geoffrey Hunter was discomfited. This poor white
woman annoyed him. Yet he could not tell why. He
got up hastily and walked once or twice across the
room nervously. Betty Certain sat still and looking
at the fire nonchalantly. Her demeanor angered him.
What right had she to call him to account for his
conduct? Was it any of her business what his relations
were with his own servant? He would let her know
her place.

"So you came to read me a lecture, did you, Miss
Betty? If you expect to become my guardian it is
certainly time you sought quarters elsewhere."

It was a harsh speech for a man of culture and
refinement to make to a woman, but this woman was

no longer young, and was only a " poor white " at
best.

"It 's not the fust time 's trouble brought me here 'n
crime druv me away," said the woman quietly.

"You do n't mean to accuse *me* of crime, Betty
Certain ?" said he, hotly.

"Oh, I did n't come here to argy with a lawyer as
tu what 's crime an' what aint. Mebbe you do n't
think it 's enny crime tu stain the white soul ov that
young cretur in yon, an' send her into hell, coz she
thinks you an angel, strayed away from home, an' be-
lieves that wickedness can 't live in yer heart. An'
maybe I was wrong in callin' it by that name; but
it 's what 's bro't the bad name to Lovett Lodge, an',
in my 'pinion, has caused all the crime an' blood that 's
been done an' shed here. I kin remember, Geoffrey
Hunter, when ye were n't out of frocks an' Arthur
Lovett lived here, with the prettiest yaller gal I 've
ever seen 'cept Toinette—an' somehow she 'minds
me of her often. Ther' never wuz a better man
lived 'twixt soil and sunshine than that same Arthur
Lovett, and I 've no more idee thet he tho't ther' was
any more harm in takin' that gal fur his mistress, at
fust, than you would in marryin' one ov the neighbor's
gals. But it led from this to that, quarrelin', an' fight-
in', an' lyin' to the poor crittur, till it all ended in
blood and death—Arthur Lovett's blood an' death, too.
I 've always hearn that two as travels the same road is
likely to come to the same eend. An' you 're follerin'
in Arthur Lovett's tracks, shore! But that 's your affair
and not mine."

The allusion to Arthur Lovett and reference to his death awakened Geoffrey's curiosity, and he remembered the connection of Betty Certain with that event, and the mysterious relation which seemed to have existed between that murder and the one attempted after he came into possession of the Lodge. He determined at this time to gather such further information as he could from her, to see if, by chance, it might not shed some new light upon the crime with which he was himself more intimately concerned. He would speak her fair, therefore, and pay no attention to her reflections upon his life. So he said:

"Well, Mrs. Certain, we will not quarrel, now that we are about to part company. What do I owe you?"

The woman seemed somewhat surprised at his tone, and, after a moment, replied:

"If I 've been wuth anything to Geoffrey Hunter he knows the vally ov what I 've done, better than I do. I 'll not make any barter about the matter. I did not come here for money, ez I said afore, an' I 've been treated well in this house, that I hev, an' I shall hev no complaint to make with what ye 're a mind to pay me, for kind o' holding things straight an' snug-like. Then, tu, ther 's a feelin' about this house ther' ain't no whar else, an' it 's wuth suthin', to me, to live in it."

Geoffrey was surprised at the evident earnestness and feeling of this declaration. This low-down woman always surprised him. Collected, cool, self-poised at all times, she seemed to have none of the insecutiveness which ought, in the estimation of the favored portion of mankind, who constitute the best society, to mark one of her station in life. She seemed even to have not a little of that delicacy and refinement of feeling which Geoffrey had supposed to have been monopolized in the creation of the self-indulgent Brahmins of his own caste. So, having paid her liberally for her services, spoken of her future plans and preferences, as she seemed about to retire without herself introducing the topic of peculiar interest to him, he finally said:

"I have always thought, Mrs. Certain, that the relation you sustained to Arthur Lovett, and the scrutiny you gave the circumstances attending his death, as well as your observation of Toinette's wound, and knowledge of its surroundings, must enable you to form a better and more tenable theory, as to these strangely connected acts, than any one else. I have never given up the hope of detecting the perpetrator of these crimes, for I am of opinion that the same hand struck the blow in both instances; nor, to tell the truth, to get rid of the apprehension that the same may be attempted again. Would you be willing to make a confidant of me, so far as to tell me whatever you may know of the former?"

Betty Certain sat in deep thought for a time, and then said slowly:

"I dunno, Geoffrey Hunter, I dunno. It's been several year ago, an' I had 'lowed never to say anything to a livin' mortal about it. Your father tried his best tu make me tell suthin', and I du believe Manuel Hunter was Arthur Lovett's friend, tho' he had n't many this side of Heaven. I dunno. It's a long story, an' not over pleasant, leastways to me, an' it aint wuth nothing without yer hear the whole; for I

do n't know nothing positive, only guesses and sur-
mises from some circumstances that nobody else knows
about, put along with them y've been told of. I can't
give yer an answer now, but if I determine to do it,
I 'll come over in the morning, a bit after sun-up, an
tell yer all I know. Ef I do n't come, then ye may
know that Betty Certain 's concluded not to tell anything about this matter, but just let time and eternity
settle it as they may; an' ef she makes up her mind
that way, you may be sure of one thing, she 's going
tu keep a close tongue while she 's got her senses, an'
she won't lose them, till she 's nigh about ready for the
t'other world herself."

MR. GEOFFREY AND BETTY CERTAIN.

"'I've come, ye see,' she said sharply as she sat down, drawing her chair
close to the fire."—p. 169.

CHAPTER XVI.

OUT OF HER SPHERE.

AT the time she had intimated that she would
come, if she came at all, Betty Certain entered
the library again. She looked pale and worn. She had
evidently been thinking of the past, and a night of
sleepless misery had given her a dull and haggard look,
which showed how deeply the memories she had come
to relate were wrought into her life.

"I've come, ye see," she said sharply as she sat
down, drawing her chair close to the fire, for the morning was a chill autumn one, and gazed absently at the
flames. She paid no attention to Geoffrey's respectful
greeting—in fact, did not seem to hear it. After a time
she looked up and caught his eye curiously scanning her
dress, for she had laid off the more elegant style which
she had adopted during her residence at the Lodge
and gone back to the coarse linsey and heavy shoes of
the poor white, which she had worn two years ago.

"Yes, Mr. Geoffrey," she said, somewhat bitterly,
"I've gone back to linsey-woolsey, an' I reckon for the
last time. Pity I ever laid it off. All the trouble of
my life has come to me in good clothes. Ef I'd allus
staid whar natur' put me, an' never tried to be anything
better than 'a poor Poll' all my days, I should n't
hev been here to tell ye what I know of Arthur Lov-

ett's life and death, whatever other crimes I might hev hed knowledge on. I 've sometimes thought thet Providence designed my troubles ez a punishment for trying to git above · the sphere He 'd placed me in."

"But your family is not so low, Miss Betty. I find upon inquiry that it is one of the oldest in the State. An ancestor of yours came over as agent for the Earl, and was afterward a man of large estate, for the country and times, if I am not mistaken."

"Oh, ther 's no mistake about that, but the family hez kind of run out sence that time. Ye see Gran'ther Ezra—that 's the one yer mean—did n't come as the Earl's agent at fust, but was brought to Virginny when a boy and sold for his passage-money. Ye see, he was stole from his people in Glasgow, by the captain as brought him over, who pretended that he had agreed to pay for his passage. Of course he could n't pay, bein' but a lad, an' stole from home at that. So he was sold for the money an' had to work for the man that bought him like a slave, till he was one-and-twenty or more. That 's the way we come to hev the name of Certain. You see he was articled to the planter as bought him, he bein' a mere boy of eight or ten years old, as a 'certain boy,' the name bein' left out entirely —whether by mistake or not, nobody ever knew. When his master found it out, he just called him 'Certain' for a nickname. After he got his freedom, he just put his given name Ezra to this nickname and went as Ezra Certain always atterward. He found out soon after that he wuz of good family in Scotland, but he

never would give up the name he hed made for himself, but left it to his children, and, as you sed, he
growed rich while he was agent for the Earl, an' hed
his pick of the land hereabouts.

"But he never would own a nigger. He sed he'd
been a slave once hisself, an' it wor not right nor Christian tu grow rich off another man's labor an' not pay
him for it. An' he could not see ez the color of the
man's hide made any difference with the right or wrong
of the matter. So he wouldn't hev a slave, an' taught
his boys arter him to hev the same notions, an' we all
kep' livin' on here, generation after generation, kind uv
between the hammer an' the anvil, growin' poorer an'
poorer while our neighbors growed richer and richer,
till we weren't of no more account beside them than
a black-jack beside uv a white-oak. That's how we
come to be poor; but ef we hain't growed rich by
slavery, we've ginerally missed the sins that come from
it—leastways, a part of them. An' I don't know but
Gran'ther Ezra wuz right in the long run. Time an'
eternity together, may be it's better to be poor then
hev more souls then one to account for in the end.
But that's neither here nor thar. I wuz alluz poor.
The first I remember we lived, mother an' I—for my
father died afore my memory—on what was left of the
old Certain Tract—a little, pore plantation about the old
spring, which Gran'ther Ezra picked out as the prettiest place he'd seen to live on. It *is* pretty, as you
know, an' a pretty price you've offered for it more nor
once, but it won't be sold while Betty Certain hez any
need for a home

"While I was a right young gal Arthur Lovett came from somewhere down in the low-country and settled here. There was no one with him then—of his family I mean—except the gal Bella ye 've heard so much about. He put up the log kitchen fust, an' lived in that while this house was building. He was mighty perticklar, an' hed it all done under his own eye.

"I do n't know how I fust became acquainted with them. Just accidentally, I s'pose. They were our nighest neigbors, you know, an' I was a young gal and sort o' lonely staying at home with only ma. So I used to come over here an' chat with the gal at first. By-and-by he got to noticing me, an' seemed to be pleased at the interest I took in the house he was buildin'. His books came afore this part was done, an' he had some light shelves made an' put them up in the parlor. I 'd never seen but a few books afore, but I wuz desperate fond of reading. So one day I made bold to try and borrow one. 'What,' said he, 'can you read, Miss Betty?' And then he asked what I had read, and laughed till he like to have died when I told him the few simple books which had fallen in my way. I was angry, and told him I did not want his books at all if that was the way he treated poor folks. I was going off in a huff, but he called me back, looking very sober, and begged my pardon for what he termed 'an act of inexcusable meanness.' Then he requested me to make free use of any books I might find in his library. I was too hungry for the wonders of the world of printed thought at that time to hold my pique, and there 's few books on the shelves yonder that I 've not looked inside their lids and took in what I might of their messages of good or evil."

Geoffrey uttered an exclamation of surprise.

"No wonder you're surprised, Geoffrey Hunter. You think a 'poor white' has little right to know more than a nigger."

"I wish you would not call yourself a 'poor white,' Miss Betty," said he.

"But I am, and can't forget it if I would. There has been twice that it almost slipped from my mind, but it never will again. Time brings it out clearer after each lapse.

"Do you mind your horse—Polydore, that you bought of Mr. Duke? He was branded when he was young on the left shoulder. It don't show when he comes sleek and glossy to your library door for you to mount in the morning. He is just wrapped in gleaming silver then, and the badge of ownership and service is hidden. But when he has been ridden a day, and dust and heat have soiled his coat, and he comes home sweaty and drooping, then the brand stands out plain 'D.' He is your pet horse now, worthy of the finest stall and keeping, but he was once Mr. Duke's scraggy foal, and slept in an old field without his supper. The brand tells that tale on him when he sweats. So when trouble comes on me the mark comes out strong, and I show the 'poor white' brand. It's on my tongue and in my heart, Mr. Geoffrey, an' will be while I live on earth, and after I go to Heaven too, if people who own niggers and put on airs come there."

Unconsciously she had forgotten, as she often did, the vernacular of the "poor white," and her diction showed something of the culture which her words implied. She checked her excitement after a moment, and pursued her narrative quietly.

"Well, in that way I became a pretty constant visitor at the Lodge. Arthur Lovett was the mildest, tenderest-hearted man that ever lived, of slender make, with a dark, irregular face, great brown eyes, waving hair, which one could hardly say whether 't was black or brown. He was retiring and modest, almost timid, and seemed to be half afraid of the rest of the world. He seldom went away from home, but stayed here with his books and Belle and their little ones, just as contented as if she had been white and they were lawfully married. The neighbor people made a heap ov talk for a time, but it all mostly died out after a few months till he had been here some two or three years. Then it sort of leaked out that the woman 'Belle' that he wor' living with was not a slave, but just a free-nigger. Then it was that the people said this was not to be borne. It was bad enough for a man to live with his own slave, and be the father of children that were to be sold on the block. But this might be tolerated. The necessities of the institution and the country demanded a certain laxity in regard to some things; but the idea that the moral and high-minded people of Cold Spring county would endure the spectacle of a white man defying the laws of God and man by living openly with a free-nigger, whose offspring would also be free, and the mother not subject to execution for the debts of the father, was altogether preposterous! Public policy, decency, and religion, cried out against it as an outrage. The church met and fulminated against him. The people met and passed resolutions. He was formally notified that he must send the woman away, or the just anger of an outraged community would fall upon him. They were mistaken for once. They could n't skeer Arthur Lovett by no such means. They miscalculated when they thought that shy, bashful man was a coward. He sent them back a letter that stung like an adder, I should say, daring them to put their cowardly threats into execution.

"Not long atterwards, as I were going on home one night, just arter dark, I heard voices afore me in the wood path, and stopped behind a tree; for I did n't care to meet strangers thar in the dark.

"As they passed whar I stood I made out from ther chat that they were going to whip that free-nigger that Arthur Lovett wuz keeping. I knew, from their voices, that several in the crowd wuz the most rascally desperate characters in the country round, and I knew that before they could do this they would hev to kill Arthur Lovett. The idea made me deadly faint. I did n't stop to think, but just turned an' run down by the branch, an' along the farm-lane, to the Lodge, and told Arthur Lovett before they got here. He was sitting in this very room, and when I told him only smiled, an' sed, 'The cowards! I expected it, and they will find me ready. Thank you, Miss Betty,' he added, pleasantly, 'you 'd better go home the other way; they might be rude to you.'

"So I run out by the back way into the orchard, an
stopped by the oat-stacks to see the end on 't. I do n't
believe I knew it till that minute, but I found it out
then—when Bill Price rode up and hailed the house,
and Arthur Lovett came out on the porch an' answered
as calm an quiet as ef he 'd bin settin' in the chair here,
a' talkin' to me—I knew then that I loved Arthur Lovett; that a hair of his head was dearer to me than all
other lives on earth. He stood there on the porch in
his slippers and wine-colored dressing-gown, an' Bill
Price called to him to come down to the gate.

"'By no means, gentlemen,' said he, ''Light and
walk in.'

"So they dismounted—those who had horses—and
all came in. I watched them as they came through the
gate toward the porch. There was seventeen of them—
strong, reckless men. I thought ther would be trouble,
an' ef ther was I could not leave Arthur Lovett. I
would hev been right glad to die to serve him then.
So, I started round to the wood-yard for the axe, to be
ready when the time came. Just then the first one was
about settin' his foot on the porch, when he said:

"'Gentlemen, I know your errand, and you will
please listen to me, before you come further.' I had
crept over the fence an' got the axe, an' crawled up by
the house corner yonder by that time.

"'I know your errand,' he repeated, 'and desire to
aid you in its performance. You have come to inspect
and regulate my domestic arrangements, to make them
conform to the highly moral and respectable standard
which you so fully and ably represent. Your charac-

ters, gentlemen, are a sufficient guarantee that your efforts are entirely in the behalf of a most laudable and exalted public virtue.' He spoke as quiet and calm, an' with a cold, hard sneer, which I had never heard in his voice before. It froze me where I stood, and I crept close to the house, still holding the axe, and wondering what would come next.

"'Mr. Bill Price,' said he, 'you seem to be leader and spokesman for this crowd of high-toned gentlemen. Will you please to station a certain number, so as to prevent egress from the house, and allow me to conduct you, and such as you may select, through the same?'

"So three or four men went on each side to guard the house, and the others went inside with Lovett.

"I could hear him as they went from room to room, taunting and twitting them in a manner most wonderful to me, who knew him to be so mild and gentle.

"He made them get down on their knees and look under the beds, peep into the wardrobes, move out the sofas, and go from top to bottom over the house.

"Then he came back with them all upon the porch an' kep' on talkin':

"'Gentlemen,' said he, 'accept my thanks! It is not everyone who can have his household affairs regulated by a committee of high-toned gentlemen. Won't you look under the carpets, gentlemen? Did you find everything right, gentlemen? Did you look in all my drawers and chests? Of course no one would suspect you if anything should be lost. Very happy to have met you, gentlemen. Will you examine the kitchen now?'

"'Yes, by God!' says Bill Price, 'we will. You can't bluff us off in that way. We know the gal's here an' we're bound to hev her. Come on, men!'

"An' they started with half-a-dozen candles right round by the corner where I was, for the kitchen—Arthur Lovett with them.

"I knew they'd see me if I staid, an' then I knew what ud be said about it; so I broke and run, still holdin' on to the axe. The fellow who was set to guard that corner called out at once:

"'Here she is, here she is,' as he saw me start. Then I was close on him and hit him with the axe— the eye, not the edge, or it would have killed him on the spot—but he kinder started back and his cheekbone got the heft uv the blow.

"I jumped the fence, an' they all tuck after me like hounds follerin' of a fox. When I came to cross the branch in the meadow I slipped an' fell, an' afore I could get up they hed me an' was pullin' me back towards the house afore I could offer any resistance.

"When we got nigh the house Bill Price called out:

"'We've caught your bird, after all, Mr. Lovett. Here, fellows, bring a light and let's have a squint of her face. She's a lively wench, anyhow, and fights like the devil. We'll see if a hundred or so, well laid on, wont tame her a bit.'

"'She's nigh killed Mike Garner with the axe,' said another, 'and ought to be hung for it.'

"'Whom have you there?' said Arthur, coming up just as lights were brought by some others. He was very pale and spoke anxiously—I thought it was for

me, and fear and shame were forgotten in an instant.
My heart beat wildly with unexpected joy, and my face,
as I looked up, must have reflected the pleasure I felt.

"He shaded his eyes with his left hand and peered
at me as the lights came up.

"'My God!' said he, 'is it you, Miss Betty?' Then
they all stared into my face, and Bill Price said:

"'Derned if it aint Bet Certain, boys. Why, gal,
ye 're gettin' into business young, aint ye?'

"At that they all laughed, and one of them said:

"'Blast her! let 's switch her anyhow. She 's nigh
killed poor Mike, and ought n't to be playin' agin a
free-nigger nohow.'

"Then Bill Price spoke up an' sez, 'No, gentlemen;
no. Ef a gentlemen chooses to amuse himself *as* a gentlemen, we 've no right to interfere. We 've come to
break up Mr. Lovett's disgraceful connection with a
free-nigger, but if he 's cast her off and took up with
Betty Certain we 've nothing to say, except to congrat-
ulate him on the improvement of his taste, beg his
pardon for our untimely visit and wish him good evening;' and with that he let me go.

"I had not thought of this view of my situation
till he spoke. Then I put my hands over my face
an' sunk down with a groan. Arthur Lovett came
close beside me and said:

"'Gentlemen, I pledge you my word that I was un-
aware of the presence of this young lady on my plantation. As you know, she is the daughter of my
nearest neighbor—of a family poor but respectable;
and I believe her to be as pure as any lady in the

land. I cannot explain her presence here to-night, but am confident it was with a good motive. You are aware she has no father or brother, and you must now apologize for your aspersions of her character, or answer to me personally for the same.'

" ' Mr. Lovett knows where to find us,' said Bill Price, ' an' any of us will be happy to accommodate him. Good night.'

" ' You will hear from me in the morning, sir,' said Arthur.

" Then they mounted their horses and rode away.

" Arthur Lovett raised me gently from the ground and led me into the house."

CHAPTER XVII.

LOVE'S LOGIC.

"I WUS sorter staggered at the turn things had taken, and when we got into the sitting-room only had a sort of confused notion of all that had been going on. Arthur gave me a glass of wine, and waited till I had recovered myself before he spoke.

"'You're better now, Miss Betty,' said he; 'you have been badly frightened.'

"I could not say 'yes' and would not say 'no.

"It was not the fright that upset me, but the idea that every one would soon be speaking of me as Arthur Lovett's mistress. I suppose something like this showed in my face, for he came up an' put his hand on my head tenderly ez if I had been a child, and says:

"'Miss Betty, how did you come to be here? You had plenty of time to have escaped before these scoundrels arrived.'

"I thought there was a little touch of reproach in his voice, an' it hurt me. I loved him too well an' hed suffered too much for him that night to endure reproof. The tears came into my eyes and choked my words as I replied:

"'Oh, Mr. Lovett, I was afeard they might do you some harm, an'—an'—an'—'

"'And so you came back with that axe to aid in my defense, did you?'

"I hung my head an' my face burned, but in my heart I was glad that he would know of my love. He might not return it. I had no idea that he would; but it was an honest, brave love, and I felt that he could not despise it.

"'Did you think,' he continued, 'that it would endanger your reputation and might imperil your life?'

"I looked him full in the face and answered, 'I didn't care, sir. I was bound you shouldn't be hurt.'

"He started, took his hand quickly from my head, and turned away with a disturbed, anxious look upon his face and walked the floor for some time in deep thought. I watched him silently. How noble he seemed as he walked back and forth in utter forgetfulness of my presence. His lips were close shut, his features flushed, and his form seemed instinct with busy thoughts. I knew he was thinking of me, though he had forgotten my presence. I was glad that he knew of my love. He, at least, would respect me, and I had told him the simple truth. As to others, his regard hid all the obloquy which they might cast upon me. He was *my world*.

"I had no idea that he would ever return my love. The thought of any tenderer relation with him than I had before enjoyed had never once entered my mind. To feel that he was my friend, that I might look upon him and know that he would condescend to remember me with kindness, that he would sometimes think pleasantly and tenderly of the risks I had undertaken for him that night, was more than enough for my new-found love. I could not help blushing, but I was not ashamed. I had all that I desired, and so I sat and waited for his moody fit to pass, that I might hear what he would say.

"At length he threw himself upon the sofa and buried his face in the pillows. I wished I might go and smooth his hair, but I dared not. After a time he got up and came toward me. His face was pale and his eyes bloodshot. For the first time he seemed to have become aware of my presence.

"'Miss Betty,' said he, 'I beg your pardon. I had quite forgotten that you were here. I am in trouble. I cannot thank you now for your kindness to-night. I shall not forget it. Let us say no more about it now. Permit me to accompany you to your home.'

"He gave me his arm, and we went out into the moonlight and along the wood-path to our house. He spoke of everything but the occurrences of that night. I do n't know what was said, whether we made haste or loitered. I only know that he left me at our door, lifting his hat with profound courtesy as he said:

"'Good-night, Miss Betty. With your leave, I shall call in a short time to express my gratitude for the heroism you have displayed to-night.'

"Then he was gone. I saw his form disappear along the path we had just come, and then I sat down upon the old door-stone and wondered why the world seemed so different to me from the one the sun had set upon.

"The moonlight was certainly brighter and softer than I had ever known before. I was, of course, the same Betty Certain, but somehow I did not feel the same. All was so bright and yet so strange. I sat and thought a long time, but yet the mystery remained. I went in at last and sought to sleep, with a strange medley of pleasant and unpleasant things in my mind.

"I saw nothing more of Arthur Lovett for several days. Meantime there had come a report that he and Bill Price had fought a duel at the Neck; that Price had been seriously and Lovett slightly wounded. No one seemed to know anything of the cause of the duel so far as I could learn. *I* knew that Arthur Lovett had risked his life against a practiced duelist to redeem my reputation.

"If I had loved him before, I worshiped him then. I would have done his bidding gladly if it had periled my soul. I longed to go to him, to kiss the wound he had received for my sake; but I knew that if he wanted me he would send for me.

"Besides that, had he not shed his blood to save my character? And should I peril anything so precious lightly? I did not go to the Lodge, but waited day after day for Arthur Lovett to come to me.

"I was sure he would come—he had promised that he would—to thank me. He was my debtor *then ;* now I was his, I thought. He would come, and I would thank him. Then he would go away, the rich, gifted, cultured Arthur Lovett, along the path which was marked out for him, and I—I would go my way. Once more I was to be allowed to bow at the shrine of my idolatry. Then our ways would separate forever. The thought annoyed me; I murmured at my poverty and lowliness; yet I did not dream that it could be otherwise.

"One day my mother was gone to a neighbor's, and I sat dreaming in the soft sunlight of a mild October afternoon, when there came a 'rap at the door and a shadow fell across the lintel.

"I knew who was there, and my heart beat so wildly that I could scarcely rise and bid him come in and be seated. Never did our neat old cabin seem so poor and uncouth before. I was ashamed of the rude door, hung on its wooden hinges; of the little room, and the snowy bed with its high posts; of the floor, full of great cracks; of the smoked and spotted ceiling, brown with age; of the gourd, beside the bucket at the door; of the low, cross-legged table, which we kept clean and white enough for the Saviour and his Apostles to have eaten the Last Supper from; I was even ashamed of the cosy splint-bottomed chair, in which I asked him to be seated.

"It may seem strange that I had never observed how meanly we lived at my mother's before; but, you know, one does not see the shadows till the sun shines.

"Arthur Lovett was pale and careworn. His left arm was in a sling. I think he noticed my chagrin. I know my cheeks burned. He seemed to look at me more keenly than he had ever done before. I was not altogether a fright in those days, Mr. Geoffrey, if my looking-glass told the truth.

"At length, after the ordinary chat of the day, he said he wanted to talk with me, and asked if I would walk with him. I think he saw my embarrassment,
18

arising from our mean surroundings, divined its cause, and desired to remove it.

" Down the branch, below the spring a hundred yards, was a cluster of old field-pines, with one or two of original growth, a patriarchal oak, a few cedars, and a fringe of second-growth poplars and gums. This had been my playground in childhood, and my place of refuge from the world ever since. Many an hour I had hidden away beneath its shadows and peopled its stillness with the creations of Shakespeare, and Scott, and other authors whom Arthur Lovett's kindness had put into my hands.

" I had arranged in it different resorts for various times of day and changing moods. I knew now where the evening sun was creeping in and lighting up a fairy room, whose door-way was a cedar bough, and whose walls were of impenetrable evergreen, flecked with the yellow leaves of a young poplar—which had thrust its head aspiringly between a pine and cedar but to have its ambition cruelly checked—and half-canopied by a dog-wood, which was just in the glory of its gold and crimson autumn robe. The ground was carpeted with leaves and strewn with cones.

" A great rock, with a cedar at one end and an ancient pine at the other, with a wide shelf near its base, and rising at the back ten or twelve feet above, with a crest covered with the mingled hues of a purple-leaved creeper, which clambered over it, and a dark green ivy, a spray of which I had torn from the library chimney here and planted beside my rock, constituted the sofa, the place of honor, in my dream-palace.

"Upon this seat, through the dogwood branches fell the autumn sunlight at that hour.

"You smile, Mr. Geoffrey, and no wonder. What right had Betty Certain to such a bower? But she had it, and though I haven't seen it for years, I guarantee that you would say I hadn't half done it justice—even now.

"So when Arthur Lovett asked me to walk with him, it struck me all at once that I would take him there and I said, very quickly:

"'Yes, Mr. Lovett, our castle is a rude one; but I've got a bower that is worthy of a queen. Shall we go there?'

"He smiled, a little amused or surprised, and said:

"'If you please, I should like to see your ideal of a royal residence. I have seen many a queen's bower in my travels abroad, and always felt a sort of nameless pity for the poor birds within those gilded cages.'

"Then we went down by the spring and I showed him the path around the old oak and under the alder bushes, down the little branch, till we came opposite the bower, then up among the boulders and under the pines, treading the cones in the shadows, and breathing the rich balsam odors, till we came out into the sunshine, before the very door.

"Then I stopped and asked him in what direction the house was from us, and laughed till the tears came when he pointed the wrong way.

"It wasn't so particularly funny, and I never knew why I laughed or cried then, only I didn't want to cry, and I couldn't help laughing.

"Then I lifted up the cedar bough that formed my door-way, and bade him stoop low and enter.

"He did so, and I followed him.   He looked sharply round and then, turning to me, said:

"'You spoke truly.   It is worthy of a queen.   Let me lead the sovereign to her throne.'   He turned and held out his hand.

"I sat down upon a rock, beside the door, put my hands to my face, and wept.

"He seemed distressed, and asked the cause of my grief.

"I told him I had brought him there to show him my only treasure, of which no one else knew, and then he mocked me.

"'You mistake, Miss Betty,' said he, quickly.   'Your bower is certainly a gem, and I but intended to compliment you, through it.'

"Then he took my hand and led me to the seat by the rock.   As soon as we had sat down he grew silent and moody again.   I picked up the painted leaves which lay about, and made bouquets and crowns, and watched him in silence.   Suddenly he looked at me, with a peculiar significance, and said:

" Miss Betty, were you not afraid to bring me hither?'

"I comprehended him at once, and said, slowly and clearly:

"'No.'

"'This is the second time you have placed your honor in my keeping,' said he.

"'He that guards the shadow so well will never tar-

ARISTOCRAT AND POOR POLL.

"At length he stopped before me, and flashed out: 'Betty Certain, will you be my wife?' . . . I was too astonished to speak."—p. 189.

nish the substance,' I replied, glancing at his wounded arm.

"He flushed, and was silent. Then he got up and walked back and forth, as he had done that other night in the parlor. At length he stopped before me, and flashed out:

"'Betty Certain, will you be my wife?'

"My heart stood still. I must have shaken my head, for I was too astonished to speak.

"'Hush, hush!' he said, 'don't say no; don't say anything until you have heard me.'

"So I sat still. I could not have spoken if I had tried. He walked about a moment to master or conceal his agitation, and then came back and sat down near me. After a moment, he spoke."

CHAPTER XVIII.

EXCEPTIO PROBAT REGULAM.

" ' I DO not ask you to be my wife, Miss Betty,'
said he, 'for any of the reasons ordinarily leading a man to make such a request of a woman. I
have long since passed that age when passion alone
controls our action in such matters. Even if I were
younger, my experience of life has been such that I
would long since have disowned such motive. Neither
is the course which I have adopted a hasty or unpremeditated one. On the contrary, it is one which has
only been determined upon after the most mature and
earnest consideration. .But before you can fully appreciate my situation, I must detail to you the circumstances which have led to it.

" ' As you are aware, I am the only son of one of
the wealthiest planters in the eastern portion of the
State. From my boyhood nothing has been denied
me that I desired. I was the autocrat of Heptwilde
(my father's plantation) from my birth. Pampered and
petted in everything, I passed my boyhood in the
usual freedom of plantation life. I have promised that
you shall have a full recital of my life, and I shall
extenuate nothing. I passed my collegiate course with
steadiness and credit, and did not become involved in
anything serious or discreditable until the summer of
my twenty-third year.

"'At that time, my two sisters returned home from boarding-school, bringing with them a young girl whom my father had purchased at the special request of the elder, some three years before, and who had since then been her maid. She had been much petted by my sister and her companions on account of her exceeding beauty and intelligence, and had been permitted (perhaps it was necessary to stimulate my sister's indolence) to pursue the same studies as her young mistress, which she had done to far better purpose. Her mind seemed to have an instinctive aptitude for acquiring knowledge. The sciences of which my sisters had but a cursory knowledge, she had in a measure mastered, and the languages their tongues refused to pronounce were as music upon hers.

"'From the moment I saw Belle, I loved her, not with the degrading passion of a favorite, but with a deep, holy tenderness, that would lead me to give my life for her happiness without hesitation. From that moment, I have never ceased to love her. Every possible means was taken by my family to break off the attachment, but it has only grown stronger with every obstacle which has been placed in its way. For a time I tried to break away from the spell of her beauty, and the charm of her love, for I knew that our attachment, contrary, as it was, to the laws, both of Church and State, could only bring sorrow and trouble ; but I was too weak to adhere to my good resolutions.

"'Months grew into years, and I was still the devoted slave of my father's servant. Meantime my father had given me a plantation near his own, and

we lived there for some time in comparative quiet.
Then we were indicted, and the whole country was
in a ferment over our relation. I wonder now that
I should have been so mad. Yet I could not help it.

"'My father agreed to compromise the prosecution
if I would give up the girl. This I agreed to do on
condition that he would emancipate her and her child.
He agreed to do so, and I went to Europe and traveled
for two years.

"'On my return I found that Belle had been taken
to New York and emancipated according to the laws
of that State. She had afterward returned and lived
in the town of N————, though this fact was unknown
to my father. He was so delighted at what he considered a final rupture of my disgraceful connection,
that he at once gave me a deed of gift of quite a number of slaves, and added a codicil to his will devising
certain property to Bella for her own use and occupancy. It seems he had some years before provided for
her emancipation by will.

"'I was too weak to avoid the connection which
Bella was nothing loath to resume, and so sold my plantation and, taking Bella and her child, came and bought
the plantation here and built the Lodge—as you know.

"'My family at last abandoned me to my infatuation,
but with sorrow and shame. They had used every
means to reclaim me, but in vain. I was an only son,
and used the power which this fact gave me without
scruple to secure compliance in my shameful course.

"'Bella has lived with me ever since. Instead of
one child we have now three. My father has lately

died insolvent, and the deeds of gift which he made to me are void against his previous creditors. This will take away a large portion of my estate. Already they have demanded Belle and her children. I shall resist their claim to the last moment, but fear they will ultimately succeed. If so, my cup of misery will be more than full. I cannot live to see my children slaves or the woman I have so fondly loved under the lash of the overseer.

"'I do not know what may be the result of the case now pending, but my mind is made up to this: Belle must be emancipated, and she and our children freed. They must be sent to some Northern State and comfortably settled. My relations with them must cease entirely, for I have not only them to provide for but my own impoverished sisters. My counsel thinks the creditors will undoubtedly hold all the slaves I received from my father except Belle and her children. This will leave barely enough upon the plantation to support my sisters. Thus impoverished, I can do but little to free Belle and the children, or provide for them, and at all events must draw upon the confidence of friends to obtain money to liberate them should they be held by the executor.'

"Arthur Lovett ceased speaking, and I sat looking at him in silent wonder.

"'You have followed me, Miss Betty?' he said at length.

"I nodded in the affirmative, and he went on.

"'I presume you see in all this no reason why I should ask you to be my wife, or that you should con-

I

sent to do so, but on the contrary, abundant reason why you should not. I told you at first that no common motive actuated me. Several years ago I had the design of going abroad, taking Belle with me and marrying there. I examined the matter while in Europe, and concluded that the legality of such a marriage was at least doubtful. At any rate, I did not do it. Perhaps for no better reason than mere inertness of purpose. But at that time I took a policy of insurance upon my life for a large sum, which is payable in the first instance to my widow, should I die leaving one, and if not, to my heirs-at-law, who in that case would be my two sisters.

"'You see at once that I had intended this for Belle —poor girl—and her children. Should she be sold for the benefit of my father's creditors I may be unable to buy her and she may yet be in dire need of this provision.

"'Now, Betty Certain, you see why I have asked you to be my wife. I have studied you closely, and feel that I can rely upon you. Your word, once pledged, will be sacred. I cannot offer you love or purity of life heretofore, but I can give you the highest respect, and you need have no fear of future infidelity. I shall think no more of poor Belle, except to study how I may remedy the wrongs which have been imposed upon her. It is almost a necessity that I should marry, if I would accomplish this, which I believe to be a holy purpose. If I die unmarried, this money will go to my sisters, who charge Belle with what they are pleased to term my ruin, and they would gladly see her and her children in bondage.

"'You love me, Miss Betty. I respect and revere you. Will you aid me in my distress?'

"I sat silent. My idol was being rapidly transformed to my eyes. Yet why? I had known all the time of his unholy love. Was he less worthy now that he sought to shake it off, than when he gloried in his shame? It could not be. Yet I was silent.

"'There is another view to be taken of this matter which I would urge were it not ungenerous to do so,' he said again.

"'What is that?' I asked.

"'Could I not imagine?' he asked. 'How would the world associate our names after what had been witnessed by so many? He could and would defend my honor, so far as it lay in his power, whatever might be my answer; but as his betrothed wife no tongue would dare to wag against me. That relation would be an unimpeachable guarantee of purity.'

"It struck me oddly then; but it was true, entirely true. His smutched garments would be a shield to my unsoiled virtue. I knew it, and I was grateful to him for what he had already done for me. Besides that, I thought I could help him, and—God, forgive me—perhaps I was tired of being a 'pore white.'

"At any rate, when he said again, solemnly and slowly:

"Knowing all this, Betty Certain, will you be my wife? Will you take the bond of faithfulness to one who has given the freshness of his love to another? And will you be the almoner of my bounty to the

Hagar of my youth, when death shall have palsied my hand and sealed my lips ?'

"Then I looked up at him, and answered, 'I will.'

"He gazed at me searchingly a moment, and said, 'In very truth ?'

"'In very truth,' I replied.

"Then he fell upon his knees beside the rocky seat, and, with streaming eyes and quivering lips, thanked God that He had opened a way for him out of his calamity, and had prepared a means whereby the load of his sin might be lightened. I never heard another such a prayer. And when it was over he rose, and, putting an arm about my waist, drew me to him, kissed my forehead, and said :

"'God bless you, Betty Certain, God bless you! You do not know what you have saved me from; and you have won more love than I thought it possible to give.'

"He looked into my eyes, from which the tears were streaming, and, reading there the joy that filled my heart, he clasped me closer, and said :

"'And you are happy? Thank God! I know now that He will give me a new love, stronger than the old passion, and pure and bright.'

"Then all was light, and my heart danced to the melody of Love's holy hymn until the great shadow fell upon my life. The hope that Arthur Lovett would, or might, one day love me, even with a heart scarred and blasted by an unholy passion, was enough—I asked no more.

"After a moment we went out of my old summer

palace, by the cedar-bough door, through the pine thicket, by the spring, to the house. The pathway has grown up now, and I have rarely been there since. The world seemed different when we came out from what it was when we went in. It had blown up cold and bleak. The sun still shone, but dully and chill.

"When we came to the house my mother was at home. She had never liked Arthur Lovett, and met us coldly. Arthur told her I had consented to become his wife, and asked her acquiescence. She replied 'that she should neither consent nor oppose, but she thought his previous course promised but little happiness to the wife he might marry; that she never did like the idea of rich and pore folks marrying together—but little good came on 't generally.'

"She never opened her lips about the matter again. In all the trouble of the future she never uttered a word of blame, nor asked a syllable of explanation.

"So he bade me good night, and went away, and I, the betrothed wife of Arthur Lovett, stood in the door of my mother's humble cottage and watched him as he went towards his home. I did not think I had yielded to his prayer because he was so much above me in society—though I was mighty tired of being poor Betty Certain—still less had I consented on account of a plea he had put forth for Belle, though indeed I did pity the poor girl with all my heart. But I think it was mainly because his whole story had been a cry for help. I loved him so that I would have gone to the world's end to do him the slightest service   Why, then, should

I not accept the way which opened to me the sanctuary of his heart?

"I shivered as I went in. The future seemed dark and chill as well as the closing autumn day. But yet I was strong and firm, and happy, too—for I meant that Arthur should love me some day, as he said he might."

CHAPTER XIX.

TRANSITION.

"THIS was the beginning and end of our court-ship. Arthur had but two requests to make. The first, that we should be married as soon as possible, the other, that I should spend the time intervening at the Lodge, with his sisters, who would come in a few days. He said the first request was for his own sake. He had an impression that he would not live many months, and he wanted to be sure that his desires would be fulfilled in case he should not. At all events, having determined upon this course he did not wish to omit any chance for its failure. He therefore desired the arrangement consummated at an early day, and he wished me to come and live with his sisters for my own sake, as, if our relation was thus openly acknowledged, there would be less inclination to scandalous reports upon the part of our neighbors. I had no opposition to offer to either proposition.

"His sisters came the next week, and the week after it was decided that the Executors of his father's estate could hold the slaves in dispute. Your father came home from court and wrote to Arthur upon the subject at once. Arthur received his letter on Saturday, we talked it over that evening, and on Sunday your father came here and had a long conversation

with him. His idea was that Arthur had better let the
slaves be sold, and then deal with the buyers, thinking
that if it were known that he was interested in the
bidding the creditors would run them up on him, in
order to get money on their debts. Arthur told him
of our intended marriage, but without explanation as to
its cause. I think from your father's subsequent demeanor towards me, that he thought it the trick of a
'poor white' woman, to get a husband above her.

"Your father was a good man, Mr. Geoffrey, and I
am not sure that I did right in not confiding in him
after Arthur's death. But I could not trust any one
then, all was so confused and strange.

"Well, your father's advice was taken, and Arthur
promised to give up possession of the slaves without
remonstrance. The matter was clearly understood with
Belle, as he told me, that she and the children were
to be sold, and, after a short time had elapsed, he was to
buy them back, take them North and set them free; so,
when they were again demanded by the Executor, they
were surrendered without opposition.

"Arthur's sisters, who were now at the Lodge, were
weak, vain women, rather past the prime, and quite
inclined to attribute their solitary condition to their
brother's irregularities. The insolvency of their father's
estate had not tended to improve their tempers, and
the knowledge that their brother—after breaking off
with Belle—proposed at once to marry a poor girl of
the neighborhood was altogether too much for their
aristocratic instincts; and the welcome they gave me
was far from cordial. I endeavored, at first, to mollify

their resentment, but, finding that mildness was thrown away upon them, I took up my own defense and answered scorn with railing, to so good purpose that in a short time they were forced to ask a truce for the mere sake of quiet. That was all I expected, or, indeed, desired—for, to tell the truth, I had no use for Arthur's sisters. They were selfish and insincere, but I did not think so hardly of them until after his death. I have reason to believe that, although they ceased all direct assault upon me, they, nevertheless, continued to assail me to Arthur, and constantly opposed our marriage. I have always thought they were instrumental in putting it off, from Christmas, when it was to have taken place, until the following Spring, and I have never been quite free from the impression that they also caused his death—though my confidence in this suspicion has been considerably shaken.

"Well, we lived here at the Lodge while the preparations were being made for our wedding—Arthur, his sisters, and myself. Arthur had made your father his agent to conduct the affairs relating to Belle, and we were to proceed upon our trip at once after the marriage. It was intended that we should be absent three months or more, and in contemplation of this absence Arthur had carefully arranged all his business matters and had also made his will. He conversed with me freely upon all his matters of business, and seemed to lean upon me as if he found me very necessary to him. He seemed to think my plain, blunt sense was worthy of consideration, and we came to converse of all our affairs with the cool matter-of-fact manner

4

which rarely comes till after marriage. There was no love on his part, at least he said not, though it is a comfort to me now, to think that his feeling toward me was far warmer than he thought. For me, I was so far below him that my regard' was more like worship than love. I cannot tell you how it was, Mr. Geoffrey, but when I saw that every thought of his life almost was to put that woman Belle and her children beyond the danger of servitude, and when he even asked me to be his wife in order that he might have a still stronger motive to put them away, wishing thereby to pledge his honor to me, as well as his love for them, for their good—somehow, after that, he seemed glorified to my eyes as no other mortal ever was. Then, too, the reason was plain why he had chosen me. Not because he loved me, but in order that he might shield me from ill-repute, thus again sacrificing his own interest, and perhaps happiness, for my honor. To say that I loved him would but faintly express my feelings toward him. I know now that God only should receive the veneration which I gave to him. I do n't suppose another woman would have felt so, but I could n't help it. I had lived a sort of odd and lonely life at best, having to do with few, either men or women, and had filled my world more with those people one meets in books and fancy than those who really live on earth.

"I loved Arthur Lovett, not wildly or passionately, but with the steady adoration which might be given to one immeasurably a superior. So it was almost like a foretaste of heaven when he would say, after our supper at night:

"'Betty, come into the library for a little while, I want to consult you on some matters.'

"I thought then, as I know now, that he did this knowing how much pleasure it would give to me, rather than get my poor notion upon whatever he was intending to do."

"You said that he consulted you about his will," said Geoffrey. "Did you see it in its completed form —or as near completed as he left it?"

"Oh, yes," she replied. "They would never have found it at all if it had n't been for my telling your father where it was. I knew it was not signed, and did not suppose it could be of any value. So I thought for a time that I would just leave it where it was till I had an opportunity to get it out and keep it myself in memory of his trust and confidence in me, and also of the kindly heart he bore towards those whom it seemed he could not help, alive or dead, do what he might. But then I thought it was but right to let his sisters and the world know what he had intended to do, even if he had failed to accomplish it. I was in hopes, too, that they might regard his wishes far enough to have the gal and her children set free, even if his will was not lawful."

"You knew that his will was not signed, you say. How did you know that?" queried Geoffrey.

"Well, you see we were to have been married the next day. That was the 10th of April. His sisters, as I told you, had succeeded in putting off the wedding, on one plea and another, but chiefly, they said, because my clothes were n't fitting; which, indeed, was true

enough, for we poor folks do n't often need anything
better than linsey, and if we did, hav' n't the where-
withal to get it. Besides that, I was n't much given
to dress at any time, and until Arthur took an interest
in me, cared but little what I wore.

"Arthur agreed that his sisters were in the right.
and that I ought to have a good stock of dresses
made up before we married. So we 'd been all this
time buying, and sewing, and getting all things ready.
I should not have taken much interest in it if Arthur
had not seemed to watch every preparation with a boyish delight. His sisters hated me powerful, but they
had a heap o' pride and wanted me to make a proper
show. So they planned and fussed till one would have
thought they were going to be married themselves.

"That last day, in the evening, all the bride's dresses
had been taken into the library for Arthur to look at,
and they were left all about the room at night. After
supper we had our usual chat there, and a very gay
one it was, too, for us. He laughed at my rusticity,
because of all the dresses I preferred a certain gray
one, which was intended only to travel in, and said he
would teach me better taste before we returned from
our tour.

"He told me that he had finished the final draft of
his will and burned all the others; that the next day,
the first thing after we were married, he meant to sign
it, and have your father and the minister witness it.

"'And then, Betty,' said he, 'I shall put it here in
this drawer'—pointing to one in that very desk—'which
no one else knows of, and where it will be perfectly safe

1 will show you how to open the drawer, so that you can find it if I should die on our journey; but you must be sure and have Mr. Hunter, or some other reliable person with you, when you open it.'"

"But there is no secret drawer in that desk," said Geoffrey.

"Did n't your father tell you, Mr. Geoffrey? He must have forgotten it. Let me show you, then," said the woman.

"Now, you just unlock that upper drawer, and open it half way or so. Now put your hand inside and run it along the inside of the upper part, until you find a little knob. Now press this toward you and a shallow drawer will fall down."

Geoffrey did as directed, when the concealed drawer, or tray rather, fell down on its hinges. It disclosed a folded paper, which he took out and found to be in his father's handwriting—and to this effect:

"April 15, 1845.

"I opened this secret drawer in the desk of Arthur Lovett, this day, on the information of Betty Certain, in her presence, and in that of George Rawson and James M. Dixon, and found herein the unsigned holograph will of the said Arthur Lovett, and opened and read the same in the presence of the parties above-named. (*Signed*) MANUEL HUNTER."

"So this is where the will, which I received from my father, was found, is it?" said Geoffrey, musingly. "Poor fellow. It is a pity it could not have been carried out. He seemed so much in earnest about it. Do you suppose he anticipated any special danger?"

"I do not know," she answered; "he seemed very much concerned about the condition of his affairs, in case he should die, and talked of it a great deal in a way that made me shiver with dread. I am quite sure he did not expect to live very long; but whether he anticipated disease or violence I could not say. He was sometimes very low in spirits, and took a very gloomy view of the future. At such times one would have thought he apprehended almost immediate death."

CHAPTER XX.

BEFORE THE WEDDING.

"HE seemed to be constantly apprehensive that his favorite scheme might fail through his unexpected death. I think his will would have been properly executed before, but he had somehow reasoned himself into the belief, or got the belief without reasoning, that he would leave me as his widow, to settle and arrange affairs as he desired.

"I do not think he expected to outlive his marriage a great while. He said to me once that he would give me his hand in marriage in order to make me his hand in death. I feared that he intended suicide, until he once said to me that no man was worth saving who could not endure his lot upon earth until it pleased God to call him to leave it. Knowing his strong faith which had outlasted all irregularities of life and all the scath of error, I at once abandoned this idea.

"It may seem presumptuous, Mr. Geoffrey, but I have often thought that Arthur Lovett had a clear forewarning of his end, though his mind was no doubt troubled as to its cause and source. This may be only a notion, but I can account for his acts in no other way.

"As I said, we were to be married the next day, and the new dresses were here in the library. Among them

was the soft gray one, which I admired so much, and
Arthur had laughed at me for preferring over the richer
and gayer ones. It was hanging over a chair at the
other end of the table, and I kept thinking while Arthur
was talking to me about the will and such matters that
it would become me better as his wife than all the rest
of the finery there.

"I never spoke of it to a human soul before, Geoffrey Hunter, but I am as sure as if I had seen it with
my own eyes that Arthur Lovett was killed by a woman's
hand. I don't know how it was managed, and I won't
say what woman did it, but this you may be sure of,
it was a woman's hand that took his life."

"A woman's? What makes you think so?" asked
Geoffrey, surprised at her earnestness.

"Because no one but a woman would have taken
from the room what the person who murdered him did,"
she answered.

"Why," said Geoffrey, "I always understood that
nothing was missed from the room."

"There was not, by any one but me," she replied.

"And what did you miss?" asked Geoffrey.

"The one who murdered him took away that gray
dress," she answered slowly.

Geoffrey started, and as his mind comprehended fully
how powerfully this circumstance pointed to the sisters
of Lovett, he said with a shudder:

"You say that this dress was the least valuable of
all those which were in the room?"

"It was, and not of a value or appearance to tempt
any one, beside the others," Miss Betty replied.

"You think, then, that the taking of that dress pointed to a hostility toward yourself?" Geoffrey asked.

"I prized it more than all the rest. Depend upon it, Mr. Hunter, it was a woman who took it, and one who knew my fancy for it, too. She took *that* dress to show me that the blow was aimed more at me than at Arthur Lovett," was Miss Betty's earnest reply.

"Who knew of your fancy for this dress?" Geoffrey asked.

"Arthur Lovett and his two sisters," she answered, steadily and coldly.

"No other person?" he asked.

"No other person," was the reply.

"You think, then, that Lovett's sisters caused his death?" Geoffrey said.

"I was *sure* of it once, now I do n't know what to think," said Miss Betty, slowly.

"Why did you not speak of this at the time?" asked Geoffrey.

"You forget how I was placed," said Miss Betty. "It would simply have been deemed an insane attempt on the part of a poor white girl, who had beguiled a gentleman into a promise of marriage, to wreak her disappointment by trying to throw suspicion upon two respectable ladies of unquestionable character and motive. No, Mr. Geoffrey, I knew nothing about law, but common sense taught me that. So, when I saw I was struck, I did not squeal, but sat down to watch and see if time did n't put the rest of the threads in my hands. I always thought I should see my way clear some time, and I have not lost faith yet."

"But you said you did not know what to think now," said Geoffrey. "You are not, then, so sure that a woman did the deed?"

"Just as sure that it was a woman," answered Miss Betty, "but *not* so sure what one it was."

"*What* one!" said Geoffrey in surprise. "What one could it be, if not one of his sisters?"

"I don't know," she replied, "and yet I am not sure it was one of them."

"What has occurred to change your mind on this subject?" asked Geoffrey.

"The knowledge that the same person who killed Arthur Lovett attempted Toinette's life!" said she, looking earnestly at Geoffrey Hunter.

"What!" exclaimed Geoffrey, springing from his chair. "The same person! How do you know?"

"She wore the dress which was made for me, and which was in Arthur Lovett's room when I left him on the night of his murder, and was taken away by the person who killed him," said Miss Betty, slowly.

"What! wore your dress! What proof have you?" cried Geoffrey, with a look and tone of horror.

"I am not in the habit of saying what I cannot prove," said Betty Certain, with a sort of testiness in her tone. "If I had been, I should have told a good deal years ago. I had chance enough, goodness knows, with Manuel Hunter begging at me early and late, in public and private. I am sure he thought I might have put my finger on the murderer if I had been so minded; and I thought I could then myself, but I don't know now. But if you want to know what sat-

isfies me that the woman who killed Arthur Lovett
was the one who tried to kill your Toinette, it 's just
this : I picked up this in the passage where Leon
fought with the woman," and she took from her pocket
the fragment she had picked up in the hall and handed
it to Geoffrey.

"You see," she said, "it is part of the left sleeve—
and, if you will look closely, you will see by the fresh
color that there has been some trimming on it about
half an inch deep, and sort of diamond shaped."

Geoffrey looked at the fragment, which was some
four or five inches long, and about three inches wide
at the bottom, and somewhat triangular in shape, having
evidently been torn out by the dog's teeth, catching at
the upper angle. He saw evident marks of the trimming spoken of, and also drops of blood. This mystery appalled him.

"That trimming was velvet ribbon, and that is a
piece of my grey dress which was taken from the
library here the night he was killed," said Miss Betty.
"I remember everything about that dress as though it
were yesterday. I could not quite call it up at first,
and kept turning the piece round my finger, that
morning I first saw it, till it all came as plain as
day, when Toinette first opened her eyes on me, as I
sat by the sofa. That 's the main reason why I came
here, Mr. Geoffrey, and one reason why I have stayed.
I knew Arthur Lovett's murderer had been here
once since his death, and hoped she might come
again."

"Hoped she might come again!" said Geoffrey, in

surprise and vexation.　"You did not want any one else killed, did you?"

"Certainly not," she replied, "but I *did* want to find out the murderer, and I thought if she came I would see her, and perhaps know her, and be able to bring her to justice yet."

"It's a pity you have been disappointed," said Geoffrey; "though, I must say, I am not sorry that a woman of such inclinations should decide to stay away from my house."

"She has not stayed away!" said Miss Betty.

"Not stayed away?　How so?　Have you seen her?" he asked, hurriedly.

"I have," she replied.

"When and where?" asked Geoffrey.

"Last night, upon the porch, at the window of your sitting-room," continued Miss Betty.

"How did you happen to see her there?" asked Geoffrey.

"After my conversation with you yesterday," said Miss Betty, "I went home, but, somehow, when I got to thinking of these matters of which I have told you, I thought I ought not to leave you in ignorance of what I knew, even for a single night.　It troubled me so that I finally started over here.　It was perhaps an hour after daylight down when I left home.　When I got here, I climbed over the side-fence into the front yard, instead of going round by the gate or back by the quarters.　As I came along under the trees and among the shrubbery, I heard some one singing in the sitting-room.　I came around the end of the porch, to the

steps, and looked up at the windows of the sitting-
room, which were lighted, and there I saw a woman
looking in and shaking her head and clenched hand
at some one on the inside."

"Did you see her face? Who is she?" asked
Geoffrey, impetuously.

"I saw her face plainly," she answered, "but I do
not know who she is. One thing I do know, however.
She is not either of the sisters of Arthur Lovett."

"Describe her appearance," said Geoffrey.

"She is a woman of near my height, of sharp, regular
features, and with hair as white as snow that falls down
to her waist," said Miss Betty.

"And her dress?" asked Geoffrey.

"She had on the dress of which you have a piece,"
she answered. "I noticed that especially."

"Well, what became of her?" he asked.

"I do not know," she said. "I was so beat by
seeing her there—though I had watched for her many
a night—that I think I must have fainted, for when I
came to myself again I was sitting in the angle of the
porch-wall and the steps, and the light was out in the
house. I am not much accustomed to fright, Mr.
Geoffrey, but I was terribly frightened then. While I
stood there thinking what I ought to do, I heard a
step, and saw the figure of that woman come out from
under the other end of the porch and go down to the
lane. I followed carefully, but lost sight of her in
the old field beyond. Then I came back here and
watched till day, but she did not come again."   .

"Strange," said Geoffrey, musingly; "that was precisely the impression produced on me the night of the assault on Toinette. It tallies with her description of the woman she saw looking through the window, which Maggie also saw and I caught a glimpse of as she passed by, and exactly fits the negroes' tales of the *Ghost of Lovett Lodge.* Mistress Certain, you have undoubtedly seen the ghost," he added, jocularly.

" Mr. Geoffrey," she replied, " I know nothing about ghosts, and do n't believe in them at all; but if I. did, I should know this—that it was no ghost I saw last night. It was a real, flesh and blood, woman, and an angry and dangerous one, too."

Geoffrey did not reply, but rose and walked the room in troubled thought. It was very strange, this baffling mystery. He had tried to grasp it for two years, and yet it came and went about him with impunity. His enclosure, his house, even his most secret hours were open to this gray-clad specter. Toinette had seen it, and Maggie. He doubted not that only the purest accident had saved the former from death. He, himself, had had a glimpse of it, and now, at last, strong, cold-blooded, sensible Betty Certain had been scared half out of her wits by the apparition. It had been unseen for a year or more. Now it had reappeared. And still it had Toinette under surveillance. Why did it follow that girl so persistently, or was it not the girl, but himself, who was shadowed? If himself, why should he be an object of resentment? And whether himself or the girl, why should the assassin of Arthur Lovett pursue them? These questions he could not answer.

Betty Certain sat with her elbows on her knees, regarding the fire attentively, and Geoffrey could not help appealing to her in his extremity.

"What does it mean, Mrs. Certain? Who *can* be dogging either me or Toinette in this manner?" he asked, anxiously.

"It's hard to say *who*, Mr. Geoffrey, but it is very evident that it means no good to one of you. As it was Toinette before, I think it's likely to be her now. If she stays here I don't see how she is to avoid the knife that came so near taking her off before," said Miss Betty.

"That reminds me," said Geoffrey, "that I wanted to show you that knife, and ask if you knew anything about it."

"I noticed it," she answered, "that first morning on which we met, in the drawer of the desk, which was open when I came in, and again when you showed it to the doctor. It was one that used to belong to Arthur Lovett. I have heard him say that it was the dirk of some foreign robber, perhaps an Italian, which had been the instrument of a great many murders before he got it. He bought it when abroad as a curiosity. Yes, I recollect there was an Italian legend upon the hilt, something in this wise :

> "'Revenge seeks not the form to mar
> With reeking wound and gaping scar.'"

"It is here now," said he, as he opened a drawer of the table-desk and examined its contents. "Why, how is this?" he continued. "I am sure I placed it here. Who could have taken it out?"

"Depend upon it, Geoffrey Hunter, the hand that took
it w³ll find a use for it soon; and your Toinette will not
come off so easily next time," said the woman earnestly.

Apparently, the absence of the dagger impressed
Geoffrey with more anxiety than all the conversation
with Miss Betty had done. He sat turning over the
various articles which the drawer contained, in an absent, puzzled manner, for a time; then turning to the
woman, he said, suddenly:

"Mrs. Certain, I cannot bear that any harm should
befall Toinette from her presence here. It is not right
that I should expose her thus to danger. Our conversation about Arthur Lovett has given me some fears
that I might travel the same road. I do not think I
am a coward, nor was he; but there seems to be the
same dark fate about my life that hung over that of
my predecessor at the Lodge. I have a mind to liberate this girl, Toinette, and take her North at once.
You have spoken of desiring to go with her, Miss
Betty. Do you still wish it?"

"I cannot go now, Mr. Geoffrey," she answered.
"When the mystery of Arthur's death seemed far beyond my reach, or rather when I thought I knew its
cause and could not bring the criminals to justice—
because they were his sisters—I was anxious to go away.
Now I am satisfied that it was not those sisters, but
another woman, and I cannot go away until I have
stripped the vail from her face, and unraveled the mystery of his death. I must stay here and watch. But
I do hope you will do as you say before further harm
befalls the poor girl."

"I will," said Geoffrey. "This very day she shall go to Perham, where I shall have to stay until I can arrange the business; after that I shall take her at once to some part of the North, and leave her as comfortably settled as I can."

Betty Certain seemed strongly moved at this declaration. She stood up and took hold of Geoffrey's arm. Her lips quivered, and tears were in her eyes, as she said :

"God bless you, Geoffrey Hunter! You will make Heaven brighter for your dear old mother, if you do. Oh!" she continued, "if Arthur Lovett had but had your determination he might have been alive and happy now. Alive, at least," she continued musingly; "he hardly could have been very happy away from that girl."

Geoffrey Hunter was not one to let a resolution grow cold before it was acted on. He instantly ordered the carriage to be brought around after dinner, and directed Toinette to be ready to accompany him to Perham.

Returning to the library, he said :

"There are some papers referring to Arthur Lovett's affairs, Mrs. Certain, which I wish to leave in your hands until my return. They are in this package and were given to me by my father. But," he continued, "we have not settled yet. Here are two hundred dollars. Do you think that sufficient?"

"Too much, sir," she answered, "for I was about to ask a privilege which I shall hardly dare to do if you pay me so liberally."

15

"What is it?" asked Geoffrey. "I will grant anything you wish, for I know you would not make an unreasonable request."

"It is that I may occupy the Lodge during you: absence," said Miss Betty.

"Are you not afraid to do so?" asked Geoffrey

"Now that my old notion of Arthur's death has proved false, I do not see why I should fear his murderer. But whether I am in danger or not, I am determined to find out who did it, and think myself more likely to succeed here than anywhere else," she replied.

"Certainly," said Geoffrey. "You are welcome to occupy the Lodge, but I fear you will have cause to regret your request."

"Thank you, sir," she replied; "I will go now and see that Toinette is ready in time."

THE OLD COUNTY CLERK.

"*His white hair still bristled full and fierce above his forehead, and his sharp gray eye looked forth from under bushy brows with undimmed keenness.*"—p. 219.

CHAPTER XXI.

IN THE CLERK'S OFFICE.

THE next day Geoffrey Hunter went to the office of the Clerk of the Superior Court for the County of Cold Spring.

The clerk was George Rawson, one of the parties who were present when Manuel Hunter took the will of Arthur Lovett from the secret drawer in the desk. He had been for thirty years the clerk of the Court. Two or three generations of lawyers had gone through the treadmill of legal routine under his eye. He was a patriarch of the Court—a man of giant frame and evident strength in his younger days, grown full and rotund in his later years and from his sedentary life. His white hair still bristled full and fierce above his forehead, and his sharp gray eye looked forth from under bushy lids with undimmed keenness, apparently to demonstrate that the gold-bowed glasses on his nose were only a joke which he played to show how lightly the years sat upon him. The only triumph which Time seemed to have achieved over him was in his hearing, which was slightly impaired, as the ready use of his hand as a sound-gatherer testified. The office was in the court-house, upon the lower floor, and paved with brick. The court-house itself was an ancient structure, and the office contained records reaching back into the

ante-revolutionary days, when strange judges sometimes
sat upon the bench and administered a wild justice
which has scarcely its counterpart. The king's judges
of assize had once entered by the door and gone out by
the window, greatly to the detriment of wigs and robes,
but glad to escape with life minus the emblems of
dignity from the hands of the Regulators. There were
entries in those quaint old dockets which the clerk
had made with trembling hand and with the muzzle
of a pistol at his head—entries in which the forms
of law were mimicked and its officers assailed with a
quaint wit and ludicrous profanity combined. In this
old office, with its dusty shelves, shattered cases, and
mouldy records, sat George Rawson, C.S.C., beside
a table of stained and grimy pine, before a smoulder-
ing fire within the capacious chimney-jaws, smoking a
clay pipe, with the inevitable long reed stem of the
country.

He seemed, like his records, to be a relic of a past
generation—a messenger sent by the old Colony to the
young State, who had lingered to see the effect of
the message he was charged to deliver. Those old
papers were as boyhood's playmates to him. He knew
their lineaments and purport at a glance. He was a
noble type of a race fast passing away, which grew
slowly into positions of trust and then held them for a
lifetime, despite the changes of party. He was a kindly
man of the justest impulses—the guardian of all
widows and orphans *ex-officio*, or, at least, by color of
office, and " Uncle " to three or four generations of boys
and girls.

No sooner did he see Geoffrey Hunter, on the morning of which we. write, and exchange the customary greetings, with especial inquiries as to the health of the senior Hunter, than the old man said :

"I was just thinking of you, Geoffrey. Sit down here and fill up. I must have a talk with you. Shut to that door and turn the key, for I don't want any one coming in to interrupt what I have to say."

Geoffrey protested that he was in great haste and much pressed for time, evidently thinking that the old man's social habits were about to make him the scapegoat of a morning's loneliness.

"Oh, bother your hurry ! I 've got something to say to you that is more important than anything you 're likely to find of record here, I 'll wager. So sit down and be quiet while I tell it."

Geoffrey at length complied, and when he was fairly settled to a smoke with one of the old man's genuine " Powhatan " pipes, sending forth clouds of incense from the fragrant Kinnikannick, the old man, drawing down his brows and looking up at his unconcerned auditor, asked abruptly :

"You 're livin' at Lovett Lodge now, are n't ye ?"

Geoffrey was all attention in an instant.

"Yes," he answered, "why ?"

"You 've heard, of course," resumed the old man, "a great deal about Arthur Lovett and his oddities, if I may call them so, for I never could make out in my own mind rightly, whether he was absolutely crazy or just peculiar and eccentric. And, queer enough, that is just what bothers me now, and has for some time

gone by. If I were just sure now," said he musingly,
"that the man was plum crazy, so to speak, I should
know just what I ought to do; and if I knew that he
was only rattle-brained, odd-like, I should know just
what I ought not to do."

Geoffrey remarked that he did not see how the
mental condition of a man who had been dead almost
a score of years could influence any one's action now,
or at least alter his duty.

"More than you think, young man; more than you
think," said the old clerk. "Though, by the way, you
may be right, in a sense. It may change facts and
results; but, perhaps, it ought not to affect my action.
It cannot alter my duty. The law must decide upon
that. You know that Arthur Lovett was the owner
of Lovett Lodge; that he lived there and died there—
a very mysterious death, too. But you may not be
aware that at the time of his death he was about to
marry a neighbor of yours, one Betty Certain. You
had heard of that too, eh? Yes, he was all ready. The
wedding clothes were bought, and he had got his license
a week before, and made me promise to come down
and see them made one. It was an odd move, and I
could not understand it, and told him so, when he
came for the license; but he said he did not need a
guardian, and if he chose to marry my grandmother he
supposed he had the right to do so without telling
every upstart why he did it.

"I told him I had no intention to reflect upon his
right, but only repeated the usual comment on his
match. in the hope that he would be at liberty to tell

me something with which to stop the mouths of mischievous talkers.

"I said this just to smooth matters over with Mr. Lovett, because he was not one that I wanted any fuss with. But, just as usual, he went off contrary-wise to any one else, and took it all in dead earnest, and said:

"'Just so, Mr. Rawson. Well, since you suggest it, I will do so. You may say to all inquirers that I marry Betty Certain, first, because I know her to be an honest, right-minded woman, and, secondly, because in her extreme devotion to me, she compromised her character to save me from danger and trouble.'

"'But you certainly paid that debt when you fought Bill Price on her account,' I said.

"'I stopped the tongue of slander,' he replied; 'I wish to kill it dead, which I can do only by making her my wife.'

"So I made out the license and he staid some time in the office talking with me of his affairs. He was in mighty low spirits, and said he had no idea that he would live any great length of time, and if his wishes could only be carried out, after he was dead, he would not care to. In fact, I thought he was about the most dolorous bridegroom I had ever seen.

"After he had finally left the office he came back and made me promise to come down to the wedding, as he would have some business for me to do before he went off on his trip. So, it was arranged that he was to send in a led-horse for me the night before, and I was to go out to the Lodge on the day of the bridal. He was so depressed, however, that before he left he made me promise that, if it should ever be in my power after his death to promote what I knew to be his wishes, without injury to myself, I would do 'it.

"I had no idea that I should ever be called to do anything of the kind; but it is this very promise which has been weighing on me for months, and would be yet if it had not been for your remark that *his* state of mind could not affect *my* duty. No more can it. If his desires were sane and reasonable, it is, of course, my duty to speak out about them. If they were otherwise, the law will refuse to carry them into operation. In any case, the law must decide—*my* duty is plain.

"Now, you see," said the old man, between long puffs at his well-lighted pipe, "as I told you, I was present when your father took the will of Arthur Lovett from the place Betty Certain showed him, and read it over to us—Betty Certain, Mr. Dixon, and me. He found it in a sort of secret drawer that let down on hinges, like some of these new trunk-covers, on the inside of the upper drawer of the desk.

"The drawer into which this tray fell, when the spring was touched, was locked, and the key was found in Lovett's pocket. In this drawer was found all the money he is supposed to have had in his possession at the time of his death—something to the rise of two hundred dollars—and the only two notes that he is known to have held against any one—one of these was against an insolvent party, and the other has been collected by the administrator, and amounted to some three or four hundred dollars more. His accounts with his factors

in Richmond, check-book and bills of sale for all of **his slaves, were** in this drawer, neatly tied and filed, as **well as a great** many other papers whose value might **be a question.** These seemed to be all 'the valuable **papers and effects**' that he had, and I have not heard that any others have ever been discovered. In the upper or secret drawer there was no other paper, except a sealed package directed to the gal Bella that he was so bewitched about—by the by, she was a most remarkable nigger, and if any one was ever excusable for such foolishness, it was Arthur Lovett. There were some little trinkets also in it, but nothing of any value. The place for a signature and a scrawl seal, as well as an attestation clause, showed that he intended to have executed it formally before witnesses, and, I am inclined to think, that was the business he wanted to see me about the morning of his marriage.

"The woman, Certain, claimed that he had told her that was his intention, the night before. I never knew how much reliance to put in what that woman said about the matter, or anyone else, in fact. There is one thing, she was certainly clear of all suspicion of having caused his death, for all her interest depended on his living to execute the will at least; and, for aught I can see, afterward too; for the place of Arthur Lovett's wife was one she might well be proud of, even with the incumbrance of the gal, Bella, who, by the way, had before that been sold by his father's executors, and gone, no one knew where.

"Your father got me to try and trace her up, but I never could get beyond the day of sale itself.

I went to N———, where the sale took place, and after some inquiry found that the man 'Edwards,' whom the sale-list filed in the Clerk's office showed to have bought the gal Bella, was a poor, no-account cuss that lived in the pines some four or five miles out. Of course, everybody knew that he never had money enough in his life to buy half as likely a nigger as this gal, Bella, and consequently, that he must have acted for some one else.

"I learned that when the girl was knocked off to him at the sale, some one made the remark that he was not good for the price, and the executor told him that he would be required to give undoubted security. But he stepped up and said he didn't want any credit, and just paid the cash in hand for the gal and took her off before the sale was over. I inquired of some of the man's neighbors how long he kept her, and was surprised to learn that he had never been known to have a slave at all, nor would they believe that such was the case. He was just a poor cracker-cuss, hardly better than a nigger himself.

"I took occasion to go by his house, and called for a drink of water—if the flat, warm, swamp-settlings they drink there can be called water. His wife came out with a gourd and piggin, both, I must allow, clean and tidy, which is more than I could possibly say of her.

"She was a big, gaunt woman, who wore about No. 9 shoes, and stood with hands on her hips while I drank and talked. In return for the water, I offered her a drink of whisky from my flask. She finished a good bit of it, and in response to a question said she

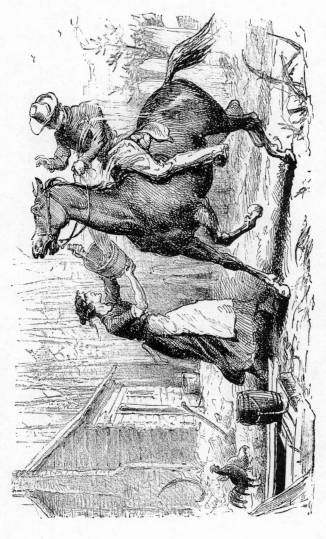

SUSAN EDWARDS AND THE LAWYER.

And with that, before I could turn my horse in his tracks, she threw that piggin of water over me." —p. 227.

had no 'terbacker,' but had some of the best 'rozzum'
one ever stuck a tooth in. As I had never learned to
like rosin, I did not find whether this was true or not.
When I thought I had put myself on terms with her
to entitle me to do so, I broached the subject of the
nigger. She seemed completely dumbfounded, but I,
thinking it was all put on—for I was now satisfied that
her husband was made an agent simply to conceal the
real buyer—put my foot in the soup by asking her finally,
straight out, what had become of the nigger gal her
husband brought home and kept for a spell.

"Do n't you ever make such a mistake as that,
Geoffrey!

"The woman flew up in a minute. She said she
would have me know that Susan Edwards was n't one
of that sort. She did n't harbor anybody's runaway
niggers in her house; and if her husband ever brought
any black sluts around there, she 'd h'ist 'em, that she
would—and she 'd h'ist me, too, if I did n't make off
about my business; and with that, before I could turn
my horse in his tracks, she threw that piggin of water over me, gourd and all. The last I saw of Mrs.
Susan Edwards, she was standing in the middle of the
road, holding her empty piggin, sticking her black
fangs into that good 'rozzum,' and cussing about the
worst soaked 'stranger' that ever run from a she-
cracker. Well, I found Mr. Edwards himself afterwards,
and with a deal of difficulty and not a little good whisky,
got him to tell me what he knowed, which was n't much
after all. It seems a man had come to him that
morning and got him to bid for the woman, and per-

haps one or both of the children, and handed him the
money to pay for them, taking care to keep him in
sight till the purchase was complete. That night he
met the gentleman at a low sort of eating-house in
the town, who paid him for his trouble one hundred
dollars in bank-bills, and as much whisky as Mr. Edwards could comfortably dispose of, which, if I may
judge by what I saw of him, was a right smart fee in
itself. He said that the stranger made out the bill of
sale, and he signed it; but could not remember his
name or where he was from. Had an idea that he
belonged in Alabama; but did not know why. Said
that he spoke of 'toting' things to the stage-house,
as he was going away that night, so I gave up the
idea of his being an Alabamian, who would have said
'pack' instead of 'tote'; and I could never get on the
track of the gal or the buyer after that, though your
father kept me at it for the best part of a year, whenever I could be spared from the office. He always
insisted that this fellow Edwards bought her for Buck
Lloyd, and would have me go to attend the Administrator's sale of his property, to see if I could not learn
something of the gal; and 'twas there I bought his
cook, Mabel. It must have cost him right smart first
and last—his search after that girl and her children—
and I never knew rightly what he did it for. I never
thought he was foolish enough to want to get them
just to free them, even if Arthur Lovett was his
friend and very anxious about the matter. Manuel
Hunter was never the man to indulge in any senti-
mentality at such a cost to himself."

"My father has been a man of much more tender susceptibilities than many suppose," said Geoffrey, sententiously.

"Now, look here, Geoffrey, do n't fly off in that way," said the old clerk, his eyes sparkling with humor. "Every one knows that a man who had his own way to make in the world, and made it as your father did, did n't go about throwing his money away on other people's whims. No, sir; he had some reason of his own for wanting to get hold of that gal. Of course it was n't the same reason that Lovett had for not wanting to let her go, for, in that case, he would not have been so anxious about her children. Now, Geoffrey, can you imagine why your father should want to own that woman and her children?"

"I think he had a very laudable desire to carry out the wishes of an unfortunate friend," said Geoffrey.

"Oh, I thought we had disposed of that before," said Rawson. "He was not the man for that. It's true he did free the boy when he got him—or said he did. I was never quite sure of it."

"I have seen a copy of the record," said Geoffrey, angrily.

"Well, well," said Rawson, "I won't deny it; but do you know what bargain he made with him, before he turned him loose?"

"I am sure I do not," said Geoffrey. "In fact I do not see how he could have made any. A contract to pay for an intended liberation would not be good, nor any other agreement made with a slave."

"Oh, of course not," said the other. "But did you

never hear or know of any contract or release executed by the boy?"

"It is simply impossible that there should have been anything of the kind."

"Of course the boy was then a minor, and any bargain with him would have been worthless—but it may have been done since."

"Mr. Rawson," said Geoffrey, "I have the utmost confidence in the belief that my father liberated this boy simply because it was his friend's dying wish he should be set free. In fact, I know it."

"Pshaw, pshaw, my son; haven't you got over that yet? Why, then, did he not manumit Toinette, as he promised your mother to do, when she was dying, instead of giving her to you to re-enact the tragedy or comedy, whatever you call it, of 'Arthur and his gal Bella' at Lovett Lodge?"

"Stop, Mr. Rawson," said Geoffrey, rising; "I cannot permit you to speak thus of my father, who is now so stricken by disease as to be the same as in the tomb, so far as the defense of his own acts is concerned."

"Sit down, sir, sit down," said Rawson, severely. "I am too old for you to gain anything by quarreling with me; besides, every one knows that George Rawson owed your father too much good will, before you were born, ever to speak of him with unnecessary harshness. And I must say, young man, that if his son had half the sense his poor father has lost, he would know that he was disgracing his father far more by openly living with that girl, than I could if I were to talk slanders of him all the time. Manuel Hunter was too proud, as

well as too good, a man, ever to have brought shame
upon his family in that way."

"You judge me harshly, Mr. Rawson," said Geoffrey,
flushing nevertheless.

"Well, well, that's none of my business, of course,"
said the old man in a pacificatory tone; "but you provoked me a little by thinking that I could slander your
father. But we were talking about his motive in wanting to get these Lovett niggers. I've thought of it a
good deal, but asked no questions. Your father knew
me well enough to know that I would do his business
without meddling with his reasons. Nevertheless, I
am satisfied that he had reasons of his own, and as he
is now past telling them and you are the one interested
—at least having the same interest that he had, or will
have, under your father's will afore many a day—I will
tell you what I think they were, and it's my opinion it
will pay Manuel Hunter's heir to listen and remember
too!"

He then gave Geoffrey a detailed account of the
relation which Belle and her children sustained to the
Lovett Lodge property through the deed of trust made
in her behalf to Arthur, of which the reader is already
informed.

At its conclusion Geoffrey informed him that he
had been made aware of these facts by his father, and
had that morning come to his office to examine the
records in regard to the matter, and he would be glad
if Mr. Rawson would assist him.

"Wait, wait," said the old clerk, somewhat pettishly, "I am not through yet. Wait and hear all that I

have to say. You can examine the records afterwards.
No, no; fill up and sit down," he continued, as Geoffrey
again pleaded haste and business.

"As I said before, you are not likely to have more
important business, as Manuel Hunter's trustee and
heir, for many a day, than listening to me about this
Lovett matter.

"I have already told you," he continued, when
Geoffrey had done as he had bidden, "how this holograph script, purporting to be Arthur Lovett's will, was
found. At that time I do n't suppose any one had an
idea that it could by any possibility be established as
such. I know your father had not, or his course would
have been different, for he had not only been Lovett's
counsel, but was his best friend. There seemed to be
a strange attraction about the shy and peculiar young
Lovett for the hard-headed, busy old lawyer, your father. The recreation he seemed most to enjoy was a
half day's chat with Lovett in his library.

"I never could imagine what they found to talk
about; but they were certainly great cronies, which was
the more remarkable from the fact that your father
had very few intimates and favored associates. He
lived in his business—that 's how he came to succeed
so well. I 'm mightily affeard his son won't keep up his
reputation.

"But that 's neither here nor there. I was speaking
of this will. Your father had no idea it could be sustained, and as the only parties interested in it were
Bella and her children, who I do n't suppose ever heard
of it, and could have done nothing if they had, and

this woman, Betty Certain, who was ignorant of the matter, and who, I must admit, did not seem to care anything about the property now that Lovett was dead, it was never offered for probate, and nothing was ever done about it.

"I remember that the only question Betty Certain asked of your father was, whether there was no way by which Lovett's wishes in regard to the gal and her children could be carried out. She did n't seem to think a word about herself. Your father said he would do all he could. I asked him before the administration was granted in the estate whether he was going to offer the will for probate. He replied that he had looked the matter over carefully, and was satisfied that it did not come under the statute, not being found among the valuable papers and effects of the deceased, and it was useless to incur unnecessary expense on account of it. I agreed with him then, thinking him entirely right, as he was mighty apt to be on a matter of law that he looked into carefully. Right lately, however, I 've taken to thinking the other way. You may not have seen it; but the Supreme Court at its last term decided a case as near upon all fours with this as one could well be. I have received the volume within a week or two—which, by the way, is shockingly printed—and have read the case three or four times very carefully. I can 't see how a case could be made to fit this closer. There were two drawers without locks, but having a common cover fastened with one. In one of these was the valuable papers, money, etc., of the deceased, and in the other the will with some loose

papers of no account. Now they say that the fact of
their being under one common lock justifies the conclusion that these two drawers may be taken as one,
and constitute a proper depository for a holograph will
under the statute.

"The case of Arthur Lovett's will, to my mind, is
quite a bit stronger than this. Don't you think so?"

"Certainly, certainly," answered Geoffrey, absently.

"And if that will should be proved," said the old
man, with a little surprise at Geoffrey's demeanor in
his tone, "what do you think your title to Lovett
Lodge would be good for?"

"Not much, certainly," said Geoffrey, quietly.

"Not much? Not much?" said Rawson, excitedly.
"It wouldn't be worth the paper it's written on!"

"Of course not," assented Geoffrey.

"Well, I must say you take it quietly for one who
has a smart chance of losing a fine estate. Now, do
you know what I am going to do in this matter?
You reminded me a while ago that circumstances
could not affect duty. I am going to apply that idea
now, and if your ox is gored, you must remember it is
your own bull that did it. I am going to inform
Betty Certain of the facts I have just told you."

"That is evidently your duty, Mr. Rawson," said
Geoffrey, "though I shall do it myself, probably before
you have an opportunity."

"That's right, my son; that's right. I see you've
got some of your old father's shrewdness, for all you've
kept still so long. By all means see her and make
the best bargain you can in the matter."

Geoffrey smiled. "Will you loan me this volume?" said he, pointing to the one Rawson had referred to.

"Certainly. The case is Robertson *et al. vs.* Carter and Others, page 592," Rawson answered.

Geoffrey bade him good morning, and went out.

"Ah!" said the old clerk, looking after him, "there's a heap of come-out in the Hunter stock yet."

CHAPTER XXII.

THE HOLOGRAPH PROVED.

GEOFFREY HUNTER was as good as his word. He examined the case which the clerk had re- ferred to, and compared it with the provisions of the statute on which the will depended for validity. By this it was provided that a will might be established and be valid to convey real and personal property, al- though not executed in the presence of witness, if certain requisites were complied with. These were:

1st. That it must be wholly in the handwriting of the person whose will it appears to be, being thence denominated a holograph.

2d. The name of the testator must be subscribed thereto or inserted in some part of the will.

3d. It must be found *among* the valuable papers and effects of the deceased, or have been lodged in the hands of some person for safe-keeping.

After this comparison he was surprised that there could ever have been a doubt as to the validity of the will now in his possession. There evidently could not have been but for the very narrow construction previ- ously given to the clause, "among the valuable papers and effects" of the testator. This, having been found in the secret drawer, was effectually separated from all his valuables. The very just and reasonable construction which was applied in the case last before the Court removed all doubt.

That very evening he went to the humble dwelling of Betty Certain, and informed her of the facts he had learned from Rawson and explained their probable results. He added, that after having himself read the case, and carefully examined the subject, he had no doubt that if she offered the will for probate it would be sustained, and she would be allowed to qualify as Executrix. He farther stated that as there seemed little probability of the discovery of Belle and her younger children, a large portion of the estate would revert to her. The information did not seem to elate the woman at all. Poor white as she was, she listened calmly, and only remarked that she had always believed that Arthur's will in regard to Belle and her children would some time be carried out.

"You see, Mr. Geoffrey," she said, "I believe that Arthur Lovett sincerely repented the sin and weakness of his course toward the gal Belle, and earnestly desired to make all reparation in his power and avoid further error. That is why he would have married me. He was not a man to break his plighted faith, however weak he might have been in other respects. He wanted a wife, in order that his vows to her might free him from a temptation he could not otherwise resist. He chose also to marry me because he could thereby discharge what he regarded as a debt toward me, though I did not. I knew or felt this, in a dim sort of way, when he said to me, 'Betty Certain, will you be my wife?' but I have seen it clearer since he died. And

I could not but believe that the good God would remember the prayer of one who was striving so earnestly
to do right. Now I see that He has.

"But," she continued, after a moment's thought,
"how will this affect you? Will you not lose what
your father paid for Lovett Lodge?"

Geoffrey admitted that this would be the result.

"Then," said she, "I will repay you out of such
portion of the estate as falls to my share."

Geoffrey protested that his father had bought it as
a speculation with his eyes open, and that he could
claim no reparation if he lost. Betty Certain would
not hear a word of it. The poor white woman was
determined that it should be as she decided, or she
would not move in the matter at all. So the young
aristocrat became the object of her magnanimity, and
it was arranged that she should repay the purchase
money, and that the profits of the plantation and his
improvements should offset the rents during his occupancy, should the will be established and the purchase money not be recovered from the heirs of Lovett.

The necessary legal steps were soon taken under
Geoffrey's advice. The heirs, seeing that the case was
hopeless for them, compromised upon terms very favor-
able to themselves, and the will was shortly afterwards
admitted to probate, and Betty Certain, as Executrix
of the will of Arthur Lovett, became the rightful possessor of Lovett Lodge.

Toinette had some time before bidden adieu to her
kind old friend Betty Certain, and had been staying
with her mother at the Hunter Home, awaiting the term

of Court at which her emancipation was to be completed.

Her reception by old Mabel was very peculiar—a sort of tender pity, united with cold sneering unbelief in the professed intentions of their young master, marked her conversation and demeanor.

"Do n't set yer heart on freedom, pore chile," she would say, " cos Geoffrey Hunter won't never part with ez likely a gal ez you in no such way. Do n't believe a word of it, honey. He 's jes' telling you that to fool ye, and git ye to go 'way with him peaceably, that 's all; an' directly when he get 's ye off you 'll find yourself belonging to somebody else, an' Mass'r Geoffrey coming home with the money ye brought in his pocket. He 's jes' got tired of ye—wants to marry likely, or else wants to put ye off before a baby in yer arms spoils yer market.

"Wants the child born free, ye say? What does he care for the child of my Toinette? If he did n't want a slave child, what did he ruin a slave girl for? Answer me that. Oh, you poor innocent! I know how it is. The lying, deceitful villain has made you love him better than your own soul. You would rather be a slave all your life, and bear slave-children too, if he would but love ye, than go away and be as free as he promises. Now, is n't it so, chile?"

Toinette hung her head, and between blushes and sobs admitted that it was true.

"My pore, pore child," said old Mabel vehemently, as she took her in her arms, "do n't do it! Do n't trust to your pore, weak heart, nor the word of any

man that owns a slave. Your old mother did that
when she was young and pure, and almost as fair as
you. She believed a man whose lightest word was
better than the oath of any Hunter that ever lived; and
yet he lied to her, basely and vilely deceived her.
Yes, he sold me for gold when I had borne him children, shared his toils and evils, and loved him better
than all else in Heaven and earth. Yes, honey, you
are his child—you have his features more than mine,
and his ways too.

"Oh, I loved him, chile, better than my own soul.
I thought his promises were truer than the Word of
God; yet he sold me—who had suffered and borne for
him more than the most devoted wife could—sold me
for gold, sold me on the block with you in my arms,
darling! He was as false as the hell to which he went.
So are they all, Geoffrey Hunter among them. Do n't
tell me; I know, chile. An' now, when I' m growing
old, I have to wear this cursed badge," tearing the
turban from her head, "and serve in the Hunter kitchen,
and watch my darling, the last of all my children, going the same hard road of sorrow, suffering, and crime
It has made me a devil," she added wildly. "God
knows what it will do for you.

"But remember this, honey. If Geoffrey Hunter
does serve you in that way, he sha n't ever enjoy the
gold you bring him. Your old mother 'll look out for that.
She has been wronged, but she 's been revenged too, an'
Geoffrey Hunter 'll find that old Mabel knows how to
pay him back all the wrong he does her Toinette."

Toinette shuddered, as the long, gray hair of her

mother, unloosed by the removal of the turban, flowed free about her shoulders—and gazed with a startled look of doubting fear at the weird figure before her. She seemed to be trying to recall some frightful memory.

Old Mabel caught the look, and seemed, for a moment, to hesitate as to the course she should pursue. Her eyes lost their wild gleam, and she gazed thoughtfully and tenderly upon her child.

"Not yet, not yet"—she muttered, and winding the long gray locks about her head, she replaced the turban, remarking, "They were not always gray, Toinette, and it is not age that has made them so now."

She busied herself with her work for a time, and then said:

"We will not say anything more about these things now, Toinette, only promise me one thing, child : When you go away, you must write to me. You can do that. No matter where you are sold, you can get a chance to write to me, or have some one do it for you. Send the letter in care of old George Rawson. He will read it to me—remember that. The slave-girl must not be able to read or write. If Geoffrey Hunter does by you according to his promise, sign your letter 'Toinette.' If he does not, sign it 'Antoinette,' and then, no matter what else you may write, old Mabel will know what to do."

Toinette gave the required promise, and then relapsed into abstraction. Old Mabel observed it, and, with evident anxiety to divert her thoughts, she said:

"But who will have charge at Lovett Lodge now that Mass'r Geoffrey is going away?"

L

"Why, have n't you heard?" answered Toinette. She then informed her mother of the recent occurrences, by which Lovett Lodge had passed into the hands of Betty Certain, under the will of Arthur Lovett.

"Betty Certain! Betty Certain!" said old Mabel, when she had heard the whole story, with Toinette's warm praises of her old friend. "Betty Certain, a low-down, scheming, poor white woman, queening it at Lovett Lodge! She has rare luck indeed! She has been working for that this many a year, and has finally got it. She carries a high hand, no doubt?"

Toinette hastened to assure her, that, on the contrary, Betty Certain did not seem at all elated by her good fortune, but only anxious to discover Belle Lovett and her children, that she might carry out the will of Arthur Lovett.

"No doubt, child, but she pretends so, and no wonder that you believe her. She was always a complete hypocrite. She is no doubt anxious to find Belle Lovett and her children—not to set them free and give them half that estate, but to make sure that they never get free at all, so that she can keep the whole."

Toinette warmly protested against this aspersion of the motives of her old friend, but in vain. Old Mabel still shook her head incredulously, and declared that she "knew Betty Certain. She could n't fool her." "And that reminds me," she said, "that there is one thing more I ought to do. I have been hesitating about it for some time; but now my mind is made up."

She went to the hearth of the kitchen, and after

some trouble took up one of the bricks. After dig-
ging for a moment in the ground beneath, she took
out a small tin box, and, opening this, selected from
among its contents a flat parcel, carefully wrapped in
a piece of snuff-bladder, which had been securely sewed
around it. Replacing the box, she came towards Toinette, and handing her the package, said :

"You may have heard that old Manuel Hunter
pretended that he had found and emancipated Arthur
and Belle Lovett's oldest child, Fred. I have never
been right certain whether this tale was true or not,
though I heard him tell the missis so when he came
back, but I have heard him lie to her at other times,
and he might have been doing it then. He promised
her to set my Toinette free as soon as ever she died,
an' instead of that he gave her to Mass'r Geoffrey for
a plaything.

"But if he did set him free, and if Geoffrey fulfills
his promise to you, you may be able to find this boy,
Fred Lovett. If you can, do so, and give him this
package, and tell him to open it in your presence. If
you should learn of his death, you may open it yourself.
By all means keep it with the utmost care till you are
freed, or meet with Fred. Let no one know that you
have it, and keep it always about your person. Not
there, not there," she said, as she saw Toinette about
to put it in her bosom. "Do you think it would be
safe there if you should be put upon the block? Sew
it into the folds of your frock, and keep it as if your
salvation depended on it. Who knows but it does?"
she added, dreamily.

CHAPTER XXIII.

BOND GIVEN AND COSTS PAID.

IT was the eighth Monday after the first Monday in September, and was Court week in Perham.

Geoffrey Hunter, sitting in the easy-chair which his father had occupied so many years, heard through the open door of the office, about the hour of ten, the voice of the crier, as he proclaimed:

"Oyez, oyez, all you good people who have anything to do or to sue in this Honorable Superior Court of Law and Equity, this day begun and held for the County of Cold Spring, come forward and give your attendance and you shall be heard."

Looking up at the venerable structure which had so long served for the dispensation of justice, he saw the rotund face of the crier framed in a portion of the window-sash from which some mischievous urchin had broken the pane, beaming with good nature, self-importance, and the lurid effulgence resulting from immemorial potations of apple-jack, while his wheezing, broken tones went out in the bright October morning through the sleepy streets of the village. The knots of idlers heard it, and slowly wended their way to the court-house.

Geoffrey Hunter heard it, and, remembering the business which of late had so engrossed his attention, took from a drawer of the table two bonds, which had been previously executed, and followed the crowd to the place of justice.

Upon the first opportunity which presented itself, Geoffrey's counsel rose and called the attention of His Honor, the Presiding Judge of the Court, to the fact that at Spring Term, 1858, a petition had been filed by Manuel Hunter, praying for permission to emancipate a certain female slave, "Mabel." His Honor would find the necessary facts set forth in the petition. Due notice had been given by advertisement, as required by law, as appeared from the certificate of the publisher. Since that time, the petitioner having become "*non compos*," the guardian of his estate, who was also his son, desired to obtain leave of court to complete the act in which the petitioner had taken the initiatory steps before being stricken with disease. He was ready to give the necessary bond for the good behavior of the slave while in the State, and her removal therefrom within ninety days, as the statute required. The learned counsel admitted that the application to amend the proceedings by making the guardian a party was somewhat anomalous. He was not aware of any precedent directly in point. But as the proceedings had been begun before there was any suspicion of intellectual decline on the part of the owner, it seemed but just and proper that his charitable design toward a servant-woman of mature age and meritorious and faithful services should not be defeated by his misfortune.

His Honor, having duly considered the matter, felt constrained to deny the motion for leave to emancipate.

He regretted that what was apparently the will and purpose of so eminent a citizen as the petitioner should be defeated; especially, while he suffered under such terrible affliction, which he sincerely hoped would yet prove to be temporary in its character. Yet, in fact, it was this very affliction, and consequent mental disability of the Petitioner, which rendered it necessary for the Court to deny the prayer of the petition. The tendency of legislation and judicial decision was certainly adverse to the emancipation of slaves. The unfortunate agitation of the questions affecting our rights as citizens of the Southern States to hold and control our own property, by the Abolitionists of the North, had led to the imposition of restrictions hitherto unknown to our law. The course of these fanatics, instead of tending to ameliorate the condition or improve the chances of freedom to the slave, for whom they professed such unnecessary and undeserved sympathy, had an opposite effect, and he feared they were doing much to render this sacred relation of master and slave the evil thing they chose to represent it. He was sorry that restrictive legislation had gone so far, but, of course, retaliatory measures were but natural to a people who had been so foully defamed, oppressed and robbed. Recent events, in his opinion, presaged still further trouble. His Honor hoped if the North persisted in her insane attempt to force upon the South a President so obnoxious to her people as the low-down fanatical demagogue who was striving for the place, against the voice of the entire Southern people—for he was sure no Southern man would vote for such a creature—that they would be taught that brave men would not submit to such indignity.

Under these circumstances, and with these views, the court was of opinion that the guardian of the Petitioner could not be made a party, and the manumission perfected under this petition. Emancipation by devise was now forbidden. His Honor thought this was a case coming within the spirit and reason of that statute, if not within its terms ; and he did not think that emancipation was an act which the courts ought to encourage by a too liberal construction of the laws. Our domestic institutions would be in great danger unless protected by the courts.

In the case of Geoffrey petitioning in his own behalf for permission to free Toinette, no such ground, nor, indeed, any reasonable ground, could be urged to defeat the prayer of the Petitioner, and it was granted. Geoffrey immediately gave the bond required by law, paid the costs of the proceeding, and directed a copy of the record, duly certified, to be made out and furnished him.

That night he handed this copy of the record to Toinette, thereby sundering the claim his father's bill-of-sale had given him over this "likely chattel," and transforming the slave-girl into the freed-woman. The interest he had acquired in Toinette by sale in the market overt of Love was not so easily terminated. The reason of the failure of the application in behalf of Mabel was duly explained to that old worthy, who merely listened with an incredulous smile.

A week afterwards Geoffrey Hunter left Perham,

having the freed-woman Toinette in his charge, and was absent a month. When he returned he brought to old Mabel a letter from her daughter, dated at Oberlin, Ohio, and signed "Toinette."

CHAPTER XXIV.

A REVIEW.

A T the date of our last chapter the muttering thunders of approaching revolution were beginning to
be heard in the land. The old Whig Party had been
shattered by the loss of confidence in its leaders consequent upon their support of the Fugitive Slave Law,
and acquiescence in other measures of a similar nature,
distasteful to a large majority of its adherents. The
avowed Abolitionists, as they were called, of the North,
were comparatively few. Almost the entire mass of the
Northern people acquiesced in slavery; at the same time,
there was a latent animosity toward the institution which
existed all over the free States, and embraced, probably,
three-fourths of their voting strength. In theory, these
men agreed with "the fanatics," that slavery was a crime
and a wrong, both to the free citizen and the slave. In
practice, they held with the pro-slavery party, that with
slavery, in the States where it was already established,
the General Government could not interfere. They were
opposed to slavery, but they regarded the Constitution
and the precedents and practice under it, as legalizing
the institution in those States, and they believed these
States alone, had the power to abolish it. On the other
hand, too, it had come generally to be accepted that the
people of the North could not be compelled to aid in

supporting, defending, or propagating this institution.
The Fugitive Slave Law, and the course adopted by the
Government towards the new Territory of Kansas,
therefore, thrust upon the people of the North the most
unwelcome issues. The former made every freeman
the agent of the slavery propagandists, in its support
and protection; it imposed upon everyone the duties
of a special policeman and informer, to prevent the escape of slaves from a bondage which was believed to
be unholy and infamous, and made him the upholder
of a system which only his reverence for the Constitution had restrained him from destroying. The latter
was equally distasteful, as it thrust slavery, even by
fraud and violence, into territory which had been until
that day consecrate to freedom. It was the harpy claw
of slavery tearing and befouling our national domain.
From the moment the first of these measures received
the sanction of a Whig administration, that party was
doomed, and from that moment the passive Abolitionists
were mainly transformed into active ones—a vast majority of the North were willing and anxious to do all
that legitimately could be done to curb the aggressions
and destroy the power of slavery.

Hence, the Republican Party and its triumph in the
election of a President, with a majority of the members
of Congress, undoubtedly meant the repeal of all this
peculiarly odious legislation; and their zeal, in all probability, would have gone further, much further, in reac-
tionary legislation.

The South was right in the claim that the organi-
zation of the Republican Party, and the nomination of

Abraham Lincoln for the Presidency, as well as his subsequent election, meant hostility to slavery. It meant opposition by every legitimate means to the system which had long been a disgrace to our flag and an insult to every freeman of the nation. It was the protest of the people of the North against a great wrong which they had long merely tolerated, confessing its evil character but pleading their own inability to prevent. The leaders of the Party denied this, but the logic of human action affirmed it.

When the Presidential nominee declared, " I would to God that the foot of the slave did not rest upon American soil," not only the vast audience who listened to him applauded the sentiment and said "amen" in their hearts, but the great majority of the North re-echoed it. And when he added, "But, having been established and recognized by every branch of our Government, I do not see how the General Government can interfere with it in the States where it now exists," the heart of the free North again beat responsive to his words—a sorrowful assent. Politicians denied this fact, of which they were the creatures, and declared that the North did not *desire* the abolition of slavery— that they only wanted the Fugitive Slave Law repealed because it invaded their own sacred rights. Poor fools! they could not see how the index finger had moved on the dial of history since the mob of Boston struggled and hustled each other in her narrow lanes and alleys, raging in a hot ferment for the blood of Garrison and Thomson. They had forgotten that thirty and odd years had elapsed—thirty years of growth and fruit, of

patient inquiry and close observation—since every member of the United States Senate, under the lash and
spur of the imperial-minded Calhoun, vied with each
othe: in their adulation of slavery, and in denunciation
of the seditious fanatics who would destroy that patriarchal institution and turn the course of society from
the way ordained of God—winning thereby the applause
of the entire press, and the approbation of a large majority of ,he people.   They did not recognize the growing strength of the underlying feeling of Abolitionism—
the conviction of the unrighteousness of slavery.   They
did not perceive that the logic of a people wonderfully
prone to question and decide for themselves, had re-
jected the absurdity of the human-brute.

For eighteen hundred years Christianity has striven
to make comprehensible the problem of the God-man,
Christ Jesus.   Reason rejects the anomaly.   Religion
appeals to Faith and flies to the Holy of Holies, which
is veiled from vulgar view by the mystic formula, "I
believe."   Reason has no weapons to oppose to this
unseen and intangible foe.   She is stricken in the heel
and dies.   Resistance ceases, and the inquirer becomes
a convert.   No other subject can stand upon this van-
tage ground.   Reason is omnipotent except where Faith
is supreme.

So, when the touchstone of human reason was applied to the fabric of chattel slavery—property in human
beings—it fell.   The mind may accept the miracle of
the Holy-Child, but not the abomination of the human-
brute.   Thus the problem presented itself: Given the
form of man, the instincts and passions of man, the

reason and soul of man, the powers and attributes of man—what is the creature? And the unhesitating voice of reason answered—Man. And if man, what is his position, what his rights, privileges, and duties, his relations to his fellows and to God? And again reason answered in a triumphant tone, "Those of his fellow mortals, varying only in degree. Of him to whom little is given, little shall be required."

Slavery sought to hide its deformity with the veil of faith, and take refuge with religion in the sanctuary of simple belief. It would not do. Reason was jealous of her attributes, and religion fearful of too much companionship in her sacred seclusion. So reason and religion—in the main—struck hands in denying the claims of slavery.

Thus far had the people walked in the light. The politicians—still infused with the formularies of years of artful dodging of the momentous issue—denied this flank march which the people had made while they slept in darkness, even when the triumphant hosts came wheeling into line with shouts and banners, bearing onward to the seat of power the incarnation of their own idea, the enlightened conscience with the uncertain hand, the ready will groping for a possible way—Abraham Lincoln, the clear-eyed, giant-limbed child of the great North-west.

The South was not deceived. Their politicians read the mystic symbols, which the hands of groping millions thus unconsciously had traced, with surer ken than their brethren of the North. They saw that it was a portentous mustering of uncounted forces against their

Moloch. They only erred in supposing these legitimate and unavoidable consequences of their acts to be consciously and immediately intended by their promoters. At once they sounded the note of alarm and prepared to do battle for their idol—on the stump first, and in the field afterward, if need be—and among the foremost and most zealous of them all was Geoffrey Hunter. His quick and subtle mind caught the logic of these events with unerring certainty. Regarding slavery, as he did, as both legally and morally right, except in peculiar instances, he considered the course of parties at the North as an unjustifiable assault upon the constitutional rights of the Southern States.

WASHINGTON SQUARE—RICHMOND.

"*Around this regal city for four years was to rage the combat of which it was
itself the prize.*"

CHAPTER XXV.

REVEILLE.

WHEN Geoffrey reached Richmond on his return, he found that city and all the country beyond aflame with excitement. The chain had been severed which bound the States into one common nationality. South Carolina had seceded! Secession, war, Southern independence, *pro* and *con*, were the staples of conversation. As yet, it was not clear that the other States would go with the pioneer in revolution. Experienced politicians were of the opinion that they would not. The most influential journals were, as yet, uncommitted to the doctrine of rebellion. Only the newsboys, the train-haunters, and loungers about the depots spoke positively upon this point. They saw the tendency of feeling—they knew that nearly all they met either favored this movement or opposed it upon some paltry quibble that was not worth a moment's consideration. It was like stubble in the pathway of the devouring flame.

Through the first hot blast of the coming sirocco, Geoffrey Hunter came to his home. As the fierce breath of the desert storm scathes the lineaments and crisps the beard which feels its wrath, transforming youth into maturity and manhood into age in a few brief seconds, so in these few days did the storm of war bring out the stern, bold man which had slumbered beneath the soft exterior of Geoffrey Hunter.

He flung himself into the foremost rank, and with tongue and pen, incessantly and unweariedly, urged the appeal to arms. As the winter passed the war of ideas grew more fierce, and for a time the result seemed doubtful; but as the spring opened the obstacles were one by one removed, and before summer had assumed her throne a united South were ready to do battle for what they counted as sacred rights.

There were some few who thought the very show of force would be sufficient to secure their object. Geoffrey was not of this number. He knew that they had an enemy slow to anger and not given to bravado, unstinted in devotion to the views they entertained, fertile in expedients, unbounded in resource, and unyielding in purpose. He knew that the war, at all events, must be long and bloody, and the issue doubtful. His only hope was that by promptitude of movement the seat of government, with perhaps one of the great commercial centers of the Atlantic coast—the ganglia of trade— might be seized before the huge leviathan of the North could rouse himself to resist.

Acting upon this idea, he was one of the first to enlist. He was elected captain of the Cold Spring Greys, a company of young men every one of whom was worthy of a commission in any well-appointed army. They were the best scions of the best stocks in the country, the bravest sons of the first families. The young attorney, whose name alone — herited from an honored sire—was a power at the bar, stood side by side in the ranks with the gifted young politician who had risen, almost in a day, from the dim obscurity of the academic grove to places of honor and power. Wealth and learning, youth and patriotism, ambition and valor, were linked with every name which graced the roll of the Cold Spring Greys, with Geoffrey Hunter at their head.

It was strange how he came to outrank all his fellows at the very first. It was not because he had greater wealth—for money could not buy the suffrages of that gallant band—nor because he had any advantages in position—for prouder names and more successful men, in the ordinary affairs of life, stood among the undistinguished rank and file.

It was not even from any greater inherent capacity for military affairs, for more than one who now tipped the cap to him in deference, as a superior, rose afterwards to wear more stars and achieve a brighter renown. It was simply because Geoffrey Hunter was gravely and seriously in earnest. He expected war, rugged, harsh, red-handed, cruel, unrelenting war, and he was ready for it. He did not expect to achieve fame. He did not enlist to avoid political ruin, or to build up a mole from which to fight with advantage the wordy conflicts of the hustings, in the future. He had no ulterior motives. He did not go into the war because he was ashamed to stay at home, or afraid it would hurt his interests, to win applause or avoid ignominy. He went to fight,—and this earnestness showed in his words, looks, and acts. It gave his youth the dignity of age, and his inexperience the practical sagacity of the veteran. It aged him in a day. It impressed his fellows, and, without previous

personal popularity, he was from the first *facile princeps*
where it was an honor to be even the *socius.*

It was just as the spring was yielding her tender
beauty to the fierce ravishment of the fervid summer,
that this band of youthful patriots mustered in the
streets of Perham, *en route* to join the Army of Virginia. All was music and rejoicing. They went to
the battle with the joyous rites that are wont to attend the return of victors. But few thought of blood,
or suffering, or defeat. The enemy was a myth and a
jest, the war a pleasant picnic, and the "Godspeed"
they were receiving only an antetype of the "welcome
home," the soldiers might expect before the autumn
came and the crops were garnered. One saucy beauty
proffered her handkerchief—a dainty bit of lace and lin-
en—"to staunch all the blood the Yankees would dare
shed." Another, more given to the horribly grotesque,
besought her true-love to bring her back "the skull of
that old tyrant, Abe Lincoln, for a soap-gourd." Alas,
alas! how close of kin are laughter and tears!

And over all rose and fell the rollicking strains of
Dixie—Dixie, strange child of bondage and burlesque
—the refrain of the plantatio n negro, caught and linked
with livelier bars to suit the purpose of the simulated
African, in whose hands the guitar became a banjo,
and whose minstrelsy was a satire worthy of Cervantes;
Dixie, snatched from the slave and the mountebank
and sanctified and exalted by the passion of a whole
people; Dixie, the casket which the slave gave to the
master, in which to enshrine his holiest thought, the
strain which fired the Southern heart, the Grecian horse

which was brought within the citadel of slavery, and spawned a brood which broached the walls to the beleaguring fanatics.

Flowers, and garlands, and beauty, and laughter, all were there. The early roses, where the Southern sun paints every petal with a richness quite unknown in harsher climes; the jasmine, with its odor half concealing a lingering hint of the poisonous exhalations of its swampy home (was it prophetic of Chickahominy?); the feather-flower, with its white plumes drooping, as if speaking the stainless grief of the white-robed angels, with myriads of other fair hues and intoxicating odors, were woven into garlands, and wreaths, and crowns, and stars, by fair hands, inspired by loving hearts, and showered upon the anticipated victors.

Alas! alas! how quickly time changes the rose-leaf into mold!

CHAPTER XXVI.

BETTY CERTAIN had been for several months the possessor of Lovett Lodge, but she continued to live at the old Certain place, and still wore the linsey-woolsey gown and its coarse accompaniments. As she told Geoffrey, she had determined never to lay these aside again, having an almost superstitious belief that the renunciation of what she considered her appropriate habiliments would be the precursor of misfortune and sorrow. She had not yet removed to the Lodge, because she had been busy in attending to the necessary work of the plantation which was carried on by the new force she had hired for that purpose, under her own oversight. She had told Geoffrey, when he protested against this course upon her part, that she felt perfectly competent to take care of the plantation and manage it successfully, and added that she considered it her duty to so manage and economize as to put the estate in as good a condition as it was when left by Arthur Lovett, in order that his bequests might be carried out to the letter. She deemed herself merely a trustee to accomplish this purpose. She had an abiding faith that Belle Lovett and her other children would some day be found to receive their portion of the estate. She did not know what use

she would make of her own share; but she doubted
not in time to be able to devote it to as good a purpose as Arthur Lovett would have desired, and she
wished it to be capable of as much good as when he
designed to have placed it in her hands. So she gave
the most unwearying attention to every detail of the
farm management; corrected abuses and stopped waste,
which the too easy Geoffrey had allowed, and " pitched
a crop " of unusual acreage for that plantation. She
had also been busy at the Lodge, restoring everything
to the status it had borne when Arthur Lovett was
alive. The old furniture—or other as near like it as
could be obtained—had been set in the old places;
books, pictures etc., which Geoffrey had discarded or
rearranged, were put into their former positions, and
the whole premises restored " on the model of the an-
tique," as one might say. " *Arthur my King* " was the
constant refrain of her faithful heart, and she had procured and arranged everything that could remind her of
the days which she spent near him, as his prospective
wife. It had been a time of unexampled stir and industry both on the plantation and at the Lodge, and
everywhere the coarse heavy shoes and linsey gown of
Betty Certain were seen, and her firm voice and keen
eye directed all things. The neighboring planters
looked on in amazement, and said to one another that
Betty Certain was showing the same vigor and energy
that made her great-grandfather Ezra the right-hand of
the Earl upon his vast estates in the Carolinas. But the
preparations were finally completed, and to-morrow Betty Certain intended to leave her mother's cottage for

Lovett Lodge. She wondered, as she passed along the
wood-path toward her old home, if she would ever go
back to it again to live. Her head was bent forward,
and her hands were clasped loosely behind her as she
walked on with a heavy, deliberate stride, like a man
lost in thought. The sun had set, and the wood-path
was growing dark to unaccustomed eyes; but she kept
on with the confidence of familiarity, avoiding rocks,
roots and branches without thought of their existence.

She was not a lovely woman, and certainly not a
weak one. Fate had made her a strange compound.
Under different circumstances she might have graced
a throne and rivaled the proudest names in history.
She could do and dare without faltering; she could
suffer without complaining, and love without return.
There was one thing she had never yet done—forgive.
Was she capable of forgiving a great, an unforgotten
wrong? Her soul was above flattery, the lust of
wealth, or the desire of ease. Was it also above revenge? This night was to decide. The crucial test
was to be applied before the moon, now just rising,
should sink beneath the horizon. Step by step she
was approaching the crisis of her fate, but she knew
it not. She was dreaming of other days, and of the
varied circumstances under which she had passed
along that woodland path, to and from the Lodge.
First a careless girl, impelled by curiosity to see the
new comers; then an impassioned maiden, bounding to
the rescue of her unconscious lover; then upon his
arm in the moonlight; then as his affianced wife; then
an unwedded widow, in sorrow and darkness, under the

shadow of crime; and then her later migrations—always leaving the cabin in the sunshine, and coming back to it in the storm. She thought of her mother's sad predictions and their fulfillment, and she determined to go to the Lodge only as a temporary home, and to keep up the old Certain place as a harbor of refuge when the storm came—as she doubted not it would, though when or how she could not foresee. So she walked on, dreaming of the past, and wondering at the future. The moon, gleaming through an opening in the undergrowth, lighted up her form for an instant, showing her bowed and unbonneted head, with its dark hair gathered into a hard and shining knot behind.

A woman crouching behind the bole of a great oak, that stood beside the path a few yards in advance, saw her as she passed through this gleam of light, and her eyes brightened with a baleful glare. Then she listened eagerly for her steps as she came on through the darkness, and watched the dim outline of her figure as it approached nearer and nearer. The crouching form by the oak trembled with excitement. The fierce eyes flashed like gleaming coals, and the right-hand quivered with eagerness as it clutched a glittering blade. Slowly onward comes the unsuspecting victim. The figure in ambush begins to measure the distance and calculate its spring. The flexed limbs tremble for the signal of attack. Still it waits for the victim to take one more step.

Wake! Betty Certain! Wake from your dream! or the past and the future will be blended in oblivion. Stay your footsteps! Turn and fly! For once let Lovett

Lodge be a refuge from danger. Lift your eyes—the ghost, the terrible ghost—the murderer of Arthur—the mutilator of Toinette—is before you!

She knows it not. She is dreaming of the day when Arthur Lovett stood with her in her wild-wood bower and asked her to become his wife. She will go there to-morrow. She will look once more upon the scene of those plighted vows which she has kept so faithfully. Her foot is raised for the last step.

The limbs of the figure by the oak become rigid with expectancy. The right hand, clutching the knife, is swiftly raised! When Betty Certain's foot shall fall again in the pathway, the signal will thrill along the quivering nerves, the limbs will bound like loosened springs, the form will be launched upon her, the blow struck, and another chapter in the tragedy of Lovett Lodge will be at an end! But no, not yet. Ere the footfall comes to the waiting ear, ere the step is made, Betty Certain wakes from her dream, halts, and looks quickly up. The upraised dagger, passing through a shaft of moonlight, casts a brief reflection upon her dress. She sees it and starts back—awake, alert. Too late! She is still within reach of the crouching horror —the terrible mystery which goes hand in hand with death. With a cry of disappointment and rage, the figure rises and bounds upon her in the darkness. Instinctively she knows the presence that confronts her. The strong arms are raised to shield herself from the shock. She hears the cry, the rustle of garments in the gloom, and feels a sharp, prickling sting in the left shoulder. At the same time her right hand comes in

contact with a mass of flowing hair, and two fiercely
burning orbs confront her, glaring wildly in her face.
The nameless horror which for an instant paralyzed her
frame passes as rapidly away. She realizes that the
attack has been made and has failed of its purpose, for
the present at least. She knows that the murderer of
Arthur Lovett is before her, within her reach, grasping
for her throat in mad, wild haste; that the hairs which
fall over her hand and wrist are the gray locks of the
ghost and murderess. A wild joy seizes her. She
forgets that she is wounded. Now—Heaven help her!
—Arthur's death shall be avenged, and Toinette's suf-
erings expiated. Her usual confidence returns. She
does not doubt her power. The ghost of Lovett Lodge
shall be laid that night, and her own years of desolation shall be recompensed.

Her right hand closes fiercely upon the strong, thick
locks and she springs backward with a sudden jerk. The
grasp, which the murderess had fixed upon her throat
is broken, though it strips the strong linsey dress from
her breast and tears it to the waist. She feels a deadly
faintness as the dagger is wrenched from her shoulder,
partly by her own movement and partly by the act of
her assailant. For an instant all is dark and her brain
reels. Then she feels the murderess trying to free
herself from her clutch to repeat the blow.

Fear, and love, and revenge, waken in her breast
a wild medley of emotion. The instinct of self-preserv-
ation surmounts natural weakness and her wound is
forgotten.

She perceived at once the advantage which her

M

accidental clutch in the hair of the murderess gave her,
and with a half-shriek, half-laugh of instinctive joy, she
gave another backward leap, and brought her antagonist to her knees.   Her enemy was evidently a power
ful woman, and made frequent attempts to regain her
position and renew the attack.   But Betty Certain
was not only brave but desperate.   She was strong,
too, despite the surprise of the attack and the wound
she had received.   Back—back—along the flinty path
with a wild energy she dragged the prostrate woman
like a tiger bearing off its prey, never giving her time
to recover, twisting her hand in the long hair and
chuckling with an insane delight.   She saw her advantage and her heart throbbed with the wild joy of
gratified revenge.   She forgot her wound.   She thought
not of danger.   The assassin of Arthur was in her power!
What were her groans to Betty Certain?   Music—rare
music.   Bruise her? beat her? kill her? aye, torture
her she would!   Die?   She should die the most painful
death she could devise!   Had she not killed her idol?
She would drag her along the path which he had trod,
till every spot his foot had touched was bathed in blood.
Her victim clutched at roots and bushes, and clung to
them with desperate strength.   She gathered with her
left hand still more of the thick, strong hair, twisted
it about her hand again and again, and pulled with a
giant's strength to break her hold.   Then she thought
of her heavy plantation shoes, and kicked her in the
face—not deftly and easily as a man would have done,
but awkwardly, yet hitting hard and strong again and
again—thinking every blow of Arthur and his death.

Still the woman kept her hold for a time. Then she suddenly loosed one hand and snatched wildly at Betty Certain's foot. She missed it, but caught the strong linsey dress. Then she let go her hold upon the root and tried to rise. If she should get upon her feet the issue would still be doubtful. Arthur's murderess might yet escape. Betty Certain tried to tear away from her. The woman's grip was a desperate one and the tough homespun would not yield. She had grasped it now with both hands. She would soon be on her feet. Betty Certain still clutched the hair—now close to her antagonist's head. Suddenly she thrust her hands downward, falling forward herself, casting her whole weight on the neck of her enemy. The woman sank beneath her, crushed down upon the flinty path. The woman's face was turned from her, the right side of her head pressed upon the ground. Betty Certain put one knee upon her shoulder and held her powerless.

She could hold her thus, but how long? That was the question. The frenzy which had possessed her for a time had somewhat abated. She felt the pain of her wound now, and a desire to know its location and character. Once or twice a sort of faintness stole over her, but by dint of a strong effort of will she repelled it. The strange woman had never ceased to struggle. Even now she was searching with her left hand, which was still free, for something in the pathway. Her breath came hard and thick, and she sometimes groaned when her struggles proved futile, but said not a word—neither did Betty Certain. With the latter, however, it was becoming a question of importance, how long she would be able to maintain her present advantage. Uninjured, she would have been more than a match for her opponent, though the latter was a woman of great activity and with a litheness of build well calculated for endurance. The faintness which she had experienced, as well as the almost total uselessness of her left arm, warned her that should she lose her present advantage, the odds would be decidedly in favor of her antagonist. How should she maintain it with her failing strength? Betty Certain pondered the question anxiously.

She did not think of her own safety so much as the escape of Arthur's assassin. Even if she should retain her position until day, there was little chance of any one coming to her aid in that lonely wood-path. The servants at the Lodge would think her in the field, and those in the field would suppose her to be at the house, and none would be within reach of her voice. To remain in her present position until chance brought relief seemed to her, after long consideration, simply impossible. What, then, should she do? There were but two alternatives. She must either kill or disable the enemy. How could this be done? It was a difficult question, on account of the faintness likely to arise from the use of her wounded arm. Suddenly she saw something glittering in the path. The moon, now risen higher, glanced bright through the clustering branches in uncertain patches of light. In one of these, within easy reach, was something glistening strangely. At first she could not make it out. At length she knew. It was a jewel in the hilt of the dagger with which she had been struck, and to which her assailant had desperately held until compelled to release it and grasp the root, to save herself from being dragged along the path. It was this which the woman was even now groping blindly for, among the stones, with her left hand. It was just outside the circle she so carefully explored. She held her victim yet closer, and with her lamed arm reached over and seized the weapon. The woman made a fearful effort to throw her off as she did so, but in vain. Betty Certain held the dagger up in a streak of moonlight, and examined it narrowly. It was the very one with which Toinette had been wounded. Her heart throbbed with joy as she made the discovery. The woman groaned as she saw the weapon, and ceased her struggles.

"It's no use, Betty Certain," she said; "you've got the advantage of me now, and can kill me as soon as you choose. I don't blame you. I meant to have killed you. I hev stood in yer way more than once. Yer ain't Arthur Lovett's wife, an I've worn the wedding clothes you had no use for. I'm much obliged for them," she added, mockingly.

Betty Certain's frame shook with revengeful emotion. She should die—this mocking fiend—die by her hand; and she raised the dagger, then another thought seemed to strike her. She placed her right knee upon the woman's neck, and loosed the clutch she had kept in her hair. Then, taking the dagger in her right hand, she directed her to place her hands behind her back.

"Do you want to torture me?" cried the woman. "Do you want to see me hung? Kill me now!" And she stubbornly refused to move. Betty Certain pricked her here and there with the sharp dagger-point until the woman cringed and groaned, but still refused. Again and again, with deliberate coolness, Betty Certain mutilated the prostrate form to compel obedience. Human nature could finally bear no more, and the unhappy creature yielded, and crossed her hands upon her back. Then Betty Certain loosened the strong linen apron which she wore, and with the knife shred it into strips. Taking the knife in her teeth she leaned forward and bound the woman's hands tightly. Then she tied several of the shreds together, making a rope a few feet long, and attached it to them. Then she rose, holding the end of this extemporized rope, and stood over her prostrate victim. Her breast heaved with excitement; her teeth were set and her eyes flashed. All the memories of the years of blighted hope, the thought of her dead love—the happiness that might have been but for this woman at her feet, surged through her mind at once. The moonlight came through the trees, and lighted up the prostrate form. Betty Certain stooped and examined the dress narrowly. It was part of her own wedding trousseau—the grey traveling-dress which she had fancied, and in regard to which Arthur had rallied her the last time she had heard his voice. Her excitement, before intense, was increased ten-fold by this discovery; her eyes were bloodshot, her face twitched, and her voice was hoarse and trembled with anger and revenge as she rose. The woman had not moved or spoken since she was bound. Betty Certain shook the dagger yet red with her own blood above

her, and it seemed, for an instant, that the last scene in
the drama of Lovett Lodge was about to be enacted.
Then she restrained herself, and said, hoarsely, "Get
up!" The woman did not move or answer. "Get
up!" repeated Betty, spurning her fiercely with her foot.

The woman groaned, and said, "Kill me, Betty Certain, kill me! I would have killed you, but did not
mean to torture you! I did not torture *him*."

This allusion to Arthur was too much for Betty Certain. She became furious with rage.

"*Get up! get up!*" she cried, and she kicked and
stamped her victim with unbridled fury. The demon
of revenge had taken possession of her soul. She would
gladly have trodden the flesh from her enemy's bones.
The groans gave her a wild delight, and the poor
wretch's shrieking, "I will! I will!" had been several
times repeated before she desisted from her attacks so
as to allow her to comply. Even then she would not,
but her mind had formed a plan of revenge beside
which death by violence would be as nothing. She
would have a revenge commensurate with her suffering,
and her long waiting; as signal as her loss and injury
by this woman's act had been.

The woman rose to a sitting posture. Betty Certain took her by the hair, assisted her to her feet, and
bade her go forward along the path toward the old
Certain place. She obeyed, moving with difficulty.
When they reached the house, Betty Certain lighted a
tallow candle and surveyed her captive closely. Her
face was disfigured with cuts and bruises. From her
mouth and nose the blood was still flowing, and her

dress and long grey hair were dabbled with its stains.
Her eyes were swollen and bloodshot, but still burned
with a look of sullen disappointment. She seemed not
to notice the scrutiny to which she was submitted; but
her countenance lighted up with a gleam of satisfaction
despite its ghastliness, when she saw the look of pain
that came over the face of Betty Certain as she glanced
at the dress in which she had hoped to be habited
as a bride, so many long years ago. She put out her
hands and felt it softly, lovingly. Looking up, she
caught the gaze of the murderess fastened upon her,
as if rejoicing in her pain. The tenderness faded from
Betty Certain's countenance in an instant, and was succeeded by a look of stern determination. She made
her victim sit down upon a chair, and passed the rope
which bound her hands under the chair and tied it about
her feet. She then took down from a peg in the corner
of the room a coil of small rope which had been sometime used for plow-lines. Having undone it, she put
the knotted end beneath her foot and tried its strength.
She seemed satisfied with the result, and proceeded to
tie one end firmly around the crossed hands of her
captive. The other she fastened to a wooden peg in
the wall behind her. Then she poured water in the
tin basin beside the door and washed her own face and
hands, bound up her hair which had become loose in
the struggle, and washed and roughly bandaged her
wound. It was, she found, in her arm, just at the
shoulder, missing the joint a little and glancing off
backwards. It bled freely, but she judged that it would
not prove serious. The woman asked for water, and

she took her the gourd and held it to her lips while she drank. She did not speak to her. She sought about the house and gathered up some pieces of fat pine, which she split with the axe and made into a small bundle, and placed a bunch of matches in her pocket. She undid the cloth rope from her victim's ankles, and taking the end of the plow-line from the peg where she had fastened it, she made a half-hitch about the woman's neck and led her with it like a halter. Then, taking the torch in one hand, said, "Come!" The woman rose, and was led out of the door and along the path to the spring.

She walked rapidly and dragged the woman roughly after her. When she came opposite the bower which she had visited with Arthur Lovett years ago, she still kept along the bank till she came to an angle of the rocky ledge upon its crest. Upon the slope of the hill here, where it turned to the southward, the woods were more open, and a number of huge rocks, whose summits were almost on a level with the surrounding oaks, stood like a group of grizzled sentinels. In shape they were not far different from the hay-stacks of the country, and, standing but a few feet apart, were certainly suggestive of the crowded stack-yard of a thrifty farmer. From this analogy they were named and known, throughout the country round, as "the Stack Rocks." Here had been a famous deer-stand in the days of Betty Certain's father, whose old Queen's Arm had dropped many an antlered buck and sleek-coated doe, as they came dashing round the hill toward the thickets that grew along the branch below. Even at this day the patient stalker sometimes gets a shot at the same noble game when the Stack Rock drive is made.

Among these giant rocks Betty Certain threaded her way with the easy familiarity of one whose feet are following a path they learned in childhood.

She stopped before the entrance of a sort of cave, held her torch under an overhanging rock for a moment, and bade her prisoner look upward. A small patch of sky was visible between the tree-tops, with the moon, now at the zenith, and a few stars. The woman complied.

"Take a good look," said Betty Certain, "you will never see the like again."

The woman did not seem surprised, but looked again and then turned towards her leader. The latter motioned with the torch towards the mouth of the cave and told her to go in. The woman stooped and entered. Betty Certain followed, holding the rope. After a few steps the cave widened into a sort of room. There seemed to be no opening beyond. The woman stopped. On the side opposite the entrance were several rocks, on the top of which stood one which seemed to overhang its base in every direction. Betty Certain stepped forward, and, laying her torch upon one of the rocks on which this one rested, placed her hand against it, and, with little exertion, rocked it to and fro on its pedestal.

"You see," she said, "how easily it may be overturned." The woman shuddered and closed her eyes, as if she saw herself crushed and mangled by its fall.

Betty Certain laughed—a low, chuckling, cruel laugh
—and said:

"But I do not mean to push it over on you." The
woman looked up in surprise. Betty Certain laughed
again, and her victim shuddered at the sound.

"I never thought when, a little girl, I found this
cave and made it my playhouse, that it would serve me
for such a purpose. Come!" she added, in a sneering
tone, "I have not shown you all its attractions."

She seized the torch and led the woman round the
pile of rocks. Just behind it was an opening low and
narrow. One must stoop to enter. Betty Certain motioned her prisoner toward it, and said sternly:

"Go in."

The woman hesitated. Betty Certain stuck the
flaming lightwood in a crevice of the rock, and said,

"Well, if I must drag you in by the hair, as I did
along the path, I can do it," and she moved toward
her victim as if to tie her limbs. The woman stooped
and entered the aperture with a moan. Betty took
the torch and followed. The opening grew smaller,
and they were compelled to go upon their knees.
After a short distance, it expanded again, and they
came out into another room. The air seemed thick
and heavy, and thousands of bats took wing and
flew about in the yellow murky light which the torch
made in the cavern gloom. The apartment was not a
large one—not more than ten steps across. Betty Certain led her victim around it without a word. Its walls
were rough rocks, with here and there a cleft, which
showed the white hard clay or metamorphic gravel

of the hill substrata. It was evidently not one of those crevices which time and torrents cut out of the limestone of some sections; but a subterranean fissure, which had been formed by the primitive rocks having become wedged together in the last act of some great natural drama, in the early days of the world's history. Granite with veins of quartz constituted the walls and ceiling. Near the middle of the apartment was a slender shaft of granite, rising some seven or eight feet and then abruptly terminating, like a broken pillar at a dead hero's grave. Betty Certain, having finished the circuit of the cave, led the woman to this pillar and bade her sit down upon a stone, some ten or twelve inches high, which lay against it. When this was done, she passed the cord she held around her left arm, above the elbow, carried it round the rock, and after fastening it about the other, drew them tightly back and tied the rope securely; so that the woman sat against the rock with her hands fastened together behind it.

CHAPTER XXVII.

THE EXECUTRIX.

BETTY CERTAIN sat down upon a fragment of rock in front of her victim, and held the torch close to the woman's terror-stricken face. There was a strange leer upon her own, as she said:

"You will be perfectly safe here, and folks outside will be safe, too."

"What are you going to do?" asked the woman.

"Do? Nothing. Only when I go out from here I shall push over that rock which you saw before the entrance."

"And bury me alive?" the woman said with a shudder.

There was no reply.

"I cannot blame you, Betty Certain," she continued, "but it is a terrible revenge you are taking. I have done you great wrong, it is true, and would have done more. I don't ask for any mercy, but if you would grant me one request—just one—you may do what you like with me then. It is not for me so much as for another—for Toinette."

"Toinette!" said Betty. "Toinette! You tried to kill her once. Do you wish me to do it for you?"

"Do not mock me, Betty Certain," said the captive woman. "What I wish you to do is to take a package, which hangs round my neck by a gold chain, and forward it to Toinette. It contains papers of the utmost importance to her."

Betty Certain seemed incredulous.

"How do you come to have papers of importance to Toinette? Who are you? How can I believe you? Did you not try to murder her? What interest have you in her?"

"I am her mother," said the woman.

"*You her mother?*" said Betty Certain, peering suspiciously at her in the dull murkiness of the cavern. "Why, then, did you seek to kill her?"

"To save her from a worse fate," answered the woman calmly. "Had she been *your* child, would you have rather seen her dead or polluted?"

"True, too true," said Betty. "I had never thought of that. You, then, are Manuel Hunter's cook—old Mabel?" she inquired, eyeing her keenly.

"I am Arthur Lovett's freedwoman, Belle Lovett," answered the woman sharply.

"What? What did you say? Belle Lovett? Did you say your name was. Belle Lovett?" said Betty Certain in a confused, uncertain manner, which showed how completely she was overwhelmed with astonishment. Somehow she did not think of doubting the woman's declaration. There was something so consistent with all that was known of the tragedy of Lovett Lodge and explained so much that had been mysterious in it, that she could but recognize its truth.

"That is my name," said the woman.

"And yet you killed him—killed Arthur Lovett—

killed the man who loved you better than his own soul.
Why, why, did you do it?"

"Because he was about to marry you. Because he
bartered off my children, and myself, when I had been
more than wife to him, for gold to satisfy his sisters—
cruel, heartless women—and to buy gay frocks for
a poor white woman who had coaxed him to agree to
marry her. Why did I kill him? Because he was
blacker than hell with lies which he had told me!"
answered the woman fiercely.

"Poor woman! *Poor thing!*" said Betty Certain.
"You little know what love he had for you. At the
very moment when he died by your hand, his will, just
written, gave you and your children one-half of his
estate. You were jealous of me. You did not know
that almost his sole reason in offering marriage to me
was to secure some one who would fulfill his wishes in
regard to you and your children in the event of his
death."

"Is that true?" asked the woman eagerly. "Did
he tell you this?"

"It was our only courtship," said Betty sternly. "He
never uttered a word of love to me. But I loved him
better than you. I would have given up all to you had
he thought it a duty. At this very time I was preparing to seek you out to give you liberty, and with it your
share of the estate. And now I find you stained
with his blood Oh God!—It cannot be! You are
not Belle Lovett! What proofs have you? Give me
proof."

"Alas!" said the woman, "but for Toinette I would

not care to produce them. They are in the packet in my bosom. Take them and examine them."

Betty Certain put her hand under the woman's dress with a shudder. She found the packet, broke the chain with a hasty jerk, and drew it forth. It was like one which was found in the drawer with the will of Arthur Lovett, and she mentioned this fact.

"Yes," replied the woman, "there were two exactly alike. My likeness was in that one, and you will find his portrait in this."

Betty Certain sat gazing at the packet she held for some moments in silence. The harsh expression of gratified revenge which her face had worn was lost, and one of painful surprise and perplexity succeeded to it. That the murderess of Arthur Lovett should be the woman whose very name and life was sanctified to her by his love, and whom she had promised, again and again, to act towards as he would have desired she should, was a startling thought.

"I will come back," she said finally, as she took the remains of the torch, knocking off the charred end, and passed quickly out through the passage by which they had entered. Her victim gazed after her with a dull, vacant stare.

Betty Certain passed rapidly along the path they had come until she reached the cottage. She lighted a candle, placed it upon the deal table, and proceeded at once to the perusal of the papers contained in the packet she had taken from the neck of Belle Lovett. It was no easy matter to decipher them, for they had grown dim with age, and the rough usage to which

they had been exposed. Betty Certain had none of
the skill in deciphering written instruments which comes
from frequent exercise. She but rarely had occasion
to read any written document, and was unfamiliar with
the various styles of different hands. After unfolding
the closely compressed papers, she found, and, with
much labor managed to decipher, the original·deed of
manumission given to Belle by the old man, Peter
Lovett, in New York. It had the certificate of probate
and registration upon it, and she did not doubt its
genuineness. There were also several letters addressed
to Belle Lovett, all of them unquestionably in the handwriting of Arthur.

Betty Certain plodded through them carefully.

The past was now an open book to her, and she
asked herself what was her duty. What would Arthur
Lovett have desired her to do under like circumstances? She took up the packet and drew from it
the golden locket which this strange woman in the
cave yonder had worn so many years. That woman—
what should she call her? Slave? Mistress? Murderess? At least, and by whatever name, the Fate of
Arthur Lovett, linked to him by the tenderest ties.
Betty Certain recognizes that, as regards Arthur Lovett,
she is but secondary to this strange compound now
bound down in the cave. She must ask herself, if she
would faithfully perform the trust which the dead had
imposed on her, not how ought Betty Certain to feel
towards Belle Lovett, and what should Betty Certain's
conduct be toward her, but what ought Arthur Lovett,
or one representing solely *his* interest and duty, to do

17

under these circumstances? It was as the executrix, nay more, as the trustee, the representative of his inmost thoughts and wishes, that she must now act.

What had the woman done? She had taken the life of Arthur Lovett! Why? Under a mistaken, though reasonable, misconception of his views in regard to herself. How came she to consider that question at all? What gave her the right to say to Arthur Lovett, " What are you going to do with me and my children?" Could Arthur Lovett blame this woman whose life had been a series of blighted hopes and priceless sacrifices on his behalf? Could he blame her if, when she found herself for the third time a slave, and saw him quietly contemplating marriage with another, she lost faith in his promises? Betty Certain considered the question fairly, and concluded that Arthur Lovett, looking down from the rest which had succeeded his unquiet life, could not but say that the act of this woman was by no means without excuse, and she had no doubt that he would wish her to receive no punishment therefor. So, that was settled. As Arthur Lovett's representative she could not injure this woman in any manner, for the act which was uppermost in her mind.

What else had she done? She had tried to kill Toinette. Toinette was her daughter, and exposed to the very danger which had filled her own life with trouble and anguish, and which had since then actually overtaken the daughter. A Roman father had been made immortal for slaying his daughter to save her from a like fate. She could not be blamed for that. Betty

Certain even felt a sort of womanly pride in the act
herself, now that she knew its motive.

What else? She had attempted to murder her—
Betty Certain. The act was dastardly, revengeful, and
without excuse. Was she called upon to forgive that?
The lines about her mouth set clear and sharp as she
considered this question. It was evident that she did
not desire to answer in the affirmative. But, with her
old habit, she asked herself, "What would Arthur wish
me to do?" And then she thought of the woman herself, harassed and inflamed by a life of untold misery,
crowded, as it seemed, with incurable evils. And as
she sighed, "Poor thing!" the victory was complete.
Betty Certain had forgiven her bitterest enemy. She
could bid defiance to revenge. The crown, which so
many years of suffering had wrought for her, was placed
by angel hands upon her brow just as the dawn cast
its first rosy gleams through the eastern window. She
shut the door carefully and cast herself on her knees
by the bedside. Sobs and groans shook her form and
attested her utter prostration of spirit.

The "poor-white" woman, who had been a murderer in heart that night, returned fervent thanks to
the kind Providence which had saved her from the
commission of crime. She recognized the Merciful
Hand which had built up an impassable barrier between her and the temptation by which she was beset.
The mystery of the past was made plain to her in
that hour, and she sought for faith and wisdom to
guide her in the future.

At length she rose, and wiping away her tears,

bathed her face and sat down by the fire she had kindled some hours before. There was a new light, a peaceful radiance on her plain, strong face that spoke of a spirit which had come out of temptation, purified and strengthened by its fiery blast.

She lifted the locket, and was about to press the spring and gaze upon the features. She hesitated; no, she would not do it. It belonged to that woman in the cave yonder. It was her secret. The receptacle of her joys and sorrows, her kisses and tears. It was that woman's shrine. She would not mar its sanctity.

Betty Certain was not a woman to do things by halves. She wrapped up the locket and papers, and put them in a drawer of the old bureau. Then, gathering another handful of pine splinters, she started again for the cave. She walked briskly, almost gaily, like one who goes to a pleasant task. When she reached it, she lighted the pine torch and went in. The woman looked at her with a haggard but hopeless gaze. Betty Certain cut the cords which bound her arms. The woman looked up, as if she wondered what new torture awaited her.

"Come," said Betty Certain, and she motioned toward the entrance.

A terrible fear seemed to take possession of the woman's mind.

"Do n't!" she cried; "do n't, Betty Certain—kill me here! Let me stay here and starve; bury me alive; beat me, torture me, do what you will with me—I won't blame you—only do n't give me up to be hung for murder! No, no; I 'll bless you. Perhaps my Toinie 's right anyhow, and you are the good woman she thinks you. If you are, do n't give me up to be made a spectacle of by a brutal crowd. You are a woman—spare me. You know I am counted only a nigger, but I am human and have some claims on your mercy. If I did kill Arthur Lovett, just think of the life I 've led. And oh, Miss Betty, if you ever loved him, think that he once loved me, and spare me, and Toinette, his child, from the degradation of a public death, for his sake. Please, Miss Betty, please!"

The woman had thrown herself on the ground at Betty's feet as she made this appeal, and it was with difficulty that the latter could stop the torrent of words she poured forth. At length she said:

"I have no intention of giving you up to anyone. I want you to go to the house. I cannot talk with you here."

"Is there no one waiting for me?" asked the trembling prisoner.

"I have neither seen nor spoken to anyone but you since sundown last night."

The woman followed her out and went with her to the house. Arriving there, Betty Certain at once provided for removing all traces of the night's rencontre from the person and clothing of the woman. Her face was washed, and its cuts and bruises poulticed. The dress which she wore was exchanged for one of her own linsey gowns, and then setting a cup of warm coffee with some biscuits before the strange guest, Betty Certain addressed her thus:

"I have read the papers you gave me and have de-

cided that it is my duty to act towards you strictly as
Arthur Lovett would desire were he present.

"Your great crime was against him, and was the
outgrowth of a relation more sinful upon his part than
upon yours. I am confident that he would desire me
on his behalf to overlook this act, and if I cannot
forgive that stroke which has shrouded my life in
sorrow, at least to take no step looking to its punishment. No one but myself knows or suspects your
connection with that act. Your other crimes having
been merely attempts, I do not consider it incumbent
on me to disclose.

"You are, therefore, safe; but it is necessary that we
should have some further conversation, in order that I
may exactly determine upon my duty towards you, as
the executrix of Arthur Lovett. We are neither of us
in a condition to consider that matter now. You can
stay here, entirely undisturbed, to-day. You will find
all that you wish in the cupboard, and your papers are
in this drawer. You can lock the door if you desire. I
must go to the Lodge, lest my absence arouse inquiry.
I will come to see you at sundown. Rest as much as
you can, for we have much to think of and decide
upon."

Betty Certain went to the Lodge, and faithfully observed the directions she had given to the woman she
had left in her cottage. She sought simply rest and
recuperation. It was a matter of surprise among the
house servants that Miss Betty found time that day to
sleep. The affairs of the plantation were left for once
to take care of themselves.

As the sun went down she set out for the old cottage. Arriving there she found the door closed, but not locked, and, on entering, she found it empty. The fire was still burning on the hearth, and there were evident indications that the woman had prepared a meal during the evening. Betty concluded that she had become suspicious of a design upon her part to betray her to the authorities, and was in hiding somewhere in sight of the house at that instant, and would probably come in when she found her suspicions unfounded. In this surmise she was correct· and, after sitting by the hearth a few moments, she heard footsteps carefully approaching the house.

"Come in," she said, in a loud tone; "if I had intended to do you an injury you would not have seen the sunshine to-day."

The woman came in very much abashed at the baseless suspicion she had displayed. Betty motioned to a chair opposite, and she sat down in silence. The two women scanned each other narrowly a long time before either spoke.

CHAPTER XXVIII.

HAGAR.

AFTER a time Betty Certain spoke. It cost her an effort to master her repugnance to the blood-stained woman before her; but she conceived it a part of her duty to inform her of all that could affect her interests or those of her children. So she said:

" I have brought with me all the papers in my possession referring to Arthur Lovett and his estate which may concern you."

She took a bundle from her pocket and read—one after another—the will of Arthur Lovett, the letters of Manuel Hunter, and a copy of the record in the case in which Bella and her children had been declared the property of the estate of Peter Lovett. Then she told her all that had been done in the matter since Arthur's death, so far as she knew it.

Then she handed to Bella the packet found in the drawer of Arthur Lovett's desk by Manuel Hunter. The woman had been sitting upon a chair in front of Betty Certain, but as the latter read, she bowed her head lower and lower, until she finally slid from the chair to the floor, and was now lying with her head bowed upon her knees at the feet of Betty Certain, her form convulsed with sobs and groans.

It was with difficulty that she could be induced to

take the packet which was offered her. She shrank
away from it, protesting that she was not worthy to take
anything which Arthur Lovett's hand had touched.

Betty Certain was angry at what she deemed the
woman's hypocrisy.

"But he was not too good for you to kill!" she said
sharply.

"I would have died before I would have harmed
him, if I had known all this," said the woman flushing
up; "and I ought to have known it, too, for he had
never deceived me—*never*. It was just my own wickedness—all my own. Why did n't you kill me, Betty Certain, and not let me live to know all this? It would
have been mercy. Nothing could be worse than what
I suffer now—*nothing!* No, I 'm not taking on. What
did I do it for? Well, I 'll tell you, Betty Certain.
You sha' n't have a worse opinion of me than I deserve,
an' that 's bad enough. It 's no use now. All the
harm 's done I could ever do; but I 'd like to tell you
how it all happened. Besides, I want to show you just
where and how I 've lived, so that my children may
have the benefit of that will you 've just read. I was
bought for one of Arthur Lovett's sisters when only a
chit of a girl. She saw me when they were going
through Richmond taking her to school, an' took a
fancy to me, an' nothing would do but she must have
me to wait on her. I was, perhaps, fourteen, and she
a year or two older. Her father paid a round price for
me, you may be sure, for I was counted a fancy article.

"Miss Nannie was n't the brightest of gals, nor the
most studious. In order to spur her up to greater effort,

N

the teacher would frequently say that 'Belle could get
such lessons without trouble;' that 'Belle would excel
her, if she had a chance,' and all such talk. I heard this,
and, being naturally proud and ambitious, I got the
stupid girl to teach me what she knew, and very soon
was leading her in her own studies. Instead of being
angry or ashamed at being thus outstripped, Miss Nannie was gratified at the fact of being spared some of the
labor of study by my ability to assist her. It became
one of my tasks to learn and repeat her lessons to her
until she partly understood them. She used to boast
of me among her companions as her 'pony,' and I was
frequently called upon to show off my acquirements
before a few of her particular cronies, and was sometimes subjected to punishment for failing to make her
understand my explanations. I had my revenge by refusing to assist her at all, and threatening to disclose
her conduct, in teaching me what I had learned. This
threat was sufficient, and, in the main, I had a very
agreeable time with my young mistress at the school.
When she finally graduated and went back to the plantation, after three years, the slave was far better educated than the mistress, and I was treated by her more
like an equal than a servant.

"I was petted, proud, and vain. I did not know
what slavery was. I knew that I belonged to my
mistress, and that she could sell me if she would—or
her father, for I did not even know who owned me; but
I did not dream that I could ever be anything but a
petted servant. I had the run of the old house at
Heptwilde. My sojourn at the school had given me a

love for books, and the library was a mine of joy to me. Here, buried in a great arm-chair, made of broom-straw by some ingenious plantation hand, I used to spend hours at a time. My young mistress, jealous of her rights, would not allow any one else to claim my services, and ' Miss Belle,' as the other servants called me, was never required to do more than attend to her wants. When my light tasks were over, I was sure to find my way to the library. The members of the family who were at home were not much given to reading, and I was nearly sure to be undisturbed in the dusty, cobwebbed old room. I learned that the books themselves had been mainly the property of an old bachelor uncle of my mistress, who had died years before and had left his library to his nephew and namesake, Arthur Lovett, who was then at college.

"And here one morning, sitting in that old arm-chair, Arthur Lovett came upon me. I had on one of my mistress's dresses which she had given me, and was reading a volume of poems—Byron's—I remember. He came and rested his arms upon the back of the chair, and said, in a quizzing tone:

"'Is that the literature they read at Belleville?'— which was the name of the school my young mistress had attended.

"I started up in confusion and tried to utter some excuse, but could not.

"'I beg pardon,' he said, as soon as he saw my face, 'I thought you were my sister Nannie, whom I have not seen since my return. Excuse my rudeness, and allow me to present myself—Mr. Arthur Lovett, at your service. I was not aware that any young lady was staying with my sister.'

"'I am not a young lady,' I managed to say.

"'Not a young lady!' he rejoined, with an amused smile. 'Then, pray, what are you?'

"He evidently took me in my fright and embarrassment for some overgrown child, who had only self-possession enough to deny young ladyhood. The reflection piqued my pride, for I had not unfrequently compared myself with my mistress and her companions, both in appearance and demeanor, and arrived at conclusions by no means flattering to *them.*

"I answered humbly enough, however, 'I am Miss Nannie's girl Belle, if you please, sir.'

"'What!' he exclaimed, 'you my sister's maid? You a—a—a slave?'

"I answered, 'Yes, sir,' and for the first time in my life I felt the degradation of my position.

"He gazed at me awhile in silence, and then asked:

"'And do you read Byron, my girl?'

"I answered quickly that my mistress had allowed me to learn to read at school, but she knew nothing of my coming to the library.

"'Well,' he said good-naturedly, 'you shall pay for trespassing on my dominions by reading to me till I see fit to dismiss you. Sit down,' said he, motioning to the old arm-chair while he took another, 'make your own selection and go on. I may be allowed to smoke, I suppose?' he added, as he lighted a cigar.

"There was not much in it. I had served a simpleton for years, and had been the creature of another's

whims and caprices all my life. I do n't know why,
but I had never felt what it was to be a *slave* till
that moment. I had never been so debased before.

"'Well, girl,' said my new master, 'begin, or I shall
think you were just shamming.'

"My blood boiled. I know my face must have
flushed. I would let him see that I was not a fool if I
was a nigger. I would read, as his own sister could
not. I opened to 'Mazeppa,' and read its marvelous
measures until hearer, library, servitude, and life were
all forgotten, and I was the impassioned but helpless
burden of the wild horse, borne 'away! away!' to
love and empire in the wilderness.

"I finished the poem before I stopped. Then I
looked up and blushed, for I had forgotten his presence
and had been reading to myself. His cigar had gone
out and he was holding it absently in his fingers.

"For a while he was silent, then he said:

"'And you say you are my sister's maid?'

"'Yes, sir.'

"'And your name is Bella?'

"'Yes, sir.'

"Somehow I could not say 'Marse Arthur' to him,
though I tried all I knew to do it, then and afterwards.

"'Well, Bella, you are at liberty to come here as
often as you like and read any book you choose. This
is my den and no one will interrupt you.'

"He rose, and, with as courteous a 'Good-morning'
as if I had been the finest lady in the land, left me
there alone.

"From that moment I loved Arthur Lovett with all
the intensity of a wild, ungoverned nature, and I spared
no pains to secure his love in return. What had I
to lose? My good name? I was only a slave and
had no use for a good name. I loved Arthur Lovett,
and Arthur Lovett *should* love me in return. That
was my thought.

"I will not try to tell you all the means I used to
secure his love. Enough that I was not scrupulous.
I played for a kingdom and an Antony at once, and
with no chance of loss in case of failure. Of course I
won—you know that. I gave a fierce, wild, jealous
love, and received a warm, tender, self-sacrificing devotion that counted everything as dross except that which
ministered to my enjoyment. Arthur Lovett became a
servant of servants unto his sister's maid. I was proud
of my conquest. I boasted of it, and through the love
of the only son I became queen regnant at Heptwilde.

"You know, I suppose, what followed; *much* I am
sure you do. I might have had freedom then, but I
despised it without Arthur Lovett. I was determined
to have him for my own. I did not care for freedom
till after we had children. I did n't mind hardship
or indignity so long as I had Arthur and he was true
to me. His father and his sisters schemed in every way
to separate us. You have probably heard the story.
It was in vain. All the force and tenacity of his tender, trustful, careless nature seemed absorbed by his
passion for me.

"When we came to have children, I loved them

hardly less wildly and fiercely than I did him. I trembled at the future which lay before them. His friends thought they saw in this a means by which they might separate us. They offered me and my children liberty if I would go away from him and remain absent. I agreed to do so. I did not intend to keep my bargain. I thought that if I was once free—I and my children— I could never be enslaved again. I always thought so until the Court decided otherwise. I thought that was a shame then, and never really believed it till you read it to me to-day.

"Well, they took me North, to New York, and I was liberated. A year after I returned, and Arthur came back to me as readily as a piece of loose iron to a magnet. They told me it would endanger my freedom if I staid; but I laughed at them.

"After a time we came up here, and you know what our life was. I believe you never liked me and I certainly never trusted you. It would have been well if I had. But I did not hate you until I had been taken away and sold by the executor. Before I went I agreed that if Arthur would buy me and my children, as he promised he would, and take us North and emancipate us, I would stay there. He did not say a word about you, and I did not know that he had any intention of marrying at all. I thought that if he took me North, I would find a way to keep him there, though I had agreed that he might come back to his sisters.

"We had had a heap of trouble first and last, as you **know.** And although it had come through my own

wickedness—perhaps for that very reason—I had lost
confidence in every human being except Arthur Lovett,
and at last in him also. I thought I had been injured,
persecuted, deceived, and dragged about, all because I
happened to be a slave, and the man I loved was
free.

"I never could make it out, Miss Betty, why you
should have the right to marry Arthur Lovett, if you
were both agreed, and I should not. I felt that it
-was wrong; that God made me to love Arthur and
him to love me, and so I fought and suffered, and
would not give up when all the world was against me.
And Arthur, he was just wax in my hand. I would
have been content to have been his mistress and have
remained a slave forever, but for the children.

"Oh, Miss Betty, if you had children bright and
beautiful as mine, how would you like to see them
doomed to the life I've led, or a lower one, if not
quite so bad?—*brutes* instead of *devils*—that's the difference.

"Well, I went peaceably to be sold by the executor. Toinette was in arms then, you know, so we
were sold together. We were bought by a poor white
cuss for Buck Lloyd, who had a plantation over the
line in Virginia, not more than thirty or forty miles
from here, though he lived in Alabama. He brought
us first to his plantation, mighty careful and secret-like.
I thought he was just acting as Arthur's agent, and so
made no remonstrance when he changed my name to
Mabel. He probably did not give me credit for knowing half as much as I did. I am satisfied now that his

object in buying and hiding me was to speculate on
Arthur's attachment for me. Thinking him Arthur's
friend, however, I complied with his wishes and remained entirely unknown except as his cook, Mabel.

"After a while, I heard a rumor among some of
the niggers that Arthur Lovett was about to marry.
Then it struck me that all this executor business was
a made-up thing to impose on me, get me out of the
way, and off his hands, and at the same time raise a
little ready money. I heard it was *you* he was going
to marry, too, Miss Betty, and I remembered his duel
with Bill Price, and that affair with the Committee, and
it all came up to strengthen my jealous suspicion. I
don't know but I could have stood it to have had him
marry, if he had first freed me and my children, or if I
had known he would do it—though that would have
been hard enough to bear; but coming with the idea
that he had betrayed and sold me and my children,
made me mad—raging mad.

"I left Toinette in my cook's hut and came to see
if it were true, prepared to do whatever the circumstances would allow—anything and everything that a
woman well nigh, if not quite, crazed could do.

"I came to the Lodge after nightfall, stole into the
secret room, and opened the door into the wardrobe.
I was there and heard your talk in the library. I
heard him laugh and jest with you, about the dress
you fancied. I saw him caress you and bid you
good-night—for the last time, he said, lightly—and
then I determined that his words should come true—
that so it should be. All my fears and suspicions had
18

been confirmed. He had sold me and my children into slavery to get us out of your way and his sisters'. Perhaps those very clothes were bought with the price of our blood. He filled his pipe and lit it. I knew he would sleep before it was smoked out. He had given me when he came back from Europe a triangular Italian poniard, which had belonged to a noted brigand, with the remark that I might need it sometime for defense. It had generally been in the drawer of his desk, for I seldom carried it; but when I went to be sold that last time, he brought it to me and told me to take it, as insult or injury to myself or children might demand its use.

"So I had it hidden then in my bosom. You know, Betty Certain — *bitterly* know — what followed. When the deed was done, I thought the weapon had well fulfilled the purposes for which it had been given me.

"After that I gave up pretty much all hope of freedom. I resigned—no, not resigned, but abandoned myself to the idea that my children must just follow in my footsteps and gather only the bitter fruits of slavery and sin.

"My new master, despairing of any speculation by reason of my connection with Arthur Lovett, took me to his home in Alabama, where he died soon after, but not before he had learned to *fear* me and, because of this mainly, to treat me well.

"I had always kept the deed of the plantation at the Lodge, which was made in trust to Arthur Lovett, for my use. I had a notion that some time it would be of value to my children—I had given up all hope for myself—though I had lost sight of the two older ones. During this time I scarcely felt a regret for the terrible crime I had committed, though I was not unfrequently very anxious in regard to my own safety. Considering Arthur to be guilty of all the wrong and treachery which I supposed to have been practiced toward me, I easily convinced myself that I had only meted out to him the justice he deserved.

"At the sale of Lloyd's estate I was bought by an agent of Manuel Hunter, George Rawson—who was on the search, he said, of Belle Lovett and her children. He had known me well when we lived here at the Lodge, but my hair had turned gray with sorrow, and he did not recognize in the care-worn Mabel Lloyd, the noted cook of Buck Lloyd the gambler and speculator, the once blithe and handsome Belle Lovett, mistress of Arthur Lovett and queen of Lovett Lodge, as the people around us used to call me.

"He asked me a great many questions about the woman he was after, and I made up a story about her which he fully believed, and which I am satisfied put them finally on the wrong track. As I was going cheap at the sale on account of my old appearance, as well as my reputation as a girl of desperate temper, he bought us on a speculation, I think—me and Toinette.

"I was brought back to Perham and subjected to the closest cross-examination by old Manuel Hunter. He had also seen me frequently at the Lodge, as he was the close friend of Arthur Lovett, but he did not recognize me at all. I repeated my story about Belle

Lovett, and deceived him as easily as I had Rawson. He took me from the latter and put me in the kitchen, as I had a great reputation as a cook, which, indeed, I deserved, for I had studied cookery to please Arthur, who was something of an epicure, as were all his family.

"During this time I had carried about in my slave's bundle the dress I had taken from the library that night. I took it just to spite you, to let you know that I meant to hit you as well as him, and I used to gloat over it by hours at a time, as the token of my revenge. I thought a thousand times I would burn it up, lest it should betray me, but yet I did not. If my bundle had been searched by either Rawson or old Marse Manuel, I should have been lost.

"As it was, I was in constant fear. I thought the motive of Manuel Hunter was to discover Arthur Lovett's murderer, though it would seem from what I have since learned, that it was to get possession of the deed of trust, and so perfect his title to the Lodge.

"I also took with me part of the keys which I had in my possession as housekeeper at the Lodge. I did this not with any idea of using them afterwards, but from a sort of jealousy, to prevent their falling into the hands of any woman who might come into my place. They seemed a sort of badge of the ownership which I had in the premises. They were to me what the crown is to the sovereign. When I wanted to get at Toinette and Geoffrey Hunter afterwards, I found that instead of new locks. duplicates of the keys had been procured, and I could therefore enter the Lodge at pleasure. The belief that the house was haunted, arising from my having been seen a few times during my nightly visits, greatly assisted me in my designs.

" One side of the fire-place in the secret room opens outward under the building upon strong hinges by means of a handle fastened into the soapstone of which it is made. On the inside it is worked by moving the right andiron to one side. It was made by Arthur on purpose to afford a safe concealment of our relations, and a secure place of retreat in case any danger should threaten, as on that night when Bill Price and his gang searched the house. I was in there with my children all the while. It was the only time we were compelled to use it for that purpose, but it was our ordinary rendezvous, and in its security were passed the happiest moments of my life. It has been my haunt whenever opportunity served since, and possesses a horrible fascination for me, though I have never entered it since that night without the most overwhelming terror. I always seem to see Arthur Lovett coming through the door in the wardrobe, with his great dark eyes fixed upon me in the deepest sadness. He never seems angry at me, only so sorrowful and pitying—oh, God ! I now know why he should be sad rather than angry. How could I wrong him with the thought of treachery !

" As years went on and Miss Ruthy got Marse Manuel's promise that Toinette and I should be freed, at least when he died, I began to hope once more, but when he gave Toinette to young Marse Geoffrey, and he brought her here to Lovett Lodge, I was just frantic. I determined to kill both Geoffrey and old Manuel as

well as my child—I would kill her first though. She
should never tread the path which I had come. I
would send her soul white and pure to heaven before
vice and crime had smutched it, if it separated us
forever. I thought I could not be worsted; I was
doomed now—I knew that; but she, my last, my darling—she should be saved!

"You know I failed in the attempt I made to do this.
When you came and watched over her that discouraged
me. I used to come and look at her, and would sometimes think that I ought to carry my first plan into execution, but I never tried to harm her afterwards, nor
indeed any one until you came into possession of the
Lodge, and I thought you were enjoying what was
justly and truly mine—the fruits of a robbery of which
we were the victims, I and my children. I meant to
have killed you and then to have destroyed myself.

"And, now, Betty Certain, you know just how bad
Belle Lovett has been. I can't thank you for sparing
me last night, for I'm sorry you did it; but you are
better than I ever thought you, or you could not have
done it. There is one reason for my telling you this
story that I have not spoken of before—I have a request
to make of you: that you will never, unless their interests
shall absolutely require it, reveal to my children the
atrocity of my acts. I shall not live to see them. I do
not wish to; but you will find them. You will give
them what their father intended them to have. Promise,
now, that you will tell them nothing that will make them
think worse of their mother than they have done before.
Will you do it, Miss Betty?"

"Poor woman," said Betty, sadly; "you can hardly be blamed, though you committed an awful crime. So far as I am concerned, I forgive you freely, and will do all that I can to hide your act from the knowledge of your children."

"Thank you, Miss Betty," said the woman, humbly; "I could not have asked forgiveness from one whom I had so deeply injured, but my heart feels lighter, now that you have granted it."

"Now, then," said Betty, as if she would leave an unpleasant subject, "we must talk of the future. You remember the will provides for your emancipation, as well as that of your children."

"Does it?" said Belle, absently; "I had forgotten. I'm getting mighty dull at best. Would you mind letting me take that packet and these papers, and leaving me until morning? Perhaps I could think of something that should be done by that time. It's a long time since I have read or written much; but it seems as if I could make out almost anything in Arthur's hand."

Betty Certain immediately rose, laid the papers in the chair before the woman, and prepared to depart. As she approached the door Belle called to her, and said:

"You will not *forget*, Miss Betty?"

She turned and asked,

"Forget what?"

"What you promised me," said the woman.

"Certainly not, and I will come back by an hour after sun-up in the morning."

"And you are sure you forgive me?" asked the woman, tremulously.

Betty Certain came back and stood beside the bowed and shrinking figure on the floor. Reaching down she put her hand upon her head, and, raising her eyes, said solemnly:

"Only as I forgive thee, poor deceived woman, may God forgive me, who might have been worse than you, had I been thus tempted."

The tears burst from the woman's eyes, and, seizing the hand which rested on her head, she covered it with kisses, murmuring between her sobs:

"God bless you! Good-by, Betty Certain! God bless you!"

"Good-by," said Betty Certain confusedly, and hurried away. "Thank God, her blood is not on my hands," she said, as she came near the scene of the last night's encounter. "God judge the poor creature. For my part, I can't make out whether she is more sinned against or sinning. She has done wrong, undoubtedly, much wrong; but, surely, somebody before her did not do right. I don't know how it is, but, the more I look at it, the more it seems as if nothing but evil came out of slavery. I 'm more 'n ever of the notion Gran'ther Ezra was right—'It 's better to be poor than to have more souls than yer own to answer for.' Somebody's responsible for Belle Lovett being what she was, an so becoming what she is, an I 'm thankful that *that* somebody's not Betty Certain, any way. Poor girl! poor girl! though, after all, I was wrong to think of stepping into her place, an' bein' Arthur Lovett's wife. She was his wife, I 'm sure of it now, in God's sight. I know he always felt so; but I thought it was only his kindheartedness. He was weak, not bad. He did not mean to wrong Belle, nor did I, and yet perhaps we did. An' so God punished us—all at once—Arthur and Belle and me, and the somebody or something whose agency was long before ours—who sowed the seed, of which this was the harvest—all in that one act of hers. Poor girl! Poor girl! I was half afraid I was doing wrong to hide her crime and cheat the law, but now I know that only God can judge aright such as she is. Poor woman!"

The next morning, when Betty Certain went, "an hour after sun-up," as she had promised, to her old home, the door was shut, and there remained no sign of life therein. Her heart stood still with foreboding. Had the woman died of the injuries she had received in the struggle. Her head was terribly swollen, and her face disfigured, yesterday. Betty's heart misgave her that she had not attended better to her condition. She remembered then, the tone in which the woman had said, Good-by. It was the hopeless, solemn one, in which we bid farewell to those on whom visible is the seal of death.

She hurried on and opened the door. The room was still and empty. On the chair by which the woman had sat was the bundle of papers she had brought yesterday, together with those she had taken from Belle Lovett's neck, the envelope which had been around the packet she had given to Belle, and a small locket. She took up the latter and opened it. It was the duplicate of the one Belle had worn, and contained a portrait of her when she was young.

A slip of paper dropped out, on which this was written :

"I desire that this may be given to my daughter, Toinette.   BELLE LOVETT."

The handwriting was delicate and refined, though it had the constrained and uncertain appearance which characterizes that of one long unaccustomed to the pen.

Betty Certain closed the locket, and looking again at the bundle of papers in the chair, saw a note addressed to herself in the same hand. She took it, and read as follows :

"MISS BETTY :

"One hour after sun-up to-morrow I shall be no more. I have done so much evil to those whom I have loved best, that I am only anxious to end a miserable and sinful life. God forgive me, perhaps this act is more sinful than any other. The poniard Arthur gave me will at least find its true mission, when it pierces the heart which has been the worst enemy of

BELLE LOVETT.

"P. S.—If you will push over the rock, you will at once afford me burial, and remove all danger of inquiry, or need of revelation on your part. God bless you, Betty Certain, whom I have hated for so long. I am almost happy at the thought that I shall soon be at rest and at peace with all.   B. L."

Betty Certain opened the drawer. The dagger was gone.

"Oh dear! Oh dear! More blood, more blood,

THE OLD RIVALS.

"She flashed the torch above the prostrate form. . . . . 'God rest her soul,' muttered the 'poor white' woman, as she bent over her rival in the love of Arthur Lovett." – p. 307.

more blood !" she exclaimed. "Oh God ! will the
shadow of crime never be lifted ?"

Then she was seized with a sudden hope. The act
might not yet be committed.

The woman might have hoped to deceive her into
becoming an involuntary actor in her death. She flew
along the path which led to the cave—among the
stately rocks—through the outer room—until she stood
before the mystic rock which guarded the opening to
the inner cavern. Here she stopped to gather the frag-
ments of the torch she had thrown down at her former
visit, and light them with a match. She then made her
way further into the interior. She emerged from the
low passage, and went up to the pillared rock in the
middle. In the dim light she almost stumbled over the
object of her search. She put her hand down to save
herself from falling, and it touched the woman's breast.
It was warm and wet. Betty Certain lifted her hand
with a shudder, and held it near the torch. It was red
with blood. For a moment her strong heart was faint.
Then she flashed the torch above the prostrate form.
The head was resting on the low rock, where she had
sat before; the eyes were closed, and the countenance
peaceful.

"God rest her soul," muttered the "poor-white"
woman, as she bent over her rival in the love of
Arthur Lovett.

Then she went out and put her strong shoulder
against the strangely balanced rock and swayed it back
and forth, until it fell over with a crash, and sealed
the tomb of Belle Lovett until, upon the resurrection

morning, the angel shall again roll away the stone from the sepulcher.

Old Mabel had been so accustomed to periodic absences, that her final one was not considered anything very remarkable, until several days had elapsed, and then the search that was made revealed no trace of the fugitive. The death of Manuel Hunter about this time, and the dispersion of the household at the Home soon after, distracted attention, in a great degree, from the unaccountable absence of the old domestic. As time went on, it was generally conceded that she was dead; and a great freshet which occurred about that time was usually credited with being the means of her death.

Of all that she had learned concerning Toinette, Betty Certain informed her in a letter which, with difficulty, she procured to be forwarded through the lines of the contending armies, a long time after, through the influence of Colonel Geoffrey Hunter. She did not, however, feel called upon to convey this information to the latter individual, rightly concluding that the matters she desired to reserve would be better kept by communicating the information she had received from Belle to none except those to whom her duty implicitly required that she should relate it. She gave Toinette no further explanation of the manner in which she had learned these facts, than that they were revealed by her mother just before her death; leaving it to be inferred that nothing of an extraordinary character had accompanied her demise.

She also sent a complete and systematic account of

the condition of the estate and of the two-fold claim
which the children of Arthur Lovett and Belle had
upon it—the one arising under the deed of trust which
might yet be declared valid, and the other under the
will of Arthur—and made inquiries in regard to the boy
Fred, whom Toinette then first learned to be her
brother.

CHAPTER XXIX.

NOT VOUCHED FOR.

THREE years have elapsed since the slave-girl Toinette was transformed into a freed-woman and settled upon the free soil of Ohio.

The liberality or conscience of Geoffrey—let us not question the motive too closely—had provided for her support, first, by purchasing a small house for her occupancy, and, secondly, by providing that a certain stipend should be annually paid to her. She had improved the knowledge which she had derived from " Mass'r Geoffrey " to an extent that made her capable of supporting herself and the bright young boy, who called her " Mamma " and answered to the name of Geoffrey, by teaching, when, during the last year, the annuity had ceased. No one imagined that the refined and elegant woman, known among her neighbors as " Mrs. Hunter," had ever worn the garb of the slave; nor did any one of them dream that there was any taint of impurity in her blood; while her modest demeanor and strict propriety of deportment had prevented any suspicion of illegitimacy on the part of her child. She was regarded as an intelligent and attractive young widow, in somewhat limited circumstances. That was all.

She was a universal favorite in the community where

she lived, as from her amiability and good nature she well deserved to be in any. The same animation and sprightliness which had attracted the notice of Geoffrey Hunter brought her many friends, and she came unconsciously and without other deception than complete silence as to her past to be received as an equal in a society which, for intelligence and virtue, has not its superior in the land. Educated and refined Christian ladies and gentlemen were her familiar friends. Of course, it was all upon the hypothesis of an unmixed Caucasian descent. While a few of them would, perhaps, have esteemed her no less had the bar-sinister of that unfortunate race, whom the tipsy patriarch is supposed to have cursed with an efficacy which could hardly have been expected from a drunkard's anathema, been traced on her brow; yet the major part of them, while they would have given her credit for her accomplishments, would have shrunk at once from association with her, even without further knowledge of her past life. With this revealed, and her descent known, she would have been as much a Pariah in that part of the nation, which boasted of its freedom and equality, and even in a community of the most ardent fanatics, as in the very hotbed of slavery. That marvelous anthropophobia, superinduced by integumentary duskiness to which the American citizen is so strangely subject, pervaded all ranks and classes. Some professed to be superior to its influences, but they were *raræ aves*, and were not unfrequently supposed to be themselves infected with the malady they professed to despise. The fanatics claimed the slave to be a

"man and a brother," but he was a brother who had
neglected his opportunities—a poor relation who was
only recognized when extreme genealogical accuracy
was required.

So Toinette passed under false colors, but they were
colors which she had no part or lot in claiming. It was
all the fault of those heedless, great-hearted people of
the Northwest, who are not given to questions of ante-
cedents. The thoughtless creatures receive every one
who comes into their midst at their face-value, without
examining closely as to the grade of alloy. Everything that has the impress of humanity's mint goes
there at par, until the base metal shows its color.
Every piece is good enough until the corrupted coin-
age tarnishes with use. Every soul is counted white
until its stains appear.

Now, as God had written purity upon the soul and
brow of Toinette, and sealed it with the spotless offspring which she cherished so fondly, and as form and
feature were cast in the fairest mould of that cream
of the Caucasian—the Anglo-Saxon-American of the
XIXth century—the *chef d' œuvre* of created humanity,
in the ineradicable convictions of every individual of
that favored family—it is hardly to be wondered at that
these unsuspicious people should never have detected
the infinitesimal trace of the dusky Orient, which
Ariel himself might have failed to discover. Neither
is it strange that they should not have discovered the
trace of Sin, when her only transgression had been but
as the unconscious indelicacies of rollicking childhood.

The knowledge that she was heir in her own right

to a considerable portion of the estate of Arthur Lovett, how much it was difficult then to say, seemed to the inexperienced Toinette a direct interposition of Providence in her behalf, a visible confirmation of the position among her fellow-mortals, in which events over which she had no control had placed her.

At this time occurred an event which tended not a little to strengthen these new ideas. She saw in the columns of a daily journal the following :

An Incident of the Massacre at Fort Pillow.—We had a conversation yesterday with Col. J——, of the —th Colored Infantry, one of the regiments which surrendered at Fort Pillow, and which was massacred almost to a man, with the utmost disregard of the terms of capitulation. He spoke of some most signal instances of devotion to the cause and the flag, upon the part of those brave men who are fighting for the liberty of their race.

Col. J—— was fortunately absent on leave at the time of the capitulation, but visited the scene of carnage a few days afterwards.

He found without difficulty, he says, the place where his regiment stood in line and were shot down by their inhuman captors, after having laid down their arms and surrendered. The scene, as he described it, must have been horrible in the extreme ; but the most touching incident was connected with the color-bearer of his regiment.

He was a young man of splendid figure and bearing, having scarcely a trace of the African in color or feature. He had been a slave, but was emancipated when quite young, and had acquired a good education, which, with his fine soldierly qualities, greatly endeared him to his fellow-soldiers, and made him a universal favorite with the officers of the regiment, many of whom also shared his fate.

He seems to have determined to save the colors of his regiment from the hands of the enemy at all hazards, and had accordingly torn them from the staff, and wrapped them around his body, before the capitulation. He was found with his hands clasped tightly over his breast ; and the thoughtful colonel, opening his jacket, to find some memento for the friends of his dead favorite, found there the colors, which he had given into his hands a few months before, with an earnest injunction that they should never be surrendered. Three bullets

19

had passed at once through the flag and the faithful heart which had striven to protect it from dishonor.

The poor fellow was buried with the honors of war, shrouded in the flag which he had so nobly saved from the hands of a brutal enemy.

In his breast-pocket was found a photograph of President Lincoln, wrapped in a copy of the Emancipation Proclamation, also a deed of manumission in favor of Fred. Lovett, "a mulatto boy, aged twelve years, the property of Manuel Hunter, of Cold Spring county, N. C." This deed seems to have been admitted to probate and registered in Lorrain county, Ohio. Col. J—— left these articles at this office, where they may be claimed by any friend of Sergeant Lovett.

The barbarism which could slay such men in cold blood, when they had honorably surrendered after a brave struggle, is too infamous for comment.

Toinette saw this in a journal which was printed in a neighboring city. She did not know whether it was true or false, but she wrote to the publishers, and said : " Send the papers found on Sergeant Lovett to me. I am his sister." And they came—the deed of manumission, the proclamation, and the sad, uncomely *carte* of the great liberator—all stained with blood.

Then she believed. She felt that her brother had died a hero, in the great struggle for the liberty of his race. Her boy was thoroughly ennobled now—first by descent from one of those knightly heroes who battled for the unrighteous and doomed cause of human bondage, believing it to be the side of Liberty and Right, instead of Slavery and Oppression ; and again by kinship with that brother, who had proved himself worthy of knighthood, though born a slave.

Toinette may have been mistaken. So was, perhaps, the editor of the popular journal. Fred Lovett may have been no hero at all. He may never have fought bravely, surrendered honorably, or been butchered treacherously. We do not know. History must settle that. We have nothing to do with the matter. We are only concerned in the death of Fred Lovett, and the influence of that fact on Toinette and her fortunes

There may have been no —th Colored Infantry, no battle at Fort Pillow, no surrender, no horrible massacre—whose recital chills the blood—there may have been no Fort Pillow at all, in fact. We only know that Fred Lovett died—that thus the editor wrote at that day—however history may teach—and thus Toinette believed.

After she knew this, she opened the packet which her mother, old Mabel, had given her for Fred Lovett, and found it to contain a deed from " Thomas Gray to Arthur Lovett, as Trustee for Belle Lovett, free-woman of color," of the premises she had known as Lovett Lodge.

Whether she was an heiress by her father's will, or her mother's right, she knew not.

CHAPTER XXX.

CHRYSALID.

THE beauty of form and feature which had marked the childhood of Toinette had ripened with years into a rare loveliness. Her sunny temperament still prevailed, and gave to every event a cheerful significance. She had never lost faith in the love which had gladdened her young life. She knew it had no legal sanction—that it bore the stain which makes the purest love the keenest disgrace. Yet she cherished its memory. Her love for Geoffrey had been of that all-sacrificing character which does not ask advantage, require recognition, or demand its right. You may call it degraded and servile if you will, it is that love which woman not seldom gives without question, without fear, without hope. As the years had elapsed, and she came to realize more clearly the relations in which they had stood to each other, she began to be grateful to the Power which had separated them, though she yet clung to a vague, foolish hope that time would bring a remedy for the evil, and yet leave her the joy of love. As the fierce struggle of the national war passed through its preliminary phases, and finally disclosed the Divine message which it bore of freedom to all, this vain hope began to take a more tangible form in the mind of Toinette. The poor creature loved so blindly that she could not think that

the object of her adoration had never once contemplated the hypothesis of which she dreamed—perhaps had
never even desired its possibility. But she did not
know—she did not wish to know—she *would* not know.
"When this war is ended," she said to herself, "then he
will have no slaves—there will be no slavery; and—
and, if I have improved, if I am as refined and lady-
like as others, then he will love me still. He cannot
help it, when he sees our beautiful boy;" and then she
would caress the child. Day by day, hour by hour,
she wrought to make herself the fit companion of the
man she loved. No task was too severe, no study too
exacting. For hours before the day-break on the cold
winter mornings, she pursued with unwearying assiduity
her musical studies and practice, that she might give
the entire day to other duties. Her progress was amazing. She came very soon to be regarded as a musical
prodigy, even in a community of skilled musicians.
Every department of science and literature she laid
under contribution to her hopeless and insane love.
Every day should have opened her eyes to its absurdity,
but, on the contrary, each day seemed to strengthen
her delusion.

As the war progressed and the end grew nearer, her
heart became more and more wrapped up in her vain
fancy; as the clasp of the giant grew closer and closer
upon the throat of the Rebellion, as the thundering at
Petersburg grew louder and louder, she could not resist
the yearning which impelled her to go to the scene of
combat. She knew that he, Geoffrey Hunter, her idol,
was there. She knew that he was fighting for the cause

of Rebellion and Slavery, and she knew that he would
be beaten; that his cause must fall; but yet she gloried
in his courage. It stirred her pulses with a wild joy to
know that the man she loved could yet fight bravely for
a cause which he knew to be doomed. As, day by day,
she read the reports of that heroic defense, half-trem-
bling lest she should find that death had robbed her of
her idol, her heart bounded with pride as she thought
that one of that proud band of dauntless heroes was the
father of her boy. She did not stop to ask, she did
not think, whether the matrimonial bond had cast its
halo of respectability around that curly head or not.
She knew that kindly nature had marked its parentage, in the deep blue eye, the broad, fair brow, the
bright brown locks, and, more than all, in the imperious mouth, the soft, clear tone, and the proud and
haughty carriage. If her slave-life had made her less
regardful of the marriage sanction, who shall blame her?
Purer offering was never laid on the altar of love than
the bounding pride with which she told to her young
boy at evening the story of his father's heroism. She
painted the perils of the siege with the prescient accuracy of love—snatching from the briefest hints the whole
horrible truth. The want, exposure, the constant fire,
the unexpected attack, the gallant repulse—and in it all
she painted the form of her hero, foremost, manfullest
of all; the sire of that fair boy, his second self, who listened with wide-eyed wonderment to the tale he could
not understand.

And so she went on, ever filling her heart with fond
hope, until it could beat no more so far away from the

scene of her hero's exploits. Every moment was agony until she could be near him, could see his danger, and share in part his peril. So it came about that in the early autumn she left her son with some kind friends, telling him that she went to seek his father and bring him home to his boy. For so the silly child cheated herself into believing she would do. And she went away and became one of that noble army of women who brought the sunshine of heaven into camp and hospital. They would have kept her at this post or that, but she would take no denial, and pressed on until she found herself under the very guns of the beleaguered city. There she did her work quietly, cheerfully, praying ever for the cause of those she served, and gazing lovingly toward the long lines of gray earthworks which showed the enemy's position, and trying to picture the place and occupation of her idol. How ardently she longed for the end. Of course the city must fall — she never doubted that — and the unholy cause with it. But her idol—he should be like the house of Rahab. She would find him and shield him. He should be her part of the plunder when the final assault was made. She would save his life and give him hers; not upon conditions, oh, no! but freely, gladly. It was his already. She wondered if he knew or ever would know how fully, how completely. She was sure he would. Perhaps he was sick. She would nurse him back into life. Perhaps he was wounded, or would be when the end came. She had an impression that he would be. She would work very hard—she would be very faithful in the hospital— that she might learn the more skillfully to bind up his wounds and bid the soul that was so dear hold its place in the shattered tenement. Oh! she would find him—just over there—and he would be hers. Her Geoffrey—her— The warm blush told the word she would not even whisper to her own fond heart. Poor, silly, loving woman! How merciful would have been the bursting shell that had brought a message from beyond the pearly gates to that pure, trusting heart—too pure to know its own impurity.

CHAPTER XXXI.

STRICKEN.

HOUR by hour the end approached. The lines grew longer and longer; and one of them grew daily thinner and weaker.

Still it did not break, till one day in the early spring. Sheridan with his troopers, and Warren with his footmen, had been for days passing on to the southward by the hospital, where Toinette sat and watched them. She knew by a sort of intuition that the last throe of the gigantic rebellion had come. She watched silently, praying for the success of liberty, and at the same time hoping that the enemy would crown their long resistance with an heroic struggle, and that one of the gray-coated braves at least would go up from the field of battle unscathed. For days she could not sleep. The busy preparation for new patients at the hospital filled her with horror. At length the day of days came—the day to which all had looked forward with dread or anticipation, when there came the sound of heavy firing away to the southward.

The blow was struck, and the blue line swept round to the South-Side, cutting off the aorta of the rebellion. But two courses were now before the master-mind who had so long conducted the defense, immediate and perilous retreat before a flushed and victorious foe, or one more blow, desperate and all but hopeless, which only transcendent genius and superhuman courage could render successful. There was only one chance in a thousand—nay, only one in a million. Yet, there was something in its favor. The cause for which the defenders had fought so long and bravely was doomed. Lee knew *that*, so did all his captains, so did every soldier, so did all thinking men. Retreat without a counter-check was almost instant death. The end could not be far off, at best, but the chances for such combinations as would make a further series of Fabian operations possible, were very few indeed, if the victorious army of his wary and tireless opponent were upon his heels. Whatever hope of success there was left to Lee lay in so paralyzing his enemy that no immediate pursuit could be made. If this could be done the struggle might yet be prolonged. He provided, therefore, for a counter-check which, if successful, would so cripple the huge leviathan that lay stretched out before him, as to give an opportunity for successful retreat, and end the most famous of defenses with the most brilliant achievement of a shattered army. If it had succeeded, the coming ages would have looked back with ever-increasing wonder upon the mind which conceived and the men who executed the daring stroke. That was the critical moment for the fame of Lee as a soldier. In that hour he failed to write his name, as he might have done, beside that even of the great Napoleon. The policy of desperation was foreign to his mind. Had Jackson *then* been at the head of that be-

leaguered army, there had been another page of Confederate history to write—not successful, it is probable,
nay, almost certain—for exhaustion had already proceeded too far, but certainly more brilliant than any
other.

Lee showed that he comprehended the opportunity,
but feared to risk all in taking advantage of it. He
saw the chance and counted the odds. But in the very
moment of its accomplishment his nerve failed. He
could not risk all upon one throw. The spirit of his
great Roman exemplar was so strong upon him that he
could not resist preparing for the contingency of failure.
So he took a handful only of his decimated forces and
hurled them in the gray of morning upon one of his
enemy's strongholds. Just where the opposing line was
weakest in numbers, and most difficult to reïnforce,
he tried to thrust in a wedge which should divide
the vast trunk and menace both extremes. Time and
place were each chosen with exquisite skill. So signal
was the success of this little band, that it shows all
the more clearly how great was the error which he
made, who entrusted to so few the only remaining chance of winning a transcendently glorious future.

On, on, came the last column to which was committed the final opportunity of an army crowned with
the unsurpassed glory of an unequal contest. It seemed
as if the inspiration of their message to posterity had
swelled every heart and strung every nerve to deeds of
unprecedented valor. Their onset was as the lightning
flash in its brilliancy, and like its scath in results.

Over the mighty works they clambered, and their enemies' ranks fled before them like the mist before the
morning. When the sun cast his full radiance over the
scene, the line of Grant was broken in twain, and the
divided trunk was shivering in both its threatened members-
bers. As the fog rolled away, it was seen how trivial
was the force which had thus imperiled a whole army,
and the Federal troops, burning with shame at their
cowardly retreat, rushed forward in a mighty wave of
flashing steel to retake the lost works, and hurl the presumptuous foe back to his hiding place.

Then it was that the tide of battle ebbed and flowed
for a brief space, the reddest and wildest about the walls
of Steadman. Then the brave force of Confederate as-
sailants, crippled and broken—the few who had come
still fewer by half as they returned—fell sullenly back.
Their work had been accomplished. Charged with the
final protest of a failing cause, which had been long sustained with unparalleled bravery against overwhelming numbers, they had delivered its last defiance with
heroic valor, and now fell back to rejoin their companions of the doomed army of Northern Virginia.   Lee
had touched the very summit of military skill, and at
the instant when about to write his name side by side
with the proudest in the history of arms, his hand had
trembled and his spirit failed. He showed that he could
comprehend the glory of that transcendent genius, and
could follow with his intellect the victorious footsteps
of the mightiest of warriors, but had not the fortitude
to pursue them in deed. He saw his opportunity, but
withheld his hand from the tempting cup.   That day

the soldiers of the Army of Northern Virginia crowned
themselves with an immortality of glory, and the Commander of that army only just missed the acme of
military renown.

Had his life ended with the struggle in which he was
engaged, the world had never known how much greater
than the greatest of mere warriors was the Christian hero
whose genius was the soul of the Confederate cause.
The hand, which on this last day of promise could put
away the glittering bauble of military fame, was strong
enough also to thrust aside the temptation of personal
aggrandizement, to put upon his brow the thorny crown
of self-forgetfulness, and make himself a great exemplar
to the people whom he loved.   It was the years that followed the hour of failure, which gave the key to his
whole career, which made his name one of the proudest of which our nation, or the world, can boast—as
representing one of the few in all the ages who could
resolutely subordinate his own glory to the good of his
fellows—his fame, to what he deemed his duty.

It was the unnoted years at Lexington which crowned the life of Lee with its brightest halo.

No sooner had the struggle ended than the wounded
victims of this last spasmodic effort of the dying cause
began to pour into the hospitals in the rear of the Federal lines.   In one of the nearest of these was Toinette.
She scanned each new arrival with nervous anxiety, and
though she attended to her duties as a nurse with a
marked effort at assiduity, yet it was with an absent-
mindedness that spoke little in favor of her compe-
tency.   The surgeon in charge noticed it, when she

failed to comprehend and obey his instructions in regard to a poor fellow who was under her care.

"You are too weary and excited to-day, Madame," said he, "to be in the hospital. The attack has disconcerted you. You have not been out so long as many of us, and I do not wonder at it. You had better not try to remain."

"Oh no!" she answered hastily, "I would not go away now for the world. This is what I came for."

"But your services will be equally needed after you have rested," replied the doctor, "and you will pardon me for saying they will be much more valuable then, for you seem now to be much excited—indeed quite ill," he added, eyeing her keenly.

"Oh, I could not rest, doctor, while I knew that these poor wounded men were being brought here every moment, needing care and attention." The kind old doctor, with that ready perception of the finer traits of human nature which is a characteristic of the profession, saw at once that she had some especial reason for remaining at her post, and surmising that it was anxiety with regard to some one in whose safety she was particularly interested, remarked:

"Well, if you will remain, you had better attend in the receiving ward. You will have enough to do there to keep your thoughts from wool-gathering. Though," he added, seeing her suddenly growing paler, "most of those who are brought here are Rebs. Poor fellows, they seem to have suffered terribly this morning."

Poor Toinette's brain reeled for an instant as she

thought of the all terrible details of the morning's fight which she had heard. She could not help thinking somehow that her idol was in that shattered forlorn hope which had been hurled against the leviathan in order that the rest of the army might escape. With a heart heavy with fearful forebodings she went to the receiving ward.

The ambulances were there discharging momently their loads of suffering humanity. Hour after hour the number of maimed and bleeding forms increased. Among them passed the surgeons and nurses, the former inspecting with practiced celerity the condition of the various sufferers, removing those most seriously wounded at once to the operating ward and directing the action of the nurses in relieving the less critical cases. It was not a romantic place for a woman to be. The fine lady whose heroism exhausts itself in sopping her lover's aching head with a wet handkerchief, or binding up his bruised hand, would have fared badly in that low, grim tent which they called the Receiving Ward of Hospital No. — of the —— Corps of the Army of the Potomac. Some of its inmates were upon stretchers and some upon the ground. Blood, flowing or clotted, was everywhere. Dirty, powder-blackened faces were smeared with it. Unkempt, tangled heads of hair were still more closely matted with the crimson ooze. Some gaping wounds were already sealed up by nature's own bandage, the hardened fibrine, while the regular spirt which showed the arterial flow from others marked the heart-beats as life ebbed away into eternity. It was the place for tender, careful hands and willing hearts; but they must be joined with unshrinking eyes and callous nerves. No faintness, no qualmishness, no sentiment, no delicacy there, except delicacy of touch and the sentiment which will endure all things to relieve suffering humanity. The matted locks must be cleansed and smoothed, the clammy brow bathed, the grimy face washed, the fevered tongue cooled, the wound dressed, the bleeding staunched, death in its most horrible forms faced, and every sense made the messenger at each instant of some unpleasant overture which death and suffering send to the living and the whole.

The canvas tent-wall alone separated the receiving, from the operating, ward. The half-whispered words of hurried consultation, the grating of the saw, the keen shudder-bringing rush of the sharp knife deftly wielded, the groan, the curse, the gasp, and, amid all, the sickening, fearful drip, drip, of the ever-flowing blood from the operating-table—all came with fearful significance to the ears behind the canvas screen. The surgeons, red-handed, perhaps with red drops upon the face and clothing, passed to and fro. One whose face had been literally bathed in the jet from a severed artery, stopped to examine the wound of a new arrival, whose only anxiety on earth seemed to be to pick the clotted blood from his clammy hands and from under his long nails. When the horrible pictures separated, Toinette washed the stiffening hands and pallid brow, and received a look of gratitude from the poor shattered clay. Then she folded the hands over the quiet breast and closed the stiffening lids over eyes that should see no more.

Death had come while she yet ministered to the sufferer.

"Ha! what have we here?" said the chief surgeon, as towards the close of the day he stopped beside a stretcher on which had just been laid a new arrival.

The wounded man seemed unconscious, though his open, moving eyes and regular breathing, with a certain nervous twitching of the fingers, showed that he was yet alive. His sword was still lashed to his wrist, and his uniform showed him to have been a colonel in the Confederate service.

The surgeon passed a hand rapidly over his face, close to his eyes, and seeing that he did not wink, said to himself, "Blind, unconscious—strange. It must be some injury of the brain." For upon first glance no wound was apparent, and there did not appear any hemorrhage to indicate its locality. The surgeon turned his head upon one side and discovered under the temple, behind and below the lower edge of the eye, just where the walls of the skull join the pillars of the cheek, the small round wound where a rifle or pistol ball had entered.

"Here, Jones," he said to an attendant, "bring me a probe."

A set of these instruments was soon placed in his hands, and he began one of these wonderful explorations by which the skillful surgeon tracks with unerring certainty the hidden course of the most vagrant missile. How admirable the art which puts an eye upon the end of that flexible wand and bids it follow the enemy of life in its dark and tortuous path among the shivered

20

tissues, until it has traced it to its lodgment! As the surgeon with unhesitating, but skilled and delicate touch, thrust ·in the probe, he muttered to himself:

"Just below the upper angle of the left malar, at its juncture with the temporal. Through the ethnoid," he said as the probe passed on. "Why, Jones, it must have come out."

He withdrew the probe, and turning the patient's head, examined the other side with care. In passing his hand over it, a slight swelling attracted his attention.

"Oh, here it is. A knife and a pair of forceps, Jones."

They were brought. Two or three quick, steady strokes and the forceps were thrust in, and a battered bloody piece of lead drawn out, and laid on the patient's breast. Then several small pieces of bone. Then the old surgeon cleansed the wound with water, laid a wet compress upon each temple, and put another across his forehead. Then he felt his pulse again, and again passed a hand over his eyes. The sun came in at the tent-door, and lighted up the face of the doctor and his reclining patient.

Leaning against the tent-pole, and gazing at them with a pallid face and sinking limbs, was Toinette. *Her* hour had come. The wounded officer was Geoffrey Hunter.

She came forward as the Surgeon finished his hasty dressing of the wound, and said, in a voice which she meant should be natural and steady:

"Will he live, do you think, sir?" The Surgeon

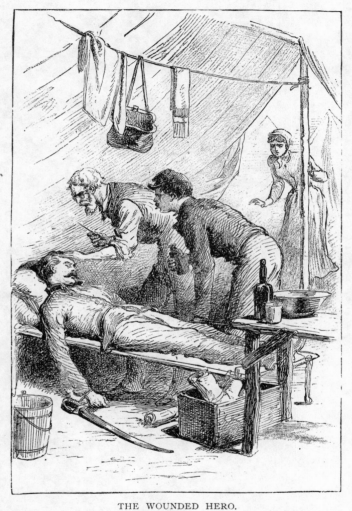

THE WOUNDED HERO.

"Leaning against the tent-pole, and gazing at them with a pallid face and sinking limbs, was Toinette."—p. 330.

looked up suddenly and sharply into her face. The tone had not escaped him, and in her pallid cheek and anxious, yearning eye he read the confirmation of his morning's suspicion.

"So this is your secret, child," he said to himself as he turned his gaze upon the face of his patient. "Poor child! a rebel, too! Well, it will probably make but little difference in a few hours!"

But to her he said, after a moment, "He may, if he is carefully nursed, though the chances are very few. It is a very unusual case, and it is hard to say just what the danger is. Certainly, it is very great. It might be better for him that he should die than recover."

"Will you tell me what to do, Doctor, and let me nurse him?" she asked. "You need not fear; I shall make no mistakes, and will take the best of care of him."

"I have no doubt, my child," said the Surgeon, kindly; "and the first thing you have to do is to maintain the same self-control you are now exercising," and he looked at her meaningly.

His look and tone very nearly destroyed the demeanor which he praised. Her lips quivered, her bosom heaved, and her voice was hoarse and tremulous, as there, amid those scenes, she grasped the blood-stained hand of the old doctor, and said:

"Thank you, sir."

Then she stooped down and kissed the upturned brow of the unconscious form between them, and rose up again, pale but collected, waiting for instructions.

The old doctor's eyes were dim, and his voice husky,

as he said, "Never mind, now, he is doing very well.
I will see you again presently," and he walked quickly
away.

Then Toinette sat down upon the side of the
stretcher, unfastened the sword-knot from his wrist, and
laid the weapon reverently by his side. Then she
brought water and bathed his hands and face, his neck
and ears, and combed and brushed his matted beard.
Then she sat by him and held his unconscious hand
in hers, till the daylight faded into darkness, dreaming—
fondly dreaming—forgetful of the fateful current which
circled in her veins, and made a gulf betwixt her and
her idol deeper than hell itself, and so wide that nothing
but sin could over-leap it. She forgot that freedom and
refinement could not make her white, and that virtuous
love would fly astonished from the embrace which sinful passion sought.

She hid the battered bullet in her bosom. Well for
her if it had been hidden in her *heart*.

The kind old surgeon had Geoffrey removed to a
wall-tent, apart from the rest, and there, day after day,
Toinette attended the stricken man.

With unwearying devotion she supplied the wants
and attended to every desire of the invalid. No labor
was too great, nothing too severe for her. And as he
began to show signs of recovery, her step grew lighter,
and her eye beamed with a clearer luster.

She was cheating herself with fond hopes that when
delirium had left his disordered mind he would recognize her. She had not a doubt that he loved her.
Then her happiness would be complete.

CHAPTER XXXII.

DARKNESS.

AT length it came. One bright morning when the earth was aglow with the beauty of the advancing Spring time, when the songs of birds flooded the soft air with enchanting melody, she came just at daybreak to the tent of Geoffrey Hunter. Upon the topmost limb of a dense cedar, which stood a few yards from the tent, a mocking-bird was swaying to and fro, and pouring forth his morning love song—the truest expression of the master passion nature or art has ever produced; now, glowing and confident, it rolled forth in exultant notes, which seemed to crowd upon each other in a burning haste for utterance; anon, plaintive and low, as a discarded angel might have pleaded with his earthly love in those primal days when heavenly lovers wooed the daughters of men; then, freighted with a bitter, mocking hate, the very essence of jealousy—and ending in a calm, clear, caressing carol, bespeaking the boundless bliss of wedded love.

Toinette stopped at the tent door and listened to this wonderful songster, her heart the while interpreting the cadences of his song. She thought—as he rose and soared away in the dim morning light, making the balmy spring dawning resonant with the matchless melody of

love—poor fool! she thought that it was but an omen
and prognostic of her own rewarded devotion, a type
and prelude of the music which should fill her future.

She had been wearied with many wakeful nights,
and another attendant of the hospital, touched by her
devotion, had persuaded her to take one night's rest.
A few moments before this friend had called her
and informed her that the patient had slept quietly
the whole night, and now seemed to be entirely without any symptom of the fever which before had been
hanging about him. Toinette's heart had leaped with
joy at the announcement. A night of calm, peaceful,
natural rest meant restored reason, as she thought,
and the ever present love sprang up in her heart,
buoyant with the hope of recognition. So she had
dressed with unusual care, endeavoring to make herself as attractive as her moderate conveniences would
permit. "I wish that his first sight of me should be
as pleasant as may be. He used to say that I was
handsome. I wonder if he will think so now? I am
sure I am much prettier than I was then," she murmured, as her little mirror disclosed the soft, rich complexion
of the perfect brunette, charged with its wealth of color
ebbing and flowing like the tide, almost imperceptibly,
with her varying thought—never flushing, never pallid,
on the instant and a wealth of wavy hair just far enough
removed from black to match the eyes of melting
brown, in whose liquid depths sat the image of the
fairest soul and purest love that had ever strayed from
Heaven. Every charm was heightened a thousand-fold
by the love which throbbed and bounded in her bosom

Every motion, as she dressed, was an utterance of
affection. She petted her hair as she combed and
brushed it; her face as she bathed and burnished it in
the coarse towel. The rustle of her dress as it fell
about her (it was one she had brought in the hope of
meeting him, and had never worn before at the hospital)
was music to her ears which ached for the sound of his
voice in approval. She felt as light of heart as the
happy warbler who had awakened the echoes of the
morning by his sweet caroling without. Her feet spurned
the earth as she crossed the open space to the tent
where her idol lay. Her heart ached with the fullness
of ecstacy as she raised the curtain and entered. She
pressed her hand upon her breast and held her breath
as she advanced to the side of the rough cot in which
he lay. It was not yet quite light in the tent, but she
could see that he was sleeping calmly. His easy,
regular breathing showed that he was free from pain,
and her heart overflowed with gratitude as she thought
that reason had regained its throne. Glad tears flowed
from her eyes, and joyous murmurs—half sobbings, and
half laughter—came from her lips.

She stooped over the sleeper and pressed upon his
lips a tender, trembling, burning kiss—one of those
embraces which might overturn a kingdom or found an
empire.

The sleeper woke with a start. The eyes opened
and gazed wonderingly about. She had raised his head,
and stood bending over him, her face beaming with
expectancy, ready to repeat the embrace upon the first
sign of recognition. But it came not.

"Where am I?" came in a querulous voice from the lips which had just received that baptism of love.

"He is only half himself," thought the fond heart, with ready excuse for its idol. "He does not know me yet." So she answered, and her voice sounded unnatural to herself even, from the restraint she was forced to exercise :

"You are with friends—in the hospital. You were very badly wounded, and have been sick for some time. You are very weak, and must be quiet, now."

"One question," he said.

"Now he will ask. He has recognized me at length," said the fond heart to itself, and a flood of joy mantled neck and brow. "Well?" she said, and her tone was a bar from the mocking bird's final strain.

"Did we take the Fort?"

Poor heart! Not yet.

But then he did not know. It was but natural that the hero should ask about the battle which was raging when he was stricken down.

"Yes," she answered patiently; "but after you had held it for a time your men were assaulted in turn, and it was retaken."

"And held by the enemy?"

"Yes."

"I am then, a prisoner?"

"Yes."

And still he did not ask.

"Be still, fond heart, lest your beatings disturb thy idol. Wait—wait—thy time will come." So whispered love—fond love—blind love.

"What makes it so dark here?" asked the sufferer.

"Ah, that's it," said the trusting watcher to herself. "His eyes are unused to the dim morning light as yet. I will open the tent and let in the sunlight."

With nimble fingers she undid the fastening and threw back one-half of the tent front, letting the bright sunlight stream in upon the sufferer's face.

"What a beautiful sunrise!" she exclaimed with rapture in her tones, as she went back to the couch. "It has been a long time since you have seen one before."

"Sunrise!" he said in a tone of astonishment, "it is dark, I tell you, quite dark."

The sun was pouring his full radiance upon the staring eye-balls, but they saw it not.

Toinette comprehended it in an instant, and with a low moan fell upon the camp-stool by the cot. This unexpected horror, coming so suddenly in the very footsteps of anticipated joy, quite unnerved her, and bitter sobs burst from her lips.

She quite forgot that he had not recognized her voice or rewarded her love, and only remembered the affliction which had fallen upon him.

He heard her sobs, and partially understood their cause.

His face blanched, his lips quivered, and the clasped hands closed quickly together in a trembling embrace, as his heart prepared itself for the saddest of all tidings to the soul of a young, brave, and aspiring man—the doom of darkness—a doom with which few hearts can wrestle. Well did the ancient poet represent the "*mon-*

P

strum horrendum, informe, ingens," who threatened all who touched his barren island with destruction, as being disarmed and rendered powerless and contemptible, by the doom of impenetrable darkness.

Few, indeed, are the Samsons who can tower above this terrible fate and show themselves more majestic and potent under its visitation than before. Now and then a Homer and a Milton walks proudly and confidently to the pinnacle of fame with sightless orbs, but to few is the inner light of such transcendent genius given. Even Milton, fearful of his fame, paid his entrance fee to Westminster. Blind, indeed, was he when he did so. Most frequently the halting feet grope their way more deeply into obscurity, and the head which might have been crowned with honor is laid ungarlanded in the nameless grave.

At length he spoke with trembling lips, and a tone in which the plaintive inquiry of blindness already prevailed—that unconscious prayer for help that lives upon the tongue of the blind as well as in the step that questions the pathway before it is completed.

"Is the sun shining?" he asked.

Toinette mastered her emotion and answered in a tone firm and unshrinking, yet freighted with a rich sympathy:

"It is."

There was silence in the tent. The stricken soul was wrestling with its fearful doom. Toinette rose quietly and went with heavy footsteps to her own little apartment. The birds sang as merrily as when she came, but she did not hear them. She almost hated the sunshine because it would not enlighten the darkness in which he lay. She took off and laid aside the pretty dress, silently and sadly and donned again the soft grey hospital habit.

Then she sought the surgeon-in-chief and asked him to visit her patient. She informed him of his return to consciousness, but said nothing about the discovery that had been made. Poor child! she hoped it might not be found so bad by the doctor, as it seemed to her, and she feared to ask lest her worst fears should be confirmed. The surgeon went into the tent, but she staid without, walking to and fro and sometimes sitting upon a wooden seat in the bright sunshine. She could hear the two men talking now and then, but did not catch their words. She would have given worlds to have known their purport, yet she would not go nearer.

Nay, she moved further off, in very dread lest she might hear what she was dying, almost, to know. It seemed an age that the doctor remained. At length he came out. She knew by his look that his message was one of evil. He would confirm her worst fears. And yet she must ask. She must hear him speak the terrible words. Certainty must be made doubly sure. So she met him and said pleadingly:

"Will he ever see again?'

"I am afraid not," he answered tenderly and gravely.

She caught at the uncertainty which was intended only to break the force of the blow, and asked with a sudden up-springing hope:

"There is then a chance?"

He shook his head sadly, and answered:

"I am sorry to say, I think not."

"Oh, it was terrible! She could have endured death, because she was prepared for it; but this — The world grew dark to her own bright eyes, as she thought of this terrible doom.

The surgeon regarded her kindly, as she struggled with her emotion, and finally said, gently:

"You have met this man before, Mrs. Hunter. Pardon me for asking; but is he a friend—a relative of yours?"

Toinette was about to answer "Yes," when all at once the truth flashed upon her as it never had before. She was no longer the slave-girl whose position had half-excused her sin. Geoffrey Hunter was no longer her master, and compliance with his will was no longer but making the best of evil circumstances. Her love was no longer the garland which crowned the Thyrsus, hiding with its loveliness a harsh and inevitable fate. She was now Mrs. Hunter—so she was called —regarded as a widow, educated, free, with a young life committed to her charge, whose pure soul she must not smutch with evil influence. Her old life was dead. The Geoffrey Hunter of the past was dead to her, too. This was another, a stricken stranger, in yonder, who had no stronger claims upon her tender ness than the terrible nature of his affliction.

In that instant she was born again. The menial nature died in her soul. The spirit and thought of the slave-girl departed, and the free woman, pure and **noble, self-reliant** and brave, stood forth in her stead.

The warm blood mounted to her brow—the blush of unconscious modesty, violated by her own thought— and her eyes fell as this young mother, for the first time conscious of the usual instincts of maidenhood, said to the watchful inquirer:

"I—don't—know.—That is—. Please don't ask me now."

"Certainly," he answered; and his kind old face was full of sympathy. "I would not intrude upon any private matter of Mrs. Hunter's; but remember, if you should ever want a friend, in any matter, great or small, I shall be happy to serve you. And if at any time you should deem me worthy of your confidence, you will find it not misplaced. Meantime, let your patient yonder be kept as quiet as possible for the present. No excitement—no conversation that can be avoided. Shall I send another nurse?"

"No, if you please. I will remember," she said, quietly.

"Well, good morning, then,"—and he went away, wondering what the secret was, but verifying the adage that truth is stranger than fiction, by imagining nothing half so wonderful as Toinette's actual relation to Geoffrey Hunter.

CHAPTER XXXIII.

BEGINNING OF THE END.

EVERY day brought wonderful changes now. The army had broken up the quarters so long occupied and changed the base, which had grown in a few months from an almost deserted landing to be a busy metropolis. The long lines of works were silent, and the deserted guns grinned at each other an impotent defiance. Now and then a fort was left with a small garrison, and here and there a force of Veteran Reserves or a body of light-duty men was still encamped. The vultures, and the poor from the fallen city, came forth and prowled lazily about in the late bustling camps A stray dog or a lame horse, with here and there a broken caisson or wrecked army wagon, was all that remained except the long lines of low, daubed chimneys, the tent-poles, the shabby bunks, and the hard-beaten paths which marked the "company streets," to show that thousands upon thousands had teemed amid that solitude but yesterday.

The hospitals change, too; but more slowly, and with more apparent effort. When the order for the troops to march is given, the various surgeons send their regimental invalids, actual and prospective, to the division hospital. Here the Surgeon in charge, after an unusually thorough inspection, sends as many as he can back to their commands on "light duty," and forwards the rest to the appointed depots for the sick and wounded, while he prepares to follow his command unless detailed by the Medical Director in charge of the hospitals.

Such were the scenes of desolation and turmoil through which Geoffrey Hunter and his faithful nurse passed soon after the events of the last two chapters. The god of war had gone to other fields upon which now hour by hour were being worked out the closing moves of the great problem in which two mighty powers had been so long engaged. From every side the forces of Grant were centering upon the doomed remnant. Horse and foot seemed omnipresent. Wherever Lee thrust out his *tentaculæ* they touched a bayonet or a saber, or the whizzing shell or pattering grape cut off a groping member, and it spake by its absence of an encircling enemy. Lee was straining every nerve to accomplish one thing, to reach one spot. He had ordered all the captains of his shattered corps to meet him there. And at that very point, with the strange prescience of true military genius, Grant had directed his own generals also to concentrate.

So that at this moment Virginia presented a strange spectacle. Richmond and Petersburg, for years the looked-for prize of contest, deserted, and the enemy, without waiting for a "God speed" from any one, fall away from the coveted booty and rush along the road which the real prize has taken. And in the very midst of the thronging columns of blue—eager and anxious for their prey—trembling and shattered, sullen and almost hopeless, plodded the wavering, melting column of gray.

The man who rode the noble "Traveler" at their front has not quite given up hope. The instinct of his soldiers is truer this time than his wondrous forecast. He would not risk everything at Steadman, because there was a chance for him to make the movement which he is now striving to accomplish. Behind him comes the great presence—the smoking Sphinx whose puzzle he has failed to read—the remorseless destiny which pursues him everywhere and upon every flank road his lieutenants. Blue and gray couriers ride here and there in inextricable confusion across the country. The dispatches meant for Gordon are in the hands of Warren, while Sheridan peruses those intended for Longstreet. On the other hand, those of Ord and Wright inform the Confederate commander of the dangers which surround him.

Every road but one was held. Lee hoped that was open. Grant knew it was sealed. Finally there came a message from the Smoker's lips. It was only a suggestion, a hint, that the result was inevitable. Might it not as well be here as there? The gray-bearded cavalier saw the fate which menaced him. Yet his Fabian nature would not give up. He would try the gate and prove whether it was closed and guarded. He plodded on—one day more, only one. He found the gate then and grim war-dogs beside it whom he dared not attempt to remove, and so the man who would not take the offer of a matchless immortality at Fort Steadman—lest he might lose the chance of victory on other fields—gave up his army a bloodless prize, like a wolf in the hunter's snare.

And while these great events were being worked out by the master-minds who were matched on this great field of empire, in a way and manner to themselves unknown, which is to all a mystery except to the shoulder-strapped disciples of Esculapius, Geoffrey Hunter and his nurse, Mrs. Antoinette Hunter, had passed from Division to Corps, from Corps to Department, and from Department to the General Hospital at City Point.

Although his sight was destroyed, the recovery of Geoffrey Hunter from the effects of his wound was otherwise wonderfully rapid. He had remembered, in part at least, the determination with which he had set out in life. His pleasures had always been those which would not vitiate his powers of enjoyment. He had indulged in no intemperance or excess, and now the strength of a sound constitution, with the reserve vitality which only a life of activity and prudence can give, enabled him to recover speedily from a wound which would ordinarily have proved mortal or have required months to effect its cure. The case was what is known in surgical lore as a healing "by first intention," which seems to be a recovery in which nature is not balked in her beneficent designs by human depravity. Of course, the old Surgeon was not inclined to have his art entirely lost sight of, and in his statement of the case the skill of the attendant and the devotion of the nurse came in, perhaps, for a larger share of credit than nature, a correct life, and a strong constitution; and who shall blame him if he was somewhat partial to his calling?

21

CHAPTER XXXIV.

TYPES.

IT was the 4th of April, 1865—five days before the end came, and the heroes surrendered to kindred heroes at Appomattox. Richmond was the seat of empire no more. The brave men who had upheld the glory which for a time she knew were either buried in the harsh, arid, bloomless soil of wasted, desolated Virginia, or were the disheartened victims of the unsuccessful struggle. The truculent horde, who had thronged her streets while war promised even a dubious hope of plunder, had vanished.

The city, queenly in its location and advantages, had gained nothing by Confederate rule. The metropolis of the rebellion, it reaped only a sorrowful prominence in disaster from its fall. Want and misery, disease and crime, had walked hand in hand with prodigality and profligacy while blood flowed for its safety. The poor had grown more abject and dependent, the vicious more abandoned and depraved, while the rich had reveled in fictitious wealth.

There had been a marvelous show of opulence. The ordinary means of estimation had almost failed. The unit of value had shrunk first to one decimal place and then to another in quick succession. What represented value by the legal fiction was more plentiful than many of the ordinary articles of daily use. Only the gifts of God were so abundant. Luxuries of the table were sometimes worth more than money, bulk for bulk.

Want at times had pressed so close that bands of women, gaunt and hunger-pinched, defied the hand of power, bore down the guards about the public stores, broke locks and bolts, and, shouting like frenzied bacchanals, possessed themselves of food. Aye, even tore the clothing from their limbs there in the garish light of day—the chill winter day—to make extempore sacks in which to bear a portion to their children.

Around this regal city for four years had raged the combat of which it was itself the prize. More than once the camp-fires of the enemy had gleamed in the eyes of its affrighted citizens. Once it was almost begirt by their lurid glow. They were the funeral torches of the mightiest of those now dead. In their glare the soul of Jackson had departed. Then, in her suburbs, within sight of the windows of Libby even, were seen the blue-coated cavaliers making good their way along the streets of the city. A few more sabers might have conquered.

During all these months and years her artisans had toiled night and day. That grand old giant, the turbid, growling James, fitly god-sired by the testy king, had given them his aid. The furnace-fires glowed, the mill-wheels turned, the burrs rolled ceaselessly, and the busy spindles whirred like points of quivering light. All was action, effort. But the war-god had swallowed up the results. Instead of growth and prosperity, decay and destruction had set their marks upon the haughty

capital. To crown all came the flame. Poor Richmond! No heart exulted in thy downfall while looking
on this ruin! Pity drowned all other thought!

The little great man whom accident had made the
head of a mighty political movement; whose audacity
was equal to the task of attempting to out-rank such
men as Jackson, and Lee, and a host of others, upon
whose brows was written immortality—this seemingly
successful pigmy had betaken himself to dishonorable
flight with the gold which he had hoarded. Already
was opening the fathomless chasm of impenetrable obscurity in which his innate mediocrity was finally to
seek its level, along with the fit companions whom his
jealous imbecility had associated in his administration.
Fortune turned terribly against this miserable gamester
at the eleventh hour. From others she had taken king-
doms and power, and given them instead—renown.
Many whom she has shabbily treated in life she has immortalized in death. This man had been her favorite
always heretofore. He had won upon the weakest hands.
Merit, ability, learning, devotion, all were nothing before
his barefaced luck, and ever-winning impudence. He
was made the head of the Confederacy with overwhelming unanimity, though a thousand overtopped him in all
the requisites of leadership. But the scales turned at
length, and he fell so low that his humblest enemy
could not but pity him. War and defeat brought him
neither death nor glory. Ignoble in his fall as he had
been unworthy in his rise, he whined and paltered,
sniveled for sympathy in his woes, fed on the charity
of the people he had ruined, and sank fussing and

fuming into that deepest hell, a living tomb—the oblivion which engulfs a worthless life before the mantle of charity is cast about the memory of the dead.

The slender, gray clad figure, erect and lithe, which had so long been known to dwellers in the city as "the President" was gone, and in his stead there came one of a different order. The elegant and courtly chief of the Confederacy—the lordly planter of Great Bend, the favored child, nourished and cultured by the Government he had endeavored to subvert—to the last moment retained the trappings and the pomp of power. He was an aristocrat—one of the few selected and ordained to rule—whose mission it is to govern. He boasted that he belonged to a class who were born to command, even as the slave was born to serve. He knew that a thousand must live and die as paupers, or slaves, in order that one "gentleman" might exist, yet he counted them cheap, even at that price.

For those who waged the war which his class had inaugurated—who did the fighting, while they reaped the profit and the glory, if profit or glory resulted from the struggle—the great substratum of the people, "the poor white trash"—he had the most sovereign and supreme contempt. They were the clods upon which he walked, the stones which paved his pathway to renown. They were but as the dust of the balances to such as he. Yet from this class came the Avenger.

Two days before, in the gathering Sabbath twilight gloom, the hoof strokes of the flying Aristocrat had awakened the wondering echoes of the almost deserted streets. Now, along the same roughly paved street, in the mild sunlight of the April afternoon, came the tall, angular form, and coarse, dark features of "the Great Uncouth"—that man into whose hands the destinies of millions had been committed; whom Liberty had chosen from her myriad sons and consecrated, half against his will, to the fulfillment of her noblest, holiest work— Abraham Lincoln—the "rail splitter" of the Sangamon country—the "poor white" of the Kentucky "knobs,' —walking in triumph along the way his high-bred opponent had ridden in defeat.

Unaccompanied save by the friend on whose arm he leaned, and the wondering lad who clasped his hand, along the streets of the fallen Capital, paced this strangely compounded being; the head of a conquering army, yet not of it; the ruler of a victorious people, yet desirous only that victory should be forgotten; in the proudest of earthly positions, yet clothed with humility; the chosen instrument of chastisement and vengeance, yet overflowing with mercy; the appointed victim of disappointed hatred and ambition, yet anxious only for peace and reconciliation; the representative "poor white," the embodiment of a triumphant democracy, gazing on the ruined seats of a defeated oligarchy "with malice toward none, and with charity for all." Since the Nazarene wept over Jerusalem Time has not limned on the canvas of history another scene to compare in its elements of moral grandeur, and in completeness of detail and surroundings, with Lincoln entering the Capital of the Confederacy before the glare of the contest had paled, or its thunders were hushed.

He strides absently along with a sad, pitying look

upon his face—grand in its very uncouthness, scarred
and furrowed by the buffetings of fortune—regarding
with strange inquiry all that surrounds him. His sham-
bling, uncertain gait is strong and rapid. The friend
who walks beside him pants with the fatigue of unaccustomed exercise. The great, grim presence knows it
not. The boy begs him to slacken his walk. He hears
him not. He does not heed the half curious, half sullen
stare of the loungers in the streets, among whom the
rumor of his identity is already afloat, nor the occasional
cheer of knots of freedmen who thus tender their thanks
for the indefinite bliss, which they have hardly tasted—
the freedom which is linked forever with the name of
Lincoln. He hears and lifts his hat, absently and
silently. In thought, as usual, he is questioning the
future. He is asking of toppling walls, decaying houses,
and neglected, half-paved streets what lesson they have
to give him of the future, of this land whose destiny he
would trace and shape aright.

Thought stamped upon his homely features long
since the index of a mighty query, and his life has been
one of ceaseless questionings. He has not delved much
in books, nor worshiped science and philosophy; but
of men and events he has ever sought the reason of their
existence and development. His genius was not forma-
tive but extractive. From laurel and thistle he gathered
alike the truth they bore, and it became at once, by
instant assimilation, a part of himself. He did not
meditate—continuous, consequential thought was irk-
some to him. He did not see events afar off; but he
caught the signs of their approach, he read the storm-

signals of the near future with a wonderful accuracy and ease.   Man or nature never passed unchallenged before his eye.

Perhaps it was from this natural bent of his mind— perhaps it was the stupendous questions with which he had to deal, but for some reason, certain it was that after he assumed the Presidential chair, the mind of Mr. Lincoln seemed constantly groping after the Infinite, feeling after the Omnipotent.   The truth that was to be wrought out by the Rebellion, the purpose which existed in the Infinite Mind and in accordance with which that mighty conflict began and proceeded, seems to have dawned upon his mind only by piecemeal.   Day after day and month after month, he hesitated and shrunk from the course which the first battle of Bull Run made inevitable, as thousands of minds had clearly discovered before.   Even in the fall of 1862, when he saw the path of freedom, clearly defined and opened before him, his cautious mind built up a bulwark of hypothetical threats behind which he might retire in case it should become necessary.   It was not necessary.   Indeed, that public feeling which he feared (was it the creature of that Omniscience which he distrusted?) very soon so blocked up his backward path that he could not but go on.   As the future showed, this indecision was his greatest source of strength.

And now another and a greater question faced him. The Rebellion was virtually ended.   In a few days, as he believed, the Confederacy would be a thing of the past.   The reconciliation of the hostile moieties of the republic was a far more difficult and delicate task than the prosecution of the war, which was to **restore the** ancient unity of its territory.

As he crossed on foot, that April day, over the turbid waters of the James, the river spake to him. It was the remonstrance, sullen and angry, of unused power or unimproved opportunity which it had for two hundred years been crooning to the dwellers upon its banks. The quick-eared child of nature heard and comprehended its complaint as he leaned over the parapet and looked at the swollen torrent. Then he turned and gazed sadly at the lone island where so many thousands had died for the cause which would render his name immortal. He passed on and saw the scath and havoc of the flame. The last foot-print of the departing war-fiend. His brow was troubled and dark. His deep, anxious eyes were filled with brooding care. His right shoulder drooped more than its wont, and he stooped from his grand height as if borne down by the burden which was laid upon his life.. The "poor white" was walking among his kindred. The problem of his birth came before his manhood for solution.

As he strode along facing this great problem, questioning eagerly all that passed before his eyes in that hour of a nation's second birth, the sound of music was heard—the fife and drum—and a marching column passed before him, at its head the starry banner. In column by platoon, it swept along the broad and silent thoroughfare.

Blue-clad, but dusky-faced, the steel-crowned ranks pressed forward to the time of that weird melody, which burst spontaneously from patriot hearts when freemen first mustered for the struggle with slavery, and moved the people ever onward to the fulfillment of its own wild prophecy.

As they passed on in the long, swinging step, this grandly measured air inspires the uncertain groping Figure, which stood upon the curbstone and gazed at them, as if he would grasp from the strange medley its true significance. The deep, yearning glance rested on those sable soldiers of liberty, as they passed, with kindly questioning. There was no love in his glance, no gratitude—scarcely respect—only grave, kindly wonder. He gazed at them as a chemist might at a new element which he had cast among the discordant contents of a bubbling crucible, uncertain of its effects —expecting little from its action—caring nothing for its fate. It was a column of Weitzel's colored troops proceeding to their quarters as the garrison of the city. Suddenly the associations of the place and time became too much for the impressionable soldiery, and from a thousand throats burst the wild anthem of liberty, and the glorious chorus,

"Our God is marching on,"

swelled from end to end of the swaying column.

Some subordinate, as he passed, recognized the potent presence on the curbstone, and brought his detachment to the "Shoulder arms," in token of respect, as they passed. Those in the rear imitated his example, and an extempore review was the result.

The "Poor-White" President did not take to ceremony and parade as kindly as the aristocrat who had fled before the power he represented. He had

THE MAN—ABRAHAM LINCOLN.

"As he stood there, and watched the allies whom freedom had armed in her own defence, the darkness and boding care faded out of his eyes."—p. 355.

not been taught in childhood to receive reverence
himself, but to yield it to others. The lordly wave
of the hand—the courtly nod of the superior—never
came naturally to the uncouth genius of the new West
Yet he felt this tribute of respect. He knew that it
was to him—the man, Abraham Lincoln—and not to
the ruler, that it was offered. He would return the
greeting. And he did it, as he did all things else, in
a way peculiar to himself—not with the touch of the
visor, which the Regulations prescribe; but by taking
off his hat with a grave courtesy, and standing un-
covered while the soldiery passed. And as he stood
there, and watched the allies whom freedom had armed
in her own defense, the darkness and the boding care
faded out of his eyes, and only kindly sympathy and
trusting hope shone there instead. Why was it? Had
he solved the problem which the future presented?
Perhaps, dimly.

The companion of the President was also a man of
historic name—a name linked inseparably with every
great question and phase of our national progress for
many a year. His mind had stamped its impress upon
every measure of the party of freedom, and his burning
eloquence had scotched, like a tongue of flame, the in-
famies of slavery. No danger could daunt, no suffering
subdue, this leonine child of the East. His voice might
be hushed by the brutal hand of the desperado, but
his eye never lost its defiance, nor did his spirit quail
before the haughty power which ruled the nation with
a rod of iron. He, too, was not an originator. He did
not go before and show the way to coming ages and

peoples; but he had the skill of the Indian hunter for
the trail, which other minds had made.   He had conned
the lessons of history to exhaustion.   He adopted instinctively that course of thought which those furthest
in advance of their fellows had indicated as the truest
and best.   He was not the engineer who followed
the compass of thought through the dark wilderness of
coming events and marked out the path of future empire; but he came in the very front of the onward march
of events.   His eagle eye discerned the " guides and
pointers " which showed the line of right, and he made
plain and broad the way in which the nation should
walk.   To him the slightest vestiges of truth and freedom were apparent.   He traced their faintest footsteps
as the ordinary mind pursues the simplest formulas of
mathematics.   His ruthless logic and keen analysis, united to an eloquence whose overwhelming force was like
the lava-tide which bursts from fierce Vesuvius, swept
away all obstacles, and showed the pathway clear and unmistakable, to the dullest mind and most unwilling feet.

His mind was not groping and tentative, like his companion's.   It was not speculative, not assimilative, but
demonstrative.   He was a prophet who had just witnessed the fulfillment of his own predictions.   Others
before him, it is true, had traced the line of thought
which had pointed to the end they had just witnessed.   The flying enemy, the conquered capital, the
vanished power, had all been foreshadowed by other
minds—the pioneers, whom truth had sent into the wilderness—but he had most clearly demonstrated it; had
marked it so plainly that he who runs might read.

Even those who would not see it could not ever afterward hide it from their sight.

It is said, that very early in the war when the great, troubled heart of the President had pondered the course he should adopt in an important crisis through all the tedious watches of a sleepless night, he came very early in the morning to this accomplished co-worker and said:

"I have determined on my course. I shall do so and so. Is there any authority for it?"

And the Scholar had answered doubtfully: "I will consult the oracles and learn."

And thereupon, he read and pondered the sages of the law, and found that the collected wisdom of the ages pointed to the same conclusion to which the instinctive prescience of the Pioneer had led.

Thus the heart and conscience of the West linked hands with the knowledge and culture of the East to accomplish the great work which was set before them.

During the entire struggle this bold, positive, decided mind supplemented the hesitating, fearful, doubting one of the President, not by leading or controlling, but by confirming. It is doubtful if the keen, questioning frontiersman did not generally go before the polished child of the East, but while he was running the course again and again, in doubt and uncertainty, perplexed with difficulties and variations, this other great mind of a different order came to his aid, and so confirmed his conviction and cleared his view, by citing the examples and precedents which history affords, that he could no longer hesitate.

He was the Fanatic.

Did he, too, learn in that hour of the completest triumph which is ever vouchsafed to man—the triumph of ideas to which he has devoted life and strength —as he looked upon the wreck and scath of that war by which that triumph had been wrought, did he learn that lesson of abounding charity which had wrought out its perfect work in the heart of his great chief? Did he learn that abstract right might be the sorest evil in the concrete, and that the most grievous wrong might be linked with elements of the noblest manhood and most admirable virtue? Were the seeds in that hour planted in his bosom which in the future should fructify in statesmanship inspired and impersonated with the divine message of Christianity shrined in that holiest of words, " Forgive "? . Perhaps; but he is of sterner stuff than the compatriot whom Providence has made his chief in position, though of less commanding intellect. He is of the fine white marble of Carrara, on which the graver must work long and patiently to trace his chosen design.

It was all there in its appropriate symbols—the grand allegory of the nation's second birth—the Poor White President—the Fanatic of the regal mind and leonine mien—the ranks of armed freedmen, and the conquered Capital devastated by fire and awaiting its further doom, half-sullenly, half-hopefully. Away to the southward the arm of the Laborer, the silent Hammerer, was pounding away at the lordly crest of the flying Cavalier. All were types, and grand ones in their way, of the Past and Future, of which that moment was the connecting and dividing Present.

CHAPTER XXXV.

THE HOSPITAL.

IT is the convalescent ward of a General Hospital.
The patients are Confederate officers and soldiers
wounded - in the last battles around Petersburg and
Richmond. The row of clean, white beds and the well-
swept floor betray the order and neatness of a permanent hospital. The breath of Spring comes through
the open windows, and some are sitting up in their
cots gazing out upon the fair scene below. A busy
city of tents and rough plank buildings, put up in dépôt
style of unplaned boards, long and narrow, with a crowded wharf, and a swift-flowing river dotted with all manner of craft—all flying the stars and stripes—while city,
wharf, and shipping are alive with thousands of blue-
clad men, rank and file, line and staff, of every grade
and branch of the service. This was City Point—
Grant's dépôt of supplies in the Spring of 1865. There
is not much cheerfulness in this ward of the great hospital. The greater part of its inmates are heart-sick, as
well as suffering under bodily affliction.

"It cannot last much longer," says one gray-coated
invalid to another. "Uncle Bobby Lee can never get
to Johnston, with all the force which Grant has in pursuit of him. It's my notion that the jig's about up,

and, for one, I 'm glad of it. It would have to come in the end, and may as well be now as later.''

"What shall we do now?" asked his comrade querulously. "The niggers will all be freed, and we shall only have a few acres of poor land left, with nobody to till it.''

"Oh, bother the land, that may be confiscated, too, for all we know, and go along with the two-legged chattels-real.''

"That is true; and then what will we do?" responded the other.

"Do? Hanged if I know," said the first speaker. "But I 'll be bound we find something to do. We have as good a chance as the niggers, any how. For me, the first thing I am going to do, if ever I get out of this, is to turn Yankee, and take the first job that offers. I 've dug ditches for the Confederacy without pay—or as good—and now I will dig for any one that will pay.''

"Don 't be too certain about the future, Captain," said one of his listeners. "Old Abe may set you up in the hemp business before he gets through with you.''

"That 's so," said the first speaker, "or if Lee should make the trip and unite with Johnston, we may be sent to Point Look-Out or Bull's Island, till ' this cruel war is over,' if we should chance to out-last it. Well, it 's what we enlisted for, boys; and as far as hemp-pulling is concerned, I reckon we have all done enough to entitle us to a share in that business.''

"By the way," said another, " have you heard that Lincoln is here?''

"No!" answered several, "is it so?"

"That's what the Doctor told me just now; and Lieutenant Goldwin, who went out this morning on parole, said that he saw him but a little time ago, walking about without any escort, talking with every one he met."

"And whittling, I suppose, like every other Yankee,' said one.

"I wish he would come here and get off one of his little jokes, to liven us up some," said another.

"I would like to see him, any how," said a third, "just to know what he is like. Wouldn't you, Colonel?" turning to Geoffrey's cot and speaking to him.

For the moment they had forgotten his blindness, but as they looked at him and saw his sightless orbs turned toward them, and the look of painful anger that swept over his face, they regretted the unfortunate forgetfulness, and were not surprised at the bitterness of his reply:

"I am more fortunate than the rest of you, for I am in no danger of seeing the monster."

Knowing that he was brooding upon his affliction, his comrades made an effort to divert his attention from 't.

"You have another piece of luck, too," said one of them, gaily; "you have quite cut us all out with that little Yankee nurse. She has neither ears nor eyes for anyone but you."

"That's so, Colonel; you have made a conquest there, certain," said another, "and it's a pity you cannot see what a prize you have taken, too,"

23

"The trimmest piece of dry-goods I have seen in many a day," chimed in a third.

"A lady, gentlemen, a perfect lady, if I ever saw one," said a brusque lieutenant from the opposite cot, "and for my part, if she has a special fancy for Colonel Hunter, I can't blame her, for, indeed, boys, he deserves it."

"I say, God bless her, anyhow," said a gallant captain; "the very sight of the sweet creature bustling about and making things tidy for us, with such a demure, modest look, has been worth more than all the doctor's stuff to me."

Geoffrey Hunter raised himself upon his elbow and listened with a show of interest to the remarks of his fellow-officers upon the nurse. He recognized the kindly sympathy which had induced this cheerful badinage, and was anxious to humor it, that they might think themselves successful in the diversion they had attempted.

"Hold on, gentlemen," said he, "you will make my misfortune unbearable, if I am to hear the praises of this goddess and not to see her. Could n't some of you lend me your eyes? Edgerton, what is she like?"

"What is she like!" said Edgerton, a gigantic artillery captain, bearded like the pard. "Like—an angel who stays below here out of pity for human woe, and brings the air of heaven with her!"

"Too ethereal by half," said Geoffrey, laughing. "Not being accustomed to the lineaments of female Yankee angels, your description is lost on me. Brig-

den, can 't you tell me something more of her person⸗
elle? Let me not burst in ignorance."

Brigden, thus appealed to, gave a minute description
of Toinette, adding similar laudations, declaring his
absolute envy of the fortunate colonel, and saying that
he would willingly lose his eyes if he could only have
as pretty a pair watch over him as tenderly.

One after another added a touch to Brigden's description, and, in a tone of light but respectful badinage,
pictured the pretty Yankee woman to Geoffrey Hunter.

Determined to promote the mirth, he answered:

"It won't do, gentlemen; I can 't make her out.
Now, would you believe it, the only personage your
description calls to my mind is a very likely yaller gal
I used to own."

"Hear him!"

"The sacrilegious brute!"

"Compare a Yankee angel to a she-nigger! Gad,
Hunter," said Edgerton; "it 's well you 're blind. If
you could see, I 'd have you at ten paces for that, as
soon as we could hobble."

"Take care, Hunter," said Dancey, " I expect you
will regret any such reflection in the future. I 've been
inquiring with regard to the *dea certa*—by the way,
I imagine our ' dear creature' is but a corruption of
that phrase—at least, it 's only a free rendering of it. I
find that her name is Hunter, too, and that she is a
widow. I presume she married some far-away cousin
of yours, and looks upon you as the predestined suc-
cessor of the dear departed. Had n't you any Yankee
cousins, Colonel?"

"Certainly," said Geoffrey, now thoroughly interested; "a large number of them. Did you learn what part of the country she was from?"

"Yes, I saw it on her travelling bag, as we came here. It was marked:

> "MRS. ANTOINETTE HUNTER,
> "*Oberlin, Ohio.*"

Mrs. Antoinette Hunter! He had never heard of such a person. Yet somehow it seemed familiar. He felt puzzled and exhausted, so he lay down with that strange disregard of observation, which at first accompanies blindness, and began to move his hand nervously and inquiringly over the blanket. Nature was beginning that peculiar training by which she makes amends for the loss of one sense, in a measure, by supplementing the power of another. His comrades, thinking that he was wearied, ceased their badinage and he thought over what had been said without interruption. It was queer this pretty nurse's name should be "Hunter;" but then there were a great many Hunters in the North. Antoinette Hunter. That was a pretty name. It was strange she should take a fancy to him, and be named Antoinette, too. That was Toinette's name—when it was written in full, it was only Toinette for short. He remembered writing it "Antoinette," in the deed of manumission. He recollected just how it looked then—how every letter was formed, "Antoinette, woman of color, born May 4th, 1844; dark hair and eyes, light complexion, very likely." That 's the way she was described in the bill

of sale he had received from his father. He had n't
thought of her for a long time, hardly since the war
began. That was one nigger Lincoln did n't get the
chance to free. He smiled grimly to himself as the
thought struck him.

He wondered how she was getting on. Her young
one must be three—four—yes, better than four years old.

She had written that it was a boy—as if he cared!
He had got the letter but a little time before Lincoln
cut off the mails. He wondered how he would have
answered it, if the war had not relieved him of the
necessity. It was strange he had been so infatuated
with the girl. She was handsome, though. And she
just filled the description given of this wonderful
nurse, though his fellow-officers did laugh at the idea.

It *was* amusing. Hair, complexion, eyes, figure, all
fitted exactly. Her voice, too, was like Toinette's, now
that he thought of it. It would be odd if she should
turn out to be a relative. She had certainly been
very attentive and watchful towards him. All his
comrades seemed to have noticed that. It was pleasant
to be the object of a pretty woman's solicitude, even
if she was only a Yankee nurse. They all agreed
that she was very much of a lady, too. That made
it nicer yet. That was the reason she was so quiet
and delicate in her ways. How tender and patient
she had been towards him; never uttering any remonstrance or reproach, however much he had fretted or
scolded, or whatever hard things he had said about the
Yankees. How kind and faithful she had been. She
had hardly left him for a moment, until he was put

into the convalescent ward. There were so many here, she could only come occasionally, and could only pay him ordinary attention when she did. Of course not— it would not be proper. Though she still combed and brushed his hair, and did a hundred little offices which she might have omitted without neglecting her duty, but which all made him more comfortable and happy, if one in such darkness could be termed happy. Every touch was a caress, too. She must be an angel, as they told him, and a sweet-tempered one at that. She must be beautiful, too, by Brigden's description. Somehow, he had always thought she looked just as they had described her. He seemed to have known her before. So like Toinette, too. She could hardly have been prettier. He wished he could see her. Really, he was half in love with the little mystery. Pshaw! a blind man in love! A woman would n't look at him a second time! Toinette herself—a free nigger—would n't care for him now.

This woman had shown wonderful sympathy for him, though. He remembered now, that he had heard her sobbing at his bedside when she thought him asleep. He did n't know why, but he had always believed she was crying on his account. What a tender touch she had. She would sit and fondle his hand for hours in silence, and he was sure that he had felt tears dropping on it at such times. Once or twice she had kissed it— softly, sorrowfully he thought. Somehow it had thrilled him strangely. It seemed, too, that once—when was it? —or was it a dream in that long night which had fallen on him? No, he remembered it now. It was that

morning when he first learned that the sun would shine
no more for him. He had heard her, (as he lay, half-
dreaming) come into the tent noiselessly almost. Then
she bent over him and kissed his lips—a trembling,
fervent, dewy kiss, freighted with hope and love. His
blood bounded at its memory. He had been so absorbed in his affliction that he had forgotten it till now.
What lips! How they spoke in that silent pressure! It
was a hymn and prayer in one. Gratitude for the past
and hope for the future were syllabled to his soul in its
trembling, tender eagerness! He had never felt but
one kiss like it, and *that* was Toinette's. He thought
of the first time he had kissed her. The girl had
exquisite lips. A Sybarite could not have helped
kissing them, if she *was* a nigger. He remembered
thinking she was only a pretty pet; yet, somehow, he
trembled when he gave her that first kiss. Then he
remembered how it became a habit, and he always
claimed one, if she came into the library when he was
there. He remembered, too, how her kisses ripened
from simple childish jests, to tender, clinging endear-
ments. They were wonderfully like this Yankee nurse's
stolen embrace. He did not know that kisses were so
much alike. Well, if she had Toinette's lips they were
nearly matchless—full, tender, mobile, and exquisitely
cut and penciled. He remembered now that last kiss
she had given him, when he left her a free woman,
waiting for maternity in her new Northern home. She
hung around his neck, and her lips had the same clinging tenderness, only it was a burden of beseeching which
they bore. There was no eager joy in them. It liked

to have broken him down. He was sorry enough for
the poor girl, off there alone, with such a dreary prospect and among strangers, too. He came very near
waiting till her trial was over, just out of pity. He
thought he would have done so but for the news that
came from home—the tidings of coming war. What was
the name of that free-nigger town where he left her?
Oh yes, Oberlin! Oberlin? Oberlin? Why that—yes—
that was the name Brigden saw on the nurse's traveling
bag! It could not—yes. He saw it all now. Strange he
had been such a fool. The jade had taken his name, and
passed for a widow—and a white woman, too! Probably
called her brat Hunter! Perhaps named it after him, too
—Geoffrey Hunter, Jr.! Mistress Antoinette Hunter,
forsooth! It was a sharp game she had played! And
she had even tried to entrap *him!* Had been kissing
him, and coquetting about him before his brother officers.

Geoffrey Hunter's face showed the most extreme
disgust. It actually sickened him that a free nigger
should impose on him and his fellows so successfully.

"A lady? Ha! ha! ha! that was a good joke anyhow! He'd teach her better than to put on airs and
pretend to be white, the huzzy! He'd show his brother officers, too, that a blind man could see better than
them all. Of course, it would cut her up mightily.
She deserved it, too, trying to pass herself off as white
and associating with white people. To be sure, she had
taken mighty good care of him, as she ought to have
done. She would have been an ungrateful huzzy if she
had not. Did n't he treat her well when he owned her?
No other nigger woman in Cold Spring county was

dressed so well, and she had nothing to do but just take her ease and enjoy herself. If ever a nigger was well treated, she was. Besides that, he had given her freedom. It is true, his mother had wished it and his father promised it, but that did n't oblige him to do it. She was *his* property and he gave her up. Made her a present of herself. No slight thing, either; a cool two thousand, cash on the nail. Of course she ought to nurse him. And he would admit she had done so faithfully—no doubt of that. He could realize, too, that she deserved the encomiums which her beauty had received from his fellow-sufferers. It was no wonder they had thought she was white. He had had doubts about there being any black blood in her veins, himself. She had deceived them handsomely. He would expose her, the brazen-faced impostor! Trying to pass for white, eh? God! if I had not happened to have been here, she might have married some of these good, impressible fellows! Who knows!"

Geoffrey Hunter's face grew white with horror as he contemplated this fearful contingency. He lay in silence awhile arranging his plans.

Then he called to the red-whiskered artillery giant who had termed Toinette an angel. Somehow he thought it would do him good to pluck his angel before his eyes. Of course, it was a mere matter of duty, just to unmask the cheat.

"Edgerton, did n't Brigden say that the little Yankee nurse hailed from Oberlin?"

"I reckon so, though I do n't mind the name," answered Edgerton.

"Is n't that the place where there is a school for free-niggers?"

"Really, I do n't know," said the giant, good-naturedly. "Is it?"

"Yes, it is," said Geoffrey, peevishly; "I was there once and saw them—niggers going about as important and saucy and well dressed and as much thought of, they do say, as any one."

"Well, we shall have no others but free niggers after this, I reckon," said Edgerton, "and must get used to it."

"Yes, to seeing them around probably; but not to associating with them."

"Of course not," assented Edgerton.

"That 's what I wanted to say," said Geoffrey, awkwardly. "That woman—that nurse you fellows have all gone crazy over is—is—is a *free-nigger!*"

"A what? Mrs. Hunter, do you mean? A free nigger! You are crazy, Hunter. It is sacrilege to think of the conjunction!" said the giant.

"Sacrilege or not, it is true. I 'll wager a hundred pounds of the best Cold Spring tobacco against half as many greenback dollars that I prove it to you before night," said Geoffrey, stubbornly.

"I 'll take you," said Edgerton, "and a half-dozen more such bets. But mind you, Hunter, not a word of insult or improper language to the little saint. Damn me if I could stand that, even from you."

"Certainly not," said Geoffrey; "and if am not right, I will go down on my knees to the little Yankee, in penance for my suspicion, besides losing my wager. But I shall not do either."

CHAPTER XXXVI.

UNSUBDUED.

HARDLY had this conversation closed, when there was a stir at the other end of the ward, and the surgeon in charge of the Hospital, with a young Confederate surgeon, who had been taken with his wounded and had chosen to remain and care for them, came down the long row of cots with a figure clad in a costume very unusual in that region at that time—plain black cloth of civilian cut, with a silk hat held awkwardly in his hand. Only a glance at the honest, kindly, inquiring face was needed to convince every one, even those unfamiliar with it, except by report, that they looked upon that wonderful child of the North-West— Abraham Lincoln.

As he came down between the cots, the occupants who were able rose and returned his kindly greeting with politeness, and usually with cordiality. To those still unable to arise he addressed hopeful, kindly words in his half-humorous, half-apologetic manner as he passed on. Coming to the knot of less disabled invalids about Geoffrey, he was introduced to each by the Confederate surgeon.

"I regret, gentlemen," said he, "that the fortune of war has been unkind to you, but hope that every obtainable comfort is provided for you by those having you in charge, as I doubt not it is. I see you have your own surgeon with you, for which I am glad. One always wants his own doctor. I hope that the days of suffering and conflict are over, and that you will soon be at liberty to return to your several homes with such degree of health as Providence may vouchsafe."

After some further conversation he bade them " good morning," and was about to retire, they thanking him for having called upon them, being sincerely gratified at his earnest kindliness, when the surgeon turned toward Geoffrey, and said : " Col. Hunter, I beg your pardon, I should have given you an introduction earlier. Mr. President, this is the officer of whom you have heard, who actually led the assaulting column at Fort Steadman, though not nominally in command. He was the last one to leave the Fort when it was retaken. In fact he did not leave it ; he was wounded, just at the southwestern angle of the Fort by a ball which passed through, just below the eyes, quite destroying his vision."

" Allow me, Col. Hunter," said Lincoln, " to express my sorrow that so brave a man should have met such a deplorable misfortune."

" I do not count it a misfortune," said Geoffrey coldly.

" Not count it a misfortune ? How is that ?" asked the President.

" Because I am saved thereby from looking on the monster who has destroyed my country," said Geoffrey.

A shadow of pain passed over the dark, plain face which was gazing down in benignant compassion on the speaker, yet ît did not lose its kindliness of expression, nor his voice its tone of sympathy, as he replied:

"It is for the sake of that country, my young friend, that I regret your wound."

Then he went on, gravely commenting on all he saw which interested him. When they reached another room, he said to the surgeon:

"Poor fellow! It is no wonder he is waspish; those were glorious eyes to lose their sight so young. Can nothing be done for him?"

"I am afraid not," the surgeon answered. "If the optic nerve is actually injured, certainly not. His wound has healed so readily, though, that I am half-convinced it is mere paralysis caused by the shock and by attendant inflamation. This might be benefited, perhaps, by an operation, or by an application of electricity, if we had the apparatus for it. It is doubtful, but I think, if applied soon, it might save his sight."

"And you have not the means to perform the operation here. Could it be done in Washington?"

"Certainly."

"And you think it would save his sight?"

"I hope so."

Toinette had stood with clasped hands a little at one side, listening to this conversation. Instinctively she knew that it concerned Geoffrey. Now she came forward, and, speaking to the President, said with simple earnestness:

"Please, sir, *please* have him taken there. You *can*. Oh! be kind and do it."

"This is his nurse, sir, who has taken very great

interest in him, as indeed we all have, though he was very rude to you, sir," said the surgeon.

"He would not thank me even for that favor, I suppose, but I cannot refuse your request, Madam. He shall be removed at once. Could he endure the journey, Doctor?"

"Oh yes, sir."

"Poor fellow," said the President, "he ought to have his sight, if only to see what a pretty nurse has fallen to his lot. Good morning, Madam."

The President went to the Surgeon's Quarters, where he staid for a short time, and, by shrewd questioning, found that the old doctor had been at his post for more than four years, without leave of absence. Half an hour after he left, the surgeon was relieved from the charge of the Hospital, by order of the Department Medical Director, and the courier who brought the order handed him an envelope containing the following, in the strong, direct handwriting of the morning's guest:

"Surgeon A. C. Kirkland has leave of absence for three months, at the end of which time, he will report to the Surgeon General's Office, Washington, D. C.

"A. LINCOLN, *President.*"

Underneath was added in the same hand:

"The Commander of Dispatch Boat, No. 9, will furnish transportation to Surgeon A. C. Kirkland, in charge of Col. G. Hunter, wounded prisoner of war, from City Point to Washington, and one nurse

"A. LINCOLN."

Inquiry developed the fact that Dispatch Boat No. 9 was specially detailed to take the President and his attendants back to Washington that night. He had made room on the little craft for the faithful surgeon, the devoted nurse, and his afflicted enemy.

CHAPTER XXXVII.

IN HIS MARK.

THE surgeon at once sought Toinette and informed her of their good fortune.

"It is all through your intercession, too, Mrs. Hunter. Take the order in and read it to the Colonel. I should be ashamed to tell him after seeing how he treated the noblest man that ever lived, this morning."

So Toinette took the letter and went, with a dancing heart, and eyes all full of light and love, to the convalescent ward to read the glad tidings to her idol.

Geoffrey's wager with Edgerton had become known to every one in the ward, by this time, though no one believed he had any chance of winning it, all regarding it as a half crazy fancy, as they did also his deliberate insult of their distinguished visitor.

All eyes were therefore turned upon Toinette the moment she entered the ward.

"You are sure to win," whispered Brigden to Edgerton, as she came down the aisle towards them.

Of course I am," said Edgerton; then addressing Toinette he added:

"Your great man, Lincoln, was very chatty with us poor rebs to-day, Mrs. Hunter. He is not half the beast we thought him, but seems just a kind-hearted, plain old man. In fact, I like him."

At the mention of her name Geoffrey Hunter had risen from his pillow, and sat with his face turned toward Edgerton, with an expression of intense bitterness resting on his features.

"Mrs. Hunter! Mrs. Hunter!" he was saying over and over to himself. "The brazen cheat! how glibly she talks to Edgerton," he thought, as Toinette replied to that officer's remark:

"Indeed he is good. I have the proof of that in my hand."

She held up the letter as she spoke. Geoffrey Hunter's brow grew darker as he heard the words. The sound of her voice, so full of the rippling melody of overpowering love, had almost disarmed him at first, but a strange jealousy seized him as he heard her words.

"She had proof of his goodness in her hand." She had received some favor—perhaps a gift from the monster whom *he* thanked God that he could not see. What right had she to receive favors from any one but him — especially from that baboon. She was a nigger, but Lincoln had not freed her. *He* had done that years ago. If Toinette had gratitude to any one it was to him. No, he would not forfeit his wager. He would not cover her hypocrisy and shame. She deserved all he could make her feel for trying to pass for a white woman and a lady.

This rushed through his brain in an instant, and then, with a voice hoarse with excitement, he cried out, imperiously: "I say, you girl, Toinette! Toinette!"

Five years were brushed away in a second. Their

months of toil and study were in vain. The knowledge and accomplishments for which she had striven were blotted out. The snug little home in the free North was forgotten. The love of that brave boy was obliterated. The free, white, intelligent, interesting, beautiful Mrs. Hunter was lost for the moment. In her stead was the poor, abject, timid, pretty "nigger gal." The old life o'erwhelmed and possessed her, like the evil spirits, which entered into Magdalen. She was instantly the slave Toinette, and heard the master's voice—Marse Geoffrey's, the voice she loved—calling her in tones of angry passion. All other thought had slipped away. The world was void, except those two ideas: Marse Geoffrey; Toinette. The owner calls; the slave must answer. She saw nothing, knew nothing, heard nothing but this. The hospital, the rows of white cots, the anxious faces all staring at her, all, all, were gone. She was a chattel at Lovett Lodge again, and Marse Geoffrey in the library was calling for her angrily. She started like a guilty loiterer, and answered instantly, with the inimitable and indescribable intonation of the slave:

"Sir?"

That was all she said. It was enough. It revealed all. The brand showed. The one drop of base admixture had overtopped all else, and marred the fairest hopes.

"Sir?"

It was the knell of hope and peace and love to one poor heart. It told of blighted visions, wasted toil and squandered love. It was the mark which slavery had put upon her soul. The deed of manumission

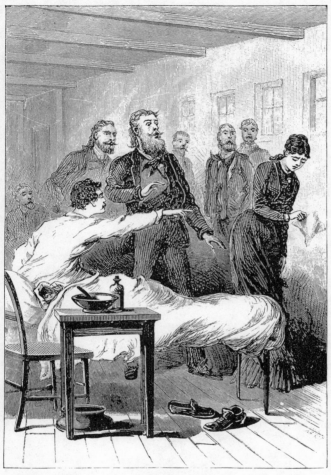

THE BRAND.

*"He cried out imperiously: 'I say, you girl, Toinette!' . . . The free
white, intelligent, interesting, beautiful Mrs. Hunter was lost for a moment.
. . . She started, and answered instantly with the inimitable and indescribable intonation of the slave—'Sir?'"—*p. 378.

had made her body free. Her soul was yet in shackles. Geoffrey Hunter had released the one. God and Eternity alone could manumit the other. It was the private mark of bondage.

To Geoffrey Hunter it was the tidings of triumph over his fellows, despite his blindness.

"Ha, ha, gentlemen!" he shouted. "What do you think now? Who can see best now?"

The words recalled Toinette from her dream. She started as one just wakened, and looked round on the anxious faces which were turned towards her. She knew at once what it all meant. She who had been respected and reverenced by all these men before was nothing to them now. She wore the garb of the Pariah. The emblem of degradation was on her. She was only the free nigger, Toinette, to them now.

Oh, it was terrible! But worse than that, it was the hand of love which had stricken her. The dream of the slave and the hope of the freedwoman were both crushed at once in that dastardly act. She had guarded him so untiringly, that disease had crept away from his life, baffled and defeated. She had waited and longed to hear those lips breathe her name, aye, her old slave name, Toinette. She would have been glad to be a slave forever, if love had only softened its accents. But now—oh, God!—it meant shame, disgrace, degradation instead. Her love was repaid in scorn—aye, worse than scorn, debasement! Her "royal gentleman" was degraded! His throne was vacant! He had striven to tarnish and debase the white soul that would have dared the perils of perdition for his sake. She felt this dimly, confusedly, as she stood stunned and stupefied by the blow. She looked pleadingly around with a dumb pale face. There was sympathy in every eye, except the glaring blind ones that blazed at her yonder. She knew they were there, though she did not see them. She had the surgeon's letter still in her hands, and was turning it over and over. Suddenly she recollected her errand. She held the letter toward Edgerton, and said, in a low pleading tone:

"Please, sir, will you read it to him?"

Edgerton took the letter, and, with a groan which was a half-shriek, Toinette fled out of the door by which Mrs. Hunter had entered.

Pity for her, and indignation at Geoffrey's course, filled every breast. Geoffrey, himself, was the only man who was not aware of the enormity of his conduct. Deprived of all knowledge of the actual change which time had made in Toinette; regarding her as only the petted slave whom he had freed, and whom he supposed had endeavored to palm off a deception of the basest character upon himself and his associates, he was only half-aware of the terrible blow he had struck and of the fair field he had devastated.

"Well, Edgerton," he cried out, "who has won, old fellow? who has the best eyes?" he shouted in glee.

"You have, sir," replied Edgerton, in a voice husky with suppressed anger and emotion; "but, by God, sir! if I had been you I'd rather have been the loser. I would not have done what you have to-day, for all the greenbacks the Lincoln government has ever issued."

There was no dissent from this by any of the others. Geoffrey was amazed. Here he had exposed a cheat, discovered an impostor of the most infamous kind to his friends—a nigger woman trying to pass herself off for a white lady—and they were denouncing him for it! He could not understand it. Had he been mean? Was it base and cowardly and ungrateful to do as he had done? Conscience told him at once that it was. But she was obtaining regard and respect under false pretenses. He had only exposed her—shown her up in her true colors. But he might have done it less harshly. He might have warned her in private conversation. He might have spared her the arrow that brought that wailing cry with which she had fled away. Conscience could not be argued off from these grounds.

But would these men who were blaming him now, would they have been more considerate in his place? Their conduct and language toward him said that they would. He wondered if it were true. Had he less manliness, delicacy, and gratitude than the great flaming giant Edgerton? It seemed so. And thus retribution came swiftly upon him. Geoffrey Hunter felt debased because he had done a mean act; not sorrowful because he had trodden under foot so fair a flower of love.

And yet Captain Edgerton and his fellow-officers were unjust in their view of Geoffrey Hunter's conduct. Every one of them would have done the same or worse had they been in his place. The difference was that they had seen the woman Mrs. Hunter, and could not conceive (although their reason assured them it was true) that she had ever been the slave-girl Toinette;

while Geoffrey Hunter had only seen and known her as a slave-girl, and did not dream that she was but the shell within which slept the woman—the lady—Mrs. Hunter.

Edgerton read the doctor's letter which Toinette had given him, and as he concluded the surgeon himself appeared and informed Geoffrey of the object of the transfer, stating that it had been ordered by the President on account of Mrs. Hunter's earnest entreaty in his behalf.

Geoffrey remembered the cheery tones of Toinette as she came down the aisle and spoke of the proof of the President's kindness which she held in her hand. He remembered, too, the wailing cry and tottering steps with which she had fled from him after he had spoken. He knew then that she had come to bring him this message of hope and joy, and that it was this which had made her step so light and her tone so joyous. And he had stricken the bearer of glad tidings. It was too bad—altogether too bad. She was a kind-hearted, thoughtful girl, and he was a brute to speak to her as he did. He remembered beating Leon once for waking him in the night by howling and whining without cause, as he thought. Even after that, however, the faithful brute had kept on his clamour, and finally tore the covering from his bed, forcing him to rise. When he did so and opened the door of his room, he found the block in which he lodged on fire. In a few minutes more the avenues of escape would have been cut off. He remembered putting his arms about the shaggy neck, when they were in safety, and begging the pardon of the faithful creature

with tears and caresses for his unreasoning harshness.
Somehow, he felt so towards Toinette now. He could
not keep back the tears which welled up into the eyes to
which the poor girl was so anxious to restore the light.
He would acknowledge his brutality, when he saw her
again, and make amends by kindness in the future for
his harshness of to-day. She was a good girl. Would
she forget his unkindness as old Leon had done? He
hoped she would. Why should n't she? Yet, somehow, he had a doubt.

He groped his way to Edgerton's cot and told him
he could not accept the wager he had won. He was
sorry he had been so harsh to the poor girl. Would
Edgerton tell his comrades when he had gone that he
regretted his meanness? He would apologize to her
himself.

The large-hearted cannoneer took the apology for
more than it meant, and responded:

"So you ought, Hunter, so you ought; for, notwith-
standing all that 's passed, I still say she 's an angel and
would almost make a heaven herself."

CHAPTER XXXVIII.

DISPATCH BOAT NO. 9.

DISPATCH Boat No. 9 was one of those little steam yachts which constituted the eyes and ears of the Federal fleets, the pilot fishes of their men-of-war, the courier-pigeons of the deep. Who that witnessed any portion of the struggle on the coast or along our great rivers does not remember these wonderful little specimens of marine architecture? Ever alert, coming and going, they seemed more like living creatures than any other mechanism that man has devised. One moment lying at the wharf with steam up—seemingly as restive of the cable and snub-post as the blooded steed of the knotted rein,—the next instant scurrying off with a frolicsome, self-important air, the crazy wheels leaving a foamy wake line far behind. What an air of mysterious reticence there was about the puffing, restless creatures! Out into the storm and darkness at night-fall, going none knew whither—with a bustling, self-conceited air that provoked a smile—breasting the billows and taking the wind in their teeth as if they gloried in the resistance of tempest and wave, or bursting at morning out of the darkness "that hung over river and lea," like creatures born of the night and the mist, they were ever the same prescient, cunning litttle monsters, with the artful, knowing leer of Venus' Dolphins, and the speed

of winged-footed Mercury charged with the commands
of Jove—riddles which the great silent sea propounded
ever to the dwellers on the land.   Like a woman they
were always stirring up a strife, yet never in it   Thread-
ing their way among looming navies like a street Arab
through a crowd.   Always ready for a voyage of an
hour or a month.   At home in the crowded roadstead
or on the billowy deep, trying the unexplored channel
or bumping their noses upon the sand bar.   Whirring
by the sentry on the fortress, casting the red gleam
of its signal-light on the distant picket, disappearing
in the haze of summer's evening, or springing, dripping
and sleety from the mist of winter's morning, the Dispatch Boat was ever the same unresting, inscrutable
little mystery.

Who that saw them has not watched them hour by
hour, trying vainly to guess the import of the messages
they bore?   Was this one outward bound, bearing
orders to Dupont or Farragut, or merely carrying some
gallant official " Salt " to a scene of revelry?   Was that,
breasting the rushing river, freighted with momentous
tidings for the silent Hammer at Petersburg, or only
bearing some favored fair one to the embrace of her
hero?   Mercury served Venus not less frequently than
Mars.

The very Queen of this fleet of Mother Cary Chick-
ens, which tossed about in the teeth of the war-tempest,
was Dispatch Boat No. 9.   Before the war, she had been
one of the most perfect and complete of the floating
palaces which Fashion prescribed as the correct thing
for the nautically inclined spendthrift and pleasure seek-

R

er. No pains had been spared in her make and equip-
ment. Little compact engines, running swift and smooth,
with perfect-fitting joints and noiseless bearings, beautiful as toys, yet strong as banded giants; full of strange
nooks and cosy corners; every inch of space improved,
and every art exhausted to fill that space with comfort;
she was in everything a wonder of skillful workmanship
and patient ingenuity.

When the war came on, her patriotic owner, having
theretofore been worth very little either to himself or
his country, suddenly made the startling determination
to offer himself and his costly toy to the Government
for the war, and, greatly to his surprise, both were accepted. So he doffed his fancy sailor rig and put on the
regulation blue, pulled down the silken pennant, shipped
a brass howitzer, ran up the triangular bunting with the
white field and scarlet edge bearing the mystic numeral,
and the queen of sea palaces and the Commodore of the
Yacht Club were transformed into Dispatch Boat No. 9
and her Lieutenant Commanding.

Upon this craft the President with two or three attendants, and the surgeon, his patient, and the nurse,
were to make the passage to Washington. All were
ready at the appointed hour except Toinette. The surgeon, fearing that she would be left, went in search of
her and found her kneeling in a sort of stupor by the
hard pallet which she occupied in the nurses' ward.
She did not seem to have been weeping, but she answered his enquiries vaguely, her eyes were heavy and
bloodshot, and her head burning with fever. The kind
surgeon, who traced all evils to a physical cause, in-

stinctively diagnosed the case with one hand upon her pulse and the other laid inquiringly upon her forehead —and this is what he thought:

Over-work, excitement, the prospect of getting this good-for-nothing Confederate fire-eater to Washington and restoring his sight, was too much for the poor woman.

"She's been a slave to him, anyhow," he muttered, little knowing how near his thought came to the sad truth which underlay her suffering. "Strange she thinks so much of him. Lucky she's going out of this malarious atmosphere, too. Threatened with congestion now."

What he did was to shake her smartly and bid her, with unwonted harshness, prepare for the journey. She obeyed him, mechanically. Meanwhile, he took his prescription book from his pocket and wrote on one of the blanks a few lines in the hieroglyphics of his profession.

Calling an attendant, he sent it to the dispensary; when she returned, he took the wine-glass which she brought from her hand, and, first shaking and smelling the mixture with professional caution, directed Toinette brusquely to "Take it, and come along."

She obeyed, and giving her little baggage to a messenger in waiting, bade adieu to the friends whom she had found during her hospital service, and leaning upon the arm of the old surgeon, went to the landing and on board the boat.

Geoffrey had arrived before them, having been brought in an ambulance, and his self-importance was somewhat wounded that neither of them was there to

attend to his wants. The surgeon had made **arrange-**
ments that he should be placed in the quietest part of
the boat, and one of its miniature state-rooms had been
appropriated to Toinette's use.

On this little craft there could not be much seclusion, but it was not until the evening meal that Toinette
came forth and joined the little company on the deck.

Geoffrey, in his narrow berth below, had several
times inquired for his nurse, and had been informed by
the Surgeon, somewhat sententiously, that Mrs. Hunter
was too sick to attend upon him.

Upon the deck the unassuming ease and cordiality
of the President, with his quaint and characteristic
humor, made this Spring evening one long to be remembered by those who were privileged to participate in
its joys.

The thrilling events of the past few days, with the
still more important results that were looked for hourly,
were the themes of conversation, and when these had
been duly canvassed the scenery through which they
were passing, and its historic associations, formed sub-
jects of pleasant intercourse. The Commander of the
little craft gave a narrative of her adventures and
escapes during the struggle. As the evening wore on
Mr. Lincoln seemed to grow quiet and moody. His
questioning spirit was asking strange things of the glorious moonlight, the flowing river, and the darkening
land. His restless, hesitating soul was throwing out
tentacles into the future. The questions which arose in
his mind were so overwhelming in their character that
they very soon crushed out the conversation, and the

great man on whose heart they rested by day and by
night sat with bowed head, and with that look of
weariness which marked the latter years of his life
watched the course of the boat as she sped on her way.
The others were hushed into silence by his solemn sadness.

After a time Dr. Kirkland broke the stillness, which
was becoming painful, by asking Toinette to sing. She
declined, out of regard for the silent presence in their
midst. Mr. Lincoln had heard the request, though seemingly unobservant, and at once seconded the desire for
a song.

So Toinette, with the thought of the great careworn,
overburdened heart before her, and the scath of the
great sorrow yet fresh in her memory, looked out upon
the deepening gloom and sung:

> Oh, why should we fear when the tempest comes down,
> And the storm glowers o'er us with pitiless frown?
> The clouds that above us so threateningly lower
> But re-echo the mandate of Infinite Power:
> > "Hush, terrified souls! as in darkness ye plod,
> > Be still, and remember that I am your God!

> "Why deem that thy burden of sorrow and care
> Is more than thy faltering spirit can bear?
> Why shrink from the task to thy moments assigned?
> He knoweth thy weakness—He tempers the wind.
> > Be still—and but think, as the wine press is trod,
> > 'Tis the will of thy Father—the vineyard of God!

> "Though the thunders above thee unceasingly roll
> His eye watches ever thy storm-driven soul;
> Though the grave yawns before, in impervious gloom
> Yet the Infinite dwells in the shade of the tomb.
> > Be still and remember, oh murmuring clod,
> > Thy Future is only the Present of God!"

Toinette's voice rang out in the darkness, mingling with the rush of waters about the tiny craft, and the cool breath which came from a dark storm-cloud that hung upon her quarter. Geoffrey heard it, and was filled with jealous anger that she should sing for other ears than his.

The gloom faded out of the face of the President, as he came toward her and said:

"I thank you, Madam, for uttering in song the truths which ought to live in my heart at this time."

He pressed her hand in gratitude. The little group broke up and sleep soon wrapt in unconsciousness her strangely gathered passengers, while Dispatch Boat No. 9 battled with the storm and sped on, with characteristic self-importance. as if she knew the precious freight she bore

CHAPTER XXXIX

LIGHT.

GEOFFREY did not meet Toinette during the trip.
He had an indistinct notion that she had bent
over his cot while he slept, and kissed him. He could
not be sure, however. It might have been a dream.
Certain it was that she did not come to him in his
waking hours. Upon their arrival at Washington he
was transferred to one of the numerous hospitals in
that city, where Dr. Kirkland left him to rest and re-
cruit his strength while he himself paid a brief visit
to his family in New York. Before he left, Geoffrey
asked him in as unconcerned a manner as he could,
why his old nurse had not been with him since his
transfer, adding that he thought the order included her
also.

"Oh, Mrs. Hunter!" said the doctor, carelessly.
"Yes, the order did include transportation for her, but
on our arrival here she said she could not stay away
from her home longer, and so went on this morning,"
he answered.

"I should have thought she might have staid to
see the result of your experiment, after having me
dragged here to endure it," said Geoffrey, petulantly.

"There is no compulsion about the matter, Colonel
Hunter. You need not endure the operation unless

you desire," answered the surgeon, quickly, with the tone of offended dignity one always employs when his craft is assailed. He resented, too, his patient's ingratitude to his devoted nurse.

"Oh, I did not mean to hurt your feelings, doctor. Of course I wish the operation to be performed, and can never sufficiently thank you for the interest you have taken in my case. I only thought she ought not to have deserted me," replied Geoffrey, apologetically.

But the surgeon was stubborn. Once started on a train of thought he was loth to abandon it. He would not let his patient off so easily, but said :

"I don't see why you should blame Mrs. Hunter for obtaining for you just what you desire. I should think that you ought rather to thank her for a last chance of recovery."

"Yes, but she knew I would be lonely and worried here, and I had got used to her ways. She ought to have staid and helped me pass the Rubicon at least," answered Geoffrey, fretfully.

"But you forget, Colonel Hunter, that she undoubtedly owes duties to others as well as to you. She tells me that she has a child of four, though she don't look twenty herself, poor dear. Of course, she is anxious about him after so long absence with the army, and you ought not to blame her for going to see him after all she has done for you," the surgeon rejoined.

Geoffrey answered nothing ; the surgeon's words were too true to be argued. How true he did not know who uttered them. Geoffrey wondered whether they had any covert meaning—whether the surgeon was aware of the true relations between himself and Toinette. He could think of no question that would cast light upon this subject without awakening suspicion, and so said no more about it.

The surgeon called an attendant and gave particular directions with regard to the diet and care of his patient during his absence. He had consulted several practitioners of eminence in the profession, and was the more convinced by a comparison of views with them that there was no actual disease of the organs of vision, but simple torpidity of the nerves connected with them consequent upon the shock of the wound and the subsequent inflammation of the surrounding parts.

He proposed to employ certain stimulants to restore the normal action of these nerves, and in case of their failure so to do, which he fully anticipated from his previous treatment, he then proposed to apply electricity, from which he hoped for good results; but in case he should fail by this means, he resolved to attempt an operation which he had long contemplated—an operation of extreme delicacy, which only one man had hitherto been daring enough and skillful enough to attempt. His counsel and perhaps assistance Dr. Kirkland expected to procure in this case.

In order that either of these courses of treatment should succeed, it was necessary that the patient should avoid all excitement and irritation. This fact was very strongly impressed both on the patient and the nurse. Having thus cautioned the man in whom he had taken such unusual interest, he departed. Upon the little slate at the head of Geoffrey's cot he left a written statement for the attending physician, giving the name and rank of the patient, and the history of the case.

Before morning came again, the blackest pall which ever enwrapt a sorrowing nation hung over the American people. In the very hour of final triumph, when gratitude and mercy filled his heart to overflowing, Abraham Lincoln died by the assassin's hand !

At the first, horror hushed every tongue. Thought was paralyzed by the terrible tragedy. Then sorrow, the most intense and solemn, swept over the land, and the Martyr-President was borne to his prairie tomb amid the regretful silence of his enemies, and the bursting grief of millions, in whose hearts and memories his name was enshrined as the noblest, the truest, the grandest of earth.

And, as the people whom he trusted and revered thronged the route of the sad pilgrimage and gazed upon that dark, sad face—rugged and grim in feature, wan and weary in life, but peaceful and benignant in death—as crowding millions came with bowed heads and streaming eyes; as loving hands and aching hearts showered on his senseless clay the emblems of tender remembrance—in that hour, there came to every heart, unsyllabled and unuttered, the knowledge that this man was of God; that the same mysterious Providence which had once rebuked the pride of Israel by choosing the lowly Nazarene for the indwelling of His Spirit, had, in these latter days, selected this halting, trembling, self-distrusting seeker after aid—this " Poor White," upon whose birth rested the blight of slavery's baneful influence—and consecrated him to the holy work which, like the Son of God, he had consummated only in his death.

Others may have been greater in gifts and learning, in intellect and will, more brilliant in action, more fertile in resource, more varied in accomplishment, more commanding in power;—but in the glory of a high and holy purpose, faithfully, trustfully and tenderly fulfilled; of a transcendent mission executed with unwearying humility and zeal, Abraham Lincoln stands the first among the men whom the ages have brought forth—that man who walked "with firmness in the right, as God gives us to see the right"—"with malice toward none, and with charity for all."

The knowledge of this tragedy came with peculiar force to Geoffrey Hunter. He was no admirer of the man who had passed away, yet he could not forget that he had received the most extraordinary kindness at his hands, and that he had requited his courtesy only with the most inexcusable insult.

As, hour after hour, the sound of mourning, the hushed murmur of affliction, which attended this calamity came to his ears, his mind could dwell only upon his brutal reply to the kind inquiry which Mr. Lincoln had addressed to him, and the favor which the President had afterwards extended to him. He would have given anything could the man he had scorned but have lived until he had thanked him for a generous act towards an undeserving foe, and begged forgiveness for his unjustifiable conduct.

It was not in the nature of Geoffrey Hunter to smother any sentiment which might obtain lodgment in his mind, and this thought so troubled him that, instead of that repose which his friend the surgeon desired, a state of the most intense nervous excitement supervened. His brain seemed on fire with a wild agony. A fierce griping pain compressed his temples as in a vice, and the course of the terrible wound, which had caused his suffering, seemed lined with seared and smoking fibers.

The optic nerves, which brought no message from the outer world, so thrilled with the terrible shock which had doomed them to darkness that they pictured constantly to the seething brain the torn and shattered fibers along the missile's course, shrinking and trembling, bathed in the lurid light which marks the discharge of fire-arms. He seemed to see the wound fresh and livid along its whole course.

The sense of hearing became also a source of torture. The waves of sound beat upon the tense membranes with a fearful violence. The most perfect silence attainable was to him instinct with terrific sound. The rustling of the clothing of his cot, the footfall of the attendant, the song of birds, the very waving of the leaves was torture the most exquisite and intense to his throbbing nerves.

To add to this deleterious excitement came the knowledge, retailed by some thoughtless attendant, that the surgeon, upon whose aid he knew Dr. Kirkland had chiefly relied in the performance of the operation which he feared might become necessary, was dead. He was the very head of his profession—"*facile princeps*"—no

hand so skillful, no eye so accurate, no judgment so unerring as his. No one else had ever been so daring as
to attempt this operation; nor had he ever performed
it, to the extent which might become necessary in Geoffrey Hunter's case. The story of his death was strangely
tragic.

He had risen to the labor of the day, which a long
life, the utmost devotion to his profession, and unparalleled success had rendered unusually onerous, and was
taking his morning meal, when his eye fell upon the announcement which clouded the land with gloom.
"Abraham Lincoln is dead!"—he exclaimed in tones of
horror, and, as if called to attend the man his soul
revered above all others, in the journey to the celestial
gates, the great physician folded his hands, as if in
prayer, and was no more.

Geoffrey Hunter felt that his last chance for restoration was gone. If the other remedies should fail he
must ever grope in darkness. It was a terrible prospect.
He prayed for death, as he had often done since his
affliction.

When he thought of the mysterious connection between the death of the renowned surgeon, whose life
was almost his only hope, and the man whom he had
so grossly affronted, and whose kindness he had never
acknowledged, it seemed to him that it was a judgment
upon him for his ingratitude and meanness. He counted
it an omen of misfortune, and gave up all hope of recovery.

In this condition the good old surgeon found his
patient when he returned. The attendants and the

medical officer in charge of the Hospital gave him a full account of the symptoms during his absence. To add to their alarming character the wound had broken out afresh, and active suppuration was in progress. The doctor sat by the cot of his patient for several hours, studying his condition carefully. With the dogged resolution of the best of his profession he enjoyed the struggle with disease when it became desperate, and hated, above all things, to yield it the palm of victory.

He did not particularly care to save this man more than any other. Toinette had nursed him because he was Geoffrey Hunter. The doctor had treated him because it was a very rare and peculiar wound—a "beautiful case" he would have said to a professional brother. Perhaps, too, he was somewhat interested in him on Toinette's account. She was a favorite of his, and her heart was evidently wrapped up, somehow, in the life of this stricken man. He was afraid the fellow had treated her badly. He had evidently done or said something which had made her anxious to avoid further contact with him, for the doctor did not believe a word of her story about her sudden anxiety to be at home. So after thinking a long time he went to the nearest Telegraph office and wrote this message:

"Mrs. ANTOINETTE HUNTER, *Oberlin, Ohio :*

"Come instantly if you would save G. H.

"Dr. KIRKLAND."

Forty-eight hours afterwards Geoffrey Hunter had been removed from the General Hospital, and was domiciled in quiet quarters, opening upon one of the public

squares which are scattered about in that beautiful
Capital, and at his bedside sat Toinette. She was again
the faithful nurse, moving noiselessly about the room,
anticipating every wish, taking every precaution, observing every direction; yet never obtruding attention
upon the patient.

In a short time her ministrations gave him rest, and
the man of science began to see points of light again
in the horoscope of Geoffrey Hunter.

Weeks passed, and faithful nursing and skillful treatment were again successful. The wound was healed,
and the patient's nerves so invigorated that the doctor
decided to attempt a restoration of vision.

The room was darkened, and the poles of a light
galvanic battery, one of which was so shaped as to fit
the orb of the eye, were applied. The mysterious fluid
thrilled along the torpid nerves and brought to the
darkened brain again the primal message of creative
power—"Let there be light."

Day after day, the application was repeated with per-
severing hope. At length the patient spoke of seeing
little quivering points of light whenever the battery was
applied; then he could dimly distinguish figures after it
was removed. Then the doctor directed his eyes to be
lightly bandaged, and the applications were made more
frequently, though not always directly to the eyes. He
wished to stimulate the sluggish nerves. After a time
he daily removed the bandages for a short time, and
little by little admitted the light; but his directions
were imperative that the bandages should not be removed for an instant during his absence.

During these visits of the surgeon he had insisted upon Toinette's taking that exercise which her close attendance upon the sick man rendered imperative to her health, so that Geoffrey had never seen his nurse, nor did she know the actual progress which he was making toward recovery. The doctor had his own notions and kept his own counsel. At length he asked her one morning, upon returning from her walk, to come into the room.

She was dressed in the pretty walking habit which prevailed at that time, gay with the bright colors of the early summer styles. Exercise and health lighted up her eyes and flushed her cheeks. The doctor thought her beautiful. Now was the time for the stroke which he had been so long meditating. He would not wait for her to remove her bonnet or gloves, but brought her in, just as she left the promenade.

The shades were drawn aside, and the morning sun was pouring his full radiance into the room. Leaning upon the propped-up pillows, with those glorious eyes bathed in the radiance of restored vision and shrinking not from the bright sunlight, was Geoffrey Hunter.

"Colonel Hunter," said the old doctor, somewhat sententiously, "allow me to introduce the person to whom you are mainly indebted for your life and for your restored vision; Mrs. Hunter," and he waved his hand pompously toward the bright vision at his side.

Toinette had, at the first sight of Geoffrey, started toward him, with an involuntary cry of joy. Collecting her thoughts, she stopped midway of the room, her hands clasped and tears of joy running down her cheeks.

Suddenly her face and brow flushed painfully, and with a low, sobbing cry she turned and fled from the room.

It would be hard to describe the expression of Geoffrey Hunter's face as the old doctor turned an inquiring glance toward him.

Surprise and doubt seemed strangely mixed with re- . gret in his flushed countenance.

The doctor had played his kindly little game and failed. He was still more puzzled that afternoon when Mrs. Hunter called at his room, and, after asking if Geoffrey's recovery was complete and perfect, and being assured that it was, bade him good-by.

But he was amazed when Geoffrey asked the next morning, "Where is—is—Mrs. Hunter?"

"Where is she? Why, gone home! gone back to Oberlin! Did n't she let you know she was going?"

The kind-hearted Esculapius gave it up then. There was something quite inscrutable about those two young people. They were clearly made for each other, and he believed by no means indifferent to one another. Yet one was a widow, the other a stupid bachelor, and both seemed only anxious to get as far from one another as possible.

CHAPTER XL.

KNIGHT ERRANT.

GEOFFREY HUNTER was forbidden excitement or employment. Weeks, perhaps months, of rest, were deemed essential to his complete and perfect recovery. The good doctor expected to remain in the city at least until the débris of the war had been cleared away and the Government was once more on a peace footing. He knew there was no way to keep the restless young rebel in reasonable subjection to hygienic rules except to represent the danger of relapse as imminent, and require his daily attendance at his office for inspection.

With the rest of his compatriots, therefore, Col. Hunter gave his parole of honor and was at liberty to go wherever he chose, subject only to the dictates of Dr. Kirkland. He owed too much to him to disregard them lightly. So he wandered about the streets of Washington day after day, watching—sometimes with amusement and sometimes with indignation—the breaking up of the great army which had overwhelmed and smothered the rebellion. He saw, without resentment, the smartly dressed, thoroughly-drilled soldiers of the East, and the bronzed and shabby veterans of the West, but when he beheld battalions of armed negroes marching along the Avenue amid the plaudits of thousands,

or acting as guards and orderlies at the Departments
and the White House, his whole nature revolted with
disgust. He became a rebel again in heart and wished
that he had never signed the parole, a copy of which
he carried in his pocket. He began to wonder, even,
if he were bound to observe a pledge given to a Government which could so infamously degrade and insult
every white man in its limits. Then he grew restive
and excitable. The atmosphere of Washington seemed
charged with a baleful electricity. He, himself, was
full of hatred and disgust. He must go away soon or
there would be an explosion which, though it might
hurt no one else, would assuredly demolish himself.

He told the old doctor so; and that worthy, seeing
that his power was relaxing, surrendered at discretion,
only stipulating for as much time as he could obtain
before delivering his patient up to the future and himself. It was arranged, therefore, that before the "dog
days" settled upon the dusty, miasmatic metropolis, he
should give his parole of prudence to the good physician
and depart.

When this time had arrived, Geoffrey approached
the doctor, whom, despite his kindness, he could not
help regarding as a Yankee and therefore as purely
mercenary in all his acts, for the purpose of offering
payment for the care which he had received from him.
He doubted not—or tried not to doubt—that gain had
been the motive of all his seeming kindness. And he
would admit that he deserved reward. He had been
untiring, faithful, and had proved himself profoundly
skilled in his profession.

With these views he called upon Dr. Kirkland and inquired almost ·pompously what he should pay` him for his services.

"What, sir?" said the old doctor in surprise.

Geoffrey repeated his inquiry.

The old surgeon laid down his pen, for he was making out his daily report, and turned his office-chair round toward his visitor.

"Colonel Hunter," he said in serious tones, "since you were brought in from Fort Hell, wounded, I have attended you faithfully, have I not?"

"Indeed, you have," answered Geoffrey, warmly; "and I desire to pay you liberally."

"Allow me to inform you, Colonel Hunter," replied the doctor, "that the Government of the United States pays me for my time and rewards my services. I attended you as a prisoner of war simply, and in my official capacity."

"I had flattered myself that I had received unusual attention," said Geoffrey, somewhat bitterly.

"Yours was an unusual case," said the surgeon, calmly.

"You will not allow me to offer you any further compensation, then?" said Geoffrey.

"Colonel Hunter," responded the doctor, "you must be aware that it would be an insult to me to offer it."

"Pshaw!" said Geoffrey. "You only wish to humiliate me by trying to insist on my obligations to the government. It is not the government to whom I am indebted, but to you, and I insist upon tendering payment,"

The doctor tapped a bell upon his desk, and said :
"Colonel Hunter, your unreasoning devotion to the
Confederacy led you to insult President Lincoln, and
drive away a most devoted nurse; and now you would
let it lead you to quarrel with me. You cannot see
that any good can come out of Nazareth. I hope time
will cure you. He is a grim nurse, but he accomplishes
wonders sometimes. Good by," he continued, as an
orderly entered—"avoid labor and excitement as much
you can, and as long. You had better travel for a
while; it will divert your mind and restore your nervous
system. My horse, John, for Colonel Hunter,"—to the
orderly, who had answered the bell. "You must not
walk so far in your present excited state, Colonel. You
can tie him before the hotel, and John will bring him
back."

Geoffrey was not a little affected and was somewhat
non-plussed by this final exhibition of regard on the part
of the old doctor. Somehow the Yankee surgeon had
surprised him. He had spoken commiseratingly of him
to his very face He had even referred to his previous
acts in language which he knew they deserved. He was
not used to being treated thus. And yet the offender
had been very kind to him. He could not be angry with
him. Was he ungrateful, or had he mistaken the character of his enemies? He held out his hand, and said,
somewhat ruefully :

"At least, doctor. I may offer you my thanks for
your services?"

"Certainly, certainly," said the doctor cheerfully,
shaking the proffered hand. "And I am right glad

they have been worth your thanks, Colonel. I have certainly never had a patient for whom I have had kinder feelings, and it hurt me that you should think that I had gone beyond my duty, for surreptitious gain."

"I meant no offense, Doctor," said Geoffrey, humbly.

"I believe you, Colonel," he answered. "You only miscalculated for the latitude. That was all. You thought because I was born north of Mason and Dixon's I was essentially mercenary, and could know no other motive. Never mind about denying. You cannot do so truthfully, and are too candid to distort the fact without embarrassment. Good by, now; the horse is ready. If you should ever have a relapse, which I think unlikely, I shall be glad to serve you. Keep out of trouble, excitement, and hard work as long as you can. If the world gets headed wrong, let it go. You can't stop it, and will only get crushed yourself if you try. Good by, again."

And with a hearty handshake the doctor and patient parted to go their various ways—each with added respect and kindness for the other.

When Geoffrey reached his hotel, he found there a letter from an old comrade-in-arms, who, at the close of our hostilities, had taken service in Mexico. It was a letter of condolence, for the writer was not aware of his friend's recovery, and, with the thoughtlessness which sometimes marks letters of this character, it was chiefly filled with lamentation for what might have been but for Geoffrey's misfortune. He painted in glowing colors the advantages of the service in which he was engaged, not the least of which was the absence of that banner which had lately flaunted in the face of their brave legions in gaudy triumph.

Geoffrey determined to answer the letter in person. The doctor had recommended travel and absence from familiar and exciting associations. Here was an opportunity, as it seemed providentially thrown in his way, to comply with his counsel. His mind was made up instantly.

Then, with strange inconsistence, his thought recurred to Toinette. She had been a faithful creature. There was no denying that. He had treated her badly, too, especially after what she had done for him. He was sorry. He would go and tell her so before he went away, perhaps never to return to his native land.

So he bought a ticket next morning for Oberlin, and; on arriving there, went straight to the little cottage which he had bought for his freedwoman five years before.

It was occupied by strangers. He could only learn that some weeks before she had sold the property and departed. The present occupants knew nothing of her destination.

It was strange that his impulses should be thus baffled. He walked about the aimless streets of this abnormally-minded little village, this pretty den of venomous fanatics, and pondered the odd circumstance.

·When he went with the self-complacent hauteur of the lordly Southerner, to pay off and recompense the priceless services and inestimable kindnesses of the

Yankee surgeon, never doubting that a sufficiency of pelf would more than satisfy the greed of one who had inherited, as he conceived, only mercenary proclivities, he was met with a sturdy rebuff, which had brought a flush of shame to his own face, and made his thanks, when finally tendered, seem cold and beggarly. He felt annoyed by it. Either he had quite mistaken the rest of the world or himself.

And now his former slave-woman, after putting him under obligations of the most exalted character, after displaying the most wonderful devotion, never remitting in her tenderness even after his unjustifiable harsh-ness, had fled from him—fled from his very gratitude as if it had been a pestilence—and left him her debtor with no power to release himself from the claim.

It seemed as if the fates pursued him with a grim mockery of his antipathies. Was he to be forever be-holden to those whom he had hated most bitterly? Was his intense Southern pride to be thus baffled and humbled, first by the man who, of all living mortals, he had regarded with the most disgust and hate—the dead Lincoln—then by the blue-coated surgeon, and finally by his former slave? To each he owed an incalculable debt, which he could never discharge. Each seemed to hold a lien upon his life. How could he ever hate these natural enemies of himself and his class as he should, when the very light that flooded his eyes was a living witness of their charity? These indissoluble obligations vexed him. He would cancel them by fly-ing from them.

A hasty visit to Perham confirmed him in this resolution. The Hunter Home was desolate. During the war his aunt and one of his sisters had died. The other had married and removed to the home of her husband, who was striving to conquer another fortune from the virgin soil of the South-west in lieu of that which the collapse of the Confederacy had swallowed up.

Not less desolate than the old mansion was the entire aspect of the country round about. Everything had changed. A blight was upon every form of life. Only the skeleton of the past remained, and even that sadly shattered and disjointed. The present seemed at outs with all that had gone before. In the expressive language of the times, "the bottom rail was on top." Society was overturned and prosperity uprooted. The future presented only the impenetrable blackness of despair.

Filled with such sentiments and apprehensions, Geoffrey Hunter left his affairs in the hands of the agent by whom they had been long and successfully administered, and himself became one of that band of self-expatriated exiles who, soon after the war, flaunted the willow of the "Lost Cause" upon foreign soil, and consoled themselves for the loss of what they deemed their rights, by taking service under a despot—revenging themselves upon the nation which had but just put down a rebellion, by undertaking a like enterprise for a government whose existence was a mere accident. While claiming to be chevaliers *sans reproche*, they became, in fact, soldiers of fortune, bartering for gold the swords they had consecrated with such high resolves and solemn vows.

25

As the bronzed and bearded veteran drove through the streets of Perham, conscious of skill and power, on the way to his new field of action, he remembered that day of early summer when he had marched along that same street at the head of a band of heroes, enwreathed as a victor and applauded to the echo. Now there was no wreath on his brow. Was it because he represented no high principle or worthy sentiment? Could it be that *he* was mercenary? The thought chafed him.

CHAPTER XLI.

THE RESCUE.

GEOFFREY HUNTER was doomed to disappointment in his new adventure. The role of a Free Lance did not comport with his nature. Besides, he soon found that the advantages, so glowingly pictured by his friend, were far more roseate when viewed from a distance than they seemed on close approach. The skies were no brighter, the air no purer, nor was the comparison between the people he had left—even after emancipation had become an accomplished fact—and the mongrel, incoherent, half-savage masses with which this tropical land of refuge abounded to be made in any manner to the depreciation of the former. If there was little hope for what these fastidious patriots fondly termed their "country," there was infinitely less for that which they had adopted.

Besides, there was not that swift decay, that utter disintegration and destruction of the Government cf the Union after the war, which they had so confidently expected and so vehemently predicted. The nation seemed a little staggered in its career of progress by the terrific shock of battle, but there was no weakness, no indecision of purpose. It was the quiet of repose. The stillness of the giant of the herd while he is gathering his strength for a fresh onset.

These over-zealous apostles of the Lost Cause were greatly amazed that the governmental structure of the nation did not crumble and fall as one by one they shook off the dust of their feet as a testimony against it, and were not a little disappointed at the result. They did not take into account the fact that the noblest spirits, the leading minds of the cause of which they claimed to be the only faithful adherer. s in defeat, had remained at home, following the lead of that Christian soldier, the illustrious Lee, whose name no American can trace without pride, and whose glory would alone redeem the iniquity of the war if self-sacrifice and unswerving devotion could obliterate the stain of a causeless conflict. These good men, as true to themselves as they had been to the Confederacy, did not count the nation lost because their cause had not prospered in its results, but felt it their duty to remain and give what aid they might in building up the places which war had made desolate, and aiding the people who had so faithfully followed their lead in the terrible struggle through which they had passed.

God bless these noble men, their names and memories, greater in defeat than they could possibly have been in victory, whose patriotism and devotion were proof against the corrupting influence of humiliation and misfortune!

One by one, in a few short months, these Hannibals of the rebellion, who had sworn eternal hatred to the Yankee, and to whom the "Stars and Stripes" were so offensive that they chose to wear the badge of despotism rather than dwell under their shadow, came dropping quietly back to the seats which had known them before. Among these patriots who early repented his excessive zeal was Geoffrey Hunter, and on the following Spring, before the white-oak leaves were as large as squirrels' ears, or the falling blossoms of the dogwood indicated the proper season for planting, he was wandering about his paternal mansion and broad plantations, moody, discontented, and unsatisfied.

In one of his desultory rambles along the river which found its way through the bottom-lands of Cold Spring, Geoffrey Hunter was startled by a cry for help. Rushing in the direction of the voice, he came out upon the bank of the river at a point where it turned suddenly from its course and swept over a half-submerged granite ledge. Upon the point of one of these rocks, in the very midst of the rushing waters, stood a boy of six or seven; fair as a lily, with long, golden, ringleted hair, which was blowing about in the Spring sunlight while he swung his blue-banded sailor-hat and shouted in delight at the wild turbulence of the mad stream, which seemed to be gloating in anticipation over its fair prey. He had gone from rock to rock along the ledge, sometimes stepping from one to another, sometimes running along the timbers of a fish-trap which had once spanned the stream at this point, and at others walking upon pieces of drift-wood which had lodged against the jutting rocks. Along one of these he had passed to the rock where he now stood. His weight, though light, had loosened the log and it had floated off, leaving him upon the rock unconscious of danger. His nurse, a colored girl of twelve or fourteen, unable to go to him,

was running up and down the bank uttering frantic
shrieks for help. Just as Geoffrey came up, the boy,
attracted by these cries, turned round and saw himself
isolated from the bank as has been described, and instinctively starting back, his foot slipped, and in an instant the little sailor-hat, floating away upon the foaming waters of the cascade, was all that could be seen
of the brave young boy.

Geoffrey Hunter did not hesitate an instant. The
fierce impetuosity which carried him, sword in hand,
over the walls of Steadman, while his men were yet
far behind, was not dead. In a moment, gun and
game-bag were thrown aside, his boots off, and he was
running from rock to rock, towards the point where
the child disappeared. The waters raged about him
exultingly, as a new victim, rushing into their insatiate
grasp. They dinned their fierce greediness into his
ears, as he stood a second, watching for some indications of the child's whereabouts. Then they flung up
a tiny hand for an instant to decoy him into their
grasp, then whirled their victim farther away. He
smiled with grim joy at the danger that offered, and
answered the challenge of the waves by a long, low
leap, stretching himself along the water towards the
point where the child had disappeared. The sweeping current caught his limbs, and drew them under
him, dashed him out of his course, and would
have hurled him broadside upon a sharp spur of the
rock, but his eye was too keen, and his arm too quick
and strong. He was borne around the jutting rock,
into the eddy where the child had last been seen.

THE RESCUE.

"Gun and game-bag were thrown aside, his boots off, and he was running from rock to rock, toward the point where the child disappeared." —p. 414.

The foaming waters hide the bottom. Their ceaseless thunder dins in his ears terribly. The spray is
in his eyes. He can see no trace of the child. What
shall he do? Has the boy been carried out of the eddy
beyond the next shoal? Or has he sunk there? He
can see nothing to guide him. He swims round and
round like a disappointed retriever, seeking for sunken
prey. All at once he feels a silken mesh about his
hand. Have the water-sprites cast a net about him?
He clasps it firmly, and raises his hand quickly to the
surface, bringing with it the dripping, blanched face
of the boy. Then he shouts with delight. But the
struggle is yet to come. The mad waters are not to
be cheated of their prey thus easily, and fling him
roughly back when he seeks to leave the eddy for the
shore. Then he gathers the strong nankeen jacket of
the boy in his teeth, throws one of the limp arms over
his neck, and with his burden thus on his shoulder, and
the strong arms free to battle with the currents, he
strikes out for the shore. The struggle is a hard one,
but the sturdy swimmer triumphs, and brings the boy
in safety to the bank.

He loses not a moment, but begins to strip the
clinging garments from the flaccid form which he lays
upon the grass, in the warm sunshine, wrapped in the
coat which he had himself thrown off, and begins press-
ing the chest, and raising and lowering the arms, to induce respiration. He hushes the clamor of the nurse
with harsh words, and, quickening her memory with a
blow, bids her run for whiskey and blankets.

"Remember," he shouts, as she flies from him,

"blankets and whiskey, or I'll throw you in where he came from."

Then an idea strikes him. There is a bed of soft, gray sand, just above the shoal, which the river has thrown upon the bank in high water. It must be heated now by the warm rays of the Spring sun. If the boy were in that his limbs would soon lose their chill. He picks him up and runs. His knees are weak and trembling, from his struggle with the river. The water rings in his ears, and his head spins with excitement and fatigue. But he pushes on. He stumbles over logs and rocks. His feet and legs are bruised by frequent falls. Once his head is cut. The brambles tear him, and the bushes cling about him, but, at length, he reaches the bed of sand. He lays the boy down, and with his hands scoops out a bed in the warm mass. Then he unwraps the coat and lays the white form upon the gray, glittering sand, in the place which he has made for him, and heaps the hot particles about it. The naked form is covered deep in an instant, all but the chest and head. He folds the coat and lays it under the boy's head, and begins again his labor of coaxing life back into the little form.

He thought vaguely how some mother's heart would bleed should the brave boy never breathe again, and labored with redoubled energy, watching for some signs of success. These came at length—first, a soft, low sigh, so low that he almost thought it but imagination, then another and another; then beads of sweat upon the brow, before so pallid and clammy; then a slight flush of the fair cheek, and finally the eyes opened and gazed at him unconsciously. He was saved.

At this moment voices came to his ears—a mother's voice, shrieking, "My boy! my boy!"

Geoffrey was weak and trembling with his exertions, but he answered the hail, hoarsely and with difficulty, "Here! Here!"

The sun seemed swimming in space, and burning his very brain. He thought that a woman came rushing along the bank and snatched the child to her bosom. She was young and beautiful, though tearful and pallid, panting with fatigue and fright.

He thought. No—he wasn't sure—yes—it was Toinette!

Then his brain reeled, and the darkness which had settled down upon him at Steadman, seemed about to throw over him again its horrible pall. He looked up and saw Betty Certain standing before him administering to himself one of the remedies which he had sent for to resuscitate the boy. It was a strange group which stood around the child he had saved, and the mind of Geoffrey could think only of the changes which time had wrought, as he was driven home that balmy evening, with the thanks of the young mother ringing in his ears, along the very road by which he had brought his pet chattel a few years before, to Lovett Lodge.

CHAPTER XLII.

IMMEDIATELY upon the recovery of Geoffrey Hunter at Washington, Toinette had returned to Oberlin, and soon after disposed of her little property there, in order that she might comply with the repeated requests of Betty Certain that she should return and enjoy that which she was entitled to receive under her father's will.

Her head was full of strange, wild notions of the future. The dissipation of one dream did not destroy all of her hallucinations. She had once been the actual mistress of Lovett Lodge, and she now longed to be the acknowledged head of the establishment. Her relations with the subject race had been so slight in reality, that she could be pardoned for half-overlooking their influence upon her destiny, in estimating the future. Yet, through all her dreams would come that ominous "Toinette! Toinette!" of the hospital.

With a strange medley in her mind, therefore, she went back to Lovett Lodge. It was her home. Her heart had clung about it ever since her eyes had missed the shadow of its majestic oaks, and she had gone away to live among strangers. More than anything else her kinship to the enslaved race was manifested in her strangely intense attachment to locality. Her little cottage at the North had never been her home. It was only a temporary abode to her. She always looked back to the loosely-built, rambling Lodge, as her ideal of a home.

To this place so eventful in her life she now returned, and soon became thoroughly domesticated in her old haunts. She did not inform her friends and neighbors where she intended to go, because she had a sort of instinct that it was not well that she should carry with her, into her new life, too much of the old.

Old Maggie and many of those who had been her fellow-servants had been emancipated by decree of the King of Kings before the Liberator had signed that proclamation which was to be an estoppel of record against the claims of every American citizen who sought to hold property in man.

Owing also to the general removal of the freedmen at the close of the war, but few were left in the neighborhood of Lovett's who could have recognized Toinette as a former inmate of the Lodge. The chances of recognition were greatly lessened also, by the secluded life which she had led as Geoffrey Hunter's favorite, and the fact that, although a slave, she had never associated much with the servants, and was only known to those who waited about the Lodge.

When, therefore, the well-dressed, refined, and attractive Mrs. Hunter, with her beautiful boy, came the Summer after the surrender and took up her residence at the Lodge, whose occupant, Mrs. Betty Certain, greeted her as an old acquaintance, no questions were asked in regard to her.

The war and its results had made strange bed-
fellows, and it was generally assumed that Mrs. Hunter
was a lady much above Betty Certain's rank in life, but
not so well supplied with the essentials of comfortable
living as the executrix of the last will and testament of
Arthur Lovett. In short, that she was the relict of
some brave man whom the war had swallowed up—a
widow in decayed circumstances. Her generally som-
ber attire strengthened this opinion, and the only remark occasioned by her presence, was that excited by
her beauty. So, she had since dwelt quietly at the
Lodge with her old friend.

Upon Betty Certain the effect of her presence was
remarkable. There seemed to be a constant struggle
going on in her mind as to the proper demeanor to be
adopted towards the new inmate of the house she had
occupied alone for five years. When they had lived
there before, Toinette had actually been its mistress, although a slave, and it was but natural that she should
now assume the privileges and familiarities to which she
had then been accustomed. To the poor white woman
this was not so easy. She could not forget that the
woman who was her guest had been a slave, and was
supposed to have in her veins a stain of African blood
—remote and obscure, it was true—but by presumption
of law and of birth, still there. She had a strange fondness for Toinette—who was wonderfully like Arthur
Lovett in form and feature, and in many of her intellectual characteristics. While she remained a slave-girl
there could be no mistake in regard to their relations,
and she had not scrupled to exhibit this fondness to

wards her. Then, too, she herself was only Betty Certain, living on the old Certain tract; not having arrived at that dignity and importance in the neighborhood which had resulted from the control of the Lovett estate in her capacity of executrix, and, as everybody supposed, sole heir of the same. Now it was different.

She had been taught to consider slavery as a wrong. "Granther Ezra" had so esteemed it, and had refused to contaminate his soul with the touch of the "unclean thing," and had enjoined this doctrine, like the commandment of "Jonadab, the son of Rechab," upon "his sons, their wives, and their children, forever." Arthur Lovett thought slavery wrong, yet practiced it, and suffered by its scath. So Betty Certain had no love for slavery, and was glad it was destroyed. But then, she had no love for the enslaved race either. She was no more in favor of their farther advancement than the proudest aristocrat of the old slave *régime.* She had been poor; her family was poor as far back as she knew it; but she was *white*, and was proud of the fact—perhaps prouder than otherwise she would have been, because she had little other ground for vanity. She could not forget this and associate with any one having a *soupçon* of the unfortunate blood in their veins, upon terms approaching to equality, without some qualms of pride, if not of conscience.

Therefore it was, that while the "poor white" woman really loved her whom she had nursed and petted as a slave girl without thought of degradation or contamination resulting therefrom, she found it necessary, as she thought, to maintain a certain distance and reserve

towards the elegant and refined creature into which time
and fortune had transformed her, lest she should lower
herself by a recognition of the social equality of one
even infinitesimally akin to the inferior race.

Toinette having unconsciously arrogated to herself
the first place in the household, Betty Certain could only
maintain the distance she deemed essential to her dignity as a person of unmixed Caucasian descent by resum-
ing the inferior one she had formerly held. So that any
one who had casually observed the ménage at the Lodge
would have taken Toinette for the luxuriously-inclined
and somewhat careless mistress, and Betty Certain for
the exceedingly faithful housekeeper and manager, who
took all care from her shoulders.

This delicate " distinction in regard to race, color,
and previous condition," in the mind of the poor white
woman, did not seem to extend to the boy " Geoffrey."
Indeed, it appeared to be somewhat regretfully entertained—as a matter of duty only—towards the mother.
Whether it was the additional strain of Anglo-Saxon,
the increased remoteness of the typical Ethiopian, the
difference of sex, the tender years, or the irresistible
winsomeness of the boy himself, certain it was that he
walked into the heart of the childless woman, and set up
a kingdom there over which he was the undisputed
autocrat. The wealth of love which Betty Certain could
not display towards Toinette because of the inherent
ineradicable antagonism of race, she lavished more
abundantly upon her child. It may have been illogical,
but it was natural. Even the subtle instincts of the poor
white could not trace in that blue-eyed, sunny-haired

young Adonis, who so strangely mingled the traits of
Geoffrey Hunter and Arthur Lovett, any hint upon which
this unconquerable and inscrutable aversion could be
based. So she assumed the responsibilities of aunthood
toward him without scruple, and outdid the young
mother in loving obedience to the imperious little
tyrant.

CHAPTER XLIII.

AS OF OLD.

IF Geoffrey Hunter came frequently to Lovett Lodge during the illness of the child whom he had saved, his visits were accounted those of condolence and sympathy.

He could not have avoided being interested in the little life which hung trembling in the balance for many days, even if he had not been aware that this fluttering soul was but an offshoot of his own existence. He had, too, somewhat of the pride of paternity, which led him to regard this brave, beautiful boy with actual solicitude. He recognized the dauntless spirit which had led him on from rock to rock, amid the mad rush of the wild rapid, as akin to the reckless daring of his own nature. As the child grew better, and he saw more of his peculiarities, he could not but recognize himself—his way and manner, in a thousand trifles, by others unnoticed. The boy's mind was an open volume to him, which he read with ease by the light of his own memory and instinct. It was a delightful study, which, by its very novelty, blotted from his mind, for the time being, the peculiar relations of the child and the mother to himself. It amused him to note how familiar the boy's mental lineaments seemed to his own consciousness. The boy's development was an open book of ever-increasing interest to the watcher, to whom, in a double sense, he owed his life, who recognized each movement, attitude, and gesture as his own, and seemed instinctively able to divine what he would do or say under any given circumstances.

Every day he called to inquire as to the boy's recovery, and long before it was completed had become a familiar visitant at his bed-side. Instinctively the boy seemed attracted to his new friend. Utterly unconscious of the relation which subsisted between them, he still seemed to recognize a kindred nature. He looked for Geoffrey's coming anxiously, and was fretful and uneasy if it was delayed after the usual hour.

Absorbed in the danger which threatened her child, Toinette had hardly time to observe who it was that brought him to her arms. During the sorrowful days that followed her solicitude was so great that she scarcely noticed the presence of Geoffrey at the Lodge. All thought of their previous relations was blotted from her mind. She had no time to think of anything except her darling boy. She had dreamed so often, too, of a glad time to come when her boy's father should acknowledge the relationship, and should share with her the joys and sorrows of parentage, that it hardly seemed strange to see him sitting by the bedside and soothing the little sufferer. Why should he not! It was his boy as well as hers. She was almost glad in this hour, when the death-angel hovered close above her darling, that another heart shared, as she believed it did, her parental anguish.

Dim, fragmentary thoughts like these were all that

she gave to Geoffrey Hunter in those dark hours, while life struggled with death for the prize of that fair form.

The keen-eyed, poor-white woman, Betty Certain, knowing nothing of the later relations between Geoffrey and Toinette, long accustomed to seeing them together at the Lodge and having unbounded love for both, was equally blind to his presence and its possible consequences. Geoffrey's upright conduct in regard to the Lovett estate, his bravery and suffering in the war, and, above all, as it seemed to her, his honorable and even generous course toward Toinette herself, had won her confidence and admiration beyond comparison with all other men, excepting always Arthur Lovett, of sainted memory. It was true that Geoffrey Hunter, having the young girl under his control, and in his charge, had used the opportunities afforded by his position in a manner altogether wrong and improper. He had no right to make his slave-girl the mother of his children. It was wicked. Arthur Lovett had erred in the same way, but Geoffrey had generously atoned for his fault. He had freed the servant woman who had shared his embraces, and had thereby discharged his debt, made compensation to Toinette, and also avoided the crime of enslaving his own offspring. Betty Certain looked upon it in no harsher light than this. Tenderly as she had always regarded Toinette, she had never properly estimated her love for Geoffrey. She had never realized that the all-absorbing, self-forgetting passion which dwelt in her own heart for Arthur Lovett might have its counterpart in that which Toinette gave to Geoffrey. She would have admitted, if asked, that the girl loved her former master, or had loved him, at least, but she would have used the term with a limited significance. It had never occurred to her that the devotion which had sanctified the years of her own life to vestal service at the shrine of a holy memory might also dwell in the bosom of Toinette.

Perhaps it is not strange. There was something so obnoxious to the mutuality of sentiment and regard which perfect love demands in the relation of slavery, that it is scarce a matter of wonder that one knowing this relation to exist should suppose love to be an impossible concomitant. Besides, she had never done full justice to Belle Lovett, who, with all her errors, had loved Arthur with a wild intensity, as sincere if not as pure as her own. She thought she did, but in her inmost heart she rejoiced that the relation between them had been that of master and menial. She put her own devoted attachment on a higher plane. It was of a nobler grade—a better rank, somehow. She had never been much disturbed by the love which he had avowed for his slave, because she *was* a slave. She was a poor creature. Arthur had wronged her; but he desired to make reparation, and would have done so, had he lived. As his agent and trustee, she would do it yet. That was all right, all proper, and it was enough. She counted the love of the slave-woman as something which could be priced and paid for. It partook in her mind of the chattel nature of the giver. Its rejection and violation were the subject matter of compensation. She would not justify—she never had justified—such conduct on the part of Geoffrey or Arthur. It was wrong for them to be the paramours of bondwomen—not because they spurned and crushed the flowers of love beneath their feet; but because the canons of decency and morality were violated. It was wrong for Geoffrey Hunter to make the slave-girl Toinette the amusement of his leisure moments, not so much because of the wrong which he did to her, as on account of the evil which he wrought to himself.

She had never contemplated it as a possibility that the girl Toinette could aspire to love Geoffrey Hunter as an equal might have done—that she should ever dream of being the one love, the all in all, the wife, of her master.

As the boy recovered, his attachment for his new friend gained strength. He rode with him almost daily. Short, careful trips at first, gradually growing longer as his strength increased. Thus the former master became again a familiar presence at Lovett Lodge.

As Toinette's care for her child relaxed with his returning health, she began to consider the embarrassments of her position with the seriousness which they required. Her eyes had been opened as well as Geoffrey's, though in a different sense. She remembered always, with unutterable horror, that scene in the hospital, and felt that an impassable chasm lay between them. She knew her position and her weakness, and felt that she could neither expose herself to the suspicions which his frequent visits would soon engender, nor trust her own heart to see him amid the surroundings of their former intimacy. She owed

it to herself, her child, the race to which she was
so strangely allied, and to the womanhood which had
sprung to life in her heart, to put an end to their
association. How should this be done? There was
but one way to accomplish it without exposing herself to annoyance and mortification. She must leave
Lovett Lodge, and leave it for good. She arrived at
this conclusion one morning while her boy was taking
his accustomed ride with his new-found friend. Geoffrey's demeanor toward her, during her affliction, had
been strictly that of a gentleman. Neither by word
nor look had he presumed upon their former relation
His courtesy had been unobtrusive and unaffected.
Instinctively he had recognized the lady whom his
comrades in the hospital had discovered in Toinette.
At first he had been at a loss for a convenient term by
which to address her. He could not bring himself to
call her "Mrs. Hunter." He felt that it would not
do to address her as "Toinette," so he had fallen back
on the indefinite "Madame," which, being very generally
used in that section, was liable to no objection on the
score of formality or affectation, as it might be in a
Northern community.

Toinette saw and appreciated this delicacy. She
regretted then for the first time that she had ever assumed the name of Mrs. Hunter, though in truth it was
a fiction which chance had put ready made into her
hands. Geoffrey had taken the deed for the little house
which he had purchased for her in the name of Antoinette Hunter, adding the master's name to her slave-
appellative, and Toinette's modesty and propriety of

deportment, together with her studiousness and the devotion she manifested to her child, so impressed her
neighbors that they instinctively termed her Mrs. Hunter, without inquiry as to the fact of wifehood. The
war which came on so soon after she had come among
them, and the cutting off of all communication between
the North and South, was accepted by all as a good and
sufficient reason for the absence of the man whom they
had assumed to be her husband. So, without a suspicion
as to her origin, they had accepted her as free, white,
and married—a woman to be pitied because of the
separation which the war had wrought between herself
and her husband.

To say that Toinette did not encourage this idea,
after it had become prevalent, would be untrue. It
was hardly to be expected of poor human nature that
she would fail to put herself on the vantage-ground
which was thus laid open to her footsteps. In doing
so, however, she was quite unconscious of an intent to
deceive, and only anxious to secure herself from remark and aspersion by what seemed a providential stu-
pidity of the people among whom she was thrown.
She was afraid now that Geoffrey would attribute its
adoption to herself and thereby infer the existence of
that secret dream which she had nourished so long, and
which had in part originated from the bestowal of this
title upon her and the rôle which she had been almost
compelled, in consequence, to adopt.

Clearly, she must leave the Lodge, and at once.
Her dream was dissipated. Her idol broken. Yet she
loved Geoffrey Hunter as fervently as ever. In justice

to herself she must flee his presence, which, however loved, could only contaminate.

Toinette did not for a moment contemplate delay, nor underestimate its dangers. She had laid this down as her rule of conduct, that if her life should ever be made known to her boy, he should have no cause to blush for any act of hers after she became free. She would keep herself pure for his sake, not only from evil, but from its very appearance and the possibility of its imputation.

She had a dim idea that she had not always been mistaken as to the nature of the regard which Geoffrey Hunter had once entertained for her. She went back over her life here at the Lodge; his fondness for her society, his enjoyment of her presence and conversation, his evident regret at her absence, even the course which he adopted in her emancipation, convinced her that his regard for her was something more than the mere liking of a licentious man for his mistress. She believed that even yet he loved her. Perhaps it was her desire that he should—her quenchless love for him—which led her to this belief. At the same time she did not think that he would ever give it the sanction of public acknowledgement. She knew the world now too well, and appreciated its prejudices too justly, to think *that*, even for a moment. His attachment, his love, she believed, to be sincere, but she felt that he would never manifest it in a form which she could recognize or permit without self-abasement and shame. She feared that he might desire to renew their former relations, and determined to go away before this insult to her love should be offered.

She sat in the library of the Lodge, in the old arm-chair which Geoffrey had so often occupied when. he was master there, in which Arthur Lovett sat when the hand of love—transformed to hate by a series of strange events—loosed the silver cord of his life.

The memories of the past came over her, and she wept at the destruction of its bright visions. She half-wished she could have remained a slave, uninformed of the nobler duties and obligations of free womanhood. The love of Geoffrey Hunter—she was sure she would have enjoyed that—would have compensated her for much. If he had but remembered his Toinette!—how sweet that name had sounded upon his lips!—she would never have dreamed of marriage—never would have thought it wrong—at least not seriously wrong. Oh! it would have been sweet to have been his—worth—*almost* the pangs and debasements of slavery!

She wept as she thought of it. Had freedom been worth its price? What had she received by it? Her-self, volition, certainly; but with isolation, friendless-ness! There was no one to love her, hardly a friend in whom she could confide. Just sufficiently con-nected with the menial race to be spurned by the dominant one, her position as associated with the one was always liable to suspicion and detection, and to identify herself with the other was to step down the ladder of development to a level which she shud-dered to contemplate. She had risen far above the mass of the lately subject race. By education and cult-ure she was the equal, aye, the superior, of thousands of the master race. She felt this, and the sting of her destiny was all the sharper for its knowledge. She was not a missionary. She did not care to devote herself to the elevation of the freed people. She loved the good things of life, her own enjoyments, light, love, music, pleasant and agreeable surroundings. She was not wide in her views. She did not care to make the world so much better for her having lived in it. She did not think she was called to do it, perhaps scarcely thought of it at all.

She was not strong-minded, only strong-hearted; did not love everybody, only a few; but those few she loved wildly, passionately—not because it was her duty, but because she delighted in loving them. She did not like hardships or sacrifice. She did not worship abstract right. The dictates of her heart prevailed always over the edicts of reason. She could endure anything, everything for one she loved, and esteem it a joy, a privilege, so to do; but she had no love for general humanity which could sweeten labor or sacrifice in its behalf. The good which was in her nature was concrete, not abstract. She loved her own, herself, her boy, her friends, and, above all, her master, Geoffrey Hunter!

Therefore it was, that while she sat and wept over the shattered memories of the past, almost regretting the slave life she had lost, when she heard the voice of her boy returning from his ride her regret instantly vanished. Her tears were dried at once. Her mother-love was the mystic solvent of her unworthy doubt. She would go away at once for his sake. She would take him where knowledge of his origin and parentage could never come—to the world's end if need be. He should

T

never know shame. His proud spirit should never be humbled and broken with the stigma of ignoble birth. She would *be* what she seemed—a lady. He should never blush for his mother. He should never know that the proud man who petted him now was his father, or that the slave Toinette was his mother. Toinette was dead! She would bury her!

It was in that instant that the iron of slavery entered deeper into her soul than ever before. She saw how it had blasted her love and shriveled her life. That terrible "Toinette! Toinette!" of the hospital rang in her ears as she heard the prattling of her boy and the footsteps of Geoffrey ascending the very stairs down which the ghost of Lovett Lodge had disappeared while she lay prostrated with the dagger-stroke so many years ago. Why had she ever risen to life again? She wished she had died!

Hastily wiping away her tears, she went to the library door to meet them as they stepped upon the porch. Her mind was made up. She would announce her decision without delay. What must be done should be done at once.

CHAPTER XLIV.

"GET THEE BEHIND ME, SATAN."

"OH, mamma!" said the boy, running towards her, his cheek glowing with restored health, and his eyes radiant with animation and joy. "Oh, mamma! may I go home with Col. Hunter? He says he has a great big house, and a pony, and a dog, and—and the dog's name is Leon, and he is the nicest old fellow— only not so nice as another Leon who died long ago— and no little boy at all. Please mamma, let me go. That's a dear, pretty mamma!" said the artless child, caressing the fair head that bowed to kiss his upturned face.

Geoffrey Hunter gazed upon the pretty picture with a strange medley of emotions. He was both proud and envious of the bright boy, whose arm encircled that fair neck and who received those caresses. He almost forgot that it was but his former slave girl and her brat. His heart was clamoring for her love, and his tongue burned to utter the prayer of affection.

Toinette having hushed the child's prattlings, rose and stood holding his hand, as she said with grave earnestness :

"Do you really desire it, sir?"

"Indeed I do," answered Geoffrey, "and if you will permit him to go, I will promise to take the best care of him while he is with me."

"I do not doubt that, sir," she replied, her eyes looking straight into his with an unshrinking steadiness, which made his own waver before their calm light, and added, with the same quiet gravity, "I know you would; yet I have one request to make before I can give my permission."

"You know I will grant any request you can make, madame," he answered quickly, almost tenderly.

"It is only that——" she hesitated, and a slight blush overspread her face, but her gaze did not lose its steadiness, nor her voice its tone of gentle dignity, as she continued: "Only that you will promise that he shall never love his mother less for granting him this favor."

There was no mistaking her meaning. The emphasis was too marked to be unnoticed. She wished to seal his lips as to the past. That past swept by him an instant panorama, as his eyes fell before hers for a moment. Then he raised them and gazed at her again, as she stood in his presence. The past was dead in her. The present and the future alone were written in her face. There was no shame, no consciousness of impurity or inferiority in her look. It was the unshrinking gaze of a candid woman, conscious of what her son might some day regard as a fault, yet full of conscious innocence and purity. There was neither reproach nor entreaty. Just the inquiry whether he would let the past remain sealed to the child. His face flushed as he answered warmly:

"You do not think I would do anything to prevent it?"

Then all at once he remembered that scene in the hospital. His eyes fell, and he added confusedly and humbly:

"I beg pardon; I had forgotten that you have reason to think ill of me. You have my promise. I had hoped that my conduct since then would have obliterated that memory."

His eyes flashed up at her a look of haughty, passionate reproach. Poor Toinette! She had not expected this. She was not armed at all points. She saw him in his magnificent strength and courage breasting the rushing stream, reckless of his own life, to save that fair-haired treasure by her side. Instinctively she sank down by the boy and clasped him in her arms. A flood of tears gushed over his golden locks, as with trembling lips she said:

"It has, it has—a thousand times. I did not mean that. You do not think I did?" she asked, as she raised her eyes, welling over with tears, to his face.

"No, no," he answered, hastily, "but will you let me have the boy for a while?"

"Yes, certainly. Run, Geoffrey, and tell nurse to get you ready." She kissed the boy, and stood before him again, self-poised and calm. "You have a right to ask it, and there will be no opportunity hereafter. But you must bring him back on Monday."

"Why so soon?"

"We shall leave here on Wednesday."

"Leave on Wednesday? Leave the Lodge, do you mean?"

"Yes."

"Where are you going?"

"I do not know."

"Do not know? When will you return?"

"Never."

His quick glance half read her thought. "You are going to avoid me," he said. She turned pale and leaned against the doorway for support, but did not answer. He turned and strode, with quick, angry steps, along the porch. Then he wheeled suddenly, and came back.

"Toinette, why do you treat me thus? You know that I love you, and am miserable without you. Have I not suffered enough for one thoughtless act? Have I not treated you kindly and tenderly ever since? You do not love me, or you would forget it."

His voice was tremulous with emotion, and his eyes burned into her very soul. She looked into them, and saw the yearning love of his passionate nature. Poor Toinette, how her own heart throbbed responsive to that fierce appeal! She knew that he loved her, loved her as he never could, or would, love any other woman. He was not speaking to the slave-girl. His manner was earnest, respectful, tender. It was the language of a thirsty soul, asking the love of its fellow, free, untrammeled, pure. He had forgotten all else. She was all the world to him in that hour of love's supremest, mastery. "Toinette"—"Toinette!" How sweet was that name now breathed in the tender, trembling accents of his lips. Poor weak heart, what wonder that the world slipped away from her view, too. Geoffrey—her idol, her *master*—bowed before her and sought her love.

Joy flushed her face. Her color came and went. The glad tears defied restraint. She uttered a low cry, half sob, half moan. She looked up at him and clasped her hands, feebly and pleadingly. She trembled, and would have fallen. Instantly the strong arms enclosed her in their fervid grasp. She was pillowed on his bosom, and his lips showered kisses upon lips and brow. Her dream was fulfilled. Geoffrey loved her. Life had no further joy. Yet even in that ecstatic moment there came over her enraptured soul a dim sense of evil. But there could be no danger. His arms were around her. She was at home. The warm, sweet sunshine lay peaceful and quiet upon the porch. The trees stood in the calm of the mid-summer noon without a leaf stirred by the wind. Nature was bathed in silence and sunshine. Her joyous heart throbs were audible in the hush of that bright mid-day. All was light and love.

"Toinette, Toinette," he murmured as he clasped her yet closer to his breast. "You are mine—mine always—you will not leave me? You must not leave me! We will live here at the Lodge and be happy, as in the dear old times."

A cloud skirted the sunbeams. How quickly the gloom succeeded the brightness. "The old times" at the Lodge with Geoffrey Hunter! What different pictures did those words bring to those two minds of the war—its anticipations, glories, hopes, triumphs and reverses, and its sad and bitter consequences swept before the eyes of one. Bondage and freedom, chattelism and self-assertion, existence and non-existence gleamed in ineffaceable contrast before the other. Slav-ery and womanhood now stood before her in the future. She must at this juncture elect the one or the other—decide to be true to herself or to go back to moral bondage.

She half released herself from his embrace, and looking calmly yet eagerly in his face, repeated:

"As in the olden time?"

"Yes, yes, my dear, why not?" with a sudden questioning glance.

"Because the past can never be again."

"True, times have changed, but we may still be happy as we were then."

"Have we not changed, too?"

"Changed! how? I have not changed toward you Toinette?"

"Yet we can never be to each other as we have been."

"Cannot! why?"

"Why? Why? Will you not see?" she cried in desperation, impetuously, at last. "Because a free woman may not lend herself to the evil which slavery might excuse."

His countenance darkened and his arms loosened their clasp.

She stood before him calm, determined, unshrinking.

"So," he cried, and Toinette remembered that terrible moment in the hospital as she heard the tone. "So you insist upon 'social equality,' I suppose. You expect me to marry you, perhaps?"

It was a harsh, cruel sneer, but Toinette did not flinch.

"I expect and insist on nothing, Colonel Hunter," she replied with dignity; "but I will not sully love with sin and shame. I demand nothing from others, but I must, I will, respect myself."

"You presume on my love," said he, angrily; "you think me so enamoured that I will degrade myself and disgrace my family openly to obtain you. You are mistaken."

He turned away and walked angrily toward the steps. As he started down them he looked up and saw her gazing after him with a sad, tearful look. He came back instantly.

"You did not mean it, Toinette. Say you did not mean it," he cried, as he caught her clasped hands in both his own. "You know it cannot be. You know Geoffrey Hunter cannot marry one who—who—has been a slave. It would disgrace him and his family forever. Besides, the law* does not allow it. Our marriage would

---

* The legal presumptions arising out of a state of slavery were somewhat peculiar, and now that it no longer exists, as a form of society, are likely to be forgotten. Many Indians, as well as negroes, were enslaved, and no doubt some persons of unmixed white blood also. The language of the old statutes upon this subject is very suggestive. They declare "all Negroes, Mulattos, Indians, Mezzotints, and other slaves who have been sold or held as such, to be slaves, they and their children, except such as may be freed for merit." From and after that time (about 1730) the condition of slavery was heritable in the female line. Every child of a slave woman, no matter what its race or color, was a slave and without legal remedy. It was a presumption which could be rebutted only by an act of manumission.

Connected with this was another and very essential presumption, to wit: That the individual who was held as a slave was presumed to be such until the contrary was *shown*. It reversed the presumption of the common law
27

be a crime, and if attempted would be void. The very
evil you seek to escape would be enhanced by it. But
I am certain you do not doubt that I love you as well
as wife ever was loved on earth."

"Do n't—do n't!" she wailed fitfully. "You would
not have me yield to sinful passion because the law pro-
hibits me a holy love?"

"Would you have me degrade myself and make the
Hunter name a badge of infamy to obtain your love?"

"Would you degrade not only ourselves but our offspring for the sake of the Hunter name? You would
not expect a sister to even listen to such a proposal."

"Do be reasonable, Toinette, and lay aside your
high notions. Wherever did you get them from? Freedom does not make you white any more than Lee's surrender made me black. You are not a lady, and need
not try to act the part of one. The barrier which na-

---

and put the onus of showing the fact of freedom upon the individual who
claimed to be unlawfully held.

Another presumption was that a person having more than *one-sixteenth
of colored blood was a slave!* It seems impossible, but such was the fact.
Reversing this too, but of less frequent application, and less clearly established by judicial construction, was the presumption of color from the fact
of slavery. Nothing else appearing, the fact of slavery within three generations made the fairest Saxon, in the eye of the law, a "colored person."
This presumption was carried to a much greater extent in common thought
than by the courts. The terms "nigger" and "slave" were synonomous
in the common mind.

This is the manner in which Geoffrey Hunter is here represented as referring to the law, which, it may be remarked, prevails in nearly all of the
States, both Northern and Southern, prohibiting the marriage of persons of
colored blood with whites, and presuming all to be colored who have more
than one-sixteenth of negro or Indian blood. It would seem that Toinette
did not fall within this category, in strictness, but the fact that she had been
a slave fixed her status in his mind as clearly as if she had borne the features of the despised race.

ture and the law has put between us matrimonially is
insuperable. Yet you know I love you. I cannot live
without you. Consider, Toinette, the difficulties. Why
can we not enjoy the substance without quarreling about
the shadow?"

Then she burst out on him.

"Because the passion which would degrade its object is alike unworthy of the giver and the recipient,
and a disgrace to both. No gentleman would offer it to
any woman he pretended to love."

"Very well, madame," said he, bitterly, "you will
find that Geoffrey Hunter will never demean himself by
marrying a nigger! You had better go back North and
try your wiles on some of the Yankees who have put
these infamous notions into your head. Social equality
will never prevail here; I can promise you that. Go,
by all means."

His brow black with the offended pride of race and caste,
Geoffrey Hunter left the woman whom he truly loved,
overwhelmed with anger because her virtue had resisted
his shameful advances. He passed down the steps and
out along the path where his horse was pawing and tossing his head with impatience.

While they had talked, one of the sudden storms of
early summer had arisen. Now the black, dense clouds
with gray-rifted rain-fronts were coming, sweeping on,
and the wild breath of the mad storm was tossing the
leaves and bending the trees in its path. Its dark, chill
presence rested majestically upon the Lodge and its surroundings, and its dull, fierce roar mingled with his
words of angry parting.

He tore the bridle from the rack, and, jumping into the frail vehicle, shook the lines, spoke sharply to the fretting steed, and, with angry imprecations, dashed along the road into the very face of the coming storm.

Upon the porch of the Lodge two figures watched his course—the boy, who wept with disappointment, and the woman, who shaded her eyes with her hand and with a calm but mournful gaze watched his course until the coming darkness veiled him from her view.

CHAPTER XLV.

GOOD-BY, SWEETHEART.

THE day after his interview with Toinette at the Lodge, Geoffrey Hunter wrote:

"TOINETTE:

"I cannot part from you thus in anger. Forgive my hasty temper, which seemed to make me do you injustice. I was wrong and you were right; quite right to refuse all love but that which proffers honorable marriage. And yet, Toinette, I cannot marry you, however wildly I love you. You know that as well as I. Besides all else there is the law, which puts an impenetrable wall between us. It is said to be based on the law of God. I do not know. It seems unreasonable, but we cannot violate it, even if willing to face all other obstacles. It would disgrace and ruin us both. But your presence makes me forget all else. I can only remember that you live—only seek to possess you. Do not go away, Toinette. Perhaps the time may come when this cruel necessity will not rest upon us God knows what of change may not occur. I would willingly give up all else for your love, but I cannot change my idenity—I cannot lose myself. Why has not the convulsion which has wrought the miracle of liberty for so many freed me also from the shackles of the past? But alas! it has not. I am still Geoffrey Hunter. I can be no other. The chains of the slave have been transferred to the master.

"Grant me one brief interview at least before you go. All will be dark afterward. That which would have made me always happy is denied me. Do not refuse me this last request, for the sake of the child I have learned to love second only to yourself.

"GEOFFREY HUNTER."

Toinette sighed as she read. Geoffrey Hunter had been her idol so long that defects in his character were like motes in a sunbeam. She was sorry he had written. He was much nobler in the fierceness of his wrath the day before. Her "royal gentleman" was discrowned. It seemed belittling his manhood to confess his love, and, at the same time, yield so tamely to obstacles. She was ashamed that her Samson was bound with the green withes of prejudice, and yielded to their restraint so readily. Why was he given that grand strength? Where was his manhood, that he should sit down like a child and say, "I would, but I dare not?" Something like contempt grew up in her bosom, yet she did not wish to indulge in such feeling. It was really mixed with sadness even now.

She was like an artisan who has wrought upon a lens for many long and weary months, hoping and expecting that it will be clearer and stronger than any which has ever before been made. Day by day he has cut and carved, ground and polished, with tireless care and a skill which only years of toil can give, and every night he has guarded his work from injury with a love as jealous

as a miser would bestow upon a Koh-i-noor. With it he
expected that the arcana of nature might be unlocked,
and the mysteries of the heavens be read aright. But
just when it is ready for the mounting, and he comes to
apply the final test, he finds that it has one slight defect. It is a *very* slight one. To any eye but that of
the scientific expert it is a perfect crystal—clear as a
diamond, exquisitely cut and finished. There is only
that little flaw where the fibres crossed and knotted in
cooling, where an imprisoned bubble produces a diversion of the rays passing through it and distorts the
transmitted image. It is only a slight defect, but it is a
fatal one. So it was with this note. It was the bubble
in Geoffrey's mind to the love-testing gaze of Toinette.

It was easier to go away from him now that he was
so ready to give her up at the demand of prejudice.
If he had held his peace she would have given him
credit for suffering and enduring silently. She had not
really expected him to run counter to all that stood in
his way—at least not after that ruthless scene in the
hospital—until he had come with his eyes open to all
that time had wrought, and had sought her love. Even
then she did not entirely expect it; but he might at
least have made an indignant protest against the shackles he was bound to wear. She would have suffered
all with him—for him—willingly, if he had bowed without yielding. She did not demand marriage, but her
heart insisted on the love which sanctifies that relation.
It was the knowledge that he would be content with
less, that he would offer a love which would debase
its object, that he would persuade her to yield herself

to shame, which cut her to the quick. She would go away before her idol shattered himself completely at her feet. She would not see him again. Henceforth she had only her boy and herself. She would be something that would take away the stigma of the past. She would win what she did not inherit—a name —a name without reproach. She was young yet— only twenty-three. How wide the world seemed! There must be something in it for her to do and win. With her boy to inspire, what might she not accomplish? Her dawning ambition made her spirit buoyant and confident. She knew too little of the world to estimate aright the obstacles before her.

So she sat down and wrote, in reply:

"Col. Hunter will pardon me for declining to accede to his request. To do so would only produce unnecessary pain."

Then she pondered long as to how she should sign it. She had the heritage of the slave—no patronymic. She had been known as Mrs. Hunter. The freedman took the name of his master. She had done the same, merely following the custom, but she could bear that name no longer. It was the badge of something more than bondage now—the name of a dead love, a perished hope. She would bear her father's name hereafter. Slavery and the past should thereby drop out of her life at once. It should serve her present purpose, too. When she went away from Lovett Lodge forever she would take with her its name. She would be Antoinette Lovett. No one would trace her by that. Even Geoffrey, if he

should try, would not think of such a simple subterfuge.
She would bury herself and her boy in the great busy
world. She would cut him off from his own past and
hers, by linking him in name with a still remoter past.
She would bear her father's name and belong to his race.
For the last time she would write the name which had
but lately sounded so sweetly in her ears, when uttered
by the lip whose accents she had heard for the last time.
She took her pen, signed the note "Toinette," and dis-
patched it to Geoffrey Hunter.

He was thunderstruck when he received it. The
petted slave-girl had made another metamorphosis. She
had not only met his love with warmth, and then repelled
his disgraceful overtures with the severity of a vestal,
but now she dismissed him with the dignity and coolness of a queen, and the grace of a practiced coquette.
Would he never learn her many-sided character? He
would see her, whether she desired it or not. He could
not part with her thus. Could he part with her at all?
The world seemed empty enough without her presence.
Why should he give her up? Disgrace? What disgrace
had he to fear. They would be few—he smiled grimly
as he thought of it—who would attribute anything discreditable to the man who was first over the walls
of Steadman — Fort Hell, they called it — appropri-
ately enough, too. He need not fear disgrace. A
few silly women might wag their tongues against him.
What did he care? His prospects? What prospects
had he to be injured by anything? The war had destroyed all hope of political preferment, and he had no
desire for any other. The fates had marked out an

even course of life for him as Geoffrey Hunter, gentleman farmer, or gentleman lounger, as the case might be.
Nothing more. Why should he not go abroad and
take Toinette with him? That was poor Arthur Lovett's plan. He would have done better if he had carried it out, too. He lacked nerve. It was not strange
that he did. It was a fearful thing to marry one's own
nigger. He felt that. He would rather have faced
Fort Hell at its hottest than do the like. Yet he was
just at this moment considering it. Perhaps—pshaw!
He would go and see her once more, anyhow. Just to
show her that he could demean himself as a gentleman,
if nothing more. She had said she was going on Wednesday. He would see her on Tuesday evening. So
he determined.

CHAPTER XLVI

A FAITHFUL STEWARDSHIP.

WHEN Toinette informed Betty Certain of ner determination, and the reasons which influenced her in its adoption, the surprise of the good woman was unbounded.

"Sure enough," she said; "the most natural thing in the world, though I am at the first of it but this very minute."

The more she considered the matter, the better she seemed to appreciate Toinette's position and honor her motives.

"Yes, certainly," she had said, "you cannot stay here any longer; but where will you go, and what will you do?"

Toinette replied that she did not know. She would go somewhere and find something to do. Of that she was sure. Betty Certain was not satisfied. She wandered about all Sunday afternoon, with her hands clasped behind her like a man, thinking it over. And when Toinette retired at night she left her still pacing backward and forward in the moonlight under the budding oaks.

"Go to bed, child," she had said tenderly when Toinette came to persuade her to retire. "Go to bed an' sleep. Betty Certain's got a heap to think of on your

account to-night, and she hopes you 'll sleep sounder for
it many a night hereafter."

Youth, health, and an untroubled conscience enabled
Toinette to comply with this injunction in spirit as well
as letter. She woke once in the night and saw that her
old friend was not in her bed. She listened and could
not hear the monotonous tramp of the thoughtful watcher beneath the trees. She wondered at it, but soon slept
again.

She little thought that the poor-white woman that night
bowed by the rocky seat under the newly-leaved dogwood
trees, where Arthur Lovett had knelt twenty years before,
to ask for guidance in her duty toward Arthur Lovett's
daughter. Did she seek for aid from God or Arthur
Lovett? It would be hard to tell. The two were strangely blended in that brave and faithful heart. Arthur
Lovett's wish was, to her mind, but the reflex of God's
will; for the essence of both was right and truth.

For a long time she communed with the past, and
when she rose her mind had grasped its relations to the
present and the future in a manner quite satisfactory to
herself. She had given up some cherished dreams, and
had prepared herself for another term of self-sacrifice
and devotion to the duty which Arthur Lovett had devolved on her as the price of his love. The next morning she asked Toinette to come into the library, and,
sitting there with the girl's head in her lap, she talked
of the future to her.

"I 've been thinking, Toinie, what I ought to do in
the course things are taking now. You know I hev just
considered myself always as only a trustee or agent for

Arthur Lovett as regards the property here, which came
into my hands as executrix. You know it was his will
that one-half should go to your mother and her children,
after the expense of freeing them had been paid, and
the other half to me. You were all to be freed, though,
'fore any division took place, if it took the whole estate
to do it. Well, as things turned out, there was n't any
need for that expense, so now the whole estate is for division. Your mother, brother, and sister are dead. I
managed to trace the latter, and found she died only a
year or two after being sold. So, you see, you and I are
the only heirs. You know I took the place in '60. It's
been a bad time to farm since then, but it hain't run
down on my hands. I hired the hands to work it the
first year, and then the war began; an' if I could ever
hev been tempted to buy a slave, I was saved from it by
the conviction, which I could never get rid of, that the
war would be a failure and slave property a dead loss
when it was over. Geoffrey Hunter tried to have me
buy, but I held off and kept on hirin'. Castin' about
for something in which to invest the money the crops
brought, I could think of nothin' that seemed to promise
a chance of safety but land. I thought that would be
here when the war was over, an' be less likely to be destroyed than any other property. So I turned the terbacker crop every year except the last one into land. Land
was high and not much on 't for sale, but I did the best
I could, an' it's turned out better 'n I expected. Most on
it joins the plantation here, so that now, instead of one
thousand acres, the Lovett Lodge plantation amounts to
nigh double that. Its all prime terbacker land, bringing

a light staple but curing up bright and even, so as to just suit the style of fine cured leaf that's all the rage now. There are a few hundred dollars due on the last purchase yet, but my last crop is in the hands of the commission merchants, and at the wonderful price terbacker is bringing since the war will not only pay this but leave a handsome surplus. It's all good quality, a fine lot of light wrappers, and the best grade of lugs I have ever made.

"One-half of this is yours, now, for I have taken the title to myself, in all cases, as executrix of Arthur Lovett, and the lawyers tell me that we are what they call joint-tenants of it all, with equal rights and powers over it. It will all be yours if you should outlive old Betty Certain—as I trust you may, many a year.

"At present prices these lands will yield a revenue that would have astonished poor Arthur, in his day. It's true the land won't bring much, nothing like what it oughter, according to its yield of terbacker. However, it will turn out enough every year for us to live on, and live well too. So that you need not have any fear on that score. You're able to live without help from Mr. Geoffrey Hunter or any one else.

"Now, I had always intended to sell out and go North with you when the war was over. Somehow, I thought that must be a more kindly climate for poor whites and free niggers than this, for many a year to come. 'What's bred in the bone,' you know, dear. Now take your ease. You are as fair and accomplished as any lady in the land; fairer than most, and better educated, in fact, than many. I have heard Geoffrey Hunter boast that you did great credit to his teaching, more than he had ever expected.

"Many a year—perhaps many a generation—must pass, however, before such as Geoffrey Hunter could unite himself with you in marriage, no matter what may have been your previous relations.. It would be social and political suicide. So, too, the time will never come, whilst I live, that Betty Certain will not be a mere 'poor poll,' because her father did not happen to own slaves. Oh! I know the spirit that lives among this people The few have lorded it over the many so long that they will cling to the scepter until the last moment.

"As I said, it has been my idea to sell out and go North with you. But the misfortune is, the lands are worth nothing now, for no one has the money to buy. So I thought we would stay here for a few years, till prices improved—as they soon will, if terbacker keeps up—and then sell and move off. In any event I meant to keep with you. Somehow, you seem nigher to me than any one else, if there *is* supposed to be colored blood in your veins,—as if you orter have been my daughter. You have your father's great, wonderful dark eyes, and his graceful, quiet, attractive ways. So I had always planned it out that after we had spent a few years here, saving and laying up as we could, that we would go away where no one would ever know that you had been a slave, or I a 'poor white,' and end our days in some cozy corner, where the outlook on earth would be brighter, and heaven perhaps a little nigher, or over a better road, at least.

"But this thing has come on me so sudden-like, that it has marred all my plans, perhaps frustrated them forever. As you say, you must go away from here at once. I know the Hunter family better than you. If there 's one quality they 've got more of than any other, it 's obstinacy—sheer, straight-out obstinacy. Geoffrey Hunter will no more think of giving you up, because you have refused to listen to his improper advances, than he would of marrying you—which he would never think of doin', unless he went plumb crazy. I see it makes ye wince, gal, an' I don't wonder, for there a' n't a spark of reason in it.

"God made you as beautiful, as pure, and as bright as He ever created woman; but He made you a slave, too, and, for some inscrutable reason, He mixed one lone drop of black blood with the warm tide that mantles to your cheek, and when He did that, He separated you and Geoffrey Hunter, so far as lawful love is concerned, further than the East is from the West.

"For two hundred years that custom which is more powerful than law has said, 'You may take the colored woman as a concubine, and raise up children who shall wear the bond of the slave, or the degradation of the free black, but neither God's holy ordinance, nor the willing covenant, which constitutes marriage in the law, shall sanctify your union, or save your children from shame.'

"Against this custom, this tradition, Geoffrey Hunter must butt his head if he would marry you, my dear, and he will never do it. He is not afraid of any danger but what he conceives to be dishonor; the loss of reputation, position, influence, he shrinks from with a mortal terror He might die for love of you, but he will never marry you, Toinette. Neither will he give you up.

Thinking that you will see the futility of your hope, and the strength of his devotion—which, indeed, I do think is very great—and will finally yield to your love, he will continue to pursue you until his purpose is accomplished.

"Well," seeing Toinette's dissenting gesture, "perhaps he might never accomplish that, but your life would be made miserable by his unceasing importunities. So you must go away at once.

"This means, too, that I must as certainly stay. Why? Because, don't you see? we are not ready to sell. You must have money to live on, and I must stay here and make it.

"No, not a word. Do as I tell you. Old Betty Certain has been faithful enough to Arthur Lovett's memory, an' wishes to claim a sort of obedience from his daughter. Has n't she? There, there, I did n't mean to blame you, child. Do n't cry, please. It puts me out to see your bright eyes full of tears and think that I have caused them.

"Well, as I said, do you go now just where you wish, and live as it best suits you, only this: you must live like a lady, wherever you are. Remember that: no scrimping, no pinching, but as a lady ought to live, and Betty Certain will furnish the money—out of your property, and what your father left her.

"Yes, I 'll come too, as soon as ever I get the last place paid for, and can sell to advantage. Betty Certain don't want to be an overseer all her life, but she will do it a while longer to help Arthur Lovett's daughter and her own Toinette Ye see, dear, I have a double

28

claim on you: your father's memory and injunction, and the love that grew up between us before I knew who you were. I have never felt towards you the same as others, since I saw you with that hole in your white bosom, so like the scar that bleeds always in my memory."

Overcome with emotion, the "poor-white" woman clasped the sobbing Toinette to her breast, and kissed her again and again, while the tears flowed like rain down her hard furrowed cheek. She had quite overcome the strange shyness which she had felt towards Toinette soon after her return, and seemed to have forgotten the prejudice arising from her birth altogether.

"There, there," she said, at length, smiling, and putting her hand over Toinette's mouth, "no thanks. Not a word. You know it is my only pleasure, and now you would spoil it all by putting me in debt for the sweet pretty ways in which you would thank me. No, no; I'm not to be cheated in that way. Really," said she, "I am almost glad there is a bar to your marriage with Geoffrey Hunter; I shall have you all to myself now, and there is nothing to prevent *my* loving you, thank God!" and she wound her strong arms about the slender girl, and laughed amid her tears.

"The 'poor-white' and the slave are too nigh of kin to marry even if we were not both women—which, thank God, we are—so we can trust each other."

"Well, well," she continued, after a short time, as she dried her eyes and repressed her sobs, "you must be thinking of getting away. When did you tell him you were going?"

"Wednesday," said Toinette.

"Wednesday? then he 'll be here afore sundown of a Tuesday evening, sure. You must take the Tuesday morning train. And where will you go?"

"I do not know," replied Toinette.

"Do not know? That means you will not tell."

"You cannot—" began Toinette in protest.

"Stop," said her companion, "you are right. It is altogether better that I should not know for the present. There is the firm name of my New York factors. Let them know your address, and write to me through them. Draw on me through them for whatever funds you may require."

And so it was done as they had planned. Toinette left a letter for Geoffrey Hunter, should he come to the Lodge; with many tears bade adieu to the faithful stewardess of her dead father's bounty, and with her wondering child turned her face again northward in search of some place where she might forget what she had been, and either begin a new life or at least decently bury the old. She clasped the child to her heart, and, young as she was, felt that she lived only in him, and so filled the future with dreams of which he was the sun and center.

CHAPTER XLVII.

THE SEAL OF THE SEPULCHER.

BETTY CERTAIN'S prediction was well proved, for the afternoon of Tuesday was but half spent when Geoffrey Hunter drew rein before Lovett Lodge once more. He noticed as he approached, under the great oaks on the lawn, that the house seemed very still —almost deserted. Little Geoffrey was nowhere in sight, nor did he hear his voice as usual. Could he be ill? It was with a strange foreboding that he advanced to the library, the door of which stood open, and beheld sitting in the great arm-chair by the table—Miss Betty Certain.

She looked up at him with dull, heavy eyes, which bore the trace of weeping, and nodded response to his greeting.

"Where is Toinette?" asked Geoffrey, in a tone of alarm.

"Gone," said the woman, doggedly. "You ought to know, you drove her away."

She was not inclined to spare him.

"Gone where?—when?" he questioned.

"I do n't know where, but she went away this morning," she answered, testily.

"Gone! gone!" said Geoffrey Hunter, "and you do not know where? Did she—that is—have you any message for me?"

"I have," she answered, "a message and a parcel for you. Here is the parcel. The message is a singular one, but I am bound to deliver it as she told me. She—that is, Toinette—desired me to tell you that it was her request that you should read the enclosure I have just handed you, in the secret room which opens off from this."

"Her request shall be law to me in this," said Geoffrey, tenderly, as he took the packet from her hands.

Betty Certain rose and left the library, closing the door after her.

After a few moments, Geoffrey Hunter opened the door of the wardrobe and touched the familiar knob. The door swung open, and he entered the secret room at Lovett Lodge. It showed signs of recent occupancy. The little table was drawn before the hearth, and a chair stood beside it. By a sort of instinct he felt that it had been lately used by Toinette. He closed the door, sat down by the table, broke the seal of the packet which he had received, and read:

"GEOFFREY HUNTER:

"I am writing this in the secret room at Lovett Lodge. You will readily comprehend why I chose to retire here to address you the last communication which you will receive from me. Little did I think, when you first disclosed to my wondering eyes this mystery of our abode, that it would ever be so closely linked with that inner life which the daily routine of existence does but hide from those who observe it only outwardly. As, trembling with the mysterious dread which your nar-

rative of all that you knew of its history had inspired,
I came with you through the door and down the steps
into the hidden room, where the sunshine through the
one window above poured down the warmth and glad-
ness of the spring-time afternoon, you cannot imagine
the strange, rapturous joy which seized my being. God's
sunshine and my master's presence made it heaven. I
did not know then why I was so happy. I do now. It
was freedom—the freedom of love. All the shackles of
the world were cast aside. My spirit was as free as
yours. The mastership which crowned your brow was
not that which your father's deed conveyed, but the
kingliness of love. The owner was shut out; the king
whom I adored alone was with me then. And you, too,
bowed beneath the yoke of love. Our souls were peers
in that blissful moment. You did not come down to
my level, nor had I risen up to yours, in the eye of the
world. We were just two souls meeting on the same
plane, mutually giving and receiving—asking and yielding a regnant love.

"From that moment I ceased to be a slave. No
shackles could have bound me afterwards. My soul
was yours by free gift—my friend, my companion. And
this hidden room was Paradise to me from that d y
Nothing could loose me from the devotion I then assumed but your own act—perhaps not even that. Love
is not easily recalled. If its treasures are once squandered they may never be regained. The bankrupt may
recover his wealth, but the prodigal of love can never
re-collect its priceless treasures.

"Do not think I blame you for aught that followed.

You but obeyed the dictates of a love whose behests are higher than any human law. Your inmost soul recognized the falsity of that social relation which placed the rod in your hand and the chain upon my wrist. I know that you are proud, Geoffrey Hunter; I could never have loved you had you not been. But I dare to tell you, now, that your soul was at its best and proudest when you brushed aside the cob-web fictions which clung about its past, and we met heart to heart in this sanctuary, peers and partners in heart. I was your equal. I did not know it then, nor indeed until of late. Now I see it. In devotion, in steadfastness of purpose, in the self-sacrifice of holy love, I was your equal—perhaps more than your equal

"And now the former slave-girl is free; free of limb by your instinct of justice; free of heart by the knowledge of God's truth. Her once master is a slave now, bound with the sinful chains which generations of slavery have forged as the safeguard of that great Moloch.

"Upon you, the master—the legitimate offspring of the dominant race—this evil, with a thousand others which will be hereafter recognized, has come to rest. That domestic love, so long forbidden to the slave, revenges itself now upon the master.

"In your passion yesterday you would have led me to trample on my womanhood. I know your reason and manhood disclaim that unholy thought, for there is but one path to happiness — one path which justice, truth and love open to your feet, and that is so hedged up that you dare not attempt it. The heart which has spurned danger in a thousand forms trembles before the mandate of exclusion which the world would fulminate against him for violation of its edicts.

"You think this is a strange farewell. It may be, and yet not stranger than that which you improvised yesterday. But you little knew your Toinette if you thought that the years which have passed since we sat here together had taught her nothing. They could not teach her to love you more, but they have taught her to love you better. She would but ill deserve even the smutched and tainted love you proffered her if she could be the willing instrument of soiling your soul with the deliberate vice of continuing in the light of freedom the course upon which we stumbled in the darkness of slavery.

"Thank God, the love I bear you is too pure to bend even to your entreaty to evil. I seemed to you at first, no doubt, to yield yesterday to your love. If I did so, it was only because I had taught myself to believe that you were so brave and true that you would tear aside the fictions of race and caste, and recognize and reward the love you knew I cherished. I ought not to have thought so. I see it now. You are but human, and that would require superhuman strength. I ought to have remembered in what mould you were cast, what influences had been around you, and how that noble nature, which my heart had discovered, was hampered in its development and crippled in its action by the traditions of the past.

"Expecting so much, I was, for a time, bitterly disappointed. Then I did you injustice. That was all—

until I received your note of this morning, in which
you cite the infamous law, which was enacted, it would
seem, simply to give an excuse for the perpetration of
crime, and to perpetuate the vilest evils which slavery
engendered. Christian marriage is forbidden in the
most solemn manner, and under infamous penalties; but
unbounded license is scarcely rebuked. If it is such a
law as this which you regard as above the sanctity of our
love, then, indeed, it is time we should separate forever.
I cannot quench my love, but I can protect myself from
temptation and shame.

"I shall leave a day sooner than I had intended, pur-
posely to avoid your presence, being satisfied that you
will seek to meet me again, despite my refusal. You
would never dream of intruding upon one whom you
would term "a lady" after she had declined an interview, but you cannot regard your freedwoman as having
even the paltry right of refusing her presence, when you
choose to demand it

"Whither I shall go, I do not know, nor what I shall
do. The world is wide, and I shall find a place and a
work that will serve my aim, which is to rear and educate our son, that he may be worthy of his father at his
best estate—his fairest possibility. I cannot cease to
love you, but, since the barriers between us are insurmountable, I shall strive only to remember those happier
days, when this room was the paradise of a love than
which earth knew no purer. I had hoped that it
might receive that sanction which would banish the
shadow of evil. It was a vain hope—God forgive me, a
foolish one—as I now see. Farewell, Geoffrey Hunter.

That reputation, honor, and prosperity may be yours, shall ever be the prayer of

"TOINETTE."

"P. S.—I shall take with me the sword that was strapped to your wrist when you were brought to the hospital. I have kept it ever since. You, perhaps, did not know that it had been preserved. I wish to tell our boy the story of his father's bravery, when he shall be old enough to be proud of it, though he may never know his name. If you are unwilling that I should retain it, you have but to inform our old friend, Betty Certain, and it will be returned.   T."

Geoffrey Hunter read the letter and then left the house, casting a sad and regretful look back at the room which had so many and such strange memories connected with it, mounted his horse and rode away.

That night Betty Certain went into the secret room and sat for a long time, alone in the moonlight, thinking of its past. Then she rose, and taking hold of one of the brass-topped andirons, moved it aside, and one of the deep jambs of the chimney, which seemed a solid slab of soapstone, fell outward upon hinges, as Belle Lovett had described, and she felt the chill breezes from without come sweeping into the room.

She moved it back and closed the opening again; then looked around the room and went out by the door into the wardrobe. Then she took out the knob which served to lift the bolt, letting that fall back into the socket, and taking a man's knife from her pocket, she whittled a piece of pine to fill the place the knob had occupied. She drove this in flush and smooth with the back of the wardrobe, and then screwed into the plank one of the black japanned wardrobe hooks of modern days, whose base covered and concealed the place which the wooden knob had occupied. Thus the inner door was sealed up beyond danger of accidental discovery or ordinary search.

"I know the other entrance," she said, "and that is enough. If Arthur Lovett never had made that contrivance it might have saved a heap of trouble."

———

The Stack Rocks still rear their gray heads to sun and storm, like a mighty Stonehenge of some forgotten race of giants; the river flows ever onward—a watery highway to the sea; the Master, the Slave, and the Poor White, late dwellers on its banks, are borne down the current of time toward the great ocean of a common humanity.

The landmarks of the Past are disappearing, but the fetters of brass which it forged are yet upon the hands which the eager Present stretches forth to that grim Sphinx—the Future—whose secret no man knoweth.

THE END.